PRAISE FOR *CALL THE CANARIES HOME*

"The concept of home,  hole again . . .
A good addition to wc

—*Booklist*

"With lush prose and vivid description, Laura Bar-row paints a picture of three sisters and their grand-mother searching to uncover a secret from the past—and heal the wounds that have, in many ways, shaped their lives. Lyrical and lovely, *Call the Canaries Home* is a stunning debut from a standout new voice in women's fiction. And Laura Barrow is officially on my list of must-read authors!"
—Kristy Woodson Harvey, *New York Times* best-selling author of *The Summer of Songbirds*

"For fans of small-town fiction and bighearted fami-ly comes a moving tale of forgiveness, loss, and se-crets told through a cast of memorable characters. As three sisters move closer toward the truth behind their sibling's disappearance, they discover deeper truths about themselves. Barrow crafts an impressive debut, culminating in a bittersweet yet satisfying conclusion. A touching, heartfelt read proving that family truly is everything."
—Rochelle B. Weinstein, bestselling author of *When We Let Go*

IF WE
EVER
GET
THERE

IF WE EVER GET THERE

A Novel

LAURA BARROW

Text copyright © 2024 by Laura Barrow
All rights reserved.

Published by Lake Union Publishing, Seattle

www.apub.com

Amazon, the Amazon logo, and Lake Union Publishing are trademarks of Amazon.com, Inc., or its affiliates.

ISBN-13: 9781662519048 (paperback)
ISBN-13: 9781662519055 (digital)

Cover design by Eileen Carey
Cover images: © Daniel Olah / Unsplash; © ysclips design / Shutterstock

Printed in the United States of America

For Grandma Vera

You don't appreciate home until you leave it and, let me tell you, you can't appreciate life till you've almost left it! Some people hope and die with their song still in them.
—Patsy Cline

CHAPTER 1
EFFIE / "SWEET DREAMS"

January 2024

On the morning of Effie's mommy makeover, an errant winter storm battered the town of Tilly, Texas, leaving its normally tidy streets littered with the splintered branches of live oaks and Bradford pears. The scene would be forever etched into Effie's mind. She'd been staring at the debris from her recovery room window at Rosehaven Reconstructive Surgery Center when her not-quite-midlife-crisis began. Like a slowly dissipating fog, the dream tugged at the edges of her memory. The light. The music. The woman in the gossamer white gown. What had it meant?

Before Effie could begin to make sense of it, Daniel stumbled through the door, scattering her thoughts. With a wary quirk of his brow, he surveyed the antiseptic room as if it might be haunted. But when his gaze landed on Effie, the muscles of his stubbled jaw tightened ever so slightly, and humiliation gripped her, wringing out her insides like a wet towel. She knew that look. It was the same face he'd made when she hadn't noticed the check-engine light in the minivan and it ended up flatlining on the highway in a puff of smoke.

Propped up by a wall of pillows, Effie felt the tingling of heat flood her cheeks as she clutched a cup of strawberry Jell-O against her paper gown. She blinked a few times to be sure she wasn't hallucinating. After the morning she'd had, it wasn't entirely out of the question. "What are you doing here?" she finally asked, her mouth gaping so that a red sugary trail escaped her lips and trickled down her chin. She wiped it quickly with the back of her hand and sat up as straight as she could manage. But the pain medication was beginning to wear off, and with every movement, she let out a sharp little gasp.

"What am *I* doing here?" He dragged a hand down the side of his face, distorting his features. "God, Effie. I thought you'd been in an accident or something."

A tiny current of hope trickled through her veins, but she did her best to appear unaffected. Would Daniel be upset if she had been the victim of a hit-and-run, fly into a blind rage until he'd exacted revenge on her attacker? But when he spoke again, his tone was laced with an irritation that eclipsed any potential concern he might have left for her.

"Some receptionist called me," he continued, "said I needed to speak to a Dr. Parker about my wife's surgery? This is the address she gave me, so . . ." Drawing his eyebrows together, he squinted at the photos on the wall—airbrushed advertisements for Botox and butt implants and liposuction. He fingered his chin and scoffed in a way that set her insides churning. She was certain Amber would hear about this, and the idea of the two of them discussing her made Effie want to disappear inside the mattress.

Deftly avoiding the judgment in his gaze, she set the Jell-O down on the overbed table in front of her. "Well, you didn't have to come all the way here," she said nonchalantly, as if she weren't lying sans underwear on a gurney. The unfortunate fact was she'd scheduled the surgery months ago, after they'd tried to work things out but before he'd packed up and left, taking with him her good set of sheet pans. This was especially perplexing because in nineteen years, Effie had only seen him operate the oven a handful of times. Honestly, she wasn't sure he knew how. Oblivious to his plans to abscond with her Farberware and her dignity, Effie had completed the hospital forms on autopilot, scribbling the familiar letters of his name in the blank, an act she'd performed countless times before. In her defense, she hadn't known then that the facility would ever need to contact him. She also hadn't known that Daniel would prefer sleeping with Amber or that a gale-force wind would sweep through the middle of town while her insides were exposed.

"I'll meet you downstairs when you're ready," he grumbled. Still shaking his head, Daniel trudged into the hallway, no doubt silently cursing her for interfering with whatever jobsite he'd abandoned. She wondered how much Dr. Parker had told him and whether he was privy to any information she didn't have. She suspected something serious must have happened for the staff to call him, but Dr. Parker had only used the phrase *mild unforeseen complications*, then scribbled out a pre-scription for a laundry list of medications. The way he'd failed to meet her eyes only made her more certain he wasn't telling the whole story.

A stout nurse helped Effie out of the bed and into a loose but-ton-up shirt and a pair of sweatpants. After easing her into a wheel-chair, she guided Effie down the elevator and through the automatic entrance doors just as Daniel pulled his white dually around to meet them. Taking note of the truck bed laden with cedar beams and slabs of Tyvek drywall, Effie wondered if he was still finishing up the model unit for Lakewood Landing. Back when she'd talked him into bidding on the project, she'd expected to be in on the interior details, down to every last tile sample. But these days, he could consult Amber about those sorts of things.

On shaky legs, Effie slid into the passenger seat while Daniel silently fumed behind the wheel. He gripped it with white knuckles, swerving into afternoon traffic. "You decided to have plastic surgery while the rest of the world is falling apart?"

Effie stared blankly at the broken tree limbs out the window, only half listening to his rant. She had drifted into the memory again, desperate to secure every detail from this morning, freeze them so she could untangle the meaning of it all later, when she wasn't high on pain meds.

But Daniel had never been the sort of man to let an argument go unfinished if he believed he had the moral high ground. "So, this is where my money is going?" He gestured to her newly stretched body, which ached and tingled in places she hadn't really felt before they'd been ripped apart at the seams and sewn back together again.

The accusation left her feeling like a scolded child, and she shrank down in her seat. But honestly, at this point, what right did he have to judge *her*? Still groggy, she lifted her chin and bravely met his gaze. "For what it's worth, I scheduled this *before* you decided to play house with Megan Fox," she quipped, flashing him an *I said what I said* look. "And anyway, Mama paid for it. When I start making my own money, I'll pay her back." Since Margie had been the one to suggest the surgery in the first place, she'd been only too happy to help out with the cost as a fortieth birthday present for her glamour-challenged daughter. Though never wealthy, her parents had recently come into a considerable sum of oil money when a reserve was discovered on their five-hundred-acre sorghum farm. The unexpected windfall allowed her mother to live the life she'd always envisioned—one that involved massages and microblading and the occasional Botox injection. For her part, Effie had always been a disappointment in the poise department, never making it past the audition phase of those insipid beauty pageants Margie had forced upon her as a child. Something about the way she swung her arms on stage. Until then, she hadn't known there were so many incorrect ways to walk. "There's nothing wrong with investing in a little maintenance every now and then," her mother always insisted without a hint of shame. "Besides, if Dolly endorses it, it's perfectly justified in my book." But the idea of going under the knife had never appealed to Effie. Not until she'd discovered those text messages on her husband's phone and a permanent weight had established residence on her sternum.

A bark of laughter escaped Daniel's chest as he maneuvered into the driveway of the white stucco home they'd once shared. "And how do you plan to pay Margie back? You suddenly got a job I don't know about?" Shifting the truck into park, he whipped his head around to face her. "Or is PTA giving you a raise?"

It wasn't Effie's fault if this divorce was costing him a fortune, and it wasn't fair to take it out on her. Every atom in her body vibrated with fury as her spine stiffened against the seat. "Not that it's any of your concern, but I applied for an administrative assistant position," she said, righting her shoulders. "At a law firm." She emphasized the word *law* as if it were something to be revered. But truth be told, it had been weeks since she'd submitted the application on a whim, and with each passing day, it seemed more unlikely that anything would come of it.

Daniel appeared unimpressed. "Well, didn't you think that I might have things to do today? Trees to cut, roofs to repair? We don't all have the luxury of staying home."

Effie rolled her eyes but remained silent. Whenever he called attention to her lack of employment, it was best to just let him finish, even if he was playing fast and loose with the facts. She'd worked right alongside him until Brody was born, performing all sorts of tasks that never earned a paycheck—designing company logos, answering phones, scheduling appointments, sorting payroll. She was also much better than Daniel at envisioning the remodels—which walls should come down to make a home feel roomier, which original floors were worth salvaging. But once the third kid had come along, it'd become untenable to maintain a household and the details of the business without losing little pieces of her sanity. Something had to give.

"That damn storm created more work than we know what to do with," Daniel was saying. "Lakewood Landing took a hit, and power lines are down on that side of town. So I've got to swing by the office and pick up a couple of generators." He ran a calloused hand through

7

his thick dark hair, recently dusted with sprinklings of gray. It made him look distinguished instead of old. It irked her.

"I had no idea they would contact you," she tried to explain. "I was planning to call Mama just as soon as it was finished, but something . . . something happened. I—" She stopped herself from telling him about the light, about the way it had made her feel like warm clay all over, soft and pliable. Instead, she cleared her throat politely and started again. "Did the doctor . . . mention anything? About why they called you?"

He gave her an apathetic shrug. "Not really. Just something about a slight hitch."

A slight hitch? She bristled. "Well, aren't you the least bit curious why he felt the need to alert my emergency contact?" she asked, studying him for any sign of concern. But he only stared back at her blankly. She filled her lungs, summoning the courage to say the unsayable. "Daniel, I realize that I may have interrupted your plans today, but has it completely escaped your attention that something potentially huge has happened to me?" Her chest felt so painfully tight, and with every agitated breath she felt her breasts ache in protest.

As he leveled his gaze at her body, his rich-brown eyes, which used to make her feel safe, made her feel exposed. "If you mean your breasts are uneven, then yes. I noticed."

She stole a quick glance down her shirt. Thankfully, everything appeared to be in the correct place, though noticeably perkier beneath her bandages. Over the past few weeks, she'd had a recurring nightmare that the doctor inflated one of her breasts twice as large as the other, then popped it with a needle to even them out. The anxiety of it all was almost enough to make her call the whole thing off. But she'd paid in advance and hadn't wanted to lose her deposit.

Daniel was trying to be funny, but considering the hell he had put her through the last six months, he no longer had the right to hear her laugh. She pursed her lips. "I'm serious. Something . . ." Her eyes flitted upward as she searched for the right word. She almost said *awful*, but that wasn't right. No, it wasn't a bad thing, and she hadn't been afraid. Strange, yes, but also kind of wonderful. Amazing, even.

"Something . . . transformative just happened to me," she finally said, accentuating the point with a flourish of her hand. Yes, that was the right word—*transformative*—the only word she could seem to manage.

Daniel cocked an eyebrow. "Isn't that . . . sort of the point?"

"Oh, good gravy! That's not what I meant. I . . . I don't know how to say this." And she didn't. She truly could not fathom how to make him understand the magnitude of this . . . *thing* that had happened. Of course, she had heard of near-death experiences, of people leaving their bodies and traveling to some alternate reality where they were greeted by smiling loved ones and ethereal choirs. She just never thought something like that would happen to her. Effie Baker. Stay-at-home mother who volunteered on the PTA and served as a den mother for her eleven-year-old's troop.

"Listen to me." Taking another beat, she tried to arrange the words in the simplest of patterns. "I think . . . I think I died?" she heard herself say in the form of a question. As the sentence left her lips, it struck her just how impossible this was. And yet, somehow, she felt certain it was true.

Studying her from the corner of one eye, Daniel seemed to mull over this information as the engine hummed in the air between them. "How could you have died?" he finally asked, his voice dripping with disbelief. "You're sitting right here." He gestured toward her plainly as if she were somehow unaware of this fact.

Effie took a deep breath. "I know it sounds impossible, but when I asked Dr. Parker if anything strange happened during the surgery, he got really cagey and couldn't even look at me. I mean, don't you think that's weird?" What she had actually asked him was *Did I die?* Dr. Parker had then calmly explained that she'd taken a little longer to wake up than the anesthesiologist would have liked and that everyone reacted differently in these situations but that it was all fine and no harm done and nothing to worry about. Except that Effie was certain that something *had* happened. A big something had happened, and it had happened to her.

And if someone else were to tell her about such an experience, she would discount it as a dream, explain it away as a pleasant aftereffect of the medication cocktail still coursing through their veins. But this. This was more than a dream. It was more real than anything she'd ever experienced. More real than giving birth. And she supposed it was a birth of sorts. Because the world had suddenly become so much bigger, so much more incomprehensible. She felt like Horton hearing that Who and realizing that he was only a speck of dust on a larger speck of dust in an endless sea of specks of dust. How on earth was she supposed to explain this to Daniel when she could hardly understand it herself?

People say there is a tunnel, but that wasn't how it happened. People also say there is a light, but that word could never adequately convey the impossible brightness. At first, it was just a tiny beam, a pinprick in the distance that grew steadily closer as her spirit swam effortlessly toward it. The light grew more expansive as it pulled her in, which she supposed could give off the illusion of a tunnel if one weren't paying close attention. Innately, she understood that anything good she'd ever experienced or ever would experience was there waiting for her, all wrapped up in warmth and memory, breathing a welcome she had no desire to resist. So, she didn't. As she'd drifted toward it, a humming grew in her ears, soft at first, then louder, until the notes arranged themselves into a pattern and she floated weightlessly on a melody she couldn't quite place. But the voice was unmistakable. As she drew nearer to the source of the music, a figure began to emerge, blurred around the edges like an undeveloped photograph until slowly, its features came into focus and a strange peace had filtered through her.

And here was the thing she couldn't bring herself to tell Daniel, because he would think she had lost her grip on reality. He would drive her back to Rosehaven and ask what medications they had given her.

Maybe he'd even claim she was unfit to care for the kids. These days, she wasn't sure she would put something so low past him. No. For now, she would hold back this one perfect memory—glorious and brilliant and entirely hers. In that effulgent moment, Effie Baker had become aware of three things all at once: In the light was joy. In the light was home. And in the light was Patsy Cline.

CHAPTER 2
EFFIE / "SHE'S GOT YOU"

"I'm just saying that maybe you could have invited him in is all," her mother said, peeling a pile of potatoes at the gleaming white marble counter. *I'm just saying* was Margie Fletcher's less-than-subtle way of preceding a topic she actually had a whole lot to say about.

"If you'd seen the expression on his face, Mama, you'd know he had zero interest in coming inside." Effie perched her bottom gingerly on a stool at the breakfast bar, careful not to jostle her sore bits. While the truck idled in the drive, Daniel had watched her stumble onto the pavement without so much as a *Feel better* or a *Tell the kids I say hello*. With her mouth agape, she'd watched him peel out down the street and turn the corner like he was racing the Indy 500.

"It's your generation," Margie went on, as if she had heard nothing Effie said. "Something breaks and you just throw it away." Brandishing a potato peeler, she waved a flustered arm around. "Look at me and your father. Forty years together and we're still going strong. You think there aren't a few days every now and then when I dream about slipping a little arsenic into his dinners? Hell, that's normal!"

Effie did not think it was normal. And despite her mother's revisionist history, her parents were never the picture of happiness, at least not from what she could remember. Her father was the softer of the two, always protecting the both of them from Margie's histrionics. In fact, she often wondered why they bothered staying together at all. It wasn't until the sixth grade, when her class was suffering through a video titled *The Miracle of Our Bodies*, that she finally worked through the math and realized her parents had likely gotten married as a result of her conception. What's worse, they had stayed together for her too. Since then, she had always felt partially responsible for their strained union. But despite everything, they stuck it out. Now they were trucking along just fine, but only because they seemed to have reached a mutual understanding where they generally steered clear of each other unless *America's Got Talent* was on.

Looking back now, Effie couldn't pretend as if those early years hadn't been full of yelling and insults and fights about money that resulted in her spending the night with Lolly on more than a few occasions. Back then, she'd thought of her grandmother as a Wonder Woman of sorts, the heroine in her story who always arrived just in time to scoop Effie up and carry her to safety before the entire house came apart at the seams.

"I wish you'd stop dredging this up." It was exhausting explaining the hopelessness of the situation to her mother for what felt like the millionth time. What's more, she'd rather not remember the images of Amber sprawled across a four-poster bed wearing nothing but the tiniest pair of panties Effie had ever seen. Or Daniel's messages to her. **God, you're gorgeous. Send more. I'm in purgatory.** Apparently, being married to Effie was purgatory—a revelation that nearly capsized her. Somewhere along the way, she'd become a cliché, the oblivious housewife blindsided by her husband's betrayal, either unwilling or too stupid to read the signs. And in retrospect, she could easily decipher them all— the late nights, the waning sex, the way he pulled away from her first whenever he kissed her goodbye. The way he sometimes forgot to kiss her goodbye at all. At first, she'd chalked it up to the kids getting older and needing him less. She'd been so naive that when Daniel's phone had chimed and she slid her finger across the screen, what she saw had stolen her breath, shaken her so hard she'd trembled from the shock.

When she confronted him in his bath towel, still wet from the shower, he just hung his head, burying his face in his hands. And she knew in her bones that he had already slept with her. For inexplicable reasons, she'd demanded to know every excruciating detail—when they did it, where they did it, how they did it. How long had they been making a fool of her? He'd cried actual tears, apologized over and over again, promised to end the relationship. And Effie had foolishly believed him because she needed to.

Margie tsked. "It doesn't make any sense. You don't just wake up one morning and decide to leave your wife. Why couldn't you two go to counseling?"

"We did," Effie pointed out for the second time. "It didn't help." After three sob-filled meetings with that baby-faced therapist who had challenged them both to *look inward*—whatever that meant—she booked the consult at Rosehaven, foolishly thinking that a surgeon could repair what had broken between them. A lot of good it did. Two days later, on a cloudy Sunday morning, Daniel left anyway, claiming he couldn't live without Amber, which threw Effie for an endless loop. He'd seemed to get along just fine without her the past two decades.

"You have to keep a man's interest, or he's liable to wander. Why didn't you try salsa lessons or . . . go on a cruise?" Margie asked, as if a vacation were the answer. Of course. Why hadn't she thought of that?

"Just forget it, Mama. We tried," she said, pinching the skin between her eyes. At least, *she* had tried. She had invested in a new wardrobe, outsourcing her fashion choices to a complete stranger over the internet, a personal shopper from a company called Fix Her Upper. She'd made him chicken piccata even though garlic made her nauseated. She'd enrolled in a Zumba class even though she hated sweating and wearing spandex in front of other people. Six new blouses, a pair of stilettos, and five pounds later—none of it had been enough. Apparently, it was difficult for Daniel to see all the progress she had made when

14

there was still an unfairly tall and impossibly thin brunette standing between them.

"He's with Amber now." She sighed, resting her chin in the palm of her hand. "I can't change his mind." Even if she could, she didn't want to anymore. They'd given it another shot, but Daniel had made his choice. As far as Effie was concerned, he and Amber could ride off into the sunset together. Right over a cliff.

"Like hell you can't." With her eyebrows drawn together in a V, Margie looked up from the mountain of cubed potatoes and fixed her sights squarely on her daughter. "Men don't know what they want. They're fickle as a feather. All you have to do," she said, jabbing a knife at the air, narrowing her thickly outlined eyes, "is put a little effort into it. Show him what he's missing." She gave a little shimmy. "When's the last time you did something with that?" She touched a pink fingernail to her stiff golden bob but was clearly referring to Effie's dishwater-blonde hair pulled into a bedraggled ponytail.

"What's wrong with my hair?" Reflexively, Effie touched a hand to her head and began tugging and straightening the flyaway strands. Unfortunately, she hadn't inherited the remarkable volume of Margie's hair or her affinity for Aqua Net. Most days, it hung like tired, dusty curtains around her face.

Pursing her lips, Margie heaved a judgmental sigh—the kind that was usually followed by a not-so-thinly-veiled criticism. "It's mousy," she said, holding up a preemptive hand, cutting Effie off before she could protest. "Now, I applaud the woman who can age naturally without a little help, but you know as well as I do that gray is not becoming on anything but a squirrel. The next time you come home, you'll visit my girl," she commanded. "She works wonders with highlights." The last time Effie had been in Kansas was over the previous summer when her father underwent a triple bypass. Daniel had graciously offered to stay behind and take care of the kids, but she'd felt guilty that he'd had to rearrange his schedule to accommodate her absence. Even though she had set up a carpool for Brody to get to soccer practice and left four casseroles in the freezer. Now she realized that her careful planning had only freed him up to spend more time perusing dating sites. How thoughtful of her.

"Mama, Daniel and I have bigger problems than my roots." Her shoulders collapsed under the weight of a sigh. "Besides, I don't think it would make a difference." A tiny stab pierced her solar plexus when she admitted this aloud. She wasn't sure if it was from the surgery or if her heart had exploded a little inside her.

She hadn't wanted the makeover to bring Daniel back, but maybe a small part of her had hoped it might make her feel like the woman he'd fallen in love with, albeit a little doughier around the middle with a slightly larger bottom. Which was only fair, since hadn't that body carried their babies, created a family? Besides, forty was the new thirty now, or so she kept hearing. Yes, she had a few more sunspots and a lot less agility, but she considered herself datable. At least that's what the Amazon delivery guy had told her. "Any man would be lucky to have you, Mrs. Baker," he'd said, no doubt registering her dripping mascara and the prolonged absence of Daniel's truck in the drive. A swath of pink had crawled up Effie's neck, settling into her cheeks, and she'd wondered if he was only saying it to be nice or to get a tip. But you weren't supposed to tip them, so maybe he had been telling the truth? She'd offered him a cold beverage, though, and perhaps this had influenced his opinion.

Shaking her head, Margie piled the potatoes into a pot, then heaved it into the sink and filled it with water. "It's just going to take a little hard work is all. Marriages don't make themselves. But if your grandparents can do it, anyone can. Fifty-nine years of marriage, and you couldn't have found a happier pair." Effie couldn't disagree with that statement. Unlike her parents, Lolly and Pop had been the poster couple for a passionate relationship full of adventure. Pop used to love to tell the story of how he'd first seen Lolly. They were at a dance, and she was brooding in a corner, wearing an outfit she detested. It was love at first sight. Before his heart attack, the two of them had spent the better part of their retirement years traveling, attending concerts and music festivals from California to the Carolinas. Stacks of photo albums were filled with snapshots of them arm in arm, smiling in front of state welcome signs and national parks—Lolly wearing a cowgirl hat while Pop donned high-waisted jeans and sandals with striped tube socks. Sometimes, they even wore matching western shirts that, of course, Lolly had chosen, often bedazzling them with rhinestones herself.

But their marriage hadn't always been easy, and over the years, Effie gleaned that her grandparents had gone through a rough patch, though Lolly could never be pressed to say much on the matter. Like most women of her time, her grandmother never aired her dirty laundry. As such, Effie was a little light on the details, but she knew that her grandmother had been obsessed with Patsy Cline's albums and had once written a letter to her during a particularly dark time. Much to her astonishment and delight, Patsy had written her back. And as a result of taking her advice, Effie's grandparents had stuck it out until the end. Of course, they had their problems, like all couples, but anyone could see how much they adored each other.

On more than one occasion, Lolly had pointed to the letter reverently and credited their successful marriage to its existence. "Patsy told me exactly what I needed to hear," she'd said. "Helped me straighten out my priorities." When speaking of Patsy Cline, Lolly only ever used her first name, as if she were an old friend who needed no further introduction. The letter still hung in a gilded frame in Lolly's living room, right next to a plaque that bore the Lord's Prayer and the Ten Commandments. It was the only material thing Effie had requested upon Lolly's death, which was hopefully a long way off. Though Lolly's mind was muddling through the early stages of dementia, she seemed healthy in all other respects, never needing to visit the doctor for anything more than an occasional bout of flu.

It wasn't lost on Effie that Lolly's history with Patsy may have influenced her vision at Rosehaven. Had she conjured the whole thing, invented her own guardian angel from a jumbled soup of childhood experiences? Maybe. But it had felt so real. And perhaps it even made sense. In Lolly's book, the holy trinity consisted of Dolly, Loretta, and Patsy, with the latter firmly at the helm.

"Speaking of your grandmother," Margie said, narrowing her gaze, "have you bought plane tickets for her birthday? It's going to be quite the event." There was a hint of judgment in her tone. "Of course, I think it's far too much excitement for an eighty-year-old woman and will only irritate her nerves, but Helen insisted." She sighed. "Apparently, the Pink Lassos have a whole set planned, but honestly, with Louisa's arthritis and your grandmother's memory, I'm not sure they'll be able to manage much more than a ballad or two."

A tide of emotion swelled in Effie's heart at the mention of Lolly's ragtag band, though *band* was a generous term. The Pink Lassos only consisted of Lolly on guitar, Helen on bass, and Louisa on fiddle. They were a far cry from famous, but the scrappy trio had provided a steady stream of notes that flowed alongside every major event in Effie's life. When her heart had been broken for the first time in the eighth grade, Lolly had wrapped her up in a hug and the Lassos serenaded her with an old Hank Wiliams tune. At her wedding, they'd harmonized a soulful rendition of "Can't Help Falling in Love." Even now, anytime Effie heard that song, she pictured Lolly's bouffant blonde hair, her thick blue eye shadow that fanned all the way up to her eyebrows, and her signature pink shirt with diamond studs along the back, fringe hanging from her arms like a bird's wings. Lolly had always understood that being a performer was just as much about the glitter as it was about the music, and she had a way of turning every opportunity into a stage. Effie was certain her eightieth birthday party would be no different, despite her waning memory. It seemed both unfair and miraculous that loved ones should elude Lolly's mind when the music remained perfectly intact. She would never forget the feel of a G chord beneath her fingers, but recognizing her granddaughter's face was no longer a guarantee.

"I'll be there," Effie promised. Lolly's birthday was still two months away, plenty of time for her body to mend. Her marriage, on the other hand, was a different story.

"What about the kids?"

"I'll ask Daniel," Effie said, deflated. "They're supposed to be with him that weekend, but I'm sure he won't mind making an exception for Lolly." He'd always adored her grandmother. Everyone did.

"Well, I can't say I like any of this," Margie noted with a shake of her head. "Dividing up days of the week like slices of pie. Children need their parents."

"They *have* their parents," Effie pointed out. "We're not dead. Just divorced."

"Not yet, you aren't! Good marriages are in your blood," Margie said, spreading her hands apart as if the matter were settled. "This is just a phase. Your father bought a second riding tractor on his fortieth. We sold it eventually, when he realized we didn't have space in the barn and the damn thing rusted out in the rain. Daniel will come around when he realizes how high maintenance that teenager is."

Just the mention of her husband's mistress was enough to elicit a bout of nausea. Amber wasn't exactly a teenager, but Effie only knew this from Instagram. She'd had to create an account to stalk her husband's new girlfriend because Facebook was no longer a valid form of social media among the Gen Zers, which she was fairly certain Amber was. Elbow deep in a rabbit hole, Effie had come across a photo of her high school graduation—Amber standing in front of giant yard letters with the number *2015*. That was the year Brody had started a Mother's Day Out program and Effie had spiraled into an existential crisis confronting her newfound lack of purpose. How old would that make Amber? After doing some quick mental math, she mouthed the number, staring stupidly into the glow of her laptop. *Twenty-seven.*

Feeling lightheaded, Effie massaged the bridge of her nose. "Mama, I can't have this conversation right now. My body feels like it's just been flattened by a steamroller." Peeling herself off the chair, she let out a groan. "I need to lie down before the kids get home from school." She hadn't told them about the surgery. And though she didn't think Jay and Brody would suspect anything, Teagan was another story. Lately she'd been giving her more sass and side-eye than the other two combined. Besides, what kind of message would it send her only daughter to see her mother cave to the pressures of a materially minded world? Hadn't she always told her that beauty was only skin deep?

"All right." Margie sighed, apparently willing to table this discussion for another day, which Effie was certain would be tomorrow. What had she been thinking when she'd agreed to let her mother fly in from Kansas and stay for a week? Seven whole days. One hundred and sixty-eight hours. The time stretched out before her like an endless expanse. She should have listened to her best friend, Grace, when she'd warned her it was a terrible idea.

Margie shot her daughter a meddlesome look. "You never told me why Daniel brought you home. You were supposed to call me after the surgery."

"Oh, that," Effie said. Amid all the excitement of the morning, she had yet to tell her mother about her inexplicable experience. Margie Fletcher had a way of minimizing life-altering events, not unlike the way she'd reimagined Effie's separation and impending divorce as a mere "bump in the road." Maybe Effie would keep it to herself for now, especially considering how Daniel had reacted. No need to give her mother any more broken areas of her life to fix. "Just a little mix-up is all. I had some trouble coming out of the anesthesia. Nothing major," she added quickly. "I listed him as my emergency contact. Before all of . . . this." Regret coiled around her heart, but she shook away the image of Daniel's face before it could undo her.

"As you should have," Margie said, nodding along. "Because as far as the law is concerned, he is still your husband until you sign on the dotted line. You still have time to make this right."

Her mother's words slammed into her, transporting her right back to her cot at Rosehaven. The phrase—*You still have time to make this right*—took root inside her heart as she summoned the memory of Patsy's face. What was it she'd said? *Not yet, hoss. You need more time to set things right.* But time to set which things right? Her failed marriage or her precarious relationship with her teenage daughter? Maybe she just needed more time to repaint the family room or sew that pile of merit badges onto Brody's scouting uniform.

Effie hadn't the faintest idea.

CHAPTER 3

LOLA

October 11, 1961

Dear ~~Journal~~ Patsy,

I suppose it's a strange thing to address this to you since we've never even met. But when I wrote "Dear Journal," it seemed far too impersonal, like the name of a stranger who hasn't earned the right to know my most private thoughts. I might as well have written "Dear Mrs. Kennedy" and it would have felt about the same. I could never share the intimate details of the real Lola Montgomery's life with something that cost me seventy-five cents at Fred's five and dime. So instead, I've decided to address this journal to you because you are exactly the kind of classy woman I hope to become someday. I'm to graduate in the spring, and my mother says I need to be thinking about these sorts of things now.

Also, if we ever met in person, I think we would be the best of friends because we have so much in common. Like you, I love to sing and pick at the piano. Truthfully, I sing better than I play, but that's only because my fingers can never seem to keep up with the music spilling out of me. Also, my mother only buys me primers with the most tedious songs that have so little feeling I can hardly be expected to enjoy practicing. But when I hear you sing, it's like you're reaching deep into my soul and pulling out all the emotions I long to feel and putting them into words. Isn't it something that a person I've never met should understand the confusing peaks and valleys of my heart?

Your most devoted fan,
Lola

CHAPTER 4
Effie / "Walkin' After Midnight"

Six Weeks Later

On a chilly Friday, Effie stood in front of the full-length mirror hanging from the back of her bedroom door. Pursing her lips, she studied herself wearing nothing but a lacy black bra and a pair of ancient silk panties. They were a bit small. In the darkness of her underwear drawer, they had faded from black to gray, and she wondered if she should invest in something sexier. But the thought of shopping for lingerie at Victoria's Secret while her husband was dating someone who looked like she might grace the cover of their catalog depressed her. *Who am I kidding?* she thought, missing the comfortable stretch of her cotton Hanes. The last time Effie felt desirable was around the year Obama was elected. The first time. She'd just found out she was pregnant with Teagan, and her body was still in that glowy, preheartburn phase when late-night sex with her husband was still preferable to whatever series they were binging.

She tugged at the silky fabric again before turning around and craning her neck to inspect her new body from behind. Her mother had flown back home weeks ago, and with the kids still at school, she didn't have to worry about anyone walking in as she sucked in and lifted in front of the mirror. During the day, it was just her and the dogs—Cletus, a giant German shepherd, and Oscar, who was just as huge but had a much lighter coat and a more nebulous pedigree. Both of them seemed entirely unimpressed and lay comatose on the bed, only tilting their heads every so often and as if to disapprove of her.

She wondered if Grace would make an appearance today. Since the surgery, she'd been routinely popping by after her shift to check on Effie's wounds, sometimes leaving dinner in the oven. Recently, she'd picked up tarot reading and had insisted on pulling Effie's card. Yesterday, she'd drawn the Fool, which Effie deemed only appropriate, considering Daniel's duplicity and her own ignorance. But Grace had excitedly insisted that it signified new adventures on the horizon and an opportunity to stretch her talents.

Despite these almost daily visits, Effie had managed to avoid telling her best friend about the dream. Or was it a vision? She still had no idea what to call it, but she'd never been good at keeping secrets, and the weight of her omission was beginning to suffocate her. Unlike Daniel, she never could have managed an affair. The crux of it was, she suspected Grace would have no trouble believing her. And therein lay the problem. While Effie had only dipped a toe in the spiritual realm, never dabbling in the occult or attending church aside from the occasional Easter or Christmas service, Grace was practically doing backstrokes in the deep end. She worried her friend would drag her back to that quack of a palm reader who had once trailed a finger down Effie's lifeline and predicted "a soulmate for the ages." That had been two weeks before Daniel left and slapped her with divorce papers.

Flattening her belly with her palms, she scrutinized her reflection. It wasn't a huge change—a modest breast lift and a little tightening around her middle—not enough to undo the damage of growing three humans or shrink her size-twelve hips. But maybe her mother was right and a little change on the outside would bolster her confidence. Even if no one else could tell a difference, she could appreciate the subtle changes, the way her breasts sat slightly higher on her chest and the flap of her jeans no longer carved a little dent into her skin when she buttoned them. So far, the kids hadn't seemed to notice; she still hadn't told them about the surgery. Margie had miraculously appeared on the very day Effie was feeling "under the weather," and they had been so thrilled to see their grandmother they hadn't bothered asking questions. When her phone buzzed on the bed, the screen lit up with Grace's auburn hair and sea green eyes. Effie reluctantly reached for it.

"Did you die?" Grace's alto voice rang through before Effie could manage a hello. If it had been anyone else, Effie would have been unnerved that someone could intuit her thoughts so well, but Grace seemed to have an uncanny pulse on Effie's inner workings. Sometimes, she could be eerily correct about her emotional states, but was it possible she'd sensed her brush with death? No, of course not.

"What do you mean?" Effie replied, a touch too defensively.

"You haven't texted me all day. What have you been up to?"

Effie loosened her grip on the phone. "Not much." *So much.* "Nothing really." *Everything, actually.* "I'm starting to feel normal again." *A lie of epic proportions. What is the meaning of normal anymore?*

"And you're all healed?"

"I'm . . . better," she noted approvingly in the mirror, though all too certain that some parts of her would never scab over. "The swelling is down, and the pain has mostly passed. But I'm not sure modern science will ever be able to put me in the same league as Amber."

"That's because she's a fetus," Grace mumbled while chewing something on the other end of the line. Effie suspected they were Red Vines. They were Grace's go-to snack when her kids weren't around. It defied the laws of nature that she should maintain the physique of a goddess when she had gone so far as to install a false door at the top of her pantry where she stored all the "good snacks" that her boys, James and Beckett, weren't allowed to have. "So, when do we get to celebrate?"

The question confused Effie. "Come again?"

"You know what I mean. Did you sign the papers yet? I'm thinking a weekend cruise to the Bahamas." Grace's voice had taken on a dreamy tone.

"No and no," Effie replied flatly, though the idea of sipping mai tais on a white-sand beach had some real appeal right now. But considering her current employment situation, there was no way she could front the cost of a trip. Then there was the matter of Daniel, who already thought she'd splurged on herself, and she didn't want to add any more grist to the mill.

"Pleeeease," Grace whined. "You'll be my first single friend in ages, and I intend to capitalize on this and live vicariously through you."

"I regret to inform you that your one single friend is going to be a little cash strapped for the foreseeable future. Turns out divorce is expensive," she noted, reflecting on the lawyers they each had on retainer. She'd hoped they could work things out amicably on their own, but when Daniel had shown up to mediation with an attorney, Grace had insisted that Effie do the same. She set her up with her brother, Steven Finley, a divorce lawyer who'd represented two other PTA moms. Though Effie wanted Daniel to buy out her half of Baker's Builders, there had been a fair amount of disagreement over the value of the company, and they had been haggling over a mutually-agreed-upon assessment for months. Daniel, who had always claimed the company was on the cusp of franchising, now asserted it wasn't nearly as valuable as he'd once believed. It was a convenient one-eighty, not unlike the way he'd decided their marriage wasn't worth saving.

"I told Steven to take you on pro bono. He owes me that much after dismembering my Barbies like a deranged psychopath."

"Even deranged psychopaths have bills to pay."

"Can we at least have a bonfire or something?" Grace pleaded. "You're not going about this divorce in a healthy way. You're entitled to a few meltdowns, Effie."

The accusation sobered her, and she flinched, remembering the way Daniel's forehead crinkled when they locked eyes across a crowded room and he winked at her. It had always been his silent cue that he was ready to leave a party, and she had dutifully followed him out the door. But this time, he'd bailed without her, and she was left scanning the sea of faces, wondering what the heck had happened. She didn't want to celebrate. And she didn't want Daniel back. She wanted to go toward the light again, let herself drift into a state of weightless euphoria where her cheating husband wasn't even a dot on her horizon. "I wasn't aware there was a right way to flush two decades of your life down the toilet," she finally said.

"Well, there is," Grace shot back. "It's called Taylor Swift and mojitos. You need to get angry!"

"Believe me, I am." Effie tried to sound convincing, but her anger was couched in so many other emotions she couldn't begin to unravel— regret and confusion and mourning for the life all of them might have had. If Daniel hadn't stopped loving her. "I promise there will be lots of time to celebrate, but right now I have to get ready for that interview I told you about."

"The secretary thing?"

"Administrative assistant," Effie corrected her.

"I don't know why you didn't apply for that job in medical records. You had an in with me, and then we could have had lunch together every day."

"Didn't pay enough," Effie pointed out. "And the firm offers health care." The kids would still be covered by Daniel's plan, but if she were taken out by a bus tomorrow, she wasn't sure who would front the cost of her medical bills. Or her funeral. She'd wondered if perhaps cremation was a cheaper option, and the kids could just scatter her ashes in the backyard next to Chewy, their old cat. So much for the joint plot they had discussed purchasing. This affair was even ruining her plans for the afterlife!

"Oh, the firm," Grace mimicked in a snooty voice. "I suppose it should be easy enough for a hotshot divorce lawyer to cover your colonoscopies."

"He's a family lawyer who happens to handle divorces, among other things. And I'm lucky to even get this interview, given the fact that my résumé has more holes in it than a block of swiss cheese."

Until that out-of-the-blue phone call yesterday, she had been certain she wouldn't hear back about the position. Before Steven Finley agreed to take her on, she'd been perusing the internet for lawyers and come across a "We're hiring" button on the Fields and Fields website. It had been a whim, something she'd done late one night when wallowing over the fact that she was alone and jobless and forty. Though Daniel would pay her a generous lump sum to be determined, Effie was astute enough to realize that money wouldn't last forever. What's more, something lightened in her chest at the thought that someone might actually want to hire her. For the first time in years, she could see her name on a paycheck—albeit a small one, but one that was hers. "I'll call you later," she promised.

"You'd better," Grace warned. "And Effie, one more thing," she added.

"What's that?"

"Under no circumstances are you to tell your potential employer about this divorce. It will make you seem desperate."

"But I *am* desperate."

"No! You're only desperate if you proclaim yourself to be. It's called manifesting!"

"Mmm . . . sounds a little too woo for me."

But Grace barreled ahead, only more enthusiastic. "It's something my therapist endorses, and I think it would do you a lot of good."

"You don't have a therapist," Effie pointed out. "Oh wait, is this that TikTok life coach you follow?" Grace was always getting sucked into the latest advice from whatever health guru had gone viral that week.

"Same thing," Grace continued, undeterred.

"You know it defies logic that you, of all people, would buy into this hippie pseudoscience." A labor and delivery nurse for twenty years,

Grace had always been the one person in Effie's life to remind her about getting a mammogram and scheduling her yearly flu shot.

"This may be difficult for you to believe, but sometimes, certain people are given special gifts, and Serenity Speaks is just one of those people. She's completely changed my outlook on life after forty."

"Oh, good gravy! The woman doesn't have a degree or any training," Effie said. "I'm better off reading my horoscope."

"Which you should already be doing," Grace chided. "Trust me, degrees are overrated. Besides, Serenity's mantras aren't something they teach in any dusty old college. The proof is in her aura."

"I'll remember that the next time I shop for a new doctor. Forgive me if I need a little more to go on than an aura." But even as she spoke the words, a seed of doubt burrowed into her mind. Perhaps she *should* let Grace in on her experience? No, she needed to sit with it for a while longer. Still, she couldn't shake Patsy's words: *Time to set things right.*

Grace let out a sigh. "Manifesting is when you put something out into the world and the act of speaking it makes it a reality," she explained. "If you want to be successful, you have to say it! You are a successful, independent woman, and you are going to get this job because, quite frankly, you're overqualified."

The idea was ridiculous, but Effie supposed a few mantras couldn't hurt. Pulling back her shoulders, she parroted the phrase to the mirror. "I am a successful, independent woman, and I am going to get this job because, quite frankly, I'm overqualified." It was a lie, but one that she would have to get behind long enough to make it through this interview.

When she got off the call, Effie opened her closet door and considered her options. "What to wear," she muttered, sifting through hangers draped in forgotten blouses. It should be easy to market herself; she'd once been in charge of marketing Baker's Builders. But that was years ago. These days, the only experience she had was watching reruns of *Mad Men*, and right now, that information was not proving especially useful. Her online personal stylist appeared to be a leftover flower child and kept sending her things that were far too boho chic for Effie's taste. Uninspired, she grabbed a white silk V-neck blouse and pulled it over her head. It was loosely fitted at the waist but hugged just enough of her rejuvenated cleavage without making her feel on display. She would be mortified if anyone besides Grace suspected her mommy makeover, especially the PTA vice president, Trisha Ackerson, who'd once whispered to Effie that cosmetic procedures were for sad women who couldn't face aging with dignity. Granted, last summer Trisha had returned from a three-week vacation to Brazil noticeably perkier. But Effie knew the rules. It was fine to have work done and social suicide to admit it.

She slid on her favorite pair of dark-washed skinny jeans, which Teagan had called *cheugy*. Effie still had no idea what this meant but had redefined the word to mean *chic*. She finished off the look with a black blazer and a pair of red suede wedges, then stumbled in front of the mirror again. Remembering her mother's criticism, she zeroed in on her flat, graying roots and winced. With a sigh, she tugged out her lifeless ponytail, flipped her head over, then shook it and massaged her scalp before flipping it back again. It was messy, but maybe that was a good thing. She didn't want to look like she was trying too hard. Yes, she would leave it—voluminous and wild like she'd just stepped out of a Harlequin romance novel and a sexy highlander had run his giant fingers through it.

Satisfied, she sat on the bed and picked up her cell, debating whether to call her mother, who was still in the dark about the extent of her *minor complications* during the surgery. She was desperate to talk to someone about it, but considering the way Daniel had reacted to her news, it seemed unwise to bring it up again. The truth was, the memory of Patsy Cline robed in white had consumed her since she'd opened her eyes at Rosehaven. It had to mean something. Like Lolly, Patsy held a special place in Effie's childhood. All those nights when her parents had rattled the walls of their home with their shouting matches, Effie had hidden beneath a blanket in the hallway and pecked out her grandparents' phone number, which she had memorized by heart. Each time it happened, Lolly would drive her old Volvo over and tuck her carefully into the back seat, wearing her pajamas and clinging to her stuffed monkey. Their nighttime drives were accompanied by a soundtrack of Patsy's rich voice crooning through the radio about love won, love lost, and love found again. Anytime Effie heard that unmistakably sweet lilt, it made her think of Lolly in her bathrobe and hair curlers. It made her remember the smile creases on Lolly's cheeks as she sat across from her, eating chocolate Pop-Tarts and playing Go Fish beneath the dim glow of the brass chandelier that hung above her kitchen table. "How you doin', little gal?" she would say after wrapping Effie tight underneath the covers and perching herself on the edge of the bed. And Effie would melt into the softness of her voice and the warmth of her terry cloth robe.

She hadn't heard from her grandmother since last week, and it was always Effie who made the call. These days, their conversations were rife with repetition and uncomfortable silences. It had been easier before Pop passed away two years ago. Always at her side, he'd been the only person who could soothe her when she became flustered over all the displaced items and people she feared had been lost to her forever. Up until the very end, he'd been her rock. Just thinking of the way Pop's sunspotted hands had tenderly sorted her grandmother's pills every morning sent a gush of warmth through her chest. Effie could never decide which was worse—to forget or to become the forgotten.

She scrolled through her cell until her finger landed on Lolly's name and photo—a candid she'd snapped three Easters ago when she and the kids had gone home to Kansas. As usual, Daniel had stayed behind to finish a project. Perched in her favorite La-Z-Boy, Lolly held her Gibson guitar, her blue eyes mirroring her signature eye shadow, crinkled in the corners. Seeing Lolly's face felt like a warm blanket, and Effie brightened. Maybe today would be a good day for remembering.

The line rang three times before Lolly creaked out a "Hello?"

"Hi, Lolly," Effie said, mustering her brightest tone.

"This is Lola," the voice on the other end clarified.

When she was little, Effie hadn't been able to pronounce the words *Grandma Lola*, and the pet name *Lolly* had stuck. When her grandfather had declared that he preferred to be called Pop, *LollyPop* had become all but inevitable. But on days when her memory was foggy, the past a sea of jumbled faces, Lolly forgot the term of endearment and responded only to her formal name.

"It's me. Effie," she said, praying for a small sign of recognition in her grandmother's voice. Sometimes she wondered if these weekly phone calls did Lolly more harm than good. Was it cruel to stir up her thoughts and confuse her just to satisfy Effie's need for connection to a past only one of them remembered?

"Effie, honey." A familiar warmth seeped from her trembling voice.

Her heart lightened, and her shoulders released. "How are you feeling?"

"All right, I suppose." From what Effie could gather, her grandmother seemed in good spirits.

"Did Mama come by this morning?" Then, remembering that Lolly seemed to do better with names than relationships, she corrected herself. "I mean, did Margie stop by?"

"Oh yes," she said. "She brought me a new pillow and a crossword and a cactus-looking thing in a cup."

Effie arched an eyebrow. "You mean a succulent?"

"I don't rightly know what it's called, but it doesn't do a thing, and it's ugly as sin. No flowers or anything, and I can't touch it 'cause it's prickly. But Margie says it's supposed to be good for—oh, what did she say again?" she asked, sounding frustrated. "Increasing focus and productivity."

A smile tugged at Effie's lips. "It sounds like something she would get you. Is it working?"

A beat of silence passed before Lolly said, "I think it's broken."

Effie did her best to cover a strangled laugh. "Is Theresa there yet? Did she give you your meds?"

"Oh yes. She's here again. Every damn day," she added bitterly. Theresa was a godsend to Margie, making it possible for her to keep up with her spin classes and brunches with all her retired friends, but Lolly viewed her the way a dog views another dog encroaching on its territory. A retired nurse and also the kindest woman on the planet, Theresa had been providing in-home care for Lolly since Pop had passed away. But Lolly could never be convinced of her use and often called Margie in a tizzy, demanding to know why "that woman" was in her home again. "I'm perfectly capable of bathing myself," she'd said resolutely. Except that she wasn't. In fact, she'd once fallen on her way to the tub and had been unable to call for help. Luckily, Margie had arrived a few hours later. That was when she had decided to hire Theresa.

"That's good," Effie replied, her lips giving way to a sad smile.

"And how are you, dear?"

Effie wasn't certain if Lolly had asked because she truly cared to know or because it was the obligatory thing to say. She wrestled with a reply, her fingernails drilling divots into the flesh of her palm. There was no sense in telling the truth. It would only upset her grandmother, if she remembered Daniel and their marriage at all. And anyway, she had asked Margie to keep quiet about the separation, which her mother was all too happy to do. She still firmly believed Daniel would return to Effie once he'd "sown some wild oats."

"I'm good," she lied. "The kids are great, and the sun is shining here, though we've had a few stray storms lately. You know how unpredictable Texas weather can be."

That seemed to confuse her grandmother. "Texas? Whatever are you doing down there?"

A sudden heaviness sucked the life from her chest. It seemed today Lolly had traveled two decades into the past, before Effie's father had provided them with the seed money to start the company. Before Daniel, the son of a carpenter, had insisted they move from the country to an up-and-coming Dallas suburb and begin their dream life in Tilly.

Though Daniel had begun his career as a handyman specializing in just about everything from clogged toilets to fence repair, they'd come a long way since those early days, scraping out a living in the barn behind her parents' farmhouse. She and Daniel had never become wealthy, but they were now firmly middle class, or what her father disdainfully called *city folk*.

Effie's heart sank, but she took some comfort in the fact that Lolly had remembered her name. Conjuring her vision, she wanted to ask about Patsy's letter, but she didn't want to dredge up old wounds and upset Lolly if she wasn't in the right frame of mind. Testing the waters, she asked, "Do you remember our nighttime drives? All those times you came to pick me up when Margie and Tim were fighting?" Silence hung on the line, and Effie worried that perhaps she had asked too much. Pointed questions usually only flustered her grandmother.

But taking heart in the way Lolly had said her name, Effie dug out her tablet from the nightstand and pulled up a black-and-white video performance of "Walkin' After Midnight." Patsy materialized on stage, decked out in a fringed cowgirl shirt and pointy white boots trimmed with silver rhinestones. Effie held the phone over the tablet's speaker and sang along as Patsy's familiar vibrato trilled out the first verse. When the chorus came around, she placed the phone to her ear again and hummed the melody, hoping that Lolly's rich alto voice would join alongside hers, that perhaps all those nights making the winding drive from her parents' house would come flooding back.

When it was over, Lolly said confidently, "That was Patsy's first hit single." Her voice was warm with affection. "The first time I heard that song, I was sitting in my parents' living room, and I knew right then and there I wanted to be just like her."

"That's right," Effie said, feeling encouraged. "I used to call you up and beg to spend the night. You always said we were going on one of our midnight walks. Do you remember?" Lolly didn't respond right away, and Effie wondered if the call had dropped.

When she finally answered, Lolly's voice wavered with uncertainty. "Who did you say this was again, dear?"

A dull ache clutched Effie's heart. First Lolly. Then Daniel. These days, everyone seemed to be forgetting her.

CHAPTER 5
LOLA

October 17, 1961

Dear Patsy,

A few days ago, I saw you sing "Crazy" on the Grand Ole Opry, and you seemed so comfortable on that stage just wailing and strutting around like it was nothing. I must admit the words of the song nearly broke my heart, but when you reached the final note, I got chills. Actual chills, Patsy! The little hairs of my arms shot straight up, and my skin turned all white and pimply. I sat there like a complete fool in front of the television for Lord knows how long, so still and spellbound you could have knocked me over with a feather! I told my mother then and there, that song was meant for you to sing it.

When the record hit the shelves at Gus's Vinyls today, he told me I was the first person to buy it from his store. Surely that must qualify me as your number one fan in the state of Kansas! Though I'm ashamed to admit here, I had to swipe three dollars from Daddy's nightstand to buy it because I'd already used up my allowance on a dress for the Senior sock hop. The point is, I needed the money because I could hardly be expected to wait another week for my allowance just to hear your voice again, so you can understand my predicament, and hopefully you'll forgive me, Patsy, as I am usually an honest sort of person.

Anyway, after I bought your record, I went straight home and pulled it carefully from the sleeve. When the needle dropped and the song washed over me, the words set my heart on fire all over again and I melted into the softness of your voice. I promised I'd only play it once a day, but for the life of me I can't stop pulling it out, trailing my fingers over the grooves of the vinyl. My mother says a record will only play a hundred times, and then it's done for, but I'm not sure if I believe her. I have a sneaking suspicion she's just tired of hearing it, which makes no sense because it is the best song I've ever heard and about a thousand times more thrilling than those tiresome hymns she's always listening to as she sips her gin and punch while my brothers run amok. (I don't think I've mentioned yet that I have three of them, and they are all younger than me, which is just the worst sort of punishment a girl could ask for. No sister to commiserate with!)

Maybe it's because I'm surrounded by boys every waking minute that I was desperate to hear a girl's voice on the radio for once. Anyway, I think a good song wants to be played out. It may sound strange, but I want to wear out my life like a scratched-up record,

get good and used up like a pencil sharpened right
down to the nub.

Yours truly,

Lola

CHAPTER 6
EFFIE / "COME ON IN"

Guiding her car in front of a strip of neat little row houses, Effie spotted a marquee bearing the words *Fields and Fields* in front of the yellow bungalow and pulled into an open space. This part of downtown Tilly had once been a thriving business center, but after years of neglect and deterioration, it had been deemed "Old Tilly" until the hipsters descended. Now a smattering of freshly painted buildings in vibrant colors dotted the main storefront road, most of which had been renovated into everything from trendy restaurants to nail salons to cycling studios.

It was unseasonably warm for early March, and by the time she spilled into the tiny refurbished office, her armpits tingled with sweat, the silky fabric of her blouse fused to her damp skin. She should have forgone the blazer. As she pushed her way past a glass door, the scent of potpourri hit her nostrils. She couldn't quite place the ingredients, but it reminded her of her obstetrician's office, cloying and impersonal. Her home usually smelled like a mixture of dirty laundry and whatever scented candle she'd picked up that week, though lately she'd been letting things slide and it leaned toward the former. A soul-crushing guilt prevented her from pushing the kids too hard when it came to helping out with chores—even though she hadn't been the one to leave.

Crisp dove gray walls greeted her as her wedges clicked against a reclaimed-wood floor.

A knot formed in her stomach as she approached the flustered woman behind the desk. She didn't appear to be that much older than Jay. With purple hair shaved close on one side of her head and a silver hoop peeking out the tip of her nose, she made Effie feel practically geriatric. Stealing a glance down at her body, she wondered if Teagan had been right about the skinny jeans after all. But, shoving down her doubts, she mustered a toothy smile.

"Hi, I'm interviewing for the assistant position," she said, doing her best to summon a tone that communicated she was serious yet friendly. If also entirely too old for this job.

"You're his one o'clock," the woman replied, nearly shouting as she removed a pair of orange headphones. It came out more like an accusation. "Sorry." Shaking her head, she spoke softer now. "It isn't my job to schedule his appointments." With nimble fingers, she rifled through disheveled stacks of files. "I'm the paralegal, but I've been pulling double duty since his assistant quit last week. Again. That one only lasted two weeks." Rolling her eyes, she tugged a slip of paper from beneath a manila folder, then tapped it with a black-painted fingernail.

The way she said *again* gave Effie pause, and for the first time she wondered if perhaps her age might be a bonus. Maybe she wasn't up to speed on legal jargon, but she was at least dependable. Clearheaded and unafraid to work hard. She wouldn't be quitting before she'd barely begun.

"Here you are. Effie . . . Baker?" The paralegal arched a thickly lined eyebrow.

"That's me." Hearing her name read aloud by a near teenager made her realize how old-fashioned it sounded, like a dowdy housewife from a bygone era.

"I'll let him know you're here." With a lift of her chin, she gestured toward a sparsely furnished lobby with a solitary floral love seat set against the far wall. "You can wait over there." She pulled her headphones over her ears and tugged open a laptop covered in stickers of skeleton emoji.

Taking the hint, Effie eyed the love seat warily, as there was already an undeniably attractive and well-dressed man occupying half of it. A year ago, she might not have noticed the way his broad chest swelled beneath his fitted button-up. But since Daniel had moved on so quickly, surely she shouldn't feel guilty about appreciating a chiseled physique when she saw one.

With one leg propped atop the other, the man was leaning back with his fingers laced behind the back of his crew-cut ebony hair. She pretended not to notice him, but it was hard not to. Teagan would have described him as *totally Gucci*. Coming from her daughter, this was not a compliment but rather a statement on the rampant commercialism of the elite who were *precipitating the demise of the planet*. Wearing a gray checkered tie and a slim-fit suit, the man was obviously younger than her by at least a decade. As she approached him, she offered a tepid smile that quickly faded when he didn't bother looking up. As her gaze drifted down to his expensive-looking loafers, a new thought entered her mind. Maybe he was her competition. If so, she had seriously miscalculated the dress code and likely had no business being here. Why had she assumed she could just waltz into a job after two decades out of the workforce with no degree to speak of? She sank into the cushion next to him, making sure to leave a respectable gap, then pretended to inspect the desert landscapes adorning the walls.

After a few minutes, the silence began to wear on her. How could a person sit less than a foot away and say nothing? They were practically knee to knee, and that was worth at least a hello, in her opinion. A perpetual people pleaser since birth, she would have done a song and dance if it made someone else feel less uncomfortable. But it seemed younger generations had missed the memo on social graces. She tried to ignore his presence, fumbling with her phone to search the news, which she was too nervous to comprehend or care about. After a few excruciating minutes of pretending to read, she couldn't stand the awkwardness any longer. "So, are you applying for the position too?" she asked brightly. The man startled, then turned his head and trained his blue eyes on Effie as if he were seeing her for the first time. The sudden attention made her heart quicken, and reflexively she fidgeted with her hair. "No. I, uh . . . I'm just a friend of Mr. Fields." Drawing a fist to his mouth, he let out a gruff cough. "I'm meeting him for a late lunch."

"I see," she said, trying not to appear relieved, but her insides loosened a little and her neck muscles relaxed. When she'd researched the company, she learned it had begun as a father-and-son arrangement. Drew had inherited the firm from Mr. Fields senior, who had passed away a few years ago, and she presumed that he would be the one interviewing her today. Half joking, she said, "I suppose you don't have any tips that would help me get this job? Since you know him and all."

"Actually—" His lips curled up at the corners, settling into a seductive grin, and Effie's stomach flipped in what she supposed was a swoon. That was definitely a new sensation. *Those dimples. That tiny cleft in his chin.* It was like staring at a work of art.

A sudden heat flushed her neck, and she hoped he didn't notice. She caught herself scrutinizing his features and briefly wondered if he was wearing makeup, because his skin was ridiculously perfect. It made her slightly jealous.

"I'd be happy to provide you with some insider information. For a price, of course," he added dryly.

Effie suppressed a nervous laugh. Was this guy serious?

"I'm kidding," he said before she could think of an appropriate response. His eyes brimmed with fresh excitement as he leaned in. "What kind of experience do you have?"

Almost immediately, the buzz in her veins dissipated. Though she'd known this question was coming, she still hadn't figured out a way to spin the substantial gap in her résumé. She'd never been an "official" employee for Baker's Builders, so she hadn't listed it. Besides, the idea of a potential employer calling her soon-to-be-ex-husband for a reference check elicited a wave of existential dread. Instead, she'd . . . improvised. "Oh here. Just . . . hold on a sec." She plunged a hand into an oversize canvas tote bag that read "Keep Calm and PTA On," then produced a piece of embossed acid-free paper and held it in front of him. She thought it odd when he didn't accept it, just leaned over and grimaced.

"You didn't have to print this, you know. If you applied online, he already has your résumé."

"Oh, I know," she said breezily, though she most certainly didn't. "I just wanted to be thoroughly prepared." Suddenly, she was overcome with nagging worry. What else had changed in the last twenty years? Were printers even a thing anymore? Of course not. Everything was on the cloud now, which was entirely too abstract a concept for her. Daniel had been after her for years to convert forgotten company contracts trapped inside a drawer of flash drives, but she hadn't gotten around to it yet.

He squinted at the words, then pulled back and cocked an eyebrow. "PTA hospitality chair?"

"Four years running now," she provided helpfully. "I coordinated the most darling gifts for the teacher holiday party. We tied the softest argyle blankets and attached little cards that said 'Sleep in heavenly fleece.'" She beamed, remembering how Trisha had told her it would be too costly and that she'd never finish them in time. But that had only emboldened her. In short order, she'd hunted down a bargain store and haggled with the owner to slash 30 percent, then single-handedly mobilized an army of Brody's soccer friends' moms to tie them during games. "The principal is still raving about them," she said, though he seemed completely nonplussed as he trailed a finger over the next bullet point.

"It says here you run a book club?" he asked, looking up at her blankly. "How is that relevant?"

Momentarily distracted by his nonexistent pores, she caught herself scrutinizing his perfect nose, then said, "Have *you* ever tried to select a book that twenty-four different women will find appealing?" Raising her eyebrows, she shook a finger. "I can assure you it's not an easy task."

"Six years spent volunteering as a den mother," he went on, a befuddled expression taking shape in his countenance.

"Yep," she said proudly. Wrangling fifteen little boys into cooking tinfoil meals without any casualties was nothing to sneeze at, but this man appeared genuinely perplexed. Judging from his immaculate clothing, Effie concluded he must not have any children of his own.

"And you did all this stuff for free?"

"Didn't earn a cent. Unless you count the hugs, which I'm all too happy to accept as a form of payment," she added with a touch of humor. It didn't feel like the right time to apprise him of her new marital situation and that, actually, cold hard cash would be much more helpful going forward.

This explanation appeared to offend his senses because the whites of his eyes grew nearly twofold. Massaging the back of his neck, he leaned forward and rested his elbows atop his knees. "All right, listen, you can't lead with any of this stuff."

"I can't?" she puzzled.

"Look, I'm going to do you a huge favor here and help you out, but you have to trust me. You see, it's all in the way you package yourself. For example"—he gestured to the space between them—"instead of *hospitality chair*, why not use a term that more accurately reflects your . . . versatile abilities? Something like . . . oh, I don't know . . . *director of events.*"

"I see." Though she wasn't certain she did. It was more than a stretch of the truth. Then again, she had single-handedly organized every "Donuts with Dad" event at the school since Jay was in the second grade. Surely there was something to be said for her work ethic, so maybe fudging the truth a little wasn't entirely blasphemous.

"And here, instead of *den mother,*" he went on, pointing to the text, "how about *educational supervisor of entry-level trainees?*" A spark of pride gleamed in his liquid eyes, making them look like rhinestones. "See how I did that?"

"Yes, I see," she said, catching a wisp of his enthusiasm. "So, instead of snack coordinator for Brody's soccer games, I could say that I'm the . . . nutritional specialist for a budding athletic team?" Admittedly, *athletic* was not the most accurate term as she had to personally dress her eleven-year-old and wrangle him into the car every game day. Brody was far more interested in playing imaginary sports via his iPad, but Daniel had insisted that each of their kids participate on a team to build leadership skills. It was annoyingly convenient for him that she should be the one to carry the burden of enforcing this rule.

Without missing a beat, the man snapped his fingers and sat up a little straighter. "Exactly."

"Gosh, this is so helpful." Her chest lighter now, she felt like a bright student who'd grasped the concept of the lesson the first time around. "After so many years at home with the kids, it's hard to think of myself as much more than a housewife."

"Uh, uh, uh." With a frown, he wagged a disapproving finger. "Domestic technician."

"Right." She smiled broadly. In nineteen years of married life, no one had ever called her that, but she had to admit, it had a certain ring. "Any other tips?" She didn't want to be too presumptuous, but as a friend of her potential boss, maybe he could provide some personal intel.

With a thoughtful head tilt, he raised a hand. "Drew . . . I mean, Mr. Fields, is a very particular kind of guy. So, you want to make sure you let him know that you'll be amenable to his demands, no matter how rigid they may seem."

Curiosity pricked at her budding excitement. "What do you mean by rigid?" Remembering the way the paralegal had rolled her eyes as she recounted the last employee's sudden departure, Effie wondered if perhaps she had assumed wrong. Maybe things had happened the other way around and Mr. Fields had driven his assistants away with cruelty. A tiny seed of worry blossomed in her gut.

"It's just that he can be . . . inflexible when it comes to certain things." He placed an arm atop the seat behind her head, angling his body toward hers as if they were old friends. But she noted the way he refrained from touching her in that annoying, overly affectionate way that some men did. Actually, she wouldn't have minded his hand grazing her knee, but admitting this made her a very bad feminist. Per usual, Teagan would be disappointed in her. *Focus, Effie. Focus!*

"He's very organized," he went on. "Likes to have his notes arranged by order of importance, so never approach him with something that's small potatoes when there's a five-alarm fire to put out first. It will only irritate him, and he'll do that thing where his eyes go dead and he looks at you like you've just said something so moronic it isn't worth addressing."

"That's helpful." Pulling her eyebrows together, Effie made a mental note. "Prioritize information," she repeated aloud, wondering if she should be writing this down.

The man snapped his fingers again, as if he'd just remembered something else. "And he only drinks Jamaican Blue Mountain coffee from Gordon's because it's the freshest. They import the beans every week. Two shots of espresso." Locking eyes with her, he held up two fingers and wiggled them, as if he needed this information to stick in her mind.

"Got it. No Starbucks," she said, overwhelmed but grateful. The tightness in her chest began to dissipate, and for the first time today, she filled her lungs completely. "Seriously, I can't thank you enough. You have no idea how nervous I was this morning. I really owe you."

"I know." A dazzling grin played on his lips, and he winked, which gave her a dose of much-needed confidence. "Oh, and one more thing," he added, his tone more serious now, his face marred by the deep line forming above his brow. His cheek muscles tightened as he stroked his chin. "Don't mention anything about his family. It's not a good situation right now. Makes him uncomfortable."

Effie nodded. "Got it. Nix the small talk," she promised, though it would be difficult, as she was the sort of person who liked to know details like that, not so much because she was nosy but because she found other people's lives interesting—far more interesting than her own, which at the moment had all the predictability of a Lifetime movie.

"Mrs. Baker," the paralegal called out. "Mr. Fields is ready for you now. Just down the hall, first door on the right."

Effie rose from her seat, then smoothed her blazer. Pulling back her shoulders, she started for his office, but she'd only made it a few steps before her southern programming kicked in. "Thank you again," she said, swiveling back to face the handsome stranger. "For the tips."

"No problem." He smoldered back, sparking a fire in places she thought had withered long ago. The last time she'd felt interest in sleeping with Daniel was last summer, right before the Amber debacle had lobotomized the libido-controlling part of her brain. Even sadder, that night she'd ditched her compression socks and stained flannel shorts for a satin nightie she'd plucked from the bottom of a pile at Costco. Not couture, but it was comfortable. Now that she knew what she'd been up against, it's no wonder Daniel had feigned being asleep.

Appreciating this man's perfect pair of dimples, she tried unsuccessfully to ignore the blood pulsing through her veins, quickly surging to her neglected loins. He might just be the most perfect man she'd ever laid eyes on, but she didn't want him to know this, so she did her best to rein in her smile, which was verging on creepy. When she made an awkward attempt to shake his hand, he seemed flustered and pulled back his own. His smile cracked, and he smoothed his blazer, leaving her hanging. Like an idiot. It was just another reminder that she was entirely out of her element. Apparently, no one shook hands anymore.

~

A man whom she presumed to be Mr. Fields caught sight of her lingering in the hallway and, with a hurried wave of his palm, motioned her into his office. Nursing a paper cup of coffee in one hand, he was standing behind a giant laptop with two extra screens, his eyes pinging between the three like an erratic pendulum.

A gruff voice scraped at her ears as she willed her feet toward the threshold. "No, that won't work."

"Excuse me?" Taken aback, she touched a fingertip to her bosom and checked behind her, but the hallway was empty.

"Are you kidding?" Mr. Fields's voice was laced with an irritation that unbalanced her. While not more than a few inches taller than her, he had an energy about him that made her feel at least a foot smaller than her five three.

"No?" she asked, unsure if she had answered the question correctly.

With a heavy sigh, he raked his fingers through slightly disheveled hair, his face muscles contracting into a scowl. "I needed those tax returns yesterday." Already, he sounded annoyed, which did not bode well for this interview.

And just like that, her newly acquired confidence melted away, coalescing in a jumble of indecipherable words. "OK, truthfully, I had no idea I was supposed to provide those, but I'll get them to you ASAP. My husband—soon-to-be-ex-husband," she clarified, "left with most of our legal documents, so it may take me some time to locate them since, as you can imagine, things have been a bit tense lately." Why was she still talking? She'd promised Grace she wouldn't mention the divorce, and it had taken all of three seconds to spill her entire life story to a complete stranger—what's more, a divorce lawyer. But what the heck did he need her tax returns for?

"Hold on a minute, Gary. Someone's in my office." Craning his neck around the biggest screen, he examined her thoughtfully. "Mrs. Baker, I presume?"

A sharp wave of heat rolled through her. "You presume correctly," she said, feeling ridiculous.

"I'm almost done here. Just hang on a sec." He held up a finger as she clocked the earbud in his right ear and immediately wished for a rock to crawl under.

As Mr. Fields continued to berate poor Gary, Effie lurked about the room uneasily. He hadn't invited her to sit yet, and she didn't want to appear too forward. Like a nervous stray, she trailed along the back wall, where a series of photos caught her attention—snapshots of Mr. Fields with a woman she assumed was his wife. With stark freckles against pale skin and fiery red hair, she was gorgeous. In one picture, the two of them sported wet suits and surfboards while a little boy beamed between them, squinting away the sun. In another, the same boy was decked out in a blue-and-white baseball uniform, brandishing a bat, with an adorable gap where a front tooth should have been. He was a perfect mixture of their features, with his father's light-brown hair and sharp nose and his mother's freckles. He looked to be about Brody's age. She wondered if this was the family trouble that poor Mr. Fields would not want to discuss. Then, remembering the handsome stranger's advice, she reminded herself not to comment on this information. What was his name again? The man in the lobby who had been so eager to help? A molten shame burned in her chest. She'd been so nervous for the interview; she hadn't even made a proper introduction. She would have to remember to thank him when she left.

A gentle whirring caught her attention, and she swiveled around as if she'd been caught snooping.

"Please, make yourself comfortable," Mr. Fields said as his desk lowered, seemingly of its own volition. Settling into a seat behind it, he gestured toward a pair of red-and-navy accent chairs, and she briefly wondered if his wife had picked them out. The office had a woman's touch about it, with a white lattice rug and floating wooden shelves dotted by framed photographs, which Effie promised herself again not to mention. Gathering her fortitude, she obeyed and settled into a chair.

"Thanks for coming in." Though he was finally addressing her, he still seemed distracted, his gaze skating across the screens every few seconds like an addict looking for a fix. Reaching for his coffee, he seemed wired and exhausted all at once, with a severe nose, a sturdy square jaw, and thin lips bracketed by deep lines. He smiled, but something about his demeanor gave her the distinct impression he was exerting a lot of energy to hold it in place. "So . . . tell me about yourself. What kind of experience do you have?" he asked, only partially paying attention. He'd never actually ended things with Gary, who was presumably still on the call.

"Of course." Like a teacher's pet at the ready, Effie dutifully dug out her résumé again and extended it toward him with a cheery smile.

"I've read through about a million of these lately," he said, pushing it away as he leaned in and clasped his hands together. "Just tell me what your strengths are. What qualifies you for the position?"

Remembering her conversation with the sexy stranger, Effie quickly filtered through her experience. "I'm . . . director of events at my son's school," she heard herself say, feeling like a liar. If Trisha could hear her now, she would have herself a rollicking good laugh.

"Really?" This appeared to pique his interest. "What sort of events do you direct?" He raised a thick eyebrow, and she noticed the faint lines taking shape on his forehead. Drew Fields was actually attractive, in a nerdy sort of way. She could imagine him as one of the mathletes at her high school who, unlike Daniel, had chosen academics over brawn. While Effie had read every book on the summer reading list before their senior year, Daniel had spent his days at the Y shooting hoops and his nights on his PlayStation playing *NBA Live*. He'd only passed their English exams because Effie had supplied him with index cards summarizing *Of Mice and Men* and *The Grapes of Wrath*. At the time, she'd been proud when he earned Bs, but now she wanted to shake her younger self for being an enabler.

Refocusing her attention on the question, she mustered what she hoped resembled a confident smile. "I planned luncheons, social activities, fundraisers . . . the occasional auction." Thinking of her book club, she chewed the inside of her lip. "Oh, and I run a literature advocacy program for adults," she added, feeling a little proud of herself for coming up with that one on her own.

"Interesting." Stroking his jaw, he appeared to mull over this information. His eyes were steely blue and determinedly fixed on her. They reminded her of a mountainscape, stony but weathered, the roughness softened by fine lines fanning out around them. The weight of his gaze made her wonder if she had remembered to put on deodorant before leaving the house. Finally, he asked, "And you're familiar with Microsoft?"

"The company?"

"The program," he specified in a way that made her feel ridiculous. "Excel, Word, the occasional PowerPoint."

"Oh, of course," she said, feigning confidence. Truthfully, aside from Word, she was no expert, though Teagan's sixth-grade slideshow had been a smashing success thanks to her Photoshop skills. No one could even tell that two students had missed class-picture day. She knew she could learn it. She *would* learn it, stay up late googling help videos, and fake her way through until she figured it all out.

Smacking his lips, he clasped his hands together. "I'm going to be really honest with you, Mrs. Baker."

"Call me Effie," she said brightly. After all, he couldn't be that much older than her. *Mrs.* felt formal and stuffy, something that only seemed right coming from one of the kids' friends. Besides, her last name was still in flux, as she hadn't yet decided whether or not to revert to her maiden name. It occurred to her that Daniel wouldn't have to worry about these sorts of details or waste an entire day at the DMV to apply for a new license.

"Effie"—he flashed her a joyless but perfectly white smile—"we've had a lot of turnover here lately, and I'm desperate to hire someone who actually wants to work. Between you and me, the last three people were complete idiots. I need someone who isn't going to put in a two-hour notice so they can focus on their social media engagement. The last thing the world needs is another TikTok star." Leveling his gaze at her, he added, "Do you understand what I'm saying?"

"Absolutely," she replied breezily, nodding along but feeling guilty about the TikTok she had posted just yesterday. Thanks to Cletus, she'd recorded a tutorial for how to remove the scent of dog urine from carpet and had received a respectable number of views. Though not a star by any stretch of the imagination, she had a small but loyal following of mostly friends and other moms from school and Brody's soccer team. She may not be a wiz at Excel, but she wasn't a dinosaur. At least not yet.

Drew laced his fingers together and leaned forward. "Educational background?"

Panic swept through her like wildfire catching dry brush, and she squirmed against her seat. "I went to Canola Heights," she managed to say.

He furrowed his brow. "Haven't heard of it. Where is that?"

"It's in Kansas . . . where I grew up," she said, hoping he wouldn't pry for more.

But, of course, he did. "Is that a two-year program?"

"Four," Effie said, wondering how much longer she could keep this going. She had wanted to go to college, had even sent in the forms, but she and Daniel, half-crazed with hormones and pie-in-the-sky dreams, had been so anxious to settle down, and he had needed her help to get the company going. She couldn't remember the precise moment she'd let her aspirations fall by the wayside, but in those early years, time and money were commodities she hadn't been able to spare. Once they discovered they were expecting Jay, the entire idea became untenable, replaced by lullabies and trips to the library and staying up late to help Daniel sort out the books. Finally, she caved, her chest collapsing under the weight of the lie. "It was my high school."

A flicker of disappointment crossed Mr. Fields's face. Was that a wince? "I see."

Though they were only two little words, the unspoken judgment was enough to graze her confidence. But gathering her courage, she leveled her shoulders. "Mr. Fields, I'm not ignorant of the facts here. I realize you don't get a lot of applicants my age for an entry-level position, but I know I can do this job. It's not on my résumé there, but I helped out my husband in our family construction company for years, doing all sorts of office work. All I'm asking for is a chance to prove myself. I'm smart. I'm hardworking. And I am one hundred percent dedicated to proving myself here, if you'll let me."

Narrowing his eyes at her, he nodded, but she wasn't sure if she'd swayed his opinion. "Of course." Straightening his tie, he cleared his throat, then stood up, pushing his seat back. "Thank you for coming in, Mrs. Baker. I have a couple of other applicants to get through today, but I'll be in touch."

"Effie," she insisted cheerfully as she stood to face him.

"Effie," he repeated with a slow nod. It was impossible to read his expression now. He extended a firm hand, which she happily accepted, relieved. Maybe it wasn't an outdated gesture after all. But when his fingers clasped around hers, a new thought entered her mind. As she locked eyes with him, it now occurred to her in painful clarity that there had probably been dozens of other applicants, each of them younger and likely more qualified. But she needed this job more than they did. Not just for the money, but to prove to Daniel, to prove to herself, that she could do it.

Noticing the sleeve on his paper coffee cup, she gestured and asked, "Don't you just love Gordon's? Blue Mountain coffee is the only way to go. I don't drink anything else."

Bingo. That was all it took for the winds to shift in her favor, and for a fleeting second, she almost convinced herself that she was every bit the person she'd pretended to be. The look in Mr. Fields's eyes sent a shimmy of confidence up her spine. It was the same look the vice principal had given her when she handed him a heavenly fleece blanket. *Thank you, sexy mystery man.* To show her gratitude, she determined to bake him dozens of her famous caramel brownies and throw in a heavenly fleece blanket for good measure. She knew that look. It was respect.

"You can call me Drew," he said, the hint of a smile gracing his lips.

CHAPTER 7

LOLA

November 3, 1961

Dear Patsy,

I suppose it's about time I introduced you to my mother, the sewing fascist of our family who is hell bent on snipping me down to size. She all but forced me to go to the sock hop tonight, which I'd like to point out I was already planning to attend. As I mentioned before, I bought my outfit weeks ago—a halter swing dress in midnight blue that flares out below my knees just like that smart little black and white number Grace Kelly wore in *To Catch a Thief*. I'm sure you know the one as you're always so well dressed. I even named it Frances because it sounds so elegant and very fitting for the style. Mitsy and Helen bought matching dresses in emerald green and lemon meringue, but guess whose mother decided that bare shoulders at a dance would be "unbecoming of a young lady."

Then today, I came home from school to find that she had utterly mutilated poor Frances with sleeves!

Sleeves, Patsy! And they weren't even midnight blue but navy with white polka dots, which I don't have to tell you is an entirely tacky look and an insult to anyone with an ounce of fashion sense. I informed her that I refused to be seen in public wearing them. Then she said if I didn't, she'd rat me out to Daddy about the three dollars I swiped for your record. I didn't know she knew about the money, but she's calculating like that, always keeping her cards close, waiting to make a move until she has a flush. She would make an expert Poker player if she didn't spend all her Friday evenings playing Canasta with the miserable housewives of her garden club.

Getting back to my poor abused dress—I was forced to wear Frances tonight in all her terrible gruesomeness, and I hated every minute of it, cursing my mother to the devil and saying the most awful things about her in my head while everyone danced around me. I started alphabetically rhyming her name with every horrible thing you can imagine. I had just made it to the P's and was feeling very clever about myself when I first heard his voice. It was low like a bass guitar, and it hummed in my ear like the flutter of bees' wings.

I know you're desperate to know who "he" is, so I'll tell you. His name is Wallace Rose! He graduated last spring and came to the dance with a friend. I'd never seen him before. I would have remembered if I had because he is entirely gorgeous with slicked back, ebony hair and a dreamboat smile that sent my heart skittering. He was wearing khaki pants with a baby blue and white striped bowling shirt that made his blue eyes dazzle like Paul Newman's. At first, I wondered if something was wrong with his vision as he didn't seem to notice my clown sleeves, but then I realized he wasn't even looking at them. He was staring at my face, smiling with a sort of half grin. It made me feel a bit bashful as I don't really like my freckles, and my hair is neither blonde like Helen's nor brown like Mitsy's, but somewhere unexceptional in between.

He asked what my name was, and because I was feeling flustered, and truthfully still a bit put out about Frances, I crossed my arms and tried to look aloof. Mitsy always says how important it is not to appear too available to boys, so I told him I wasn't in the business of giving out my name to total strangers. Then he said if I wouldn't tell him, he'd just have to guess. He bet me three dollars he could guess my name correctly—which just so happened to be the exact amount of money I had stolen and the reason I was standing there looking like a fool in that awful dress. What are the odds, Patsy? It seemed like too much of a coincidence not to be fate. So of course, I couldn't turn him down as I was certain he couldn't guess it, and also, as a repentant thief, I was in desperate need of the money.

At first, he tried Alice, and I snorted. As if I look like an Alice! Then he tried out Barbara, which made me a little heated as every Barb I've ever met has been a complete bore. And then, much to my shock, he said, "Lola. You look like a Lola." It was about then that I called him a lying sack of potatoes and outright accused him of being a stalker. You see, I'm named after a little-known actress, Lola Lane, because my mother is obsessed with every movie starring the Lane sisters. In all my years, I've never come across another

Lola in the flesh. There's no way he could have known it unless he cheated. Well, I wasn't going to have it, especially since I was already in debt up to my eyeballs.

He laughed and told me he had asked around about me when he saw me brooding by the Jell-O table. (I wasn't brooding. I was in mourning for Frances.) In any case, he told me that because he cheated in our little game, I didn't have to pay him the money, which I wasn't going to do anyhow. He said that a date would do just fine, and that he would pick me up next Friday evening around six if I was available. I was, but I didn't want to admit it on account of my pride, so I told him I'd have to ask my mother. But of course, she'll be thrilled since I haven't been on a proper date in ages, and she's always at my throat about putting myself out there when it comes to members of the opposite sex. Apparently, seventeen is plenty old enough to be thinking of marriage, which she's always droning on about as if it will be the pinnacle of my life. But judging from hers, I can't say the idea appeals to me as I would much rather go on to do something interesting and important like you, Patsy, instead of draping myself over the sofa with a cocktail glass every night.

Then again, I can't seem to stop thinking about Wallace's eyes and the way he brushed his hand against mine as if by accident. I think it might have been on purpose. If it wasn't, I sort of wish it were.

Sincerely,
Lola

CHAPTER 8
Effie / "Faded Love"

"Mom, I think I have an ulcer," Brody said, peeking up at her from his supine position on the couch, video game controller in hand.

"You do not have an ulcer," Effie replied as she glided around the living room tossing loose items into a laundry basket. "The most stressful part of your day is deciding what flavor granola bar to pack in the morning. In fact, if anyone has ulcers in this house, it's me." Come to think of it, she had been experiencing more gastrointestinal pangs since Daniel had left. Maybe she should see a doctor. But considering her experience at Rosehaven, she wasn't keen on the idea of entering a medical establishment anytime soon.

Brody crossed his eyes and stuck out his tongue in an attempt to study the anomaly in question. "Then what's this white bump on my tongue?" he asked, lisping the words, his face awash in consternation. "Do you think it's a vitamin deficiency?" Unlike his older siblings, Brody had taken after Effie in the height department and was short for eleven. He seemed much younger, with his soft, rounded face and doe eyes. When he used words like *deficiency* around strangers, they usually did a double take.

"I think it's a bump, and you shouldn't worry about it," Effie replied, trying not to sound annoyed. Brody was always inventing illnesses—a hypochondriac since he was old enough to read the side effects on his asthma inhaler. And since the separation, his list had only grown. Last week, he'd convinced himself that eating pizza turned his face red, which she supposed was a better excuse than admitting he'd forgotten to wear sunscreen at soccer practice.

"But it hurts when I bite it." He demonstrated this action and winced.

"Then don't bite it." Reaching for a stray sock on the rug, she blew a chunk of hair from her eyes, wondering if she should enroll them all in therapy. But she was too busy with work now and too tired at home to think past making dinner and slipping into a bath later tonight.

As if hearing her thoughts, Brody looked up and said, "You look nice, Mom." The compliment took her aback, and she blushed. Normally, she would not have expected her youngest child to comment on her appearance, so maybe her efforts hadn't been in vain. After all, the interview had ended in success. She would begin at Fields and Fields on Monday, a fact that still seemed too good to be true.

"Thank you, sweetie," she said, tousling his sandy hair before walking into the kitchen to start dinner. She wasn't sure if she should feed the kids before they left to go to Daniel's place for the weekend. She could picture him saying something like, "With all the money I'm graciously providing, you could have fed them dinner at least." Just to be safe, she boiled a pot of water for pasta and rummaged around in the freezer for a bag of meatballs. Tossing them in a pan, she sighed, remembering she would have to prepare Teagan's meal separately. Her socially minded daughter had been in a vegan phase since watching a documentary about how cows were the leading cause of the seventh major mass extinction on the planet—or maybe it was the sixth. Honestly, Effie had been too put out to process Teagan's reasons for rejecting the perfectly good pot roast she'd prepared for New Year's Eve.

An engine lulled to a halt as Jay's giant sapphire truck rolled into the drive. With its monster wheels and leather interior, it was a ridiculously expensive model for an eighteen-year-old, but Daniel was never able to say no to his oldest son, especially since he was currently trying to claw his way back into Jay's good graces. While Teagan appeared to blame Effie for the divorce, Jay had been punishing Daniel with the silent treatment since he'd moved out. Last week, he'd sideswiped a trash can while simultaneously backing into the side of his father's pickup, which would have sent Daniel into a tailspin a year ago. But when Effie asked about the giant dent in his truck, Daniel said it was his fault for parking too close to the garage and that insurance would cover the cost.

It always made her heart lurch when she saw her curly-haired baby climbing out of the driver's seat with his little sister in tow. Slinging her backpack over one shoulder, Teagan slammed the passenger-side door, and the two of them ambled inside.

"How was band practice?" Effie called out.

"Fine," Teagan said, dropping her backpack and trumpet by the door before making a beeline for the kitchen. She ran a hand through her shoulder-length blonde hair, then opened the refrigerator.

Jay tossed his keys on the counter, his face still covered in red splotches and his basketball jersey fused to his skin. She'd told him weeks ago to get a haircut, but he clearly hadn't because the curls hanging above his eyes were tinged with sweat. Somehow, teenage girls found this look attractive, because he had never been at a loss for dates. Effie understood. Daniel had been the same way at that age, all gangly limbs and questionable hygiene, his presence accompanied by a pervasive musky scent he'd tried to cover with too much cologne. Towering over her, sometimes Jay looked so much like his father, it stole her breath. It was like staring into the past.

"Are you guys all packed and ready to go?" Effie asked, chopping an onion. "Your dad is expecting you tonight." After discussing it ad nauseam with Daniel, she'd conceded that the kids should spend three weekends a month at his condo, with the stipulation that Amber not live there. But not everyone agreed.

Jay shot her a look. "I still don't get why you're forcing us to go. We're not little kids anymore." He opened the pantry and reached for a bag of chips before settling down at the breakfast bar across from Effie. "Layla and I had plans. If Dad gets to be with his girlfriend, why can't I be with mine?" he murmured into the bottom of the bag.

It was a fair point. For all Daniel had put her through, at least she still had their loyal firstborn in her corner, always ready to offer up commentary on his father's ridiculous new hobby. Effie tried her best not to let her satisfaction show.

"Spare me," Teagan said before popping open a can of orange soda.

"You sure that's vegan approved?" Jay asked, raising an eyebrow.

A hint of worry crossed Teagan's face as she inspected the can, but if there was anything amiss in the list of ingredients, she didn't say. Redirecting her sights on Jay, she asked, "Did you know that only two percent of high school relationships outlast high school?" making Effie reflect on her own failed marriage. If this was true, she and Daniel had beaten the odds for a time, only to become another depressing statistic. "You can survive one weekend without Layla. Stop being so dramatic."

"I'm being dramatic?" He laughed. "This, coming from the girl who wants to protest prom?"

"Wait, what?" Effie said, doing a double take between her teenagers. "What do you mean by protesting? You're not planning anything illegal, are you, Teagan?" Since her outburst about colonialism in geography class last week, things at school had been precarious. Effie couldn't go through another parent-teacher conference with Daniel, discussing Teagan's lack of respect for authority. Besides, now she had a job to consider, and she didn't want to ask Drew for time off to address her wayward daughter's disciplinary record.

"God no, Mom. We're wearing animal costumes." She tucked a chunk of hair behind her ear, revealing the strand of piercings that ran up the cartilage. "Some big developer is tearing down the old science museum to build a strip of tacky condominiums, and we're trying to raise awareness. We need six hundred signatures for the city to consider placing a hold on his permit."

A seed of pride blossomed in Effie's bosom. She had always admired that fire in Teagan that made her believe she could change the world, maybe because Effie had never felt that she had the power to change much of anything herself. But at the moment, she couldn't help envisioning Teagan wrapped in taffeta and silk, donning a giant carnation corsage. "I can't believe you're actually going to prom." Suspended in the moment, she held a tentative hand to her chest. A memory of her own prom surfaced, but she swallowed back the dry lump that sprouted in her throat. How many people could say they'd gone to prom with their husband, the love of their life? She had bought a strapless lavender dress and spent weeks trying to find a matching tie for him. Eventually, she'd given up and told him to wear whatever he wanted. He showed up on her parents' porch wearing a double-breasted tuxedo with a bow tie and cummerbund the color of amethyst, and she'd nearly cried. Years later, when people asked why she'd married him so young, she thought about that bow tie and the homemade picnic dinner his mother had made and felt sorry that they didn't understand what love was. The memory made her homesick, and she shook it away. "But you said you didn't want to go." What Teagan had actually said was "I'll go to prom when the United States addresses the reality of climate change in a meaningful way instead of just paying lip service to tired phrases of comfort." But Effie had taken that as a hard no.

"I said I didn't want to go as some guy's property." She rolled her eyes. "I mean I still object to the whole thing on principal, but Harper and I are going together. To protest, ya know?"

"OK." Effie sighed, trying to get on board. She should be grateful that Teagan was making an effort, even if it wasn't exactly how she had hoped her only daughter would go to her junior prom. "So, we'll go shopping." She gave a dainty shrug. "We'll find an outfit next weekend, something . . . epic," Effie said.

"Don't worry, Mom. Harper's mom is taking us shopping at this amazing little vintage shop in Dallas."

"Oh," Effie said, trying to sound casual, though she was certain her face had drained of all color. "I mean, it's just something I'd hoped the two of us could do together, you know. It's a milestone, honey."

"Maybe for you," she grumbled under her breath.

Shaking his head, Jay scoffed. "God, Teagan, you're such a jerk."

"Don't call your sister a jerk," Effie snapped. Though Teagan had been acting out for weeks. Lately, everything seemed to be a point of contention with her.

"I'm sorry," Teagan said defensively, turning her attention to Effie. "No offense, Mom, but I didn't think you'd wanna go. Besides, Harper's mom knows a lot more about this kind of stuff than you do. Did you know she once led a student walkout in her high school because the girls were being unfairly targeted by the dress code? Can you believe that? She's all about taking down the patriarchy."

"Yeah, that's cool. Me too," Effie said, nodding her head vigorously. Washing her hands in the sink, she blinked back the sting of tears, unsure if they were from the onion or her shattered dreams.

"Right," Teagan said. "So, like, how are you helping to do that, Mom? Getting plastic surgery and living off Dad's income isn't really furthering the cause."

In the deafening silence that followed, both kids locked eyes on Effie, and her face went slack. Apparently, she hadn't gotten away with anything, and she now wondered if she should have just told them about her surgery from the very beginning. But judging from Teagan's reaction now, maybe it wouldn't have mattered. Either way, she would have still given Effie that saucy half smile.

"Shut up, Teagan!" Jay stood up, his jaw tight. "What are you even talking about? Mom didn't get surgery."

"So, you think Grandma just happened to show up last month and Mom just happened to be sick and when she finally came out of her bedroom, she looked all . . . different?" She motioned a limp hand in Effie's general direction before taking another swig of soda.

Jay's eyes trailed over his mother, as if searching for signs of change. "She doesn't look different. She just looks like . . . Mom," he said, seeming unconvinced. Effie wasn't sure if she should take this as a compliment or an insult. Trying to stave off another argument and appear unfazed, she steadied her chin and adopted her signature mom voice, reserved for moments when her usual cheery tone wasn't sufficient. "Enough, guys! Besides, Teagan's right. I'm sure Harper's mother will help you pick out the perfect ensemble." As she said the words, she did her best to ignore the way her heart cracked in her chest a tiny bit.

~

The kids were all plugged into electronics upstairs while Effie frantically attempted to scrub spaghetti sauce out of her top. The doorbell had rung a full minute ago, and Cletus and Oscar were barking in frenzied circles. Why had she worn white when she knew there was a 60 percent chance she would spill dinner on her breast? "Fudgesicles!" She made a mental note to write this down for the internet stranger shopping for her clothes. *No white. Prone to food disasters.*

Effie startled at the sight of Daniel's lukewarm smile when she opened the door. Ungracefully, she attempted to hold back the dogs, who had seemed like a much better idea when he had been around to wrangle them. They were on him as soon as he slipped inside, apparently unoffended that he had abandoned them as much as he had her. It seemed Daniel's condo had a firm no-pets-allowed policy, which was annoying because she'd once had one too. As much as she now loved those furry giants, they were yet another responsibility that had fallen on her plate.

He bent down and patted them all over, returning their enthusiasm, before he stood and locked eyes with her. Maybe it was because of her conversation with the kids, but seeing him on her doorstep transported her back to prom night when he saw her in her dress for the first time. His eyes had gone wide, and then he'd pulled her in for a kiss so fiercely, as if he couldn't stand to be near her without touching her. It hurt to think about how different they both were back then. Young and beautiful and entirely obsessed with each other.

Vanquishing the memory, she noticed Daniel's eyes grazing her top. "You got a little something on your . . ." He gestured a finger toward her chest and the bright-red splotch that had only expanded with the club soda and sponge.

"Oh," she said, eyeing the stain. "We were eating dinner, and you know me." She shrugged but felt her cheeks flush hot. Why should she be this nervous around a man with whom she'd spent the better part of her life, the same man who had asked her to dig out an ingrown toenail on more than one occasion. And she had done it. Because that was what she thought marriage was supposed to be. She doubted Amber was willing to dig out an ingrown toenail, much less inspect a questionable mole in places she knew he'd rather her not mention.

"You fed them already?" he asked, incredulity creeping into his tone.

"Well, yeah. You never said, so I just assumed."

"That's OK." But he raked a heavy hand through his hair and sighed in a way that made Effie think it was a huge inconvenience. "I was going to go take them to Marco's tonight, but I'll just pick up something quick, and we'll go for ice cream instead."

A twinge of jealousy rippled through her. The idea of the four of them eating at Marco's without her felt personal. She wondered if Amber would be there too. Marco's, a hole-in-the-wall Italian bistro, had been *their* place. Not his. "Next time just let me know. I can hardly read your mind." That was the understatement of the century. "No offense, but why are you here?" Effie asked. One of the many benefits of having a teenager with a vehicle was that she could avoid awkward interactions like this.

"Sorry, I should have called first," he said, plunging his hands into his jeans pockets. "I was on my way home from work and wondering if

Jay had gotten any mail. Has he said anything about acceptance letters yet?"

"Not to me, but I'm sure they would have emailed him."

"Yeah. You're right." His gaze drifted to his shoes. "It's just that . . . he hasn't really been speaking to me very much lately, and I want to make sure he's making the best decision."

"You mean the best decision for him or the best decision for you?" Crossing her arms, she narrowed her eyes at him.

"Come on, Eff. You know I just want him to be happy. And that kid is in his element when he's on the court. Duke is the best place for him, and I don't want him hanging around here because he thinks he needs to . . ." He stopped before finishing his sentence, but Effie filled it in without hesitating.

"Take care of me? That is what you meant, isn't it?"

Shifting between his feet, he grimaced. "That's not what I said, but you do tend to have a certain"—he paused for a beat—"effect on him. He's got it in his head he needs to worry about you all the time. And what he needs to be worried about is planning for a future that makes the most of his talent."

It was impossible to hide her irritation, so she didn't try. Daniel did not have a monopoly on wanting the best for their children. As the person who had sacrificed her career and abdominal muscles to birth and raise them, she would know. Besides, maybe Jay wouldn't feel the need to worry about her all the time if his father had been faithful to his mother. She debated letting the words roll off her tongue, then thought better of it. "It's his decision to make. And let's just say you don't always act in the best interest of this family."

With a tight-lipped grimace, he shook his head. "I didn't come here to rehash everything, Effie. I made mistakes. I've admitted that. But we weren't happy. And it wasn't just me." This was news to her, because she had thought that they were happy. She had thought that when he kissed her goodbye every morning and said "I love you" that he meant it. She did not know it actually meant "I don't love you anymore, and by the way, I've met someone else, and we've been texting for months." Effie cleared her throat. "Fine. While I have you here, do you mind if I take the kids the last weekend this month? Lolly's turning eighty, and you know her. It's going to be a big to-do." She hated having to bring this up. Asking for extra time with her own children felt ridiculous.

Daniel grimaced. "Actually, I bought tickets to the Mavericks game that weekend. You know I'd normally say yes, but they're nonrefundable."

"Of course," she replied, trying to keep her disappointment from showing. Again, she wondered if Amber would be there and bristled at the thought of the five of them wearing matching jerseys and sharing popcorn. "I should have mentioned it sooner." Margie would be furious. Desperate for a change of subject, Effie swiveled around and called up the stairs, "Kids! Your father's here."

The thudding of feet and slamming doors filled the air. Avoiding eye contact with him, Effie ran a nervous hand through her hair. She now realized that wearing it down made her look less like a Harlequin temptress and more like an exhausted Maltese.

Finally, Daniel coughed into his fist. "So, are you feeling OK? After the . . . death thing?" He smirked, which sent her stomach lurching. She never should have told him about it.

"I'm fine." Righting her shoulders, she did her best to shrug the whole thing off, to act as if it hadn't killed a piece of her soul to know he didn't care that she'd almost died. Mortified, she forced a smile, hoping it looked genuine. It wasn't the fact that he had seen her lying makeup-less and bleary eyed on a gurney. After all, he had been there when she gave birth to all three of their children, had hugged her tight as the anesthesiologist stabbed her spine, had squeezed her fingers, dabbing away the sweat beads on her forehead with his other hand. It was the desperation of it all. Because while she told herself she'd had the surgery to boost her confidence, she had to admit that it wouldn't be the worst thing in the world if it turned Daniel's head, made him realize all he had given up. She didn't want him back. She only wanted him to *want* her back so she could properly refuse him. "It was nothing," she said finally. "I wasn't thinking clearly. I was on a lot of medication, so . . ." Whipping around, she peered up the stairs, hoping their offspring would materialize and put them both out of their misery.

"Well, for what it's worth, I'm glad you're OK. I wasn't in the best mood that day. It was . . . busy, you know. I'm sorry I wasn't more helpful."

"Don't worry about it," she said, trying to remain unaffected, though her heart lifted ever so slightly. As long as Amber was around, his intentions were perfectly clear. "I've already forgotten it."

CHAPTER 9
LOLA

November 10, 1961

Dear Patsy,

I have so much to tell you, my pen can barely keep up with my thoughts as I write. Tonight, Wallace picked me up for our date ten minutes early which I took as a sign that he was even more impatient than I was. I wore my canary yellow dress, the one with the little daisies along the hem, and the matching gloves, and he wore a smart pair of khaki trousers and a shirt the color of marigolds. You'd think we coordinated! Wallace drives a mint green '52 Plymouth he owns free and clear. I suppose it's easier to come by money when you aren't imprisoned in a classroom all day, burning up cakes in Mrs. Northrup's Home Ec. I haven't yet mentioned my abysmal baking skills, but suffice it to say I am perfectly inept in the kitchen, much to the disappointment of my mother.

Wallace took me to see *West Side Story* which I've already seen twice with Helen, though I didn't mention this to him as I didn't want him to feel bad. Afterward, we walked along Main Street, and try as I may, I couldn't stop humming "I Feel Pretty" under my breath, hoping he couldn't hear me. He told me that he loved my voice and asked me to sing it louder. But I'm not brave like you, and the idea of singing in the middle of the street made me clam up like an oyster. Wallace said I shouldn't feel bashful about it though. He said if I had a voice that people actually wanted to hear, I was committing a grave sin by keeping it to myself. Well, I thought about Matthew in the Bible and that poor little light under the bushel, and I decided that maybe he was right. So I sang for him. And not the soft kind of humming I do in the drugstore or helping my mother with the sewing, but the loud, free kind I do in the bath. It felt good to sing for him right there on the corner of the street while the cars whizzed past us. I'm sure we must have been a sight!

But that wasn't the best part of the evening. As we were walking along the storefronts, we passed Gus's, and I saw your record in the display case. And right next to it, hanging in the window was a perfect Gibson guitar with cherry red lacquer around its edges and a pair of white fringe boots painted on the face of it. When I saw those boots, I immediately thought of you and knew I had to have it. I should probably mention that I don't play the guitar very well yet, but Helen's father bought her a Martin last Christmas, so I pick around on it every now and then when she lets me. I very nearly have three chords learned already!

My mother says the piano is a far superior instrument, but I think it's ornery. You can't take it with you or have it at your fingertips if you happen to feel a song coming on. She'll never agree to a guitar, but I feel certain I can butter up Daddy. True to her nature, my mother told him about the stealing after all, and he's finally forgiven me since I sold two crocheted scarves to pay him back the money. He wasn't happy about it, but he has never been able to stay angry at me for very long when I turn on the water works. He said, "Scoop, you and I are cut from the same cloth. We both have so much passion inside that sometimes it comes spilling out of us in the wrong ways." He used to call me Sugar, but recently he's said I hadn't earned the right to that name because more often than not, I'm salty. So now he calls me Scoop on account of the fact he's never sure which way I'll swing on any particular day.

I told Wallace tonight that I was going to buy the Gibson. I've already worked out how many scarves I'll need to crochet to buy it. I'll probably have to babysit for the Weaver twins next door to make up the difference. They're even worse than my little brothers and once put a garden snake in our mailbox. But it will be worth it. Wallace just shook his head and smiled as if I'd lost my marbles. He said a hundred and forty-five dollars was a lot of money, but that if anyone could find a way to get it, I certainly could.

Sincerely,
Lola

CHAPTER 10
EFFIE / "CRAZY"

The first time Effie suspected she was losing her mind, she was standing between the frozen pizzas and the toilet paper display at the supermarket. For the third weekend in a row, she had awakened on a Saturday morning to a quiet house and an empty refrigerator, anxious to be around other people. She still hadn't gotten used to days like this, without the scent of her slow cooker breakfast casserole or her sleepy husband greeting her with a crooked smile and morning breath that was so distinctly Daniel. When the kids were small, she had wished for mornings like this, when she could escape them all for a few blessed hours. But now she was angry at herself for not savoring all those little moments of heaven.

The elderly couple ahead of her had been shuffling along at a snail's pace for the last two aisles—the man pushing a near-empty cart with a slight hitch in his step and a serious squint in his eye as he perused the shelves. The frail gray-headed woman alongside him was equally interested in scrutinizing the ingredients of every box he selected, wrinkling her nose as if she were sniffing out a lie. Every now and then, Effie could hear her quietly urging him to put something back. She caught only snippets of the woman's pleadings. "Too much sugar . . . not enough protein . . . bad for blood pressure." Near the vegetable bins, she'd convinced him to select a bag of peppers and a head of romaine. Now, the pair huddled around a foggy freezer door, mulling over the nutritional integrity of frozen pizza.

"How many times have I told you not to eat that garbage?" the woman asked, her voice grating. "The salt content is through the roof. You know if you eat it, you'll be up all night with indigestion."

Effie smiled to herself before emitting a polite cough to alert them of her presence. She'd been unintentionally shopping in their wake since the canned goods and couldn't seem to manage a graceful escape. Finally, she guided her cart around them, offering a courteous wave, but the two appeared so engrossed that neither acknowledged her. As she moved past them, a nagging realization entered her mind. It didn't sound like an argument so much as a one-sided plea from the woman. Her husband appeared wholly uninterested in whatever she was saying—his eyes glassed over as he defiantly reached for a thick-crust meat lover's over her protests.

Effie didn't usually make a habit of speaking to strangers in the grocery store, but something about their exchange made her cock an eyebrow, and she couldn't help but take sides. Daniel had always been the one to bring junk food into the house because, unlike her, he'd never had to count calories. Even with the slight belly he'd gained during her pregnancy years, he still possessed the athletic physique he'd had as a high school basketball player stealing glances at her in the bleachers. It had been easy for him to keep up a workout schedule during all those months when she was nursing in the middle of the night, then later when she had to be up early with the kids for school. Children hadn't seemed to change his habits all that much. And she had said she didn't mind, that she was happy to bear the emotional load of building a family so that he could focus on building the business.

Once upon a time, Effie had easily pictured the two of them wearing hearing aids and orthopedic loafers, arguing over items in their grocery cart. Daniel would have insisted on the Oreos, which she would have discreetly plucked out and replaced with a bag of raisins while he was busy deciding between Chunky Monkey and rocky road. But that future had been erased, swept away by a tide she'd never seen coming, and now she wondered how long she was going to be dragged along the bottom of the seabed like flotsam, unable to breathe. A fresh knot churned low in her belly, but she pushed herself forward, determined not to become the kind of woman who cried in the middle of the grocery store.

Unable to shake the image of the couple, her feet stopped, and she peeked back over her shoulder one last time. "You should really trust your wife on this one, sir. She's absolutely right. The salt content in those things is outrageous."

The man's jaw went slack, and his face turned ashen. But it was the woman whom Effie could not seem to tear her gaze from. Her gray hair lacquered into a tidy bun, she was gaping, her thin eyebrows knitted together in one deepening crease. "You can hear me," she said softly, almost in a whisper. It was a statement, not a question. "And you can . . . see me." She waved a withered hand in front of her vacant eyes as if to test out the idea. If she was being sarcastic, the joke fell flat for Effie.

"Yes." Her heart ticking up speed, Effie flashed a confused look over at the man, hoping he would back her up, but he stood rooted to the spot, his lips slowly parting in something like disbelief. Or maybe horror. Effie couldn't tell. "And I can see him." At this, a startled groan escaped his throat, and the pizza box tumbled out of his trembling hand, hitting the floor with a thud.

"This is amazing," the woman breathed. "You're . . . one of them. I see it now," she said, lifting a shaky finger. The ghost of a smile crossed her lips, but Effie was lost as to its meaning.

Trying to recover her composure, she instantly regretted having said anything. What sort of game was this woman playing? "Look, I shouldn't have said anything. I'll just go." She grabbed her cart firmly and lowered her gaze, desperate to reach the checkout lane before running into them again. She still needed eggs, but she was willing to sacrifice them to leave with her dignity. This was what she got for try-ing to be social. Unless she practiced greetings in front of the mirror, she almost certainly came off as awkward or nosy. Aside from Grace and the kids' extracurriculars, her social connections were sparse these days. Maybe commenting on someone else's marital disagreement in public was an unforgivable faux pas. "Again, I'm truly sorry to have said anything. It wasn't my place to get in the middle. I apologize if I overstepped. It's just that"—she paused for a beat, fighting back a soup of emotions—"you remind me of another couple I used to know."

If she'd kept moving forward, she would have been in the clear. She would have been free to make a run for her minivan. But just as she determined to make her escape, the man clutched a hand to his chest and reached the other toward Effie, his fingers shaking with the effort.

Now her confusion gave way to a cold panic, and she heard herself let out a little scream. "Are you OK, sir?" She checked behind her, hop-ing someone else would materialize and know what to do. Someone braver.

"He's having a heart attack! He had one two years ago," the woman yelled as the man's legs gave way beneath him. "Do something!" she said, her eyes begging Effie to act. Kneeling alongside him, she whis-pered something inaudible in his ear.

Clutching her stomach, Effie tried to slow the fear racing through her veins. If she'd only minded her own business, this would not be happening. If she hadn't been thinking of Daniel, if she hadn't been trying to live vicariously through total strangers, she would already be in the checkout lane talking herself out of buying a candy bar, instead of causing this poor man's demise.

"Call 911!" From somewhere behind them, a sales associate came barreling toward them with a purposeful look that suggested he was a person who knew what to do. Blinking herself out of a stupor, she reached into her purse for her phone and struggled to keep her shaking hands from dropping it as she pecked out the numbers.

"911. What's your emergency?" a man's voice asked.

Effie managed to mumble a location while the cashier, who couldn't be more than eighteen, prodded and tugged at the man lying flat on his back, his eyes staring accusingly into Effie's. Gazing down at him, she tried to muster an expression that conveyed *I'm sorry* but landed on something in between an apology and bewilderment.

Because when her eyes flickered back to the woman beside him, she was gone.

~

Strapped to a stretcher, the man strained against gravity, making a desperate attempt to speak. But the paramedic who held him down encouraged him to save his strength.

"What's your name, sir?" she asked in reassuring tones.

"Marty," he breathed.

"You're going to be OK, Marty. My name is Renata, and I'm going to help you get some air, OK. We've got you now. Just lie back and focus on your breathing." Her hands worked with an efficient calm while fitting an oxygen mask over his face.

"Her." Inexplicably, Marty was now pointing a finger at Effie, who had followed the scene into the parking lot, because she could hardly leave the poor man alone considering she was the reason for this whole disaster. "She"—he took a labored breath as the paramedics lifted the stretcher and tucked it away in the ambulance—"comes."

Flashing a dubious look at Effie, Renata shook her head. "Sorry. Only family." Once inside, she made quick work of attaching him to a maze of cables and cords.

Feeling like an intruder, Effie took a step back into the crowd. Perhaps in his confused state, Marty had mistaken her for someone else. A brain deprived of oxygen might imagine something or some*one* who wasn't really there. *Like a deceased country music icon, perhaps.* Or maybe he wanted to confront her, make her watch him suffer as some sort of deranged punishment for the crime of meddling. And where was his wife? She had vanished at the most inconvenient moment, leaving Effie to question whether she'd seen the woman at all. But she'd heard her voice so clearly. Maybe this divorce was taking a greater toll on her mental health than she'd initially thought and she should seek counseling immediately. That settled it. She determined to call a therapist first thing Monday morning.

"She's my"—Effie heard him trying to speak, but his voice was muffled beneath the oxygen mask—"daughter."

Effie gasped, drawing the attention of the growing crowd. Since her own father was alive and well, probably catching a college-basketball game right now and getting reamed by her mother, she was certain Marty was confused. Probably delirious. But even if he was, could she deny him the chance to hold his daughter's hand while he died? Maybe this was her penance for being a nosy Nellie.

Renata shot her a look, no doubt registering the lack of family resemblance. Even so, the paramedic waved her over, and for reasons she could not fully understand, Effie pushed her way through the crowd of bodies and climbed into the back of the ambulance as if she belonged there. Sidling up next to Marty on a bench beside the medic, she ran her eyes over the length of his birdlike frame, taking note of his chest as it struggled to rise beneath his button-up plaid shirt. Guilt threatened to undo her. How was she ever going to make this right? How would she ever forgive herself if this man died as a result of meeting her? Two hours ago, she'd woken up needing milk, and now she was providing emotional support to a stranger on the verge of death.

"I'm here," she said, finding his clammy hand and tucking it inside her own. Was this OK? Was this what a person was supposed to do when they caused another person's heart to stop beating?

"You saw her." He craned his wrinkled neck upward, his rich-brown eyes holding hers with such urgency that she couldn't break away. A shiver trickled through her veins until it settled in a tangled knot in her throat.

"She was standing right next to you," Effie pointed out, unsure how he could have missed this obvious truth. Thinking of Lolly, she wondered if perhaps he, too, had been robbed of his memories. "Surely you saw her."

"Please." His raspy voice carried a grave note, but his eyes were desperate. "Tell her I know it was her who turned off the gas last night." Effie's heart sank even as she told herself it couldn't be true. A deafening siren circled somewhere above while machines beeped and whirred in the space between them, making it nearly impossible for her to think clearly.

She wasn't sure what she was supposed to do. Even if she agreed to comply with his request, the woman—whoever she was—had vanished. Perhaps Effie could lie, tell him she would, of course, communicate the message. Refusing him in his condition would be cruel. She would promise him her soul if she thought it might help him survive this.

Just as she determined that yes, she would lie and tell Marty what he needed to hear, a reedy voice cut through the curtain of noise. It was softer this time, melodic and tinny. Like wind chimes.

"Can you believe he tried to off himself for an old biddy like me?" Effie looked up to find the woman sitting across from her, with dewy brown skin shimmering against a pale-pink dress with a Peter Pan collar, her hands clasped peacefully below her belly. And this time, Effie noticed the barely perceptible hazy aura that accompanied her, something she hadn't caught in the industrial lighting of the grocery store. She was smiling, but there was an unmistakable sadness behind her inky eyes.

"Tell him I'm here," she said, grazing the back of her hand across the creases of Marty's forehead. "But I can't stay any longer to make him take care of himself." Though she spoke the words to Effie, she never once tore her gaze from her husband's watery eyes. "It's time for us both to move on. And the kids need him to stick around a little longer."

With her mouth agape, Effie managed a nod, trying to process the task at hand, but her brain had yet to catch up with her eyes and ears. How was it possible that she could see and hear a person who was invisible to both Marty and the paramedic hovering about his head and currently throwing some serious side-eye in her direction? Perhaps she'd passed out and all of this was a result of being unconscious. Or maybe she never woke up this morning and had only dreamed that she'd had a cup of coffee and taken a shower and driven herself to the grocery store. But even as she tried to convince herself that this could not be happening, a familiar peace blanketed her, enveloping her in that same perfect warmth she had felt all those weeks ago at Rosehaven. A lump formed at the base of her throat, but she forced it down and squeezed Marty's hand. "She says you have to stay," she managed to get out, leaning closer. "Your family needs you."

Renata shot her another pointed look, and Effie bristled. She couldn't begin to imagine what this woman must be thinking of her, but she gripped Marty's hand even tighter, propelled by something greater than her humiliation. "She says she's leaving now but that she loves you." Noticing a tear roll down the curve of his cheek, Effie realized she was crying too.

"I'm not ready." The fear in his voice was palpable, and his shoulders shook as he spoke. "Not yet, Iris." Then, tightening his grasp around Effie's trembling fingers, he fell into a full sob. "Tell her to stay. I can't live without her. Tell her I love her! I should have told her that every day." The scene scraped at Effie's heart—Iris beaming at her husband's crumbling face, so serene that she seemed complete. After a few weighted moments, Marty gave a slow nod. That simple action appeared so forced, Effie worried he might break from the pain of it, but Iris only looked more radiant.

Drawing from Iris's strength, Effie placed a gentle hand to Marty's cheek before looking him directly in the eye, saying the words precisely so he wouldn't misunderstand. Though lately she had made a habit of putting her foot in her mouth, all at once the words floated into her mind weightlessly, and she knew exactly what she was meant to say. "She knows. She's always known."

A warm breeze wafted between them, and for a moment everything seemed to go still. Finally, Marty loosened his grip on her fingers, and his head rolled back onto the cot. Relief flooded through her when she saw the rhythmic rise and fall of his chest begin to even out in a steady pattern.

"His vitals are stabilizing," Renata noted, her voice assured.

"Good," Effie replied, feeling her heart lighten. "That's good."

Arching an eyebrow, Renata gave her a dubious once-over. "Mind if I ask you who you were talking to?"

Effie almost told her the truth, started to form the words in her mind, but when she looked across the cot, Iris had vanished for the second time.

"No one," she said, blinking back tears. "No one at all."

CHAPTER 11

LOLA

November 28, 1961

Dear Patsy,

I made the grave mistake of telling Mama about the Gibson, and she said it just wouldn't do for a girl; though, by all accounts I'm a woman now. I can't say I'm surprised as I didn't expect her to understand the seriousness of my situation. It doesn't matter what she says. I need that guitar. It may sound ridiculous, but it called to me from that window, and ever since then I can't seem to get those little white boots out of my head. They remind me of the ones you wore on *Arthur Godfrey's Talent Scouts* when you won the whole contest. I dream about them sometimes. I imagine I'm wearing them on stage with a matching white dress with silver fringe, and I'm singing the way I sang to Wallace that night in a sea of people, free and unafraid.

Having had no luck with Mama, I made sure to bring it up at dinner last night with my father. I said, "Daddy, if I don't get that guitar, I'll die!" He nearly spat out his meatloaf laughing, but it only made me more determined to prove my sincerity. I told him I'd already saved five dollars, and I just needed a little help to get the rest. "I'll do anything," I told him. "I'll scrub floors and cook dinners and mind the boys." When I said that part, my oldest brother Peter just looked at me like I'd grown a third eyeball. He's fourteen now and doesn't need entertaining, but George is ten, and Harry is six and in constant need of supervision. Usually, I do my best to ignore them, but I would watch countless hours of *Mister Ed* if it meant I could have the Gibson sooner.

Daddy put down his fork and rubbed his chin. "Scoop," he said, "I like your spirit. It's good to work for the things you want. Makes you appreciate them more." Then he said if I earned half the money, he would match the rest! I nearly fell out of my chair with happiness, but I could practically hear my mother dart her eyes at Daddy. She said, "Richard, you can't be serious." I shot her a cocky sort of look as I was feeling firmly in the salty category today. Then she huffed and puffed and left the table as if I'd just taken the Lord's name in vain.

Sincerely,

Lola

CHAPTER 12
EFFIE / "DEAR GOD"

Slumped over the kitchen table in her bathrobe, Effie stirred a spoon around mindlessly in her mug of ginger tea. Though she wasn't watching, the television blared from the living room and floated into the kitchen, a natural consequence of the open floor plan and vaulted ceilings she had requested when they built the place over a decade ago. When the kids were with Daniel, she needed the noise, something to trick herself into believing she wasn't alone, especially in the evenings. Since her experience with Marty and Iris this morning, she'd been too terrified to leave the house. She wasn't sure if seeing ghosts was a one-off or a regular occurrence she should now come to expect, and she didn't relish the idea of meeting another dead person in, say, the middle of her Zumba class. She was pretty sure if she did, she would pass out mid–salsa step and end up in the back of an ambulance herself.

For now, in the safety of her home with the blinds tightly closed, she could pretend it had all been a strange dream, the product of too much late-night scrolling on social media. She remembered gliding her finger across a thumbnail that featured an article on the most haunted hotels in America. She'd been intrigued. It had been late. She'd had more wine than usual. Yes, that was the only explanation that made any sense—a technology- and alcohol-induced mental break.

Yet she couldn't seem to shake the glow of Iris's face, the way the light had shimmered off her skin like pearls in the sunlight, growing brighter and brighter. And then, just as quickly as she'd appeared, she was gone.

Effie's cell vibrated, breaking her out of a muddled daze. She sighed, knowing who it was before she looked at the screen. So far, she'd been relying on Google and caffeine to deconstruct the meaning of the vision to no avail. But now that she'd gone from seeing dead celebrities to seeing dead regular people, maybe it was time to loop in her best friend. If she was experiencing a full-blown mental break, Grace was the only person she could trust to stick by her. She slid her finger across the screen to accept the call.

"Where have you been?" Grace was already midsentence by the time Effie switched on her speakerphone. "I called four times today, and you didn't answer any of my texts."

"Sorry. Things have been"—she paused for a beat, drawing a heavy hand to her head—"busy." Certainly not an untrue statement.

"So," Grace said, a note of anticipation rising in her voice. "How did it go? Did you get the job?"

With everything that had happened this morning, Effie had almost forgotten about her successful interview yesterday. A spark of pride flickered in her chest as she remembered the way Mr. Fields—who had told her to call him Drew—had shaken her hand, which had surprised her. It had been warm and firm and sent a strange flutter of tingles up her arm. "I start on Monday."

"That's amazing! I told you it was yours. So?" She paused for a beat, and Effie could imagine her waggling her eyebrows. "Is he hot?"

"He's my boss!" she shot back, though the ghost of a smile crossed her lips, which Grace would have instantly seized upon if she could see her face. Effie wouldn't describe Drew Fields as hot, exactly. More like determined. Busy. The sort of person who didn't have time to be hot. The mystery man, on the other hand, was objectively hot. She wondered if she would ever see him again, then shook away the image of his intoxicating dimples. She wasn't sure if she'd ever be ready to date again, but if she ever was, someone like him would be entirely unattainable. He'd seemed like a walking airbrushed centerfold. Too perfect for someone like Effie, who had once worn a pair of Jay's basketball shorts to Zumba. Grace would never let her live that one down. Besides, they would never work. He'd looked so young and energetic, ready to take on the world. But Effie was tired and barreling toward midlife, growing more cynical with each passing day since her separation began. "And anyway, I told you I'm not dating until the divorce is final."

Grace heaved a sigh laced with judgment. "How is that going, by the way? Did you sign the papers?"

"We're still hammering out a few details." A twinge pierced Effie's belly. Despite their drawn-out mediation, sometimes she could delude herself into thinking that Daniel was simply on an extended trip, but it only made the truth hurt worse when reality set in.

"There's actually something else I wanted to talk to you about." Effie cleared her throat, trying to build up her courage. She didn't have many close friends, and she didn't want to scare Grace away with a story that even she would deem absurd. "But I need to know you won't think any less of me."

"The only thing that would make me think less of you is if you got back together with your worthless ex-husband."

"Almost ex," Effie clarified, though she wasn't sure why. She and Daniel had unplugged the marriage from life support months ago. At this point, it was only a matter of paperwork. Who got the guest room furniture, how to divide his IRA, whether they would sell the time-share in Galveston—the particulate matter remaining after their implosion.

A brief pause passed, but it was enough to send Grace spiraling. "Oh no, Effie. I don't care what your mother has told you, but do not go crawling back to him like some 1950s desperate housewife. Shall I remind you of the ten stages of grief you went through when you found out he was cheating with Nancy Drew?"

"Amber Drew."

"Same thing."

"And I'm pretty sure it's five stages."

"For most people, yes. But with you, we went through the Ben & Jerry's phase, plus the two-week period when you wouldn't take off that horrible poncho. Ten is conservative." Effie loved that poncho. Daniel had bought it for their seventh anniversary when they'd vacationed in Cozumel at an all-inclusive resort. She'd said it made her look shapeless, but he'd liked the idea of her wearing it with nothing underneath. After he'd left, she'd found it collecting dust in the back of her closet. When she'd held it to her nose, she could still make out the faint scent of sunscreen, and tears had sprung to her eyes.

"Calm down. I'm not getting back together with Daniel. This is about"—pressing the phone to her chest, Effie cringed, debating whether to say it aloud—"something else. Something . . . happened to me. Actually, a couple of things have happened to me. And I'm not sure what's going on, but I need to get it all out without any judgment, OK?"

"Need I remind you who you're speaking to? I'm not exactly a model mother here. You stuck by me after Pottygate, remember?" Grace had raised a stink at a PTA meeting over another child peeing on Beckett in the bathroom, complained the school had done nothing to protect her five-year-old from the urinating sword fights happening in kindergarten. But during the course of the meeting, she had learned, quite publicly, that Beckett had started the game in the first place. "Well then," she'd said, donning a pair of sunglasses as she rose from her seat, "I think we've all learned something here. Clearly, this school is not meeting my child's creative needs if he's feeling the need to paint piss murals in the bathroom." She walked out with her head held high, and Effie had stood in total awe of this woman who had failed so spectacularly and owned it. Grace was tall and elegant—a natural ginger, and unshakable. She reminded Effie of a gazelle, lithe and beautiful but willing to toss her horns around if the moment called for it.

"Right then," Effie said, gathering her strength. And then the words came tumbling out of her. She told her about Patsy, about Marty, the drive in the ambulance with the dead woman speaking to her. "I don't know how to explain it," she said. "I know it sounds ridiculous, but I promise that nothing has ever felt more real to me." But maybe that was bad to admit, just more evidence that she was, without a doubt, delusional.

"Wow" was all Grace said after she finished. "That's, um . . . intense."

"Yeah," Effie agreed. She wasn't sure what she expected Grace to say. When Effie had forgotten Brody at the fair four years ago, she had only told Grace, to which her friend had replied, "I'm sure he deserved it. You probably told him a million times that you were leaving, and he ignored you because he wanted to get in one more round of ring toss. Kids are jerks like that." It was the only thing that had consoled her, and she had laughed through her mom guilt. Between the two of them, Grace was without question the more open minded, but maybe supporting your friend in her paranormal hallucinations was a step too far. Effie held her breath.

"Well," Grace said, chewing on the word. "What are we going to do about it? We can't have you going all *Sixth Sense* alone."

"You think I've lost it." Effie deflated, dragging a clammy hand down her face. "I have, haven't I? It's the only explanation." She sighed, feeling exposed. "Daniel broke me."

"I didn't say that. You are talking to a woman who has seen every episode of *Charmed*, who tried to start a high school club for witches after seeing *The Craft*."

"You did?"

"I said *tried*, Eff. Pay attention! We only had two members. It was pretty much me and Mr. Roosevelt."

"You were in a witch club with a grown man?"

"Mr. Roosevelt was my cat. The point is, I'm into it. So, let's figure this out. Call the four corners and everything. Conjure the spirits and ask them what they want. Oh, oh, oh!" Grace's voice rose an octave as she squealed like a schoolgirl. "Let's call Patsy!"

Effie would be lying if she said the thought hadn't crossed her mind. In fact, she'd already tested it out in the darkness of her bedroom, where no one else could hear how unhinged she sounded talking to thin air. Lying in her bed, she had squeezed her eyelids closed while she murmured Patsy's name, but when she opened them, she was met only with Cletus and Oscar, their heads tilted in tandem as if they were concerned about her. Against her better judgment, she'd taken to sharing her bed with them when she missed the feel of the mattress sinking in next to her.

Biting her bottom lip, she mulled over the idea. What harm could one last effort do before googling psychiatrists? "Bring candles," she heard herself say.

"On it." There was a childlike delight in Grace's tone. "Don't you dare start without me."

~

"Really?" Effie watched Grace reach into a giant Whole Foods bag and produce an assortment of tea lights and a box of multicolored candles—clearly Halloween and birthday-party leftovers.

As if reading her thoughts, Grace leveled her green eyes at her friend. "I have two kids and a full-time job. Didn't exactly have time to hit up the occult shop on my way here. Besides, they're perfect because we need three white candles and three purple ones. Do you have a cupcake or something I can stick them in?"

She looked at Effie expectantly, to which Effie replied blankly, "Are you serious?"

Planting her hands on her narrow hips, Grace glowered. "Do I look like I'm kidding? How else do you expect them to stand up?"

Effie shook her head but rummaged around the pantry until she located a half-empty container of soft-baked cookies from the top shelf.

"Here," she said, returning to the living room. "Try these."

"Lofthouse," Grace noted approvingly. "You really did have a bad week."

"Just take them," Effie said, rolling her eyes. "How do you know how to do all this, anyway?" she asked, observing Grace's work.

"Season four." Grace shoved a candle in the middle of a pink-frosted cookie, then lit the wick. A satisfied grin played on her lips as the flame danced.

"Come again?"

Grace looked up from arranging the candles and cookies in a circle around the living room rug. "*Charmed*," she said, as if this should explain everything. "You would know if you'd watched it with me instead of rewatching every season of *24* with Daniel."

"Right." Effie rubbed her forehead, suddenly rethinking this idea. "So, we're deferring to Aaron Spelling for this séance?"

Snapping her head up again, Grace raised a finger. "Never underestimate the wisdom of Aaron Spelling. Besides . . ." She reached for a blanket and spread it out in the center of the candles. "Hollywood knows all about this kind of stuff. They have to research the hell out of it to make it seem believable."

Effie balked. "Three women who go around casting spells on their exes is believable?"

"Hey, I am not the one seeing dead people." Grace thumbed her chest. "Concerned friend here trying to help."

"And I appreciate you. Did I say thank you yet for not heading for the hills?"

"No, but that will do. The IOU from Pottygate has no statute of limitations." A playful grin teased the corners of her mouth. "And you're welcome." Settling onto the blanket, Grace assumed a Buddha pose and began humming with her eyes closed. Effie sighed, drawing a dramatic eye roll from Grace, who tugged her down by her shirt to sit across from her.

"What are we doing?" Effie asked, her palms up, reluctantly mimicking Grace's body language.

"Meditating. You have to repeat a neutral syllable to generate the vibrations." Grace hummed a little louder now.

Opening one eye, Effie wrinkled her brow.

"To call the spirits." Grace shared this information hurriedly, as if Effie should already know it. "Effie, clearly the universe is trying to tell you something. Do you want to know what it is or not? Now is not the time to be a cynic. Focus!" She reached for Effie's hands, tucking them inside her own, and closed her eyes again. "Can you hear us, Patsy? We're here. And we come in peace." Not surprisingly, her pleas were met with silence. She licked her lips and resettled herself. "We want to know if you have a message for Effie Baker. Please make yourself known." Again, nothing.

"Maybe we should try playing her music," Effie whispered, half kidding. But hearing herself suggest this aloud, she realized it wasn't a terrible idea.

"Good!" Grace opened her eyes for a beat, her voice cloaked in delight. "Now we're talking. But not too loud."

"Of course not." Effie rolled her eyes as she reached for her cell. "Wouldn't want to interrupt the 'vibrations.'"

Once she'd located a playlist, the notes from "Walkin' After Midnight" drifted from Effie's phone, and a million memories came flooding back—Lolly singing along to the record player as she scrambled eggs in the morning; Pop whisking her up in his arms, dipping her, and planting a kiss on her lips while Effie looked on, entranced. They really had been the epitome of true love. She fought a lump growing in her throat, grateful when Grace interrupted her thoughts.

"Wait! I almost forgot." She reached into her shopping bag and produced a small wooden pentagram and a black-and-white photo of Patsy Cline, no doubt printed on her home computer. The ink must have been running low because there was an empty space where her left eye should have been. It gave off an unnerving vibe, and Effie shuddered as Grace propped it against the hearth and placed the pentagram next to it. Reaching for Effie's hands, she started again. "Patsy, if you're here, make your presence known."

A floorboard creaked somewhere above them, and Effie's eyes flew open. She supposed it must have been the dogs making noise upstairs but remembered that she had put them in the backyard at the start of their ghost-hunting activities.

She felt a shift in the air, and her skin prickled with fresh goose bumps. "What was that?" Before she could come up with a satisfactory explanation, the front door swung open, and Effie jolted upright, letting out an audible squeak. She hadn't believed their little experiment would work, but a small part of her assumed that if Patsy did show up, she'd enter through the fireplace or swoop through a window or perhaps just materialize out of nothing at all. Would she really be so traditional as to use the front door?

"What the . . ." An unmistakable voice emerged, and a dark figure shuffled inside and flipped on the lights, illuminating Effie and Grace and the candles and the cookies and the pentagram and the smudged photo of Patsy Cline. Effie fumbled with her phone, taking far too long to locate the source of the music, then made quick work of blowing out the candles. The cloying smell combined with Daniel's presence nauseated her.

He cleared his throat as if to make things less awkward, but Effie was certain that train had left the station. She darted for the door to meet him.

"Hello, Daniel," Grace said. From her perch on the rug, she gave a little wave, but her voice was decidedly unwelcoming.

"Grace." He nodded a curt hello. "Good to see you again." Though Effie suspected he was not thrilled to see her best friend, who had recently tagged him in a rather unfortunate Facebook event—free testing for STDs at Our Lady of Faith Hospital, where she worked.

"Wish I could say the same," Grace replied with a wicked smile. "How's your child bride?"

"Very funny. You know we aren't married."

"So, you admit she's a child?"

"Always great to see you, Grace." He saluted her before drawing Effie aside by the crook of her elbow. "Can I talk to you? Outside," he added through a forced smile. Once the two of them were alone, he let out a judgmental groan and winced. "What are you doing, Eff?"

"What are *you* doing?" she asked. "You're not supposed to enter without knocking. You don't live here anymore, remember?"

"The lights were off. I thought you were out. And Brody forgot his inhaler."

Her heart gave a little leap. "Is he OK?"

"He's fine," he said, heading her off. "Just ran a little hard at soccer practice today, and . . . you know Brody. Convinced himself and half the parents he was in cardiac arrest. They nearly called an ambulance." They shared a mutual eye roll, and Effie wondered if she would ever have that unspoken kind of understanding with anyone else. No one besides Daniel would ever know the millions of tiny details acquired from creating a treasure trove of family moments. "I thought I'd save you the trip. I didn't mean to interrupt"—he gestured behind her—"whatever that was."

Just once, why couldn't he catch her when she wasn't conducting a séance or lying on a hospital gurney? She concluded the universe was conspiring against her. The days she got a blowout, she bumped into precisely no one. How would he ever know how OK she was if he was constantly finding her at her worst? She at least wanted to appear like she was functioning well enough.

Straining his head to the side, Daniel scrunched his eyebrows together. "Does this have anything to do with the . . . death thing?"

She bristled before straightening out her shoulders, the nostalgia of the moment entirely dissipated. "If it does, it's none of your business."

"I still care about you, Eff. We spent over half our lives together, for God's sake."

"Yes, we did," she shot back, affronted. "But it obviously didn't mean as much to you as it did to me." At one point, she'd thought it had, but somewhere along the way he'd changed his mind without telling her. Probably right around the time he'd posted his profile on Match.com.

"Look," he said, gliding a hand through his hair. "I just don't want to see you getting caught up in some weird"—he swiveled a hand around in the air between them—"voodoo shit."

"Why not?" she pushed back. "You always said I should try new things."

"I meant yoga or tennis, not . . . contacting the dead!"

She considered this for a moment, wondering if he had a point. Lately, she had been in a weird headspace, and she wasn't sure she could trust her intuition anymore, least of all where it concerned Daniel. Nevertheless, she said, "Well, thank you for your concern, but I'm perfectly capable of taking care of myself. Now, if you'll excuse me." She turned and went inside the house, but when she moved to close the door, he wedged a foot in the threshold.

"Still need the inhaler." He held out an open palm.

"Right. Wait here," she said before pulling the door closed. He didn't live here anymore, after all.

When she came back brandishing a bag of assorted medicine, he tilted his head and studied it, then expelled a long sigh. "Just the inhaler, Eff. He isn't a baby anymore."

Effie's spine stiffened, bringing all five foot three of her up to his nose. "Just give him the antihistamine. It will help. And a couple of melatonin gummies before bed. They always help him sleep after he's had a scare." She pushed the bag toward his chest defiantly.

"Fine." As he reached for it, he heaved another sigh and cracked a slow grin she couldn't quite decipher. "You always were the prepared one."

At one time, she thought, that had been true. She'd been ready for anything motherhood threw at her, heading out into the world with four different kinds of Band-Aids and the number for poison control tucked safely in the back of her mind. When the middle school had hosted a parents' night on sex education, she had been one of five people in attendance. When Teagan had finally started her period, she had taken to assembling what she referred to as *lady's days care packets* and tucked them in the bottom of her daughter's backpack. She'd made sure Brody carried an extra hoodie to school in case he got cold in class, and when Jay had started driving, she'd discreetly applied a bumper sticker to the rear of his truck that read PLEASE BE PATIENT, STUDENT DRIVER, much to Jay's embarrassment.

But she hadn't prepared for some things.

She hadn't prepared to be replaced. And she hadn't prepared to see dead people.

～

After Daniel left, Effie hadn't been able to recenter herself enough to continue the séance. Instead, she watched reruns of *Buffy* while Grace created a dating profile for her on something called MeetYourMatch. com. Looking up from her phone, Grace pursed her lips. "Who do you think my guardian angel is?"

Effie shrugged. "Didn't your aunt Donna pass away last year?"

"Yeah, but"—she made a sour face—"she was more of a cross-stitching and water-aerobics kind of woman. I was hoping for someone with a little more . . . oomph."

"Like who?"

"Like . . . I don't know, like"—jutting out her chest, Grace gave a proud little shimmy—"Marilyn Monroe."

"Don't you think Marilyn Monroe has better things to do than follow you around all day? Icons like her are probably living it up poolside in a private villa instead of granting wishes to peasants like us."

A frown touched the corners of Grace's lips, and she dropped her gaze to the screen. "Well, if you get a celebrity guardian angel, it's only fair that I should too," she mumbled.

Nothing about the current situation seemed fair to Effie. Certainly not the part about speaking to dead folks.

"What about this one?" Grace held out a photo on her phone, one of Effie at a Galveston beach at least twelve years ago, before Brody was even conceived. She was wearing a yellow bikini, her skin tanned to the shade of toasted almonds, her sun-kissed hair windswept to the side as she laughed demurely away from the camera. When Jay and Teagan were small, she'd always been outside, taking them to the park or carting them off to the neighborhood pool. Back then, she'd been more confident in her skin, able to snap back into shape because she was busy chasing two small children around. It was the third one that had done her in. After Brody, it seemed a stubborn thirty pounds permanently took up residence in her midsection and thighs. What's more, nursing three babies hadn't exactly done her breasts any favors. Her children had quite literally sucked the life from her body, and she was tired. Too tired for a girls' night out with friends or that ceramics class Grace had tried to rope her into. Too tired for late-night sex with her husband after the chaos of the day. In truth, she'd been relieved when Daniel had stopped trying to pursue her because she felt guilty admitting that she preferred sleep to sex almost any night of the week. So maybe he didn't bear all the blame. Even since her surgery, she'd often felt like a more exhausted, less exciting version of her former self—one that was fueled by strong coffee and stretchy pants.

"You can't use that one." Effie leaned closer. Scrutinizing the picture, she shook her head. "I don't look like that anymore. It's false advertisement." As the words left her lips, a wave of nostalgia rippled through her. Daniel had taken the photo, coaxing her into a smile by performing a mock striptease. She'd never been able to resist him when he looked at her that way, like he couldn't wait to get her alone when the kids were asleep.

"And you don't think the men on here embellish themselves?" Grace scrolled down and landed on a selfie of a fortysomething man wearing horn-rimmed glasses and a tweed jacket. With his speckled-gray scruff, he was nerdy—not in an attractive sort of way—and holding out a mug that read I SPREADSHEET ABOUT PEOPLE. "James here says he's a data analyst for a major social media company." With a saucy smile, she narrowed her eyes at Effie and flipped the screen toward her. "Twenty bucks says that means he spends all day making creepy TikToks with this stupid mug."

Effie rolled her eyes and began cleaning up the mess, stacking paper plates of cookies atop one another as she shuffled around the living room. "It doesn't matter. I'm not going to lie to get a date." On her way to the kitchen, she stubbed her big toe on the sofa and let out a yelp. "Fudgesicles!" She sucked in a sharp breath and expelled the air slowly, siphoning out the pain through her nostrils. "Besides, I already told you I'm not ready for anything new right now. I'm not even officially divorced yet."

"First of all"—Grace shot her a rebellious look and held up a finger—"doesn't seem to be stopping Daniel. And second of all, can you please just talk like a normal forty-year-old woman instead of inventing curse words?"

"Sorry, I forget when the kids aren't here."

"And while we're at it, stop saying sorry all the time!"

"I know. Sorry. I mean . . . look, it's different." Drawing a hand to her neck, she released a frustrated sigh. "If I started dating now, it would only be to get back at him."

Grace threw out her hands. "I fail to see the problem here, Eff!"

She had a point, but it was not one Effie was willing to entertain. At least not yet. She'd known Daniel since they were teenagers, knew the ins and outs of him; that he hated cilantro and could only eat picante salsa, the way he ironed his jeans every morning because he said it made him look professional but not too highfalutin to shoot the breeze with the men who worked with him. She had reveled in the predictability of it all. But somehow, the familiarity that had been a saving grace for her had become a weight for Daniel. The worst part was that she hadn't really suspected it. If a person could spend a lifetime with someone and just fall out of love without warning, what was the point in trying it again with someone else?

"When I'm ready, I'll know," she said, sailing toward the kitchen, where she threw the cookies into the trash can and dusted off her hands. "And anyway, it's bad timing. I don't want to go out to dinner with a guy and have his dead grandmother show up to disapprove of me. I'm not sure I could take rejection from both the living and the dead right now," she called over her shoulder.

"You're right," Grace said slowly, as if something monumental had just occurred to her. "Or what if his dead wife showed up?"

Effie rolled her eyes, but Grace held up her hands.

"Hear me out. I mean I'm just saying this could come in handy when you're trying to avoid dating axe murderers and stuff."

Effie plopped down on the couch again, the cushion still warm and inviting. Pulling a quilt around her shoulders, she settled in and turned up the volume on the TV. "Can we just . . . table this? I have to figure out what I'm doing with my life first. I have to help Jay prepare for college. Teagan hates me. I'm pretty sure if I brought someone new home, she'd disown me and move in with Daniel." She cringed at the thought of Amber sharing clothes with her daughter, telling her she could stay out as late as she wanted. "I'm just saying . . . my life is complicated enough without adding a . . . data analyst."

Apparently, the finality in her tone was enough to fend off Grace's efforts, because half a glass of wine later, Grace peeled herself off the sofa, looking defeated, and stretched her limbs. "I'm gonna go. I think I need more training in the art of conjuring. Or more wine." She swirled around the remnants of her glass before setting it down on the end table and sighed.

Effie groaned and scrunched up her face. "Thanks for supporting me through my midlife crisis."

Grace reached for her purse and fished out her keys. "You aren't old enough for a midlife crisis," she declared. "Besides, friends don't let friends see ghosts alone."

"Well, thank you for being here for . . . whatever this is."

Warmth radiated from Grace's smile. "Where else would I be? We're going to figure this out." Looking her square in the eyes, Grace fixed her hands atop Effie's slumped shoulders and straightened them as if she were preparing her for battle. "Because you have to be fully sane to support me when I have my midlife crisis, which is coming up sooner than yours." Grace was forty-five—a fact she loved to remind Effie of whenever Effie complained about her aching knees or stiff back. "And you're going to have to talk me out of doing something really crazy. Like getting bangs."

Effie placed a hand over her heart. "I would never allow that to happen."

CHAPTER 13
LOLA

December 16, 1961

Dear Patsy,

There's been much talk around here lately about my future. You'd think I was an old maid from the way my mother goes on and on about my prospects after graduation. She seems to like Wallace well enough, but she gives me "the look" every time I leave the house with him, like she worries I'll get myself a reputation. She says a typing certificate will be fine, but a fiancé would be preferable. Honestly, I don't see how I'll have the time for either if everything goes according to plan.

So far, I have ten dollars and twenty-five cents saved for the Gibson. That means I only have sixty-two dollars and twenty-five cents left to go, and Daddy will chip in for the rest. I keep the money hidden in a cigar box at the top of my closet so the boys don't find it. They would waste it on taffy and chocolate coins in no time and make themselves utterly sick. Speaking of— the Weaver twins snuck a bag of marshmallows after I put them to bed last night, and one of them threw up all over my good loafers. But I reminded myself that sacrifices must be made, and the shoes are only a casualty in a much larger battle.

I've never wanted anything so badly as I want that guitar. It's been nearly impossible to learn my chords without it, so I've been practicing more at Helen's house after school. I'm able to play four songs now, including a couple of Jimmie Davis tunes.

My mother noticed my fingernails today and nearly popped a button. It's not my fault if they were getting in the way of things. I had to cut them down if I ever hope to get a better grip on the steel strings. At first, they were tender and red at the tips, but I've roughened them up pretty good, and they're starting to make a decent sound on the Martin. I think I'll have to grow a sixth finger to master the F chord, but all considered, things are going well.

Sincerely,

Lola

CHAPTER 14
EFFIE / "STRANGE"

The Fields and Fields parking lot was nearly empty when she arrived Monday morning. There was only a dusty black Honda bearing a bumper sticker that read I BRAKE FOR EMO GUYS wedged next to a sleek red Tesla. It didn't take a genius to figure out which one belonged to Drew. Noting the time on the dashboard, Effie congratulated herself for managing to arrive fifteen minutes early despite the precarious state of her stomach.

At least she hadn't run into any more dead people on her way there, but then again, she had done her best to avoid eye contact with anyone on her commute. When she'd stalled at a red light, an elderly man riding shotgun in the adjacent sedan frantically tried to get her attention, but she lowered her gaze and tugged on a pair of aviators, determined to avoid any potential delusions on her first day of work. It wasn't until this precise moment, standing behind her parked minivan, that she understood what he had been trying to tell her. In her haste this morning, she'd left her coffee tumbler atop the car. Siphoning out a breath of frustration, she noted the brown rivulets streaking the back window and cringed. "No matter," she said, righting her shoulders. Nothing was going to ruin her first day of work.

Sans coffee, Effie sauntered into the office fixing her eyes forward as if she had some pressing business to address, though she wasn't exactly certain yet what that was. Sporting a pair of high-waisted navy dress pants and a tasteful pink chiffon blouse, she clutched a brimming tote bag at her side. Hopefully she at least looked as if she knew what she was doing.

She was met by the purple-haired paralegal, who quickly assigned her to the welcome desk in the lobby, which Effie learned she had only been temporarily using in the absence of an assistant. Now that the paralegal had relocated to an office down the hall across from Drew, she seemed much more agreeable and warmly introduced herself as Lena. Effie was slightly dismayed by the news that she would be working alone. The drab lobby was devoid of any coworkers and thus any exciting office gossip. Grace would be disappointed.

Doing her best to focus on the silver lining, Effie took a moment to savor the sight of her desk—a pile of Post-its lined up by size and pens she'd sorted into various bins by color. Lena had even given her a key to the drawers, which were all tidily organized. Effie had no need to lock anything away. Still, it made her feel important to have the option, and she fingered the key reverently.

Shifting her weight around the ergonomic chair, she wondered what her first order of business should be, then restlessly straightened a stack of loose papers. She checked her watch. While she knew what time she was supposed to show up, she was still a bit light on the details after that. Drew was supposed to drop off some work for her, but he had yet to emerge from his office. Lena had given her a shiny new laptop and showed her how to set up a company email inbox that remained stubbornly empty despite refreshing the feed every seven minutes. Much to her delight, three phone calls had come in, and she had dutifully scribbled down a few notes to give to Drew later.

Her cell rang from inside her bag. Feeling guilty, Effie plucked it out and answered in a whisper. "I can't talk now."

But Grace didn't seem to compute this message. "How's it going?"

"Fine," Effie replied, though honestly, she had no idea if she was doing a good job, since Lena hadn't bothered to check on her in ages. Taking calls from her bestie on the first day was probably a bad look, especially considering her boss's TikTok spiel.

"Listen, I've been thinking about this ghost-seeing business," Grace continued, "and I've got some ideas."

"What are you talking about?"

"Just hear me out, OK. I have two words for you." She paused for effect. "Luke. Perry."

Effie wasn't sure how she was supposed to respond. "What does that even mean?"

"It means that maybe if we watch a little *90210* marathon, you can conjure him. I'll dress like Kelly, of course, and you'll be Brenda." Her excitement was reaching a near fever pitch. "Maybe we should wear matching dresses like they did in season one for the—"

"Are you seriously calling to talk to me about this right now?" There was no way Effie was going to invite Luke Perry into her midlife crisis too. And anyway, so far she hadn't been successful invoking spirits. They seemed to come and go of their own accord. But what did Effie know? None of this made any sense, so perhaps it wasn't an entirely ridiculous notion. In any case, now was not the time to discuss it. "I have to go," she said, craning her neck to peer down the hall.

"Wait!" Grace pleaded. "Don't forget that you promised to do hot spin with me today. Meet me at the studio across the street after work. And *do not* wear Jay's old basketball shorts again," she added. "You look like Grungy, the eighth dwarf."

"I won't," she promised, though the idea had crossed her mind when she'd packed her things this morning. They were comfortable and stretchy and, most importantly, covered her knees, which hadn't seen sunlight since last July.

Effie ended the call, then pulled in a fortifying breath and exhaled a small fraction of worry. Maybe exercise would be a good distraction from the strange detour her life had taken. She surveyed the room, taking note of the muted tones and sad plastic ficus in the corner. The place still had a clinical feel about it, but that would be easy enough to remedy. She fished inside her tote for the candle she'd picked up yesterday, hoping it would make things feel homier. Surely Drew wouldn't mind. After all, they were on a first-name basis, so maybe he wasn't as inflexible as the sexy mystery man had made him out to be. Unfortunately, her Good Samaritan hadn't resurfaced yet to properly thank, but she had tucked a heavenly fleece blanket and a Tupperware of brownies into her bag today just in case he made another appearance. She was aware enough to understand that she never would have landed the job without him.

She struck a match and lit the wick, and the scent of warm sugar cookies saturated the air. It permeated the sunny lobby with its giant storefront window, wafting down the hall where Lena and Drew worked with their doors ajar. Their voices thrummed down the corridor, carrying phrases like *thread the needle* and *due diligence* and *actionable items*. It all sounded very important—and boring.

After a mostly stress-free morning of sharpening pencils and setting up her new laptop, Effie straightened at the sound of heavy footsteps drawing near. A few moments later, Drew materialized in front of her desk, displeasure written over the ridges of his jaw.

"Morning, Effie." His face contorted in what she assumed was supposed to be a smile. At least he was trying, bless his heart. "How are you settling in?"

"Great," she replied. "Oh, I have a few notes for you." Locating a Post-it, she filtered through the messages she'd taken down. *Prioritize information.* Remembering this advice, she read them off in order of urgency. "Mrs. Lawrence called this morning because her husband has broken the custody agreement and taken the kids to Disney World without her consent." That would be distressing indeed. In fact, Effie had spent the better part of an hour commiserating with the poor thing and talking her out of driving down there to pick them up. It would only cause more trouble, and wouldn't it make more sense to go through the appropriate legal steps to avoid any further drama? Mrs. Lawrence had been so appreciative of the advice, and Effie had deemed it the bright spot of her otherwise mundane morning. "Oh, and some guy from the construction crew next door came over and asked if it was all right that they cut the power at seven o'clock."

This part appeared to grab his attention because he pinched his eyebrows and cocked his head. "And what did you tell him?"

A sliver of worry crept into her mind. "I told him it should be fine," she said. But the way Drew was staring at her with wide eyes made her second-guess this answer. "Lena said not to bother you if you were on a call unless it was important," she explained.

He grimaced, making her instantly realize her mistake. Though she couldn't be certain, she suspected this was the look that sexy mystery man had warned her about, because she felt entirely moronic.

"That's all right. I should have told you. Your day ends at three, but I'm usually here till dark," he pointed out in a way that made her feel guilty. She should have intuited this. "Not all of my clients are able to meet during usual business hours. I've got a meeting this evening with the Petersons, but I'll just reschedule. Can you reach out to them and move it to tomorrow?"

"Absolutely. I'm really sorry." Though she wasn't certain exactly what she was sorry about. When did he sleep? Or have time for his wife and kid? Was work the reason he was having problems in the family department? Her brain was buzzing with questions, but she reminded herself that this was none of her business.

Pressing his lips together, Drew sniffed at the air. "What is that?"

She scrunched up her face, her gaze darting around the lobby. "What is what?"

"That smell." He seemed perturbed.

Relief saturated her chest. "Oh, that." For a second, she feared she had made another mistake. "Warm sugar cookies," she replied, pulling her shoulders back proudly.

His eyes located the source of the scent on her desk, and he made a face that reminded her of a doctor about to deliver bad news. "I don't like candles in the office. Especially ones that smell like food." "But it's sugar cookies." And what kind of joy-deprived soul doesn't like sugar cookies? He must be dead inside.

"It's a mass-produced wax artificially forged in a lab to smell like sugar cookies," he said dryly. "Besides, I don't like the liability of having an open flame in the office. You might forget to put it out before you leave."

Of course, a lawyer's mind would go straight to the worst-case scenario. "But I won't," she pointed out, thoroughly confused. Leaving a candle burning was the sort of thing Brody would do.

He pressed a hand to the space between his eyes and pursed his lips. "I just settled a divorce between a couple that was married for forty-two years. Four kids, thirteen grandchildren. She left him to join a nudist colony in Florida with her lover. Trust me, anything is possible." Grazing her desk with his knuckles, he seemed to be restraining himself from saying something more on the matter. There was no denying it was a romantic tragedy, but Effie suspected that somewhere beneath all that practicality, Drew had a sad story of his own. "Look, I just emailed you an agreement that needs to be formatted," he said, ignoring her pitying look.

The task sounded ominous, but she waited for further instructions, hoping for some enlightenment.

"Oh, and you'll need to utilize orphan control," he added, as if this should clarify any confusion. It did not. Words had clearly left his mouth because his lips had moved, but their meaning evaded her. Orphan control? Whatever it was, it sounded barbaric. Even so, she pasted on a cheery smile. "No problem. I'm on it."

He rapped his fingers atop her desk and flashed a tight smile as if waiting for her to say something else. Finally, his eyes flickered to the candle, and he scrunched up his nose in a wince.

"Oh, right." Leaning forward, she blew out the candle, making a point to put her lungs into it.

Drew's lips settled into an awkward line. "Thanks," he said, not looking especially thankful. The heavy clack of his dress shoes echoed throughout the lobby as he trudged back to his office, then pulled the door closed behind him.

A sliver of outrage boiled low in Effie's chest, but she reminded herself how lucky she was to have landed the position, considering her abysmal experience. Besides, there were other ways to create a welcoming ambience that didn't involve fire. Conjuring an image of Lolly in her hair curlers, she fished out her phone and located a playlist, then turned the volume down low. A sweet country melody washed over her, and she closed her eyes, centering herself for the rest of the morning.

Lunch came and went with no sign of Drew, but Lena emerged for a quick break at the kitchenette across from Effie's desk. She popped a Lean Cuisine into the microwave and threw a curt nod over her shoulder at Effie.

Desperate for conversation, Effie seized upon her immediately. "Oh hey, I'm glad I caught you. Do you think you could help me figure out how to format these agreements?"

Lena shrugged. "Sure, what part do you need help with?"

Remembering Drew's request, she tried to piece together an acceptable answer. "Something about . . . orphans?" she said, hoping she'd heard correctly. "Honestly, I have no idea."

Lena stared back at her as if she were deciphering a crossword puzzle. Finally, her shoulders relaxed, realization settling in her eyes. "Oh, you mean widow and orphan control. It's just a way to ensure that the sentences in a paragraph stay on the same page," she said. But she must have picked up on the vacant look in Effie's eyes because she waved a dismissive hand.

"I'll send you a step-by-step guide. Don't worry about it. It's easy," Lena promised. The microwave dinged, and she retrieved her dish, then dug out a fork from the silverware drawer beneath the sink. She started for her office again, but Effie rose and bolted toward her. She'd been sitting on a burning question all morning, hoping that Lena could shed some light.

"Hey, while I have you . . . do you remember my interview last week? There was a man sitting in the lobby. He said he was a friend of Drew's."

"No." Twisting her fork around her noodles, Lena shook her head impassively. "There was no one else here."

"He was wearing a suit and tie." Certain Lena was mistaken, Effie tried harder to dislodge the memory for her. "Athletic build. Movie-star teeth. Totally gorgeous, if I'm being honest." She hated to admit this, as he seemed to be the sort of guy who already knew this about himself.

Lena only gaped with a look that made Effie question the poor thing's sanity. She and Drew appeared to have taken the same class in deadpan staring. "You were the only person on his schedule Friday."

Unable to accept this, Effie conjured a clear picture of the man's face. There was no way her mind could have invented a person that good looking. And Lena had been so distracted that day with her headphones, it was entirely possible she hadn't seen him. "He was meeting Drew for a late lunch," she said, thinking this should help clear things up. But it only seemed to make Lena more confused and irritated.

"Look, I've only been here for three months, but I've never seen Drew eat lunch outside his office. Besides, I think I'd remember a hot guy in this place if I saw one. It's not exactly crawling with prospects." With a *See what I mean* look about her face, she gestured around at the empty lobby. It wasn't entirely true, as Drew wasn't terrible on the eyes—though a little prickly around the edges. But based on the information she'd gleaned from those photographs, he seemed to be married. Or not. She was still dying to know the story there but didn't feel comfortable asking Lena about it just yet. It wasn't the sort of thing she could slip into casual conversation.

"Right, of course." Effie shook her head, though by now an uneasiness had settled in her sternum. A gnawing thought clawed at her mind.

She thought of Marty and Iris in the ambulance and the way Iris had looked at her with such desperation. Such need. The way her skin had sparkled before she vanished in front of her very eyes. There was no way her Good Samaritan could be dead too. If so, he had been far too cavalier about the whole being-dead part. She pushed the thought away, determined to think rationally.

Dead people didn't look that alive. Or that handsome.

Did they?

CHAPTER 15
LOLA

January 6, 1962

Dear Patsy,

It seems there will be no future career for me as a biographer as I am perfectly terrible at keeping a journal. But things have been so busy around here lately, I haven't had a moment to myself. For Christmas, I crocheted a periwinkle scarf for my mother and a charcoal hat for Daddy. Between school and minding the Weaver twins, I didn't have time to do anything for my brothers. Then my mother said as the oldest, I had to give them presents too, so I was forced to delve into my savings and spend three whole dollars on a couple of matchbox cars for George and Harry and a chocolate orange for Pete. Of course, I couldn't forget Wallace, so I gifted him a Jimmy Dean record. It was only slightly awkward as he didn't remember to get me a present. To make up for it, he said he'd take me to Gus's and let me buy a few picks for the Gibson. It was sweet if a little belated.

My total savings comes to fifteen dollars and fifty cents which is abysmal. At this rate, I'll be able to afford the Gibson when I'm an old woman, but by then, my fingers will have petrified to stone and my voice will be all warbled and useless. A small part of me hoped that perhaps Daddy would surprise me with it. Lord knows, I've only dropped about a million hints. On Christmas morning, I rushed to the tree and quickly found the biggest present. I knew it was a long shot, but my mind went wild with the idea. It was wrapped in butcher paper and had a strange shape about it, big and round at the bottom and long and thin at the top. But it turned out to be a Hoover for my mother. I don't know who I felt sorrier for—me or her.

Yesterday after school Wallace drove me to Gus's so I could make sure the Gibson was still there. It's torture to see it hanging in the window like a beautiful little orphan. An instrument like that deserves to be played, but I'll be devastated if anyone else takes it. Afterward, he took me to a sweet little house in a charming cul de sac across the river. He says it's high time to get out from under his parents, and this place will be perfect for him. It's a two-bedroom ivory bungalow with blue shutters and a wraparound porch with a hanging wicker swing. He asked me if I could ever envision myself sitting on that swing next to him, singing him a song as the crickets chirp around us in the evening. The idea made my neck flush and my stomach go all topsy turvy.

Sometimes I think maybe we shouldn't rush into things so quickly, but I know two other girls who got engaged this year, and they are both younger than me.

Besides, when Wallace drives me around town in that Plymouth, I feel like a bird on the wind, so free and wild, like I could do anything. He says he's going to teach me how to drive it which sounds like a perfect idea to me because it would send my mother into a fit.

I told Wallace if he rented that house, I would sit on that porch with him forever.

Hopelessly in love,

Lola

CHAPTER 16
EFFIE / "I CAN SEE AN ANGEL"

Effie made her way up the stairwell of the gentrified two-story warehouse across the street, mammoth water bottle and monogrammed chevron bag in tow. She'd come straight from work, changing into her Grace-approved gym clothes before she left—a black tank top and gray running shorts.

Out of breath once she reached the top of the stairs, she pushed past the industrial-size shiplap doors and stumbled into a sunny studio bustling with fresh-faced women and a few toned men. She scanned the sea of bouncy ponytails and messy buns in search of Grace, whom she spotted elegantly perched astride a stationary bike in the back row.

Grace's height put her a good six inches above Effie, and she looked a bit like a giraffe as she reached her sinewy arms above her head in a stretch. Grace brightened when she saw her friend, and she waved her over.

Effie meandered through the maze of exercise equipment to the back row, doing her best to remain unnoticed—an effort she practiced daily. Apprehension brewed in her mind as she passed a serious woman doing lunges, exuding the sort of confidence that suggested this was not her first rodeo. Briefly, Effie wondered if she'd overcommitted, but Dr. Parker had said she could exercise after six weeks as long as it wasn't too intense, and cycling had seemed like a safe enough bet. But that was before she remembered what ninety degrees felt like indoors. Already, a relentless heat weighed upon her skin, melting away her resolve and whatever was left of her mascara. But Grace had been such a rock the other night, so she shoved down her concern and bravely mounted the empty bike next to her friend. "Sorry I'm late. Drew asked me to stay after work a few minutes to review the HR policy," she said, gesturing toward the office building across the street.

"So, you're on a first-name basis now?" Grace waggled her eyebrows.

Rolling her eyes, Effie pulled an arm across her chest and stretched. "It's a strictly professional relationship."

Grace extended a lean biceps above her and reached it to the other side of her body. "I googled him last night, by the way," she said casually. "You didn't mention he was really cute. In a Jason Bateman kind of way," she added.

"He's . . . OK," Effie admitted. "He's also really married."

"Divorced," Grace pointed out, the word dripping with intrigue. "In case you cared to know. Going on two years now. I tried to feel him out on Facebook, but his account is practically a desert. Fortunately, my friend Stephanie just so happens to go to the same CrossFit class as him, so I asked her to check his relationship status, and do you know what it said?"

Annoyed, Effie closed her eyes, trying not to care, but a splinter of hope pricked at her heart. "I can take a guess."

"Single," Grace said, entirely satisfied with herself.

"Please stop stalking my boss. And I told you, I'm not interested in seeing anyone right now." Although she couldn't help conjuring the suit-clad stranger from the lobby and felt her skin prickle with curiosity. Had her sexually deprived brain only imagined him?

"I'm just saying there's no harm in a little flirting," Grace said.

"There is when it's specifically forbidden in the employee handbook, which is pretty fresh in my mind."

"Forbidden?" Grace teased. "God, you make it sound that much more tantalizing."

"Forget it." Ignoring Grace's sultry smile, she changed the subject. "Why are we doing this, again?" Even before her surgery, she'd never enjoyed torturing her calves. Besides, she had tried the whole fit lifestyle in the weeks before Daniel left, and it had only resulted in a pinched sciatic nerve. It was as if her body had given up the fight and resigned itself to its current plushy shape, and each time she tried to do something about it, it got angry and punished her.

"Because Kathleen said it's supposed to expel all the bad stuff. Not PTA Kathleen. Book club Kathleen," she specified. "I wouldn't take advice from PTA Kathleen if my life depended on it."

"What kind of bad stuff?" Effie pressed.

"I don't know . . . toxins, chemicals, the wine I drank the other night trying to get drunk enough to see dead people," she said, flashing Effie a secretive look. "And husbands."

The mention of Daniel diffused Effie's spirits instantly. She wished that were possible, not because she wanted to erase him—she didn't want to forget the nineteen years they had spent building a life together. She only wished it were possible to surgically remove the searing ache that throbbed in her heart each time she thought of his affair. Because she had loved him. And he, for all his cliché faults near the end, had once loved her too. "But I've never done hot spin before," Effie pointed out.

"It's just like regular spin." Grace shrugged and gave her an easy smile. "Only . . . hotter."

"Well, I'm not exactly a star student in that either," Effie clarified, looking around uneasily. The only bike she owned was a Schwinn cruiser that was presumably in the garage still attached to the trailer she'd once used to cart the kids around their old neighborhood. She could picture Jay's and Teagan's little faces as they bumped along behind her, their eyes alight with wonderment as they spotted the flowers and birds and insects she cheerfully pointed out along their trails. Back then, she'd been the center of their worlds. Now she was more like an orbiting moon, only allowed to glimpse them from a distance.

As the lights dimmed, a petite woman wearing a yellow sports bra and sage leggings bounced up to the front and settled herself atop her bike. "I realize some of you are new to this, so don't let my enthusiasm intimidate you. This is meant to be an empowering experience, a true test to show yourselves what you're capable of. So, there will be no quitting. No crying. And no excuses," she added in a militant voice that made Effie feel as if she was most definitely about to fail this test. "Now"—pressing her hands together, the instructor gave an impish smile—"it's about to get very hot in here. Let's begin!"

The weight of her words landed with full force in Effie's stomach as a techno beat filtered through the room. "How hot, exactly?" But apparently no one had heard her because when she looked around, everyone, including Grace, had begun feverishly pumping their legs like they were competing in the Tour de France. The machines thrummed in unison, and the acrid aroma of sweaty bodies drifted along waves of steadily intensifying heat. Effie imagined this was what it would feel like if hell opened its windows in the summer. She began pedaling at a leisurely pace, and the first sweat beads sprouted along her hairline. Though her confidence had begun to slip, she wiped them away, determined to power through and do this for Grace. But with each new command from the instructor, the rising heat sent her mind into fluttering fits of panic. Her body did not seem to be adjusting to the temperature as well as the others, all toned and warm and glistening with a healthy glow that did not suggest they were on the verge of passing out.

"Uphill for twenty seconds now. No phoning it in today! If it doesn't burn, you're not doing it right," the tiny woman was shouting. Her size suddenly became a note of annoyance to Effie, who now realized that it would be much easier to mirror her eager momentum if she were also the size of a malnourished twelve-year-old. She might as well have been pedaling in wet concrete. After only a few short minutes, her legs turned to ground meat.

Teetering atop her bike, she grabbed at her side to stifle a cramp until finally her legs could go no farther. As the room began to blur in and out of focus, her gaze landed on the floor covered in a spray of fresh sweat droplets she could only assume had come from her. Had she drunk enough water today to produce this much liquid? "I don't think I can do this." Dr. Parker lied! *Six weeks?* The very suggestion had been a fantasy! It would be decades before she could exercise again without wanting to curl into a fetal position. Maybe longer. Maybe never.

"Of course you can," Grace whispered. Her skin had turned the color of a lobster, but her jaw was set in a determined sort of way. "You are Effie freaking Baker. You can do anything you put your mind to. You can see dead people, for God's sake."

Placing a hand to her forehead, Effie closed her eyes and focused on emitting a tiny stream of air through pursed lips. "I'm serious. I think . . . I think I'm gonna be sick."

"It's mind over matter, Effie. Pull it together," Grace commanded.

"I need . . . air." Without waiting for permission, Effie dismounted and darted for the doors. Stumbling out into the light of the landing, she clutched a hand to her chest and tried to steady her breaths, which were coming hard and fast.

She closed her eyes against the sunlight, then dropped to her knees and dipped her head between her legs. Dragging the back of her hand over her face, she wiped away the salty mustache that had formed above her upper lip. Still lightheaded but feeling more in control of her breathing, she pinched her shirt, lifting it from her body, zealously fanning herself with the other hand.

"Everything OK?"

She startled at the realization that a man was speaking to her. Had someone followed her out here? In her hasty exit, she hadn't noticed much of anything apart from her imminent demise. Blinking against the sunlight, she squinted at the hazy image hovering above her. It was seductively familiar, if a bit blurry still. But when he smiled at her, there was no mistaking his identity. Even half-crazed with heatstroke, she would recognize those celebrity teeth anywhere. With a concerned look about his eyes, he crouched down to her.

"It's you," she said, scrutinizing him for signs of deadness. He looked completely normal, but as fuzziness gave way to sharper edges, she noticed the faintest light emanating from his olive skin. Shaking away the possibility, she attempted to stand, but her calves still felt like Jell-O.

He reached out a hand to steady her, but it passed through her back, disintegrating like glittering dust before materializing again in front of her midsection. He seemed almost as perplexed by this phenomenon as she was, flexing and studying his fingers as if he were a newborn trying to master the mechanics of a strange new body. "Damn. Don't think I'll ever get used to that." He seemed disappointed, but Effie wasn't calm enough to empathize. He'd just passed *through* her!

As she sprang to her feet, an electric jolt shocked her veins, and Lena's words from this morning echoed inside her skull with the force of a foghorn. *You were the only person on his schedule.* "Oh, no no no no no no no." Shaking her head, she crossed her arms as if to fend him off. "No no no," she said more firmly this time, pushing her hands apart. "This is not happening again!" She headed for the railing, circling around him as if he harbored a contagious disease. Leaning over, she pressed her rib cage into the metal bars and drew a fist to her chest. He was a hallucination, plain and simple. Perhaps this time she could blame it on the unforgiving heat, the lack of oxygen to her brain, just as she had experienced on the operating table all those weeks ago. It still didn't explain the fiasco at the grocery store, but she was willing to ignore that to keep herself from jumping off this landing. Hot flashes, perhaps? But she had just barely turned forty!

"I can't tell you what a relief it is that someone can finally see me." Dust-speckled beams of sunlight encircled him in a halo as a smile unfurled across his perfect face.

"I don't know what you're talking about," she lied, still gasping for air. She pressed her hands to her ears and squeezed her eyes shut, then counted to twenty Mississippi in her head. When she finally cracked one eye open, the landing was empty again. Her shoulders dropped as she let out a breath but only stiffened again when she heard the same tenor voice behind her call "Yoo-hoo. Still here." Slowly, she swiveled around to face him, then quickly jerked her head in the opposite direction as if she hadn't seen him at all. Maybe he was like the imaginary clown she'd envisioned beneath her bed at night, an irrational childhood fear, and if she ignored him long enough, he would eventually go away. She determined to appear aloof and studied the floral mural on the side of the warehouse.

Apparently, her performance wasn't convincing, because when she peeked behind, he was looking straight at her, meeting her eyes with a laser-like focus. And he did not appear amused.

"I know you can see me."

Plugging her fingers in her ears, she said, "You don't exist."

"If I don't exist, then why are you talking to me? And how did we have an entire conversation about your nonexistent work experience?" He held up a finger. "Which, I'd like to point out, I helped you massage into something resembling a résumé."

"You're a delusion," she reasoned aloud. "A figment of my imagination. A result of unbearable heat mixed with exercise and . . . and . . . I—"

Desperate, Effie filtered through those vapid Serenity Speaks TikToks she'd perused at Grace's insistence and remembered the recommended tips for grounding herself when anxious. "Something I can see," she said, scanning her surroundings with frantic need. "A tree, a mural, a pot of flowers," she said, her voice shaking. "Something I can touch . . ." She ran her hands along the railing, her fingers trailing along the bumpy paint that had begun flaking from the bars. She sucked in a cleansing breath, then released it while counting backward from ten. "Something I can hear . . ." She craned her neck in search of an acceptable sound, hoping for a bird or a car horn, but the only sound she could make out was her heart thrashing wildly in her chest.

"Me," he said, flashing her a palm. "You can hear me." He had somehow reappeared just feet away and was leaning back against the railing on his elbows, a triumphant look about his face. "Just trying to help." He shrugged.

Defeat pooled in her heart, and she rubbed her temples. "How did you know I'd be here? Are you following me?" If that was the case, she wasn't sure whether to be afraid or enraged.

"Of course not." He appeared offended and straightened his suit jacket. "I heard you talking to Grace while at work and thought it might be a good place to formally introduce myself. Didn't want to spook you at the office and get you fired on your first day since I kind of need you there."

Confusion and denial played a tug-of-war inside her fuzzy brain. At this point, she no longer trusted herself to separate reality from fantasy. Aside from the almost imperceptible shimmer radiating from his body, it was impossible to tell him apart from the living. He reminded her of a freshly printed glossy photograph. How could she have missed it before? She should have registered that perfect complexion as too good to be true—or, more accurately, too good to be alive. "I need to sit down," she said, her desperate eyes scanning the landing for a chair.

"I apologize. That was a bit too forward. I feel like we should start again." Puffing up his shoulders, he held out a confident hand.

Effie eyed it dubiously.

"Sorry." An easy laugh reverberated from his chest. "I keep forgetting. Still getting used to the rules." Drawing it back, he shook his head and patted his shirt, his smile fading into something more like nervousness. "I didn't mean to startle you, but I didn't expect you to come out so . . . early." He winced. "I'm Cameron."

Unsure what to do with this information, Effie stared back at him out of the corner of one eye. "Why are you here?"

His blue eyes came alive as if he had been waiting for her to ask this very question. "I need to get a message to Drew, and so far, you're the only person that can see me."

Was there a sign hanging somewhere above her head, alerting the dearly departed everywhere to this inconvenient truth? Questions were coming faster than she could untangle them. It must have been the surgery. That incompetent anesthesiologist had knocked something loose in her brain, and now she'd come entirely undone. And if that were true, how many other dead people had she spoken to since then? The question frightened her. Were all spirits good, or did evil ones hang around too? Most importantly, why hadn't Patsy returned to tell her what to do with this new talent?! "So that's why you helped me get the job," she said to herself, feeling like an impostor. Per usual, she'd been a pawn in someone else's game.

"Of course not. Can't a person do something nice for no reason?" He tugged at the cuffs of his sleeves. "Although, it does make it easier to ask you for a favor now. Quid pro quo, if you get my drift."

She wasn't entirely sure she did.

With a gruff cough, he thumbed his nose. "I've been unable to . . . move on or whatever you want to call it. And I think it has to do with Drew."

Curiosity softened her tone. She knew even less about Drew than she knew about Cameron, but so far, he seemed a little too uptight to keep company with the likes of this guy, so suave and self-important. They were an unlikely duo, to say the least. Enemies perhaps? Or a client? "What do you mean?"

Plunging his hands into his pockets, Cameron dropped his head and siphoned out a slow exhale. When he finally met her gaze again, he seemed to have shrunk by a couple of inches.

"Because he feels responsible for my death, and it's ruining his life."

The words drained her of irritation, and something softer took its place. Was that why Drew seemed so tortured all the time? Bless his heart, the poor man was obviously still grieving his friend. "How so?" she asked, still careful not to appear too interested. She didn't want to encourage him.

"Look, this may be hard for you to believe, but I wasn't a perfect ten, OK," Cameron said. "I had a few vices. And one night, I had too much to drink at my mother's rehearsal dinner, made a bit of a scene—you wouldn't believe the arrogant prick she married." He blew out his cheeks. "He's nothing like our father was. Anyway, I tried to drive home, got so far as to get my keys back from the valet, but Drew caught me just in time. Took them away and put them in his suit pocket. I was wasted, though, couldn't see past getting back to my apartment. When he went back inside, I followed him, and when he wasn't looking . . ." He paused on the next part, rubbing his chin. "I took them back."

So, it had been a car accident. A DUI, no less. And if that was the case, did Cameron even deserve her help? "I don't understand." She screwed up her face. "Why would Drew feel responsible for your death if he took the keys away? You were the idiot who took them back," she pointed out.

"Thank you for reminding me of my mistake," he replied, his tone laced with sarcasm, "but I think I've received punishment enough. Don't you?"

Feeling chastened, Effie offered a reluctant nod.

"The point is, Drew feels like it was his fault he didn't do more to stop me," he went on. "He's still living in my apartment, sleeping on my couch like a drifter. I heard him tell his therapist that he's the reason I died."

Drew's in therapy? Good for him. Though she pitied him for the reason he needed to go. *Time to set things right,* Patsy had said. Was this what she meant? Was Effie supposed to help her boss come to terms with his friend's untimely death? The whole situation was heartbreaking. Even so, how could she possibly set things right? She'd only just met Drew. What's more, he was her superior. Why in the world would he take unsolicited—and incredibly personal—advice from her? Drawing a hand to her temple, she said, "Look, Cameron—whatever your name is—if you are truly dead, and I'm not experiencing some sort of mental break, which—let's be honest—I have not completely ruled out, then

I'm sorry for what's happened to you. But I don't know how I can help. If I mention any of this to Drew, he'll think I'm delusional." And he wouldn't be wrong.

Cameron nodded, but his eyes drifted to the ground, and she could tell he'd gone somewhere else. Finally, he met her gaze again, and this time, his perfectly contoured face struggled not to crumble. "Effie, do you know what it feels like to be on the outside of your life looking in? Like everything is happening on a screen, and no matter what you do, you can't control any of it? Like no one knows you exist at all." It seemed as if he were speaking more to himself than to her.

Still, the words filtered through her, sending a twinge of recognition to her heart. Traitorous tears pricked at her eyes. She'd always been a sympathetic crier. "Actually . . . I do," she said, realizing that she knew the feeling intimately. How long had she been the ghost in her relationship with Daniel? The unseen hand making flash cards and healthy dinners and hundreds of brownies for people she didn't even know. Was that why Daniel had fallen out of love with her? Because he'd stopped seeing her? It wasn't like Amber had just appeared in their lives unannounced. He'd gone looking for her because he'd felt like something was lacking. She had been lacking.

Feeling guilty about her still-beating heart, she sucked in a breath, her chest trembling as she struggled to release it a little at a time.

"All right," she said, resigned. "But we have to go about things carefully. I'm dealing with a lot of my own issues right now, and I can't afford to lose this job." And she would not risk giving Drew a heart attack as she had with Marty.

"Understood." With a smile, he nodded eagerly, though his eyes were still thick with emotion. "I think it's best to ease your way into it. Get him to trust you," he said, like it should be simple. "Get him to see you as more than an employee. I know Drew. If he respects you, he'll listen to what you have to say."

Effie was unconvinced. "And how exactly do I do that?"

"Simple. Take an interest in the things he likes. And it just so happens that I know everything about him, so that will be the easy part," he said, lifting his chin.

None of this sounded easy to Effie. "Fine. But first we're going to establish some ground rules." Drawing closer, she threatened him with a shaky finger. "No more popping up in unexpected places. My pulse was already racing in there," she pointed out. "You almost gave me a heart attack! And you're not allowed in my house," she added, worried the kids might think she was conversing with a wall. It would only be more fodder for Teagan. "And under no circumstances will there be any surprise appearances in the bathroom." Crossing her arms, she leveled a steely gaze at him and added, "Or the shower."

"Trust me, that won't be a problem." He stifled a smirk, which made her want to slap him. Or blow him away. How did one go about getting rid of an egocentric delusion? "No offense, but you're not really my type."

"No offense, but neither are you," she countered, crossing her arms. She must have been temporarily insane to have ever thought this man was attractive. "I happen to prefer men with a pulse."

"Touché." He nodded once, drawing a fist to his chin. "OK, so we'll communicate at work," he decided. "Shouldn't draw too much attention since most days the lobby is empty. Drew prefers to shut himself in his office like a hermit."

For some reason, she bristled on Drew's behalf, but the terms of the agreement seemed reasonable, so she allowed a subtle nod. "All right, then."

"All right, then," he repeated, his lips settling into that dazzling smile that had fooled her once. He'd been a fraud, but then again, so had she.

Catching the excitement in his voice, she worried that she'd given him false hope. This whole medium thing was still a newly acquired talent, and she wasn't certain she had the knowledge or wherewithal to assure Cameron's salvation, much less stop Drew's self-loathing. She wondered if he'd been less rigid before Cameron's death. She didn't want to care about him, but she couldn't help herself. "The two of you must have been close for it to affect him like this," she ventured, picking up on the way his eyes flickered away from her for the briefest of moments.

"Yeah," he admitted. "I guess you could say that. He always felt this huge responsibility to take care of me, make sure I was OK." A silent heaviness hung between them, and his gaze fell across the bustling street, landing on the sunny yellow building. For the first time, she noticed the way those steely blue eyes reminded her of someone else's, and she felt her breath hitch. "Big brothers are like that."

CHAPTER 17
LOLA

February 4, 1962

Dear Patsy,
It seems my efforts to save are continually thwarted on all sides. I'm embarrassed to admit that I had to pay twenty-five cents in overdue library fees for failing to return *Jane Eyre*, which just goes to show that reading is far less productive than music making. I didn't even like the book. The only interesting part happens when Mrs. Rochester sets the house on fire, but then, like a fool, she jumps to her death. I think I would have enjoyed a cold Coca-Cola while I watched the flames from the safety of the moors, but what do I know about literature? These days, I'm far more interested in music. Which reminds me—I took the bus down to Gus's yesterday to buy your new single which set me back another three dollars. But of course, I have no regrets because the song is phenomenal. I didn't think you could outperform yourself, but "She's Got You" is my favorite ballad to date!

My mother says everything on the radio sounds the same these days, but I disagree. Most people who sing about heartache and loving and losing someone don't really perform with their whole hearts like they mean it. They don't sing the words like they've lived them. But you do. Which brings me to the next thing I have to tell you, Patsy. I don't usually keep secrets from Mitsy and Helen, but something happened that I can't tell anyone else about just yet. Especially not my mother as it would only make her happy. Also, I'm not entirely certain how to feel about it.

Last night, Wallace took me for shakes at Matty's, and afterward we walked along the river skipping stones over the water. When I ran out of rocks, I set to searching for more, but the smooth ones were few and far between. I whirled around to find Wallace bending down. I assumed he was doing the same thing, but he wasn't moving. He was kneeling and holding out his class ring, and he had a look in his eye I'd never seen before, like maybe he had developed a sudden case of indigestion. He said, "Lola, I knew you were the girl for me since the first time I saw you in those dad burned sleeves." He said he knows we have to wait until after I graduate, but he wants to start our lives together as soon as possible.

As you can imagine, I didn't know what to say! It's only been a few months, but in that moment, I couldn't think of a single reason to turn him down. Wallace has a job and car, and his parents seem to think I hung the moon. Sometimes, I can't get over the idea that out of every girl at the dance that night, he chose me in my clown sleeves. He said he loves me. And even though I'm not sure I know exactly what love is supposed to feel like yet, I let him give me his ring as a place holder until he can afford a better one. He seemed so relieved when I said yes that I let him pull me close and kiss me. It was a night I think I will always remember.

    Sincerely,

    Lola

CHAPTER 18
EFFIE / "I DON'T WANNA"

By the time she made it to the office the following morning, Effie wished she had thought to fill her metal flask with something stronger than water. One spirit had already approached her at the gas pump after she accidentally made eye contact, begging Effie through tears to contact her son and let him know where she had stowed away a second life insurance policy. The whole thing had depleted her, but she'd promised to send an anonymous text message on the woman's behalf. Since her encounter with Cameron yesterday afternoon, she'd resigned herself to being perpetually bothered by the dead. So far, it had been more of a *Casper* situation than *Poltergeist*, and for that at least she was grateful.

As if that weren't unlucky enough, there had also been a stalled tractor that slowed traffic to a painful crawl for two miles along her route. When she finally spilled inside the office twenty minutes late, Drew gave her a dissatisfied once-over from the kitchenette, where he stood pouring a sugar packet into his cup of coffee.

"Morning," he said. But his face was all edges, and the way he pursed his lips after he said it sent a wave of dread through her midsection.

"Good morning," she replied, heading purposefully for her desk. Maybe he hadn't noticed the time.

"Everything all right? You're running a little behind today." No such luck.

Steeling herself, she swallowed a lump in her throat as she settled her things at her workstation. "There was a slight delay along my route," she explained, trying to sound casual. "It set me back a few minutes." She left out the impromptu ghost conference; it wouldn't help her credibility. "But I can stay later to make up for it."

"No need." Taking a sip of coffee, he studied her over the rim of his mug. "Just curious, but where do you live?"

This was starting to feel like an interrogation. Next time, she would just wear a sign around her neck that said she was closed for otherworldly business before work, maybe stipulate office hours. "Laurel Heights," she replied. "Normally it's a ten-minute drive, but I didn't expect a backhoe to get stuck in a ditch." She forced a nervous smile.

"I know where that is. Nice area." He nodded slowly, making her feel exposed. He was probably wondering why someone in her suburban neighborhood had taken a job that paid little more than waiting tables. "You didn't take the interstate?"

"No, I prefer the more scenic route." Tugging open her laptop, she fixed her eyes forward, hoping he would drop the subject.

"But the interstate is faster," he pointed out, the line in his forehead deepening into a thin canyon. And then, as if something new had just occurred to him, he reached into his shirt pocket and produced his phone. "In fact, you should download an app. There's a great one I use that calculates the most efficient path so you never end up stuck behind an accident," he said, his fingers busily tapping away at the screen. This was perhaps the most excited she had ever seen Drew Fields.

She wasn't sure if he was trying to prove a point or make conversation. Either way, she knew she would not be downloading any more apps. "Thanks, but I like my route." This time of year, the pastures lining the winding back roads were generously dusted with blossoming wildflowers. What's more, something about the scene reminded her of those few inexplicable seconds when her soul had escaped her body—earth and sky and sun and life, all teeming together in a perfect kaleidoscope of beauty. But there was no way to explain any of this to him, so she just said, "It's . . . familiar."

"But the app is foolproof," he said, studying her as if she'd just rejected a pile of cash. Maybe he was trying to be helpful, but it felt more like judgment. Effie couldn't help but compare Drew to his younger, taller, devilishly handsome brother. It seemed that where Cameron was impetuous and extravagant, Drew was careful and levelheaded. It reminded her of her own children's pecking order. While Teagan tended to act on emotion, Jay had always been methodical, a typical firstborn child.

"It's really OK," she replied again bravely, fixing a smile to her face. "But don't worry. I'll leave earlier next time so I won't be late."

"Sure." He flashed her a confused sort of smile that felt obligatory, then reached behind him and produced a legal pad. A subtle cough escaped his chest. "While I'm here, I was hoping you could transcribe these notes for me today." He set the notepad atop her desk.

"Of course," she said, reaching for it. Now that seemed like something she would have zero problem accomplishing. But as her eyes trailed over his handwriting, confidence gave way to dread. It was entirely illegible. He might as well have dropped off a book in Korean.

But Drew must not have registered her apprehension, because he ambled toward his office, leaving Effie alone again, wishing for a Rosetta stone. Looking around, she wondered when Cameron would make an appearance. So far, he'd kept his end of the deal, and she hadn't caught him sneaking about her home or following her on errands. She'd stayed up way too late last night googling him and her intense boss. With each keystroke, she'd learned another impressive fact about the brothers. Drew had graduated magna cum laude from Stanford before returning to Tilly and joining his father at the family firm. Then, three years ago, Mr. Fields senior suffered a fatal heart attack, leaving the company to his sons, one of whom was far less inclined to follow in his father's footsteps. Judging from the photos she'd come across, it seemed

Cameron had been more interested in acquiring hot real estate and beautiful women than in finishing a degree and joining the family firm. Likely utilizing his rich-kid trust fund, he had bought and renovated an apartment complex and three trendy restaurants uptown. It was a shame he'd died so young. With that easy charisma and an apparent head for business, he would have gone far, she suspected. What's more, she learned that it had been nearly a year since Cameron had died in the accident, which meant he'd been stuck here for longer than she'd initially suspected. If Drew was the reason his brother couldn't cross over, he must be nursing a pretty bruised heart. Maybe she'd overcommitted.

"I see Mr. Efficiency is already winning you over." As if on cue, Cameron appeared before her desk, greeting her with a smolder. "How are you settling in?"

"Not so great," she admitted, stealing a glance down the hall. The last thing she needed was for Drew to see her speaking to an empty lobby, so she kept her voice low. "Your brother has asked that I transcribe his handwritten notes from court, but it's all chicken scratch." She squinted at a jumbled cluster of squiggles that resembled upside-down hieroglyphics. "Do you think he was angry at someone when he wrote this?"

Cameron made a clicking sound from the side of his mouth. "Penmanship was never his strong suit. But lucky for you, I happen to be an expert in Drewscript."

"Thank goodness," she said with a sigh. "I was worried I'd be here all night."

"I can help you finish quicker so we can start planning what you're going to say to him. I meant what I said about the quid pro quo." He waggled his thick eyebrows.

"About that." She pursed her lips, still unclear where they had landed yesterday. "How am I going to tell Drew the truth without (a) freaking him out, (b) pissing him off, or (c) getting myself fired from the first real job I've had in years? Am I supposed to just walk up to him and say, 'Here are the notes you requested, and by the way, I've been chatting with your dead brother?'"

Seeming unruffled, Cameron waved her away. "Nah, Drew is a total skeptic. All logic and argumentative reasoning, that one. Even if you did tell him, he wouldn't believe you. No, you're going to have to break through that concrete wall he's put up. But don't worry. I can totally get you in."

Considering Drew's dogged work ethic and the dark cloud that seemed to follow him around, that seemed unlikely. "You sure?"

"Of course," he said. "Want to know the silver lining of being dead?"

She shook her head, uncertain if he really wanted her to answer that question.

"I've got loads of time to think about this kind of stuff. Now"— steepling his fingers, he leveled his gaze at her—"I've been compiling a list of all the things he likes to do. So, we just need to find one that you can talk to him about."

A tiny seed of curiosity pricked at her mind. Unless Drew was discussing work or maximizing efficiency, he was pretty much a closed book. At least from an employee perspective. "Well, what kinds of things does he like?" she asked. She wasn't sure if she wanted to know for Cameron or for herself.

"Well . . . he's really into off-road biking." Cameron lifted his eyebrows expectantly.

Effie's face went slack. Considering her experience in the spin studio yesterday, off-road biking sounded awfully dangerous. In her case, potentially fatal. "Not really my forte," she said, stapling a stack of loose papers with more force than necessary.

"He likes to fish," he said, his eyes brightening. "It was kind of our thing growing up. Just the two of us out on the water with a couple of poles and a cooler of RC Colas. This one time after he'd just gotten his license, he was supposed to be out running errands for our dad, but he took me to the lake instead. I reeled in this massive catfish, and it finned the hell out of my hand." A wistful smile took shape on his face, and though no one had asked him to elaborate, he went on. As she listened to the rest of his story, it occurred to Effie that she was probably the first person he had spoken to in ages, and she felt a bit sorry for him. "Drew wrapped it up and said we would tell my parents it was a dog bite. So, we did. And they never found out about it." His eyes went misty, and he thumbed his nose as if he were trying to stave off tears, leading Effie to wonder if ghosts could cry. "That's the kind of big brother he was."

Touched by the memory, Effie felt her stony facade slipping. Nevertheless, she shook her head. "Sorry, Cameron, but I don't see fishing in my future either."

"Oh, I know." He snapped his fingers, his voice picking up speed. "He's obsessed with pickleball. Before the accident, we played all the time. He can't get enough of it. Lately, even more so." His smile faded around the edges.

Growing impatient, Effie tapped a ballet flat under her desk. "I still don't understand what any of this has to do with me."

Her reticence only seemed to energize him. "Hear me out. He goes to these indoor courts after work every Tuesday and Thursday. Now, normally he plays with a group of four, but one of the guys is on a business trip, so they'll be a man short tonight. You could offer to step in."

She reached for another stack of papers and deadpanned, "Unless you mean just physically stepping in the building, then no. I couldn't." She accentuated the point with another violent press of the stapler.

"Come on," he whined. "I can teach you the rules. It's easy. All you have to do is hit the ball. It's like oversized Ping-Pong," he added, like this would make the idea more appealing. It did not.

"Don't play that either. Again, I think you have seriously overestimated my athletic abilities."

It seemed she was getting under his skin, because he pulled in a deep breath through his nostrils. "Look, the sooner you get him to open up, the sooner you can get him to move on, and the sooner I'm out of your life. Isn't that what you want?"

He had a point, but it irritated her all the more. Plus, the name of the game had the word *pickle* in it, which made her think of sandwiches. She envisioned a leisurely game between friends, maybe something low key but kind of fancy, like badminton. With sandwiches perhaps. So maybe it wouldn't be as awful as she feared. Leveling her gaze at him, she crossed her arms. "Even if I did agree to it—which I'm not—I can't tonight."

"Why not?"

How to explain. To her knowledge, the only other people who officially marked the day were Lolly and the Pink Lassos. Cameron would never understand. "Because today is March fifth," she finally said. An image of Lolly in her mink coat floated into her thoughts, carrying with it a hint of regret.

Confusion rippled across his face. "And tomorrow is the sixth. So what?"

"March fifth is a family holiday," she said flatly, hoping he wouldn't ask her to elaborate. Growing up, anytime she tried to explain the significance of the day, other kids would stare at her the same way Cameron was looking at her now. They could never understand how someone could just make up a holiday, though none of them seemed to have a problem with Groundhog Day, which Lolly deemed not only ridiculous but an utter waste of time and an unnecessary inconvenience to the poor groundhog.

"Come on, Effie. You can't abandon me for a made-up holiday. I neeeeeed you," he said in a way that made her think he wasn't going to drop the subject. "Besides, I literally have nothing better to do than ask until you say yes."

From what she knew so far of ghosts, there was no reason not to believe him. She heaved a sigh. "Fine, I'll go. But only because you're being incredibly annoying right now."

Her phone buzzed to life on the desk, and a message from Daniel materialized on the screen. A flutter of anticipation sent her heart skittering, and she braced herself, wondering if it was about the terms of the divorce, which were still undefined—not for lack of trying on her part.

Just wanted to check in and make sure you're alright? You seemed off the other night.

Off was an understatement. She wasn't sure if she should feel moved that he still cared enough to check on her or annoyed that he had the gall to keep caring about her after everything he'd done. Reflecting on her interrupted séance with Grace, she cringed, then fired off a quick response.

Fine. Grace and I just had a little too much to drink.

Not entirely untrue.

"So, that's him, huh?" Cameron appeared behind her, peering over her shoulder intently. "Your ex?"

Bristling at the proximity of his voice, she locked her phone. She wasn't sure how much he had gathered about her personal life, but the idea of him having an opinion about it made her uncomfortable. "How do you know I have an ex?"

"Heard you the other day when you were word vomiting in Drew's office."

Remembering her completely unprompted monologue, she cleared her throat. "Not quite ex," she clarified, unsure why she felt the need to. Once their lawyers brokered a financial agreement, the divorce was all but certain. She stowed her phone in her bag. "But yes. That was Daniel."

His eyes zeroed in on the framed family photo gracing her desk, a snapshot taken last year at the cabin they'd rented for spring break in Arkansas—before Daniel had so casually discarded her heart and ripped apart their family. *Stop smiling, you idiot,* she told her old self. "He's not that hot or anything," Cameron said, interrupting her thoughts. "I mean, he looks like a regular old dude. No offense, but he has a total dad bod."

Cameron wasn't exactly wrong. Despite his daily jogging, Daniel had softened around the edges over the years, his stomach ever so slightly straining the fabric of his T-shirts. The observation should have validated her, but for some reason, she felt defensive on Daniel's behalf. She had once loved that dad bod. And though it pained her to admit it, a part of her always would. "Well, I suppose we can't all be *GQ* models."

Cameron held up a palm to head her off. "I didn't mean you guys are old. I just fail to see how a guy like that ever managed to get you."

Her throat constricted, her cheeks flushing the sheen of an apple. "That's sweet of you to say, but you haven't seen Amber." She did her best to compose herself, but just mentioning the name brought on images she wished she could unsee. Since she'd learned about the affair, she'd gone out of her way to avoid her husband's mistress. It would only add to her self-hatred, and she already had social media for that. A cold sweat sprouted beneath her hairline.

"I mean it," he said earnestly. "You've got this whole . . . Disney-princess vibe about you. Minus the hair situation," he added. Briefly, she wondered if her mother had a point about touching it up. "Seriously, he must be an idiot not to see it."

Cameron's sudden sincerity made her emotional. Fighting off tears, she discreetly dabbed at the corners of her eyes. "Yeah, well, Daniel could be incredibly charming." Once upon a time. Her phone chimed again, and she reached to silence it. Another message from Daniel.

Need a contract I left at the home office. A client thinks I'm in breach, but I'm certain we didn't sign off on these specs. Any chance you could bring it to me?

In another life, she would have packed up her things and headed to his aid, no questions asked. But this time, her initial instinct was to side with the client since Daniel had already proved himself a liar, at least where she was concerned. Feverishly, she pecked out a reply.

Can't. Not my job anymore. Thank God.

No, she couldn't send that. It was too petty, and she was determined to be the bigger person in this divorce. She chewed her lip, mentally rearranging her schedule like a game of *Tetris*. She would have to run his errand at the expense of her lunch, which sounded depressing. But wasn't Daniel's success at work every bit as important to her and the kids as it was to him? Shaking her head, she deleted the message and started again.

I have a break at noon. Can you meet me somewhere?

She was about to hit send when Cameron's voice interrupted her train of thought.

"What are you dillydallying about over there?"

"Nothing," she replied, not wanting to elaborate. "Just a favor for someone."

"For who?" He tried peeking over her shoulder, but she flipped the screen.

"None of your business." When he cut her a smolder, she relented. "Fine. It's a favor for Daniel."

Cameron pinched his face. "You don't mean the same Daniel who left you for someone else, do you?"

"That would be the one," she admitted. She was beginning to think this was a talent of his, saying the one thing that would most irritate her in the moment.

"Do you always do that?"

"Do what?"

"Come running whenever he calls."

"I do not come running whenever he calls," she protested. The nerve of this man. Who the heck did he think he was?

"Of course you don't," he replied. But the pitiful look he gave her belied his response. "Effie, do you know how I became one of Tilly's 'Thirty under Thirty to Watch'?"

"Geez. Humblebrag much?" The answer seemed obvious to her, but of course, he was probably too blind to see it. Finally, she said, "Because your parents are rich?"

"Right, Karen." He flashed her an acerbic grin. "And I'm sure being a housewife from suburbia has been a *real* struggle," he said, causing Effie to bristle. He didn't know the first thing about her life. Nevertheless, he seized upon her answer as a teachable moment. "Look, the reason I died owning more of this town than most people could ever dream is because I didn't roll over and do other people's jobs when they flaked out. You can't give in to your ex every time he asks for a favor."

"I wasn't going to give in. I was going to be . . . helpful," she said, trying to convince herself as much as him.

He leveled his gaze. "You were about to be a doormat. And doormats don't run businesses or broker seven-figure deals or lead countries. You've got to be a shark! And right now, you're like . . . a friendly dolphin."

Though the accusation brought a fiery red to her cheeks, she knew he was right. Truth be told, she wasn't even a dolphin. More like a guppy, aimlessly swimming in circles, returning to the same worm on a hook no matter how many times it fooled her. Did Daniel know that she would always do his bidding?

As if reading her thoughts, Cameron said, "Here. Type this instead: *That isn't going to work for me.*" He framed the words with his hands, allowing them to hang in the air between them like he was waiting for her to declare him a genius.

Effie let the phrase simmer on the tip of her tongue. It sounded so . . . formal. And she'd never been formal with Daniel.

She shook her head. "Daniel and I aren't like that. I help him out with work occasionally because it's always been a family business."

Cameron looked dubious. "Is this another one of those 'jobs' you do for free?"

Another irritating truth. "What's your point?"

"My point is that you don't value your time." Hands on his hips, he looked like an exasperated teacher. "And you can't expect anyone else to respect you if you don't respect yourself."

He was making a lot of sense, but she would never admit this aloud. "Fine," she conceded, and began typing out the message he'd dictated.

Sorry. That isn't going to work for me.

"Don't say sorry! Never say sorry," Cameron said firmly, peering over her shoulder. "Apologizing implies you've done something wrong, and you haven't. He's the one who needs your help. You have all the power."

Effie rolled her eyes. It was something Grace would have said. Even so, she deleted the text and started again, this time adding the phrase **I'm at work.** She wondered what Daniel would make of the fact that she was no longer "lazing about the house." When Cameron appeared satisfied, she finally hit send. Steeped in worry, she chewed a thumbnail, awaiting a response. It would only make the divorce more difficult if she made unnecessary waves, and they had enough to argue about.

Cameron must have registered her anxiety because he furrowed his brow. "Wait . . . you don't want him back . . . do you?"

"Of course not," she said, and she meant it. But her voice went high and defensive.

"You know, if he cheated once, he's probably done it before," he pointed out, as if this were an objective fact.

"What? No," she said, pushing away the idea. Amber had been the first. Daniel had been clear about that, although she supposed she had no reason to believe him anymore.

Cameron circled to the front of her desk and perched himself atop the edge. "Here's the thing, Effie. Unlike Drew over there"—he thumbed toward the hall where her boss was speaking loudly on a conference call—"Daniel and I are cut from the same cloth. We can't help it. It's in our DNA," he explained casually. "Take it from a guy who recognizes his own kind. There's no way he cheated on you just once."

"You don't know what you're talking about." Effie dismissed him with a wave of her hand, refocusing her attention on her email. "Daniel isn't like you. He'd never done anything like that before." But even as she spoke the words, a fleck of uncertainty lodged its way into her chest.

Leaning forward, Cameron raised an eyebrow. "That you *know* about."

"You're wrong," she protested, louder than she'd intended. Suddenly aware that she was speaking to an empty lobby, she lowered her voice, glancing toward the hall to make sure Drew and Lena had closed their office doors. "I know Daniel's heart. You don't." It wasn't true—at least not anymore—and she realized how unconvincing she sounded. Had she ever really known her husband? Which version of Daniel had been the truest one?

He flashed her an *I'm sorry to be the one to tell you this* look. "That's the thing, though. I do."

Unwilling to let him win, she leveled a steely gaze at him. "Yeah, well, how could you? Yours doesn't even work anymore, remember?"

He frowned, clutching a hand to his chest as if he'd been shot. "Ouch. That one hurt. I may be dead, but I still have feelings."

"Sorry," she said, guilt seeping through her. She wasn't usually the kind of person who said the cruel thing, but Cameron's arrogance was bringing out the worst in her today. "So, I take it you never settled down?"

"Nah. Had a girlfriend that wanted a ring. Total smoke show. Tall, blonde, legs for days," he said with an appreciative smile. "But no one was gonna cram the Cam Man's style."

"That tracks." Effie rolled her eyes. God, he was so asinine. "How's that working out for you?"

"Great, thank you very much." Looking affronted, he tugged at the lapels of his blazer, then smoothed out his sleeves. "Look, you of all people should understand that marriage is a sham. It's a social construct meant to keep people in bondage. Take Drew, for example, the sort of guy who finds something that works and sticks with it forever. Then his wife leaves him for some ripped yoga instructor, and he's left pining for her, still paying a shit ton of money in alimony. And for what? Reduced wages, weekends and every other holiday with his kid? No thank you."

So that was why Drew walked around like the sole survivor of a plane crash, living on his dead brother's couch. She made a mental list of tragedies—his father passed away, his wife left him, and then his dumb brother, the only person he had left in the world, went on a bender and wrapped his car around a tree. When she'd first met Drew, he'd seemed so successful and put together, but she supposed life had a way of leveling the playing field. "So, no regrets, then?" she asked, certain Cameron must have more than a few.

He put a thoughtful finger to his chin, then said, "I regret that I never made out with Summer McKee. She turned me down when I asked her to junior homecoming," he went on to explain, though Effie hadn't asked. "I always meant to look her up just so I could date her and ditch her. Of course, I have regrets." For a second, his smile faltered, but he quickly recovered. "Just not in the marriage department."

"Well, this may surprise you, but neither do I."

"Seriously?" He scoffed. "Two decades of your life wasted on a marriage that didn't pan out and you still endorse it? Daniel set you aside when someone shinier came along."

He was right, but not about everything. Effie squared her shoulders. "Just so we're clear, I didn't waste those years with Daniel. I built a life with him. I built a family. And just because it didn't work out doesn't mean I regret any of it. If I'd known at the beginning that we wouldn't make it, I would have done it anyway. Because if I hadn't, I wouldn't have the kids. Or all the memories we've made together." Her gaze flitted to the picture on her desk, and she smiled, her eyes filming over again. At one time, the thing she'd wanted most in the world was to re-create that photograph over and over until they were old and gray, surrounded by their children and grandchildren. That future was gone now, but there was still so much goodness there, so much to look forward to. A family divided was still a family, after all. "Take it from me." She drew in a deep breath. "Some things are worth failing at."

CHAPTER 19
LOLA

March 9, 1962

Dear Patsy,

My mother found out about the proposal. I made the mistake of telling Mitsy who told her mother who told her husband who works with my father at the auto factory. Then Daddy came home yesterday in a sour mood, complaining that he hated to find out about his own daughter's engagement from a coworker he didn't particularly care for, especially when he's the foreman and the person who should be doing most of the knowing around there. This, of course, sent my mother over the edge. At first, she was hotter than a pistol and demanded why she should be the last person to learn of my plans as she is always so keen to know what they are. But after a few days, it seems as if she's forgiven me and is always finding opportunities to bring up the wedding. In her usual way, she says little off-handed things like "satin is a much cleaner look than tulle, you know" and "of course, you'll wear your grandmother's butterfly broach." She thinks a summer wedding sounds perfect.

I have uninvited Mitsy from my birthday party next month.

Sincerely,

Lola

CHAPTER 20
EFFIE / "FOOLIN' 'ROUND"

Wearing a loosely fitted T-shirt and athletic shorts, Effie made her way into the gym, her hair pulled back into a decent-looking ponytail. Thank God for dry shampoo. She never would have survived the first days of work without it. At this point, she was barely running on copious amounts of coffee and processed food. Not to mention takeout. Luckily, the kids didn't mind that part so much.

At the front desk, a slim blonde woman behind the counter greeted her with an effervescent smile, then slid a sign-in sheet toward her. "Need any gear?"

Scrawling her name in a box, Effie assumed she did, though Cameron hadn't gone into the specifics of the game. He was supposed to meet her here at seven but so far was MIA. Checking her watch, she wondered if he'd somehow passed on without her help and was surprised to find that she was slightly disappointed at the idea. He was annoying, but it had been nice having someone around to help her sort things out at work today. "I'll just take a paddle," she said, in the form of a question.

"Sure thing."

With a grateful smile, Effie accepted a blue-and-green striped board by the handle, unsure what she was supposed to do with it next. It was smaller than she had anticipated. She was hoping for something more frying pan size, because while she may be able to talk to ghosts, she was not blessed in the hand-eye-coordination department.

She entered the heavy double doors to the gym, passing courts sectioned off by short nets. An eclectic assortment of people was scattered about, smacking balls back and forth—a young father with his children, a pair of elderly couples, and a rather serious-looking band of middle-aged women wearing sweatbands and bright-teal skirts. They looked a bit scary—like they'd come to take no prisoners. She scuttled past them, avoiding eye contact. So far, everyone here seemed to have a pulse, so at least there was that. Even so, she'd gotten fairly good at avoiding the gazes of strangers, just in case.

Near the back of the gym, she caught sight of Drew donning bright-yellow sweatbands, huddled with two other men. His shirt was tight and stretched just above his biceps, displaying a generous glimpse of his muscles. She had suspected that underneath all that J.Crew was a fairly toned body, but she hadn't been able to fully appreciate his athletic build until now. Stealing a peek down at her neglected physique, she felt a bit dowdy. The surgery was supposed to make her feel better about herself, and in some ways, it had. But it hadn't been a miracle, and she still lacked the confidence and the fashion sense to draw attention to the changes in her body.

The three men were dripping with sweat, a detail that unnerved her. Cameron had said the game was easy, but she now wondered if they subscribed to the same definition of the word. Doing her best to appear aloof, she sailed past them, unsure exactly where she was headed.

"Effie?" Drew called out, squinting at her as if he'd just spotted a penguin at the beach.

"Oh hey. What a coincidence," she said, trying to sound breezy, as if she hadn't just rearranged her entire evening to be here.

He peered behind her, seeming confused by her presence. "What are you doing here?" Then, locking in on the paddle in her hand, he asked, "Do you play?"

"Only all the time," she lied. "But I had to take a break for a while on account of an injury." Lies. All lies. Cameron owed her big time. Where was he, anyway? He was supposed to be walking her through all this. Aside from his vague advice to "hit the ball," he had given her little else to go on.

"This is Mark," Drew said, gesturing to the tattooed giant lumbering beside him.

"Pleased to meet you." With a warm smile, Mark extended a meaty hand nearly as big as the paddle he was clutching. Gaping up at him, she was beginning to rethink this whole idea.

"And this is Carl."

A wiry gentleman stepped forward and waved a wrinkled palm. He had a constipated look about his face that made her uneasy. Wearing knee-high socks, he had tucked his shirt into a pair of rather inadequate shorts that left little to the imagination. This was a motley crew if she ever saw one. What the heck kind of game was this?

"This is my new assistant," Drew explained. "Effie, meet the Court Jesters. Minus Ted, of course," he added. "He's in the UK till next week."

"That's a fun name for a team," she noted. Maybe Drew wasn't dead inside after all.

"We're all lawyers, so . . . it's a play on words," he explained in a proud sort of way she found slightly adorable.

Taking some heart in his excitement, she mustered a brave smile. "Nice to meet you both."

"Since we're down one man tonight, you want to be our fourth?" Mark asked, his thin eyebrows lifting. "I mean woman," he added. "Unless, of course, you're playing with another group."

Apprehension stalled her response. "Absolutely," she heard herself say. "I was supposed to meet some friends here, but it looks like I got my evenings mixed up," she lied. Mark seemed nice enough, but Carl was looking at her in a way that made her uncomfortable, like he was sizing up her athletic abilities. Or staring down a potential meal.

"Perfect." Drew smiled a real smile, the first she'd seen from him. It tugged at her conscience to receive it under false pretenses. "You can be on my team," he offered. "I'll serve first."

Fixing her eyes on Mark and Carl, she took note of where they positioned themselves on their side of the court and adjusted accordingly. "All right, 0-0-2," Drew yelled.

What was he shouting? Before she could make any sense of the numbers, Drew flicked his wrist and lobbed the ball to the other side of the court, where Mark whipped it back at a speed Effie was certain she had never encountered before. Drew saved it just in time, sending it to the other side of the net, where Carl promptly sliced it down the middle so fast she never saw it bounce off his paddle.

"That's all right," Drew said, his voice encouraging. "That was a tough one." This time, Mark served. "0-0-1," he thundered as his paddle met the ball. Why were the numbers going backward? There was no rhyme or reason to any of this! It sounded like they were just shouting area codes. Amid all his jabbering, Cameron hadn't mentioned how to keep score. She looked around, desperate to find him before it was her turn to serve, but he remained stubbornly invisible. Too late. The ball shot past her ear like a bullet, and she flinched.

"No worries," Drew said, pressing his lips into a thin line. "We'll get the next point." But they didn't. Or the one after that. Or the one after that. Each time the ball came near, her survival instincts kicked in, and she held the paddle up to shield her body. The only time she made contact with the ball was an accident that sent it clear onto the adjacent court, whizzing dangerously close to a woman in one of the teal skirts who flashed her an evil eye. Drew seemed to be growing more and more irritated with her too. Though he never came right out and said, "You suck," she caught his sigh after every ball that sailed past her head.

Finally, during an unusually long rally, the ball landed directly in front of her like a fortuitous gift, and the impossible happened. She angled her body sideways, drawing her hand back before pushing it forward until the thwack of the ball echoed like a gunshot. In slow motion, her astonishment turned to elation as she watched it sail across the net, just barely skimming the top before it made contact with Carl's racket. It was a miracle from God, nearly as extraordinary as talking to the dead. Maybe she wasn't an utter failure in the sports department after all. Cameron would be proud. Had he seen her? She was practically Venus Williams out here!

"Watch out!" Mark shouted. Or maybe it was Carl. She had no idea because by the time she registered the warning, it was too late. Everything went dark.

~

Drew's face was unusually fuzzy, disappearing and reappearing with every blink. Each time she opened her eyes, his features looked less and less like a Picasso painting. A worry crease deepened along his forehead. "Are you OK?"

Alarmed to realize she was lying flat on her back, she struggled to lift herself.

"Don't try to get up yet." He held her down with a firm but gentle arm. "You took a pretty hard hit to the head. Carl feels awful."

"I apologize," Carl said, not looking especially repentant. "I can get carried away sometimes." Who the hell is Carl?

"I should have warned you. He doesn't look it, but he's a real beast on the court."

"No worries," Effie said, though she was full of worries. Where was she? How long had she been out? Why did her head feel like someone had sliced it open and was stirring a spoon around inside it? "Where am I?" she asked, cautiously taking stock of her surroundings. The last thing she remembered was leaving work.

"You're at the gym," Drew replied. "You were playing pickleball."

"Not sure I'd call that *playing*," Carl noted with a frown. Whoever he was, he sounded like a real piece of work.

Keeping his eyes fixed on Effie, Drew waved him off. "Does any of this ring a bell?"

She dragged a sweaty hand over her head as the puzzle pieces began to slide into place. A throbbing lump had sprouted between her eyes. She was going to kill Cameron. Again. Carefully, she turned her neck to search for him, but he was nowhere to be found.

"You need to ice that," Drew said tenderly. Someone produced a cold pack, which he promptly applied to her forehead. He cradled the back of her neck, his face a mess of worry.

"Thank you. It's . . . been a while since I've played."

Behind him, Carl appeared unconvinced. "If you say so."

"That's enough," Drew snapped. "I'll take it from here." The rest of the Court Jesters trudged off, leaving the two of them alone. "Think you can stand now?"

She nodded, then let him guide her up, one hand fixed to the small of her back. "Thank you. I'm fine now. Really," she promised, though there was a buzzing in her brain she couldn't seem to quiet, no matter how many times she tried to blink away the sound. "You guys should keep playing. I'll see you tomorrow." Thoroughly mortified, she attempted to skulk away, but he followed close behind, steadying her when she stumbled.

"Sorry, I can't allow that. There is no way you're driving home in this condition. In fact, you probably need to see a doctor just to make sure you're not concussed. Carl hits the ball harder than anyone I've ever played."

"That would have been helpful information to have about an hour ago," she mumbled. Clutching a hand to her forehead, she said, "No, I don't need a doctor. But a glass of water might help."

"Come on. Let me take you out for a drink. It's the least I can do after my teammate tried to kill you. And I'm driving you home," he insisted. "I won't take no for an answer."

~

Nestled in a booth across from Drew, Effie nursed a club soda, her head finally silent.

"You sure you don't feel nauseated?" Clutching his phone, he scrutinized WebMD with all the concern of a distressed parent, and she smiled. Despite her first impressions of him, Drew Fields was probably a wonderful father. "Any sensitivity to light? Excessive fatigue? Confusion?" He peeked up from his screen and studied her carefully.

Bingo. Although *confused* couldn't begin to describe her current mental state. As he spoke, she discreetly scanned the sparsely dotted tables for potential dead people, wondering if perhaps Carl's ball had reversed whatever sorcery had befallen her on that operating table at Rosehaven. So far, everyone here appeared to be alive. Maybe she was cured. Maybe a good bump on the head was exactly what she needed to shock her back into reality.

"I feel so awful," Drew said, his features drawn in that familiar grimace. "You shouldn't come to work tomorrow. Take the day off to recover."

"I'll be fine. Besides, I've survived worse," she said, thinking of her surgery. "Please don't feel bad." She waved him off. "Also, I may have oversold my pickleball abilities . . . just a smidge." With a guilty smile, she pinched her thumb and forefinger together.

His expression suggested he agreed with her. "You know, it *was* kind of weird the way you were just standing there, staring into space."

She hadn't been staring into space. She had been admiring her perfect shot, which would have earned them a point if Carl hadn't performed some Hail Mary ninja move that sent it sailing back at her skull. "I've just been . . . distracted lately," she explained.

He arched an eyebrow. "Does it have anything to do with your soon-to-be-ex-husband?" He winced, drawing his shoulders together. "Sorry. Super personal question. You don't have to answer that."

"No, it's OK," she said, though the mention of Daniel had sucked all the humor from her tone. "How did you know?"

"Your interview. When you thought I asked you for your tax returns?"

"You heard all of that?" She may as well have announced it through a bullhorn. Her cheeks turned to lava.

He nodded, his eyes awash with sympathy.

"Let's just say"—she let out a bone-weary sigh—"it's been a rough year." She left out the part about Daniel leaving her for a younger woman, pulverizing her heart. Drew was still her boss, after all, and she didn't want him to look at her the way everyone else did—with pity.

Besides, she didn't want to talk about Daniel. The whole point of this evening was to talk about Cameron. Inclining her head, she gave Drew a thoughtful once-over and said, "You're really good at pickleball. Have you been playing long?"

His smile cracked in a way that made her wish she hadn't asked the question. "I got into it after my father died. My brother . . ." He reached for his glass of water and downed a swig. "My brother, Cameron, is the one who turned me on to it."

"Were you close with him?"

"Yeah . . ." Resting his drink on the table, he narrowed his eyes at her. "You said *were*. How did you know he died?"

Her skin prickled with heat as she realized her mistake. "Oh, I didn't," she lied. "I'm just really good at reading people. The way you said his name . . . I could just tell."

"I see," he said, though he still studied her with a hint of distrust. In any case, he went on. "After Dad died, it became the thing we did together. Then my wife left, which is a whole other sad story you don't want to hear." It was a story she definitely did want to hear, but she let it slide for the moment. "Cam was always so competitive."

From what she knew of Cameron, that seemed like an accurate assessment.

"My brother was like . . . my antithesis, I guess you could say."

Another astute point. Even so, she tilted her head and asked, "Oh really? How so?"

Leaning back against his seat, he pursed his lips. "Where Cam was tall, dark, and handsome, I've always been . . . short, melanin deficient, and . . . forgettable."

Effie did not agree with that statement at all. As far as she could tell, Drew was a perfectly normal height, of a lovely medium-beige color, and had no visible goiters or moles. She certainly had no trouble remembering the ridges and valleys of his face, the way his eyes crinkled at the corners when he smiled. But she wasn't about to tell him that, so instead she just said, "I'm sure that isn't true."

"It is," he protested. "If I got a new phone, he bought a better one," Drew went on. "If I got tickets to a Rangers game, he booked a flight and got tickets to see the Braves. Once, I bought a black BMW, and the very next day, he showed up at my house driving a better model with all the bells and whistles. Same color and everything." Smiling, he shook his head, his eyes misty at the memory. "He always had to one-up me." Then he grimaced and took another sip of his drink. "He made me play pickleball until he won, which he always did. But it wasn't exactly a fair fight. He was ten years younger. That's a lifetime for knees." A hearty laugh escaped his chest, but he quickly reined it in.

"That's quite the gap," Effie noted.

"He was a surprise. My mother was told she couldn't have any more children, and then one day, my parents come home and tell me I'm going to have a little brother. I've always felt like his protector."

"I'm sure you were."

A muscle twitched below his cheek, and his face became rigid again. "No. I wasn't."

"I'll bet he thought differently," Effie tried.

"Maybe," he said, seeming far away now. "I don't know. Cam was always getting into trouble. If it wasn't an impulsive real estate purchase, it was fast cars and an endless rotation of women. Pretty hard to tell someone like that what to do." His smile faded as he reached for his drink, and Effie could feel the weight of his pain. Talking about Cameron had killed the mood. She felt guilty to have pricked his sadness, but this was her intention in coming tonight. She should be proud that she was gaining some ground with him.

As if reading her thoughts, Drew said, "Tell me more about you. What does Effie Baker do when she isn't at the office or defying death?" He didn't know how true those words were. The corners of his mouth tugged up into a rare grin.

The change of subject flustered her. She hadn't prepared to talk about herself. "Well, I have three kids," she finally said. "And they each have about a million things going on in their lives. I can hardly keep up."

"Tell me about them." He seemed genuinely interested, and the invitation made her smile.

"Well . . . Jay—that's my oldest—he's so levelheaded and kind. The sort of kid who's popular but also sweet. He'd give you the shirt off his back in a blizzard. Unless, of course, it's his sister who needed it," she added, drawing a hand to the back of her neck. They shared a chuckle. "Then there's Brody, our youngest. He's a hypochondriac and a bit lazy when it comes to schoolwork, but he's whip smart. I call him my tech guy because he's the only one in the house who knows how to reset the Wi-Fi. And then there's Teagan. And she's . . ." How could she sum up her beautiful, ferocious, exasperating daughter? "Well, right now she kind of hates me." Teagan had always been a difficult kid, hotheaded and sassy to boot. A faint picture emerged on the edge of her memory: Daniel and her playing endless games of Guess Who? with the kids when they were small. Smiling, she pictured Teagan's pouty face, so full of outrage each time Jay guessed her person, even though she chose the lady with the gold hair and pink hat every time. Her fiery little girl had thrown her card and wailed about the injustice of it all. She'd always been opinionated, but ever since Daniel had taken up with Amber, her barbs had been especially cruel and sometimes downright vicious.

"Oh, come on. I'm sure she doesn't hate you."

"No, I'm pretty sure she does." Effie chewed her lip. "The thing is, most parents can look at their kids and see themselves. But when I look at her, I don't see any part of me. She's all Daniel, that one. Determined and stubborn. You tell her she can't do something and she sets out to prove you wrong just to spite you."

He gave a thoughtful nod, then shifted his weight. "Well, I've never met her, but . . . I think she may be more like you than you think."

She did her best to ignore the way her cheeks burned and averted her gaze. "What about you? Do you have kids?" she asked, remembering the photo in his office. Finally, an opportunity to learn about his family.

"Yeah. Samuel." His voice brimmed with pride. "He's ten. Great kid." Drawing a fist to his mouth, he cleared his throat, and his face fell. "But I don't get to see him as often as I'd like. My ex, Darcy, got married a couple years back. One month after our divorce was finalized, to be exact." Ouch. Poor Drew. "Actually, they just had a baby. Suddenly, it feels like they have this whole new family, and I'm the lonely guy that comes to entertain Samuel occasionally." He laughed, but there was an emptiness behind it. "Sometimes, I feel more like his mentor than his dad."

"He's lucky to have you," she said, and meant it. "Kids need both their parents. It doesn't matter what the arrangement is. Besides, I'm sure he looks up to you. You're smart, successful."

"Yeah." He gave a wry chuckle and downed another swig. "A divorce attorney who got divorced. How appropriate is that?"

"You can't look at it that way. You just . . . had a setback." She shrugged. "The beauty of life is the trip . . . or something like that, I once read in a Dear Abby article." A smile played on her lips.

From behind Drew, a haggard-looking waitress emerged, wearing a name tag that read "Ruby." She rested a menu on the table, then tugged a pencil from her silver bun. "Can I get you folks anything else?"

Drew flashed a quizzical look at Effie. "You hungry?"

"Actually, I'm starving," she admitted. "Do you have a chicken-salad sandwich?"

"Only the best in the state of Texas," Ruby declared with a proud lift of her chin.

"In that case, make it two," Drew said, handing back the menu.

"Oh, and a root beer," Effie called after her.

After the waitress had gone, he arched an approving eyebrow. "A woman who knows what she wants. I like it. Is that your standard order?"

"It's sort of a tradition," she admitted. "But only on March fifth."

He scrunched his eyebrows. "Care to extrapolate on that? Don't tell me you're one of those vegans who allow themselves to eat meat one day out of the year and today's your lucky day," he teased.

"Definitely not," she said, fending off a laugh. Unsure how much to share, she wrestled with a reply. Talking about Lolly would only make her emotional. "When I was a kid, my grandmother was obsessed with Patsy Cline, and March fifth, 1963, is the day she died."

"Your grandmother?"

"No, Patsy Cline," she clarified. "My grandmother always said that the president should have declared a national day of mourning. But since he never did, she decided to formally mark the occasion. We call it Saint Cline's Day." Lolly would emancipate her from school, wearing her mink coat, and take her to her grandparents' little white bungalow, where Helen and Louisa were waiting. They played all of Patsy's greatest hits. The music was always a balm to Effie's soul, the familiar twang of the strings combined with the sweet melodies they wove together. Afterward, they would eat chicken-salad sandwiches with dill dressing, and toast one another with Schlitz beer—Patsy's favorite. With a wink, Lolly would always slide a root beer over to Effie. The rest of the afternoon was filled with more music and laughter and memories about Patsy's life, so personal that at times Effie wondered if her grandmother had actually known her.

Lost in the memory, she nearly forgot Drew's presence.

He leaned back against his seat and studied her. "Interesting. That's really . . . weird."

"It's not weird," she said through a smile, though admittedly it was. She had tried to continue the tradition with her own children, but she hadn't wanted to interfere with their schooling, and the chicken-salad sandwiches had never really taken. They much preferred chicken strips and fries. At this point, the only way she marked the day was by making a sandwich for dinner and watching a few old clips of Patsy on YouTube.

Drew seemed to be sizing her up. Finally, he reached for his glass and raised it to her. "Here's to us." She lifted her own to greet it. "And to Saint Cline's Day. May she rest in peace." He smiled, and as their glasses clinked, something shifted inside her—the part of her that had believed she would never be curious about a man who wasn't Daniel.

CHAPTER 21
LOLA

April 7, 1962

Dear Patsy,

Who could have imagined that one little wedding should take so much time and energy to plan? Wallace's mother and mine have taken over the whole affair. They say I don't have to worry for a thing, and all I need to focus on is finishing my studies and graduating next month. But it seems any time I get a minute to spare, I'm being carted off to a dress fitting or a cake sampling or a free makeup tutorial at the department store.

My mother insisted on a satin gown with a lace bodice for the wedding. To spite her, I've chosen a strapless tea-length tulle number that cinches my waist so tightly I resemble a life-sized Barbie doll. Truthfully, a small part of me is still put out about Frances, and this was the only card I had left to play. But mother is relentless. Finally, we reached a stalemate in which she pretended not to notice me for three whole days and moped around the house like a bereaved widow. I told her if she let me have the dress, I'd carry a bouquet of white freesias instead of the yellow tulips she claims are far too splashy for a church wedding. I suppose concessions must be made if I am ever to be free of her. I'll bet your mother never forced you to endure these sorts of fashion atrocities, Patsy. I read in your fan newsletter, of which I am a most devout subscriber, that you design your own outfits, and your mother sews them. I am green with jealousy!

Between all the wedding talk and final exams next month, I've had little time to earn money for the Gibson and even less time to practice at Helen's. My calluses are beginning to soften, so I've been running the tips of my fingers over a piece of sandpaper before bed at night.

On top of everything, the boys found my cigar box and stole seventy-five cents for hard candies. They didn't think I'd notice, but I have a running ledger beneath the lid. As I write this, they are out hunting bottles and cans to pay me back. When they do, I'll have seventeen dollars and fifty cents put away. That's accounting for the lock I purchased this morning at the drugstore.

Sincerely,

Lola

P.S. My mother said I couldn't uninvite Mitsy from my party, so I told her I'd rather not have one after all. But she said eighteen is an important year for a girl, especially since I'm to be married soon, so she baked a coconut cake and invited Helen and Mitsy and Wallace over after dinner this evening. The whole thing felt entirely juvenile. We just sat across from one another like dolts with nothing interesting to say. I imagine you would tell me to chin up and soldier on and forgive Mitsy as life is much too short to hold grudges. Except in the case of Frances where the statute of limitations does not exist. I'll try to remember to write more.

CHAPTER 22
Effie / "I Love You So Much It Hurts"

The office was quiet the next morning when she sauntered in wearing black gaucho pants and matching flats. She'd done her best to cover the mark on her head with makeup, but it didn't erase the purplish disc protruding between her eyes.

Lena looked up from the breakfast bar, alarm written all over her face. "What happened to you?"

Touching a finger to the bump, Effie forced a smile. "Just a little mishap at the gym. Nothing to worry about." She had no intention of reliving the details of last night, at least not the part where Carl's ball had sailed directly into her skull. The second part, with Drew, was a different story. She craned her neck discreetly to search for Cameron, but he wasn't there. If he knew what was good for him, he would stay invisible for as long as possible.

"If you say so." Lena seemed unconvinced. "You want a doughnut?" she asked, covering her lips as she spoke through a mouth full of bread.

"Thanks," Effie replied. Though she knew it wasn't the wisest decision, she helped herself to a bear claw. Amid all that had happened lately, carbs were the one thing that never disappointed her. Besides Grace, of course. "That was thoughtful of you."

"Wasn't me." Lena nodded toward Drew's office door, which was uncharacteristically propped wide open with a wedge at the base.

"He asked to see you, by the way," Lena said, tucking a strand of purple behind her ear.

"Me?" Hopefully she hadn't said anything embarrassing last night after her second brush with death. When she'd woken up this morning, the whole thing had still been a bit fuzzy, and she'd been alarmed at first to find her car missing. Then she'd remembered that Drew had driven her home, walked her to the front door, and insisted again that she should stay home today.

Feeling ridiculous, she'd refused the offer flatly, promising to arrive at her usual time. Then, twenty minutes ago, an Uber had shown up in her driveway, accompanied by a text message from Drew that read Thought you might need this today. Hope you're feeling better.

She plated the bear claw and left it atop her desk, then ambled toward his office, where he stood perched behind his screens. "Oh hey." He removed an earbud. "How's the head?"

She rubbed her elbows, hoping the giant amoeba between her eyes didn't look as bad as it had the last time she'd looked in the mirror—like someone had whacked her with a shovel. "Oh, just fine," she said, as if she had merely stubbed her toe rather than lost consciousness in front of a roomful of strangers. "I woke up with a little bit of a headache. Thank you again for looking out for me last night."

"Of course."

The way he was staring made her wonder if there was another reason he had asked her in. She still had a stack of agreements on her desk to proofread and format. Cameron had become more of a hindrance than a help around the office lately, and she hoped she hadn't forgotten to do something else.

"And you're sure you're feeling up to being here?" he asked.

"I'm sure," she promised, but he continued to study her as if he didn't quite believe her.

Finally, he broke eye contact and awkwardly rubbed the back of his neck. "Look, uh, while I've got you here . . . there's a charity banquet tonight. My mother's foundation is always hosting some pet project in honor of my brother, Cameron." His face muscles contracted as he cleared his throat. "It's tonight at the Hotel Marquis at six thirty." He paused for a beat. Was this an invitation? Surely, he wasn't asking her to go with him. Per the HR policy he'd designed himself, that would be wildly inappropriate, if also a little intriguing.

"I bought a table for six," he continued, "but I'm not able to go, so if you want to invite some friends, you should take it. In fact, it'd really help me if you could," he added. Silence hung between them until finally he shrugged and said, "It's a free dinner. Should be decent food."

"Oh," she said, her voice much higher than she'd intended. "Thanks. I'm not sure if I can. I've got the kids tonight."

"Bring them," he said, as if this was what he had intended all along.

"I don't know." She couldn't imagine her children agreeing to a stuffy fundraising event wearing their Sunday best. Drew's smile died around the edges, making her feel guilty, so she quickly supplied a more ambiguous answer. "But I'll try," she added, though she was 90 percent certain there was no way she was going. The only other person she could think to invite was Grace, and that was hardly six people. "Thanks for thinking of me." She cringed. It made it seem as if he had been thinking about her when, of course, he had not. He'd probably only felt sorry for his poor lonely, single assistant.

"Well." A heavy pause hung between them until he finally said, "Let me know if you need anything today."

"Sure," she promised, though she didn't see herself asking him for anything else. The whole passing-out-in-public thing had been demoralizing to say the least, and she planned to spend the rest of the day hiding out behind the bonsai tree at her desk.

Returning to the lobby, she clocked Cameron lying supine across the love seat, and her insides caught fire. One arm was draped over his eyes as if he were blinded by the sunlight filtering through the window.

Or hungover. Could ghosts get drunk? In any case, she was too angry right now to care.

She checked to be sure they were alone before tearing into him. "Where were you last night?" she whisper shouted, cutting him a murderous look, the same one she gave Brody when he forgot to take out the trash and the garbage truck sidled past the house. "You left me to fend for myself in the bullpen, and I was practically draped in red," she said, remembering the evil gleam in Carl's eye. "I told you I wasn't athletic, and those people were cutthroat."

"I'm sorry." But he didn't seem sorry. He wasn't even looking at her. He was staring out the window, his face contorted as if he'd just swallowed something sour. "You remember the girl I told you about? The one who wanted me to propose?"

"You mean the one you cheated on?" she asked flippantly. "Oh wait, that was all of them." She settled behind her desk.

"I said I wasn't perfect," he shot back.

With a saucy glare, she crossed her arms. "Are you sure Drew is the reason you're still here? Seems like you pissed off a lot of people while you were alive," she said. She was still angry about last night. He hadn't even asked about her battle wound, and it was impossible to miss.

Ignoring her, he buried his face in his hands, dragging them down his cheeks. "I saw Cassidy last night in some coffee shop with my business partner. Joe." The way he said Joe's name, like it was dripping with bile, led her to believe they probably hadn't been drinking buddies.

"You do realize that qualifies as stalking," she pointed out.

"Yeah, well, I don't think the rules really apply to me anymore. Do they?" A strange new anger tinged his voice, making her regret the observation. "The point is, they seemed to be having a grand old time without me." He sat up straight, planting his hands on his knees. "She laughed, and not the fake high one she always did with me. A real laugh. And then, do you know what Joe said next?"

Effie had a fairly good idea, but she kept it to herself. "What?"

"He gets on one knee, and he says, 'Cassidy, I've loved you from the first moment I met you.' He says, 'Cameron never saw you the way you deserved to be seen. He never treated you the way you deserved to be treated.' Then he pulls out this gaudy ring that I never would have chosen and asks her to marry him right there in front of everyone."

"And?" Cameron didn't strike her as the sentimental type, especially considering their conversation yesterday.

"And . . . and I can't believe she actually said yes," he said, his jaw set like that of a little kid who'd been passed over for dodgeball.

"But why do you care? I seem to remember a certain someone vowing he would never settle down."

"Because . . ." He dropped his chin. "Because I think I may have . . . loved her," he admitted softly.

"But what about your big speech? 'Marriage is just a social construct to keep people in bondage' and all that crap," she mimicked.

"I know," he said, his face crestfallen. "But that was before I saw her with Joe. It . . . sucked."

It disarmed her to see Cameron's usual confidence obliterated, and she offered him a sympathetic frown. It made her think about the cloudless Saturday afternoon she'd first witnessed her husband thriving in a new life without her—Daniel placing a concerned hand on the small of Amber's back as he led her out the double doors of the department store. They'd been buying sheets. When had he ever helped pick out sheets before? She'd stood there, dumbfounded, her mouth unable to form sentences, as she tried to remember the last time he'd touched her like that. Blinking away the thought, she cleared her throat. "Cameron, I know it's hard to believe, but I really do understand how you feel."

"I seriously doubt that," he said. "Now I can't stop thinking about all the things I should have said to her. All the things I loved about her. The way she always got that little crinkle in her forehead when I said something stupid. The way she snorted when she laughed at my jokes. The way she ate at all my restaurants even though she hated fusion food." Looking exhausted, he raised his eyes to the ceiling. "I'll tell ya, it's a real shitscicle."

Effie lifted an eyebrow. "Come again?"

"I don't know!" He threw out his hands. "I think you and your pretend cusswords are rubbing off on me."

Not quite. "Cameron, I think you can rest safe in the knowledge that you haven't changed at all. But you get an E for effort."

Despite her reassuring smile, he groaned, then slunk back in his seat, defeated. "Piece of advice?"

She nodded, though she wasn't sure she would take lessons in love from someone who had died without any meaningful relationships aside from with his big brother.

"Don't wait to tell the people you love that you can't live without them. Because one day, you'll have to, and it will kill your soul to know that you never did. Knowing that you wasted the time because you were too busy or too prideful or too . . . stupid . . ."

For the first time, Effie wanted to reach out and hug him, to take away his sadness. Because, finally, Cameron was right about something. Reflecting on Drew's invitation, Effie let the idea simmer. There was frozen pizza at home, and the kids would understand if she went to dinner without them. After all, it would be her first evening out in ages. "Hey, what are you doing tonight?" she heard herself ask.

"Is that supposed to make me feel better? The same thing I do every night," he grumbled. "Wallow in pity and general self-loathing."

The people pleaser inside her wanted to fix him. And what could be better for a narcissist's bruised ego than a room full of people toasting him? Cameron needed some tangible proof that he still had plenty of friends and family who loved and missed him. "Did you know there's a charity event tonight in your honor?"

"I'm listening," he said, brightening, and Effie could tell that she'd sparked his interest.

Pride blossomed in her chest, and she pulled in a deep breath, letting the hint of a smile take shape on her lips.

~

Brody prodded Effie's arm with a finger as she lay lifeless on the sofa. "Mom, something's wrong with my elbow. It hurts when I lean on it."

Vaguely aware that someone was speaking to her, Effie tried to pry her eyes open, but they felt impossibly heavy.

"Can you break your elbow bone?" Brody was asking. "Is it supposed to wiggle around like this?" He demonstrated by pinching the nub at the tip of his forearm and wincing. "Ouch!"

When Effie responded with a muffled groan, Brody shot a worried look at Teagan, who was hunched over a bowl of cereal at the kitchen island. "What happened to Mom? I think she's broken."

Exhausted from the day, Effie's head swirled with a throbbing she couldn't seem to shake. Brody's dramatics were not helping. She needed to peel herself off this couch and get ready for the banquet. As she'd expected, Grace had been all too happy to tag along as her plus-one. The prospect of meeting a ghost, a handsome one at that, had made her practically giddy.

"I think she got a real job," Teagan answered between bites of cereal.

"I heard that," Effie called out, emerging from the haze of sleep. "Please educate us all on what you think a real job is. Since you have so much experience on the subject."

"I don't know." Teagan shrugged. "Not sitting around the house all day," she said, full of snark.

Effie shot up and whipped her head around. "And just what exactly is it you think I've been doing all these years, Teagan? Eating cookies, watching TV . . . playing Brody's video games?"

Teagan shrugged, not meeting Effie's probing gaze. "Not the video game part. That would be weird."

Heat gathered in Effie's chest. "Says the girl who quit every sport she tried." Grateful for the distance that separated them, Effie did her best to remain calm, not allowing herself to say the words that hovered on the tip of her tongue. Daniel had spoiled Teagan rotten, paid for every dance lesson she wanted until she didn't want to dance anymore, then hired a private violin instructor before she complained that it was too hard. After that it had been soccer and tennis and softball. To Daniel's great disappointment, none of them had stuck. All so Teagan could stand in front of her mother at the ripe age of sixteen and tell her she did not understand the value of work.

Effie rose from the sofa and began fluffing the pillows with an angry fist. She had chosen to forgo a career to stay home with the kids, but now she wondered if any of it mattered. Would Teagan still be this ungrateful if she'd pursued her own path? Gone for that degree in interior design instead of donating her time to Baker's Builders? "And in case it was ever unclear"—she fixed her sights on Teagan—"I already had a real job. I make your vegan lunches every morning, which, by the way, you can start doing yourself from now on. I clean up after all of you, not to mention I have to walk the two giant dogs you begged your father to get, and shovel their enormous crap." It always irritated her when people assumed that she'd chosen the easier path. The thing about being a stay-at-home parent was that people felt entitled to her time, like maybe she was bored and they were doing her a favor by suggesting she sew seventeen new costumes for the middle school production of *Annie*, even though none of her children would be caught dead in a theater class.

Teagan rolled her eyes, but Effie could tell that her words had struck a nerve, because Teagan could no longer return her gaze.

"Now can you please put a pizza in the oven for you and your brothers? Jay won't be home for a couple of hours, and I have to go to a work thing tonight."

Teagan made a face. "What kind of thing?"

"A charity event. It's for the Cameron Fields Foundation."

Shock registered on Teagan's face. "You work for the Cameron Fields Foundation?"

"Not exactly."

"Mom, do you even know how rich that family is? They're practically destroying Tilly with their 'beautification grants.' It's the whole reason the museum is being torn down." She looked at Effie as if she were somehow complicit, making her feel like an idiot once again. Parenting a social activist was not for the faint of heart.

"Honey, it's just a dinner," she reasoned. "Besides, there's nothing wrong with wanting to infuse some life in the older parts of town. It could use a facelift."

Teagan recoiled, her words dripping with sarcasm. "Of course *you* would say that." She scooped up her things and headed for her room.

Closing her eyes, Effie listened to the sound of Teagan's footsteps as they trailed up the stairs and disappeared behind a slamming door. She cringed. Effie had tried so hard to make things pleasant for the kids when they were with her, to make everything easy and happy and light because she knew how difficult the separation was for them. She wondered if Teagan behaved this way with Daniel, or if she reserved the worst parts of herself for Effie.

CHAPTER 23
LOLA

May 19, 1962

Dear Patsy,

I graduated today. I wore a blue gown and a cap with yellow tassels. And when I walked across the stage, I could hear Wallace scream my name from the bleachers. He cupped his hands around his mouth and shouted, "That's my fiancée!" I tried to pretend as if I hadn't heard him, but I've always been an easy blusher and my face went entirely red. Right next to him was my mother in her flower hat and Daddy in his good suit and all three of the boys in rare form with their hair slicked back like little rascals. Daddy had a proud sort of look on his face and flashed me a secretive grin.

When the ceremony was over, I met them at the back and pulled everyone into a hug, even Peter who tried to act like he didn't know me. Then as they were walking away, Daddy slipped a little white envelope into my hand and held a finger to his lips. I took that to mean I shouldn't tell my mother about it, so I waited until he'd left to open it. It was a crisp twenty-dollar bill and a note that read, "For my darling Lola. May you always have a song in your heart." I was glad he'd gone because I promptly erupted into a fit of tears. Maybe it was because I knew I was that much closer to getting the Gibson. Or maybe it was because Daddy always seems to know the exact thing to say when I'm feeling afraid. I have this little piece of paper now that says I'm all grown up, but I don't feel grown up. I feel like the same Lola Montgomery who once picked our neighbor's tulips and got a severe spanking from my mother, the same Lola who used to beg Daddy to pretend like a horse and trot me around in the wagon all over the yard.

All that feels like a lifetime ago. Now it feels like I'm on a conveyor belt just waiting for the next thing to happen. Pretty soon, I'll be someone's wife and after that, a mother. The idea makes my head spin like a top, but I'm excited to start a life with Wallace in my own little house with my own things. Even if sometimes I think maybe I'd rather stay that girl in the wagon a little bit longer.

Sincerely,

Lola

CHAPTER 24
EFFIE / "FINGERPRINTS"

Strands of white lights twinkled above the ballroom, giving the massive ceiling a cozy feel about it. With Grace trailing behind her and Cameron plowing gleefully ahead, Effie meandered between tables topped in white linens bearing little jars with floating candles. By the time she nestled between Grace and Cameron at their table, she caught sight of a diminutive woman with a voluminous brown bob taking her place behind the podium on stage. She was flanked by two enormous screens. One of them read **THE CAMERON FIELDS FOUNDATION** in curly green script, while the other featured a few pictures of Cameron superimposed over one another. In one of them, he was midstride in the middle of a busy street, wearing a navy suit and an expression that denoted he had somewhere important to be. In another, he leaned against a brick wall, his face turned away from the camera, knuckles resting beneath his chin in a contemplative pose. Effie suppressed a smile. It didn't surprise her that Cameron seemed to have been just as self-important in life as he was in death. Already she could tell that his mood had improved, because he was staring at the photos with an appreciative grin.

"I miss that suit," he said wistfully. "Dolce and Gabbana. Custom silk lining. It cost me a fortune, but it was worth it." He drew a fist to his chin and attempted a smolder like the one in the photograph. "It's so unfair," he whined. "Why did I have to die wearing Ralph Lauren?"

Effie rolled her eyes. "Perhaps this is a great lesson in determining what's most important in life. You couldn't take the money with you, after all."

"No. But you can take the feelings." He sat up a little straighter now. "And that suit made me feel invincible."

It was an ironic observation coming from a dead person, but Effie bit back the desire to point this out.

"What's he saying?" Grace asked, referring to their invisible guest.

"Nothing worth mentioning." Effie threw Cameron a salty smile. At times like these, it was empowering to control his communication with the living world.

"Well, tell him that suit is amazing," Grace said, studying the screen. "Keanu Reeves wore a similar one to the Academy Awards. Totally classic look."

Cameron resettled in his chair, his eyes skating past Effie and landing on Grace. "Your friend has impeccable taste. Tell her that dress is stunning. Green is definitely her color, really brings out her eyes." Tilting his head, he leaned back to study her at a different angle, framing her with his hands. "You know, if things were different, I could see myself with someone like her. Always did want to date a redhead." He sighed. "Life is so short."

"I'm not telling her that!" Effie shot back, immediately regretting her outburst. A couple at the adjacent table glanced over, looking concerned. "Besides, what's the point of hitting on a woman who can't even see you?" she whispered from the side of her mouth, hoping no one else noticed she was speaking to an empty chair.

"Tell me what?" Grace demanded, the impatience in her voice reaching a fever pitch. Grace had been happily married to Tom for sixteen years. Though she would never cheat on her adoring husband, she thrived on knowing that she was still every bit as desirable as she had been before settling down. And it wasn't as if she didn't look her age.

It was something else—a goddess-like confidence that made it nearly impossible for men to resist her charms. Effie envied that.

"Nothing," Effie said, waving her away. "Forget it."

Grace crossed her arms. "Excuse me, but I think if someone pays another person a compliment, it's only fair that said person should hear it."

"Trust me. It wasn't a compliment. Besides, you're *very* married, and he is *very* dead."

It should have been enough to settle the matter, but Grace pouted. "Fine," she relented. Crossing her arms, she leaned back against her seat. "I'll remember that the next time a handsome stranger takes an interest in you."

The slight woman at the podium tapped the microphone a few times before drawing it closer. "Good evening, friends. I'm Nina Pendergast, and I'm so honored to be here tonight to support Tilly's Women's Shelter. This is just one of many endeavors that the Cameron Fields Foundation supports. I hope all of you will take the opportunity to visit our silent auction table at the back of the atrium before you leave tonight. All proceeds will go directly to serving women in our community." Her voice was brittle but warm. Thin lines carved a spidery fan of wrinkles around her mauve lips. A string of pearls graced her neck, highlighting the deep-red lace of her cocktail dress. "As many of you know, I developed this foundation in honor of my youngest son"—her voice cracked, and it took her a few moments to compose herself. Her watery eyes trailed over the room as if she were looking for someone, and Effie wondered if she was disappointed that Drew hadn't come. After a few moments, Nina cleared her throat. "My son was a beautiful soul who was taken from us far too soon."

Effie looked to Cameron, who blinked away from the stage. A frown marred his face, eclipsing the smugness that had been there just moments ago. She'd never seen him cry, and for the second time, she wondered if it was even possible. But Cameron remained dry and silent.

"So, that's your mother," she whispered, trying to gauge his emotions.

He nodded, but there was no joy in his eyes. Only sadness.

"She's beautiful," Effie noted brightly. "I can see the family resemblance." Though she was smaller than her sons, Nina had the same strong nose and thick eyebrows.

"I'd like to thank my husband, Robert," Nina continued, "for helping me arrange this event." Cameron's jaw went rigid at the mention of his stepfather. "And all of you for being here tonight. This is a cause I know would be close to Cameron's heart."

Effie shot Cameron a dubious look. Somehow, she doubted the truthfulness of that statement. The only charitable cause she could envision Cameron championing was the Miss America pageant.

"Hey, don't look at me that way," he protested, affronted. "I've provided shelter for a lot of women over the years. One-night shelters, but nonetheless."

"Oh, good gravy." Effie shook her head. "You really are a piece of work, you know that?"

"I like to think of myself as a Warhol," he supplied with a confident swell of his chest. "An American classic."

From her perch behind the podium, Nina began spouting off a list of donors, thanking them for their contributions. Then her gaze slid over the back of the room and stalled. Effie turned around and tracked the focus of her attention. Drew was in front of the entrance, silently pulling the door closed behind him. Still dressed in the same salmon shirt and navy slacks he'd worn at work, he ducked his head and offered Nina a subtle wave. What was he doing here? All at once, Effie became very aware of her own outfit, a sleeveless purple cocktail dress she hadn't squeezed into since the company Christmas party three years ago. It was a little snug, but she hadn't had time to shop for anything better. What's more, she hadn't expected to run into anyone she cared to impress. She worried now that it made her look like a giant eggplant.

"Is that who I think it is?" Grace nudged her shoulder.

But Effie was too surprised to respond.

"So much for not being able to come," Grace went on. "Maybe *someone* wanted an excuse to see you outside of work."

"I'm one hundred percent positive that isn't the case," Effie reasoned, though a part of her couldn't deny that she was wondering the same thing. Drew had been so clear about not coming tonight. What had changed his mind? She didn't mean to stare, but it was impossible not to pick up on the awkward vibe brewing between mother and son. The way Nina was glaring at him made Effie feel anxious on Drew's behalf. Cameron must have sensed it, too, because he said, "Looks like Mom won again. She usually gets her way."

Drew locked eyes with Effie and gave her a sheepish grin and a slightly raised palm. Feeling caught, Effie responded with what she hoped was a smile, but it felt as if she'd forgotten how to flex her facial muscles, and she quickly diverted her gaze.

Waiters in black aprons trickled in, balancing trays with plates and flutes of champagne. Effie salivated when an appetizer dish bearing a smattering of grilled seafood was placed before her. At least Drew hadn't been lying about the decent-dinner part.

"This looks amazing," Grace said, reaching for a scallop drizzled in lemon butter. "Can Drew be my boss too?"

Though she couldn't help but wonder if Drew was still watching her, Effie did her best to appear engrossed in conversation. She didn't want him to feel obligated to come over and make small talk, but as she sliced her fork through a crab cake, she felt Grace's elbow jab her side.

"He's coming over!"

Before Effie could come up with any suitable conversation starters, Drew materialized in front of them. "Hi, Effie. Enjoying your evening?"

Still chewing, she covered her mouth. "Very much." She swallowed, then clumsily dabbed at her lips with a cloth napkin. "How about you? I wasn't expecting to see you here."

"Yeah, well, I wasn't planning on it, but my mother has a way of guilting me into doing things." His gaze drifted to the stage, where Nina was greeting guests with handshakes and affectionate pats on the back. "Especially where it concerns my brother."

Cameron gave a guilty shrug.

Effie seized upon the silver lining. "Well, I think it's wonderful that she works so hard to keep his memory alive."

"It keeps her busy, that's for sure. There's never a shortage of good causes to support."

"I'm sure Cameron would have been honored."

"Maybe." He shrugged, the muscles of his jaw contracting ever so slightly. "He wasn't exactly the most selfless person, if you know what I mean."

Cameron made a face.

Effie knew exactly what Drew meant, but considering the circumstances, she only nodded in understanding. Thankfully, Grace leaned forward and extended her lithe wrist, alleviating some of the tension. "I don't think we've been properly introduced."

"I'm so sorry," Effie said, motioning to her left. "This is my friend Grace."

"Pleased to meet you," Drew said, clasping his fingers around hers.

"The pleasure is all mine," Grace said. "Thank you for the invitation."

"It's me who should be thanking the two of you. It will likely save me another lecture from my mother. An empty table would have been tough to live down. She doesn't let things like that slide easily."

Effie's mother wasn't exactly the most forgetful person, either, so she could empathize with Drew's plight. "I'm happy to help. Also, I can't say I didn't get the better end of the deal. Crab cakes are kind of my Achilles' heel."

"Seafood lover, huh?"

"Guilty," she conceded.

"Then you probably would have loved Cameron's restaurants. One of them was an upscale seafood kebab place, every kind of fish you can imagine on a stick. It was incredibly overpriced."

"Sounds pretentious," Effie noted, teasing Cameron with a subtle glance.

"Sounds like Cameron."

The two of them exchanged an awkward chuckle as Cameron shot Effie a murderous look.

The levity of the moment slipped away, replaced by a lull in the conversation that neither of them knew how to break.

"You know," Grace said, eyeing the empty chairs at their table, "you could join us . . . if you're hungry."

A surge of adrenaline pulsed through Effie's veins, and it took every ounce of her strength not to whack Grace over the head with her handbag. She didn't want Drew to feel pressured to stay, but Grace was an expert in the fine art of guilt-tripping.

Drew shook his head. "I don't want to impose. Besides, I can't stay long. I'm supposed to pick up Samuel later tonight. He's staying with me for a few days."

"Oh, come on," Grace needled him. "Our table could use some lively conversation." She waggled her eyes at Effie, who bristled. "It's a dead bore over here."

Cameron looked affronted, and Effie kicked her under the table, drawing an "Oof."

But Drew must not have picked up on the violence between them, because he reluctantly pulled out the chair next to her, which just so happened to be where Cameron was seated. "I guess I can stay for a course or two."

"Don't mind me," Cameron said, looking indignant. He relocated to an empty chair across the table.

The salads arrived, and Effie was grateful to have something to do with her hands.

As the three of them worked their way through the risotto, lobster bisque, and glazed salmon, Grace regaled them with stories from work. To his credit, Drew humored her with follow-up questions, laughing in all the appropriate places. And Effie did her best to ignore Cameron's incessant pleas to work him into the conversation.

When the lemon tarts were served, Grace pushed her plate away and shook her head. "I really shouldn't. Besides, I have to get going," she said, making a dramatic show of checking the nonexistent watch on her wrist.

"Are you sure?" Effie muttered through a tight smile. She knew Grace was scheming to get them alone. She was never one to shun dessert.

"Oh, hon, you know I'd stay, but as someone recently reminded me, I am *very* married, and Tom is expecting me, so . . . I'll text you later." With a wink, she plucked her handbag from the back of her seat and thanked Drew profusely again.

Cameron snapped his fingers and pointed at Grace as she walked away. "I knew I liked her."

~

The conversation waned to a standstill, and Effie worried that Drew was growing bored of her. Mining her brain for something to talk about besides work and the food, which she had already complimented too many times to count, she focused on the screen bearing Cameron's image.

"Who do you think took the photograph?" she asked, truly curious.

"What do you mean?"

"Well, whenever I see a picture like this pop up on someone's social media, I wonder who was behind the lens. He's trying so hard to look aloof, but he's obviously posing for the camera. Did he just rope in some random person on the street to point and shoot?" She could feel Cameron's eyes on her but ignored the silent storm of anger he was sending her way.

"Good point. And knowing Cameron, the first picture wouldn't have been good enough. He probably badgered the poor soul, made them take it from no less than a dozen angles before he was satisfied."

"Three times!" Cameron protested. "It's not my fault the old bag didn't know how to operate it in portrait mode."

"You think so?" Effie replied, ignoring Cameron's outburst. It was getting easier to block him out.

"We're talking about my brother. I know so."

The two of them exchanged a chuckle, but Cameron was not having it. "Well, I can see when I'm not wanted. I don't have to sit here and take this, you know." And with that, he disappeared. Effie felt slightly guilty, as the whole point in coming tonight was to make Cameron feel better, not worse. She vowed to apologize after he'd had time to cool off.

"It's interesting," Drew said, seeming far away now. "My ex was always the one who took the pictures. I guess I never really saw the point in ruining the moment by turning it into a photo op. But now . . . well, now that she's with someone else, I wish I had taken more pictures of Samuel and me together."

A wave of empathy rippled through her chest. She often had the same regret. "I'm usually the one behind the camera," Effie said. "God, I can't remember the last picture I was in." There was Brody's scouting ceremony last week, Jay's championship game, Teagan's band concert. Come to think of it, there were probably more pictures of Brody's staph infection from last month than there were of her. If someone were to scroll through her mobile gallery, they might never know she existed. She'd been the keeper of everyone else's memories, the one leaving fingerprints on all their lives while her own seemed to vanish like letters in the sand. Of course, Grace had tagged her in plenty of Facebook pictures, but usually her eyes were closed or she was looking away, never the object of the photographer's attention. It had been years since anyone had taken time to really see her. Just her.

"That's a shame," Drew said, and Effie could tell he meant it. He was staring at her now, making her skin prickle with goose bumps.

"Well . . . let's fix that." Breaking the tension of the moment, he tugged his phone from his shirt pocket, then centered it on her and leaned back in his seat.

"Oh no, please don't," she said, drawing a hand to her neck as the camera shuttered. She never should have said anything.

But Drew was already studying the image on his phone, satisfaction playing at his lips. "Perfect," he said, making her wonder if he was referring to her or the picture. Then he tapped away at his screen, and a few seconds later, her phone dinged with a notification. "There," he said. "Now you have a picture of yourself. And you didn't even have to beg a stranger to take it."

"Thank you," she said, absorbing the image before her. Though caught off guard, her eyes unfocused with a soft hand kissing her neck, she looked more like herself than in any of the professional family photographs she had paid hundreds of dollars for over the years. None of those pictures held a candle to this one. In this picture, there was a muted gracefulness about her so very different from that younger version of herself she'd locked away in her mind like a Russian doll. Though older, with the crow's feet to prove it, she looked like a woman who was comfortable in her own skin, genuinely happy and entirely complete.

Before Effie could compliment his photography skills, Nina glided over to their table, stealing the words from her throat.

Drew stood to greet his mother.

"I'm so glad you came to your senses, dear," Nina said warmly. She embraced him, then kissed him firmly on the cheek. Lingering, she whispered in his ear. "Of course, two people does not a table make," she said through a tight smile as genuine as the cubic zirconia earrings Effie was wearing. Then Nina's eyes trailed over Effie, homing in on her forehead. "Oh dear, what happened to you?"

Effie caught a glimpse of her mother in those words and reflexively drew a hand to her head in search of the problem. She'd done her best to cover her pickleball injury, but clearly it wasn't enough. A wave of heat enveloped her.

Before she could answer, Drew touched a hand to the small of Nina's back. "Mom, this is my new assistant," he said, gesturing to his left. "Effie, this is my mother."

"Wonderful to meet you, dear." Tilting her head, Nina smiled affectionately. "So good of you to come tonight."

"Thank you for having me," Effie replied, standing up. The chair groaned beneath her. "It's a wonderful cause." She reached out to shake Nina's hand.

"Yes, well . . . it's good to know that Drew has at least some friends." Nina zeroed in on her son, her fingers still locked around Effie's. "Even if they are on his payroll," she added.

Effie wasn't certain whether this was a dig at her or Drew, but from the way he grimaced, she assumed it was the latter. It was weird seeing Drew interact with Nina. He seemed so uncertain, so unlike the decisive, self-assured boss he was at the office.

"Well, I have to go make the necessary rounds, but you two enjoy the rest of your evening," Nina said. "And be sure to put in a few bids at the silent auction." She pressed a finger to Drew's chest, before moving on to the next table.

Once they'd sat down again, it was impossible to ignore the tectonic shift in Drew's mood. He reached for his glass of champagne and took a swig, then smacked his lips and winced.

"Everything . . . OK?" Effie asked, unsure how to navigate the conversation. Just when things between them had begun to feel natural, Nina had waltzed in and set off a bomb.

"Yeah . . . it's just tough sometimes, you know?" He shifted uneasily in his seat. "With my mom."

Effie nodded, waiting for him to say more. She didn't want to pry, but she was desperate for any crumbs about Drew's personal life.

"She thinks I need to do more to contribute to the foundation. She says I never really mourned Cameron's death." His eyes glazed over his empty dessert plate, not meeting hers.

Adrenaline coursed through Effie's veins. Here it was, her chance to get Drew to open up, help him explore his feelings about the accident so Cameron could move on and she could, at long last, be free of him. "And what do you think?" she asked, hoping it was the right question.

Drew went quiet for a moment, then looked thoughtfully at Cameron's photograph on the screen. "I think . . . she will always choose to see the best of him, even when he doesn't deserve it."

"That's our job as parents, isn't it?" Effie said, reflecting on her argument with Teagan. "We see the best in them even when they treat us like garbage."

He raised an eyebrow. "Are we still talking about me?"

"Maybe." She smiled, unsure how much she should prod. But Drew's eyes seemed so tired, so full of regret that she couldn't help herself. "Look, I know I don't have any insight into your family, but as a mother, the thing I want most for my kids is for them to get along. I'm going to be gone someday, and all they'll have left is each other. So, I guess I'm saying I understand why she wants you to see the best in Cameron. He's part of you." Maybe she had said too much. She didn't have any siblings herself, so she didn't understand all the ins and outs of a relationship like that. Then again, she was supposed to be helping Drew move on and accept Cameron's death. If not now, then when?

Drew dropped his head and chuckled. He had a great laugh, warm and low. It instantly set her at ease. "You know, you shouldn't have to provide emotional guidance to your employer, but thanks, Effie. I'm sorry for unloading all of that on you."

"Don't apologize," she said. "Believe me, I know how hard it is to let people go." She couldn't stop picturing Daniel's face when she'd told him she was pregnant with Jay. He'd been so afraid and excited all at the same time—a tangled mixture of emotions. "Sometimes, it's just nice to have a listening ear. Family is . . . complicated."

"Can't disagree with that statement." As his eyes rested on hers, a string quartet began to play a soft melody. Couples drifted onto the dance floor, drawing their attention away from each other. Finally,

Drew dropped his gaze and planted his hands on the table. "Well . . . Samuel is expecting me, so . . ." He thumbed toward the door. "I'd better get going."

"Of course. Me too," she said, wishing she had said it first.

She thought she caught a trace of hesitation before he said, "Thanks again for coming, Effie."

"No problem," she replied. "It was really good to see you."

And as he walked away, it occurred to her that was the truest thing she'd said all night.

CHAPTER 25
LOLA

June 6, 1962

Dear Patsy,

I can't believe I've let so much time slip away without writing, especially considering all that's happened in the past month. For starters, my name is Lola Rose now which I think has a glamorous ring if I say so myself. It rolls off the tongue like the name of a singer or leading lady.

We had the wedding at the First Presbyterian Church because Wallace's family is religious. And since Daddy always says we're only part-time Methodists, I didn't mind the concession. Wallace wore a black suit that matched his hair with a gingham pencil tie and silver cufflinks I had specially engraved with his initials. They set me back ten dollars. I wasn't keen on spending the money as I was getting so close to buying the Gibson. But it seemed like a very grown-up thing to do, especially since he replaced his class ring with a quarter cut teardrop gold one from the Sears Catalog.

It's not very big, but it's amazing how much power that little ring can wield. People treat you differently when they know you're a Mrs. The saleslady at Macy's looked at me as if I might actually have a little money to spend. She doesn't know we're broke, but still. It feels nice to be seen as an adult all of a sudden.

Daddy cried at the wedding, and my mother nearly fainted at the sight of me standing in front of a reverend bearing my devil shoulders. By the simple act of marrying, it seems I have unwillingly fulfilled all her dreams. She's come to adore Wallace so much that sometimes I think she prefers his presence to mine. We didn't have the money for a honeymoon, so we stayed two nights in a hotel downtown and ordered room service for breakfast. I had French toast and scrambled eggs and these fancy little sausage rolls that made me feel like Queen Elizabeth. I must have eaten about a hundred of them, though I admit the rest of our stay was not at all what I expected. My mother never talked about "the marriage act" or prepared me in any way for what was going to happen. By all accounts, I was immaculately conceived. She lied. A girl should know about these sorts of things. And that is all I have to say on the matter.

I'm sorry to say this, but married life is a bit more trying than I anticipated, and I am perfectly terrible at everything I've tried to cook. My spaghetti is too watery, my rice casseroles are gummy, and I overcook the chicken nearly every time as I'm terrified of contracting salmonella. I don't want to be the sort of wife who kills her husband with a Cordon Bleu before they've even celebrated their first anniversary. When dinner rolls around, Wallace gets a strange look at the table, like he's trying to prepare himself to swallow a spoonful of medicine. It makes me feel as if I am torturing us both since I don't particularly enjoy the cooking and he obviously doesn't enjoy the eating. I suppose I should ask my mother for help, but that would only make her happy. For now, we will suffer through it together, and hopefully no one dies.

Sincerely trying,

Lola

CHAPTER 26
EFFIE / "I CAN'T FORGET YOU"

The windows of the house were dark, and the night air was quiet and warm, disturbed only by the persistent call of a mockingbird. The flicker of the porch light illuminated her hands as Effie worked her key into the lock, hoping the kids were already asleep. It was a school night, and she had told them not to wait up. Not that she expected them to, especially after her blowup with Teagan. As her fingertips reached for the doorknob, she heard an engine purring in the driveway, and she swiveled around to find blinding headlights creeping toward her. Shielding a hand to her eyes, she recognized the shape of Daniel's truck. He climbed out and gently closed the door behind him. When he caught sight of Effie in her cocktail dress, he leaned his head to the side and squinted.

"What are you doing here?" Effie asked as he made his way up the steps.

"Just dropping off Brody's tablet." He held up the sleek black square and shook it. "He forgot it at my place."

"Thanks," she said, reaching for it. "I'm surprised he lasted this long without it."

"Me too." He chuckled, his eyes traveling down the length of her dress and back up. "Sorry, I didn't realize you'd be out tonight." He seemed surprised, and Effie couldn't blame him. She didn't normally don formal wear in the middle of the week. "Oh my God," he said, zeroing in on her forehead. "What happened?"

The concern in his voice alarmed her. Then she remembered the pickleball fiasco and the purple bruise between her eyes. By now, she must have completely sweated off her makeup. "It's OK." She waved away his concern. "It was just a . . . work injury." It wasn't exactly the truth. More like a favor to her broody boss—who was slowly beginning to grow on her. She wondered if this information would make a difference to Daniel. "Don't worry," she added. "It's not usually that dangerous."

"I was wondering about that text," he said, clearly referencing her message from yesterday. "So, where are you working?" He raised an eyebrow.

"That assistant position I told you about. I got the job," she said, her confidence bolstered. The truth was, when she'd gotten the position, the first person she'd wanted to tell was Daniel. The tricky thing about marrying her high school sweetheart was that he had always been her best friend, the person she couldn't wait to tell when something exciting happened. It seemed unfair that one person should encompass so many roles. Now that he was gone, she felt utterly alone.

"You're kidding." He reared back, looking down his nose to study her.

"No, I'm not. Why does everyone assume I'm incapable of earning an income?"

"It's not that, it's just—" He shook his head, massaging the scruff of his chin. "Good for you, Eff."

She couldn't tell if he was impressed or amused. "I mean, with the kids at school all day and you gone, it just felt like I needed something of my own," she continued, though he hadn't asked her to explain. She didn't tell him that what she had really needed was a distraction from replaying the last nineteen years over and over again in her mind, trying to pinpoint the precise moment Daniel had fallen out of love with her.

"So?" He seemed to be waiting for more. "Tell me about it."

"It's for a law firm downtown." She shrugged. "Working the phones, scheduling meetings, that sort of thing. Pretty much what I used to do for you in the early days of the company." She looked away from him, hoping he didn't detect the regret in her face. "It will be good for my résumé to have something. Got to start somewhere."

"Yeah," he agreed, seeming genuine. "Well, I'm happy for you. Glad to see you're doing all right."

Effie wasn't sure what to make of that. If he'd really cared about her, he wouldn't have left her for a woman who, up until a year ago, had been eligible to remain on her parents' insurance policy. She let her eyes trail over to the swing Daniel had hung from the rafters, its wooden slats worn smooth by years of use. She used to sit out here on warm spring evenings, like the one when she'd watched Daniel and Jay shoot hoops while Brody and Teagan ran through the sprinklers with the dogs nipping at their heels. Transfixed by the memory, her heart broke all over again.

She shook her head to clear the image, not wanting to cry in front of Daniel. "It's good you're here," she said. "We should talk about the kids."

"Why?" The concern in his tone was palpable. "Did Jay hear back from Duke yet?"

Her spirits deflated, and she groaned. "No, but you have got to stop pushing him on that." Heaving a sigh, she ambled to the end of the porch, her feet tired and aching. She kicked off her heels, then lowered herself onto the swing. "I want to talk about our daughter."

Daniel sat next to her, his jeans brushing against her thigh. "What about her?"

Effie pulled in a deep breath. "Something's been off with her lately, and I'm worried. She's . . . struggling."

"I haven't noticed anything. She seems just like she always is. Moody as hell." With his long legs, he pushed the swing into a gentle rhythm, and for a moment, Effie could almost believe they were in some kind of parallel world where they were still together, rocking on their front porch as they fussed over the kids.

"I mean, don't you think she's more . . . moody than usual? The things she says to me, Daniel. They're hurtful. I need to know that you're backing me up, not bad-mouthing me behind my back." *With Amber.*

"You know I wouldn't do that, Eff." He sat up straighter, giving her his full attention.

"You wouldn't?" She studied him for signs that he was lying but came up short. "Because I've got to be honest, I'm not really sure what you're capable of doing these days."

"I'm not capable of that," he said, firmly planting his legs. The swing stopped moving, the steady groan of its hinges now silent. "I've never said anything in front of the kids that I wouldn't say in front of you." Sighing, he raked a hand through his hair. "I'll talk to Teagan, tell her she has to respect you from now on."

"Thank you." A flood of memory swept through her as she swallowed the sting of tears. "Remember when she was little how she used to have to hold my hand everywhere we went? She was so afraid of being away from me. Till she was ten. Anytime we went shopping, her little fingers would reach out for mine. And she'd hang on for dear life like she was scared to death to lose me. And now . . ."

Giving her arm a squeeze, Daniel fixed his eyes on hers. The familiar warmth of his calloused fingers sent a shiver of heat through her midsection. Had he done it out of habit, or was he just being nice? Either way, her body's response irritated her. She wasn't supposed to want his touch anymore. "She loves you, Effie. She's just"—he rolled his head around in an exasperated motion—"a teenager. There's an unwritten rule somewhere that says all teenage girls are supposed to butt heads with their mothers." He grinned at her and gave a little wink, and the familiar combination of the two caused her heart to catch in her throat.

"I guess so," she admitted. "Doesn't make it hurt any less."

The oaks rustled in the wind, breaking the silence between them. "So?" With a half grin, he nudged her shoulder with his own. "How've you been? Aside from dealing with our angsty offspring."

Caught off guard, Effie filtered through her week. It didn't feel like the right time to apprise him of Cameron or the fact that she could communicate with the dead. He hadn't exactly validated her first otherworldly experience, and she didn't expect him to change his tune now. "I'm great. Everything is . . . normal." This was an astronomical lie, as nothing was normal and would probably never be normal again. Forcing a smile, she heaved a sigh and pushed herself up by her palms. "Guess I'd better get back to the kids now."

They grew quiet, and Effie wondered if he was thinking what she was—that she missed their talks, missed the way he could coax a smile from her even when she was livid with him. He still could, and it destroyed her. As she turned for the door, his hand grazed her fingers. "Don't worry about Teagan," he said. "She'll come around. You're an amazing mother, Effie. I've never doubted that for a second." In his touch, she felt a familiar spark, the same one that had led to nineteen years of marriage and three children. It was small, almost imperceptible, but it was there just the same.

She wondered if he felt it too.

CHAPTER 27

Lola

June 27, 1962

Dear Patsy,

It seems Satan is on the loose around here. The bungalow has a few more problems than we initially suspected. Our first night there, the toilet backed up into the tub, and there's a leak beneath the sink that's warped the cabinets. It was supposed to come fully furnished, but the owner said we misunderstood the agreement and now we have no Frigidaire. Obviously, this poses a problem. After work today, Wallace asked me how much money I had saved for the Gibson, and it took me aback. How could he ask me that? I almost lied but thought better of it. That is no way to start a marriage, after all, so I told him the truth. I have fifty dollars and twenty-five cents in my cigar box which he said would go a long way in getting a decent used model. I told him I'd rather have my guitar than cold milk any day of the week, and he said I was being selfish which I suppose maybe I am. I locked him out of the bedroom and refused to talk to him for two hours. I felt bad about it as it was our first real fight, and he isn't wrong about needing the fridge. But I was so close to earning my half of the money I could practically feel the strings and the smooth finish of the wood beneath my fingers.

Wallace finally apologized and said that once I get a typing job, I'll earn back the money in no time. I know it's the adult decision to make, but it didn't make it hurt any less. After I handed my life savings over to him, I bit back tears and made dinner, which of course I burned again. Only this time, between you and me, I did it on purpose.

Sincerely distraught,

Lola

CHAPTER 28
EFFIE / "HEARTACHES"

It had been three weeks since the banquet and the inadvertent date with her boss, and since then, things at work had been a little less stifled. Though Effie hadn't made much progress on Cameron's dilemma, with each new day, Drew seemed more and more at ease around her. It probably helped that Effie had become an expert at utilizing orphan control, which she'd been relieved to learn had nothing to do with orphans. And it was nice to feel needed again. What's more, it was refreshing to return to her desk every morning, neat as a pin, just as she'd left it the day before. No dirty socks lying about or dogs to walk or unwashed dishes in the sink.

Chewing a thumbnail, she scrolled through her inbox, which had steadily filled up with inquiries over the past few days. Apparently, she wasn't the only person navigating a divorce; Drew would never be at a loss for clients. The office was eerily quiet this morning. Cameron had yet to make an appearance, and Effie suspected he was stalking his ex or sulking on a park bench somewhere. Lena had called to say that she was having car trouble and would be working from home for the rest of the week, a development that made Effie feel slightly unsettled. It was the first time she'd been alone in the office with Drew, though he'd been slammed with phone calls all morning, not even emerging for a restroom break. She wondered if things would feel weird when he did.

She pulled her gaze away from the numbing glow of her screen, then reached for her phone and located a playlist. "Crazy" floated into the lobby, and she turned up the volume a little louder than usual since Drew was tucked away in his office. When the second verse rolled around, she allowed herself to softly sing the words, even though she had never been especially thrilled to hear the sound of her voice. Lolly had always been the singer in their family. Something sharp splintered in her chest as she thought about her grandmother. Tomorrow morning, she was flying out to Kansas for her birthday, and she couldn't wait to talk with her about Patsy's framed letter. Hopefully, she could steal a few lucid moments alone to get the entire story.

Lost in the song, Effie muddled her way through the chorus and was rounding her way to the third verse when Drew peeked around the wall.

"Hey, Eff—" he started to say, catching her in the throes of a high note. When he stifled a smile, the rest of the phrase died in her throat. She swallowed a dry lump, uncertain if she would ever be able to pry her mouth open again.

Finally, she managed a warbled "Hey."

"I was just going to see if you were hanging around for lunch. I'm ordering from Lorenzo's." It seemed like he was trying to be practical, but his tone was a little more casual than usual, and it caught her off guard. "You want anything?"

"Sure." She blinked a few times, still mortified. "That'd be great. I'll take a turkey on rye, if they have it." Maybe he was trying to make things less awkward after everything he'd shared at the banquet dinner. Or maybe he still felt guilty about the whole Carl-trying-to-kill-her thing. Either way, she had to admit, she wouldn't mind the company.

~

Effie nibbled her sandwich across from Drew at the tiny kitchenette table. Apparently, the only thing more awkward than singing badly in front of her boss was eating lunch with him. So far, he had been mostly quiet, only breaking from his meatball sub every so often to ask a polite question.

"Having a good morning?"

"Mm-hmm," Effie replied, still chewing. Covering her mouth, she tried to speed along the process, then swallowed and reached for her Diet Coke. "What about you?"

"Good," he said. "The Petersons—you know, the couple you rescheduled a while back—they've decided to work things out after all."

"That's great!" Effie replied, overcorrecting with a bit too much enthusiasm. "I mean, not for you," she conceded. "I guess your livelihood kind of depends on them splitting up." She didn't mean for it to sound rude, but she wished she had worded it differently.

He chuckled, shaking his head as he reached for his tumbler. "Not necessarily. I suppose you must think I'm the grim reaper of happily ever afters."

"I didn't say that." She felt her cheeks flush. "Besides, you don't really strike me as the black-cape-and-blade-carrying type of guy," she teased, then sank her teeth into her sandwich again.

"I work on wills and trusts, too, you know. And there's the occasional adoption. Those are always my favorite." He smiled wistfully, and she could tell he was being genuine about that part.

His satisfaction was contagious, and she found herself smiling. "Must be a pretty amazing feeling to bring a family together like that."

"It is," he agreed, wiping his mouth with a napkin. "It almost makes up for all the custody disputes and detailing assets. Those are really my bread and butter. There's always going to be a market in divorce," he said, his tone a little bleaker now.

Considering that her life was playing out like a sad country song, she couldn't disagree with that statement.

More serious now, he put down his sandwich and fixed his eyes on her. "Look, I don't mean to pry, Effie, but . . . do you have a good lawyer?"

The question threw her a little. Was this why he'd wanted to eat lunch with her? To secure him on retainer? "Grace referred me to her brother," she managed to say, rearranging her face into something she hoped exuded confidence. Like his sister, Steven was persistent, and she had no doubt he would get her the best arrangement. Though she had to admit that the thought of him lawyering on her behalf reminded her of a used-car salesman or a Realtor trying to squeeze every penny out of a deal. But this wasn't a deal. This was her life. "He's good. Thorough," she added. Though she hadn't returned his last two phone calls, hoping that perhaps if she ignored reality long enough, both she and Daniel would contract amnesia and forget about the past nine months.

Drew nodded, apparently satisfied with this answer. "That's good. Just be sure he isn't sloppy," he added. "And don't sign anything until you've had time to read through it with a fine-tooth comb. I'm happy to assist you in any way . . . if you need advice . . . or anything."

The fact that he cared enough to bring this up made her want to hug him, but that would be weird. Instead, she cleared her throat. "Thank you," she replied, overcome with emotion. "Once we agree upon a fair price, he'll buy me out of the company. He'll take the kids four weeks over the summer and three weekends a month." A rogue tear carved its way down her cheek, and she swept it away quickly with the back of her hand. "Sorry." Reaching for her drink again, she forced a watery smile. "It's just that saying it out loud makes it real."

"Don't apologize." His voice was softer now, gentle but assured, like someone who knew a thing or two about bereavement. She guessed he'd been in this situation hundreds of times, consoling clients who fell apart as their dreams vanished with the stroke of a pen. Not to mention his own divorce. "It's not easy figuring this stuff out." He touched a warm hand to her arm, sending a flutter of tingles up her spine. She quickly squelched the sensation.

As if on cue, a warm gush of spring air burst into the lobby, carrying the thud of footsteps with it. Effie startled when she saw who they belonged to. Wearing a blue baseball cap, jeans, and a white polo shirt with the Baker's Builders logo she had designed herself, Daniel hovered near the entrance. He craned his neck around the lobby, inspecting the walls and floor, looking entirely out of place. His eyes twinkled when he saw Effie, and he grinned.

She felt a twinge of guilt seeing him so soon after discussing their divorce. But why? She hadn't been the one to end things.

"What are you doing here?" she asked, her lips curling into a crooked line.

"Lakewood Landing isn't far from here, so I thought I'd check in to see where you work." This was not true, as the development was a good twenty minutes east.

With his glistening arms and sun-kissed cheeks, he had that familiar sweaty, worn-out look about him, proof he'd been laboring alongside the crew today. "You mentioned working here, and I figured I'd drop by to say hello." Actually, she hadn't given him any specifics on the location of her job, and she wondered how he'd managed to track her down, as there were at least a dozen other professional offices on this street alone. Had he checked out each of them or just gotten lucky when he stumbled into this one?

"Oh," she managed to say, not sure what to do with this information. A flutter of confusion swirled inside her. She suddenly felt awkward having this conversation in front of Drew, who had begun to gather the remnants of his lunch.

Catching sight of him behind her, Daniel removed his hat and raised it toward him. "You got a real nice place here," he said, his gaze sweeping the perimeter of the lobby. "Did we renovate it?"

"I'm actually not sure," Drew replied, offering a hand. "I don't think so, but it would have been a few years ago, when my father was still running things. I'm Drew, his son. Nice to meet you."

Eyeing him, Daniel accepted the gesture with a firm shake. "Daniel," he said. "Hey, thanks for hiring Effie. Hopefully she's working out for you." It irritated Effie that he should speak about her as if she weren't standing right in front of him, but she forced a tight smile.

"Oh, absolutely. We were very lucky to get her." Drew cut her a flustered sort of look. "Effie's a great addition to the team." The compliment warmed her heart, but Drew's demeanor worried her. He always seemed so unflappable, but at the moment he looked pale, and she feared he might be sick. "I'll just, uh . . . I'll leave you to it," he said, turning for his office. "Nice to meet you, Daniel." He nodded once in her direction before disappearing down the hall. "See you later, Effie."

"See you," she called after him.

When his door closed, she wondered briefly if she should go check on him, but there was still the matter of Daniel to address.

"So, that's your boss?" Daniel asked, lifting his chin. His gaze lingered on Drew's office door. "You like working for him?"

"Yeah. Drew's great."

He arched an eyebrow. "You call him by his first name?"

"Don't your employees call you by your first name?" If she didn't know any better, she'd say he was jealous, which struck her as particularly unfair since she had hardly fallen into bed with Drew like he had with Amber.

"Yeah. You're right," he conceded. He dropped his gaze to his shoes and dug the toe of his foot into the floor. "It's good to see you."

"Yeah," she said, surprised by the slight nervousness that tinged her voice. After all their years sharing a bed, she shouldn't be this flustered by a simple conversation.

The way he was staring at her made Effie wonder if there was another reason he had come. Doing her best to ignore the warmth creeping up her neck, she gathered her resolve. "Lakewood Landing isn't anywhere near here, Daniel. Why are you really here?"

"That's fair," he conceded, dropping his head. A gruff sound escaped his barrel chest, and he started again, more firmly now.

"Listen, I, uh . . . I've been thinking about a few things, and I was hoping we could talk. You free tonight?" He looked up at her, his eyes unreadable. Was this about the kids? Did he want to alter the custody agreement? During the week, they stayed with her—an arrangement he had respected until now. Maybe she would need to take Drew up on his offer for legal advice after all.

"I get off at three, but I'm taking Brody to the dentist after school. Want to swing by before dinner?"

"I'll plan on it," he said, his lips settling into a slow grin. "Guess I'd better get back. Oh, we finished the model house today," he added. "Went with the mosaic backsplash you suggested. The one with the fleur-de-lis. I think you'd like it."

Unsure what to say, Effie touched a hand to the back of her neck. Last summer when they discussed specs for the project, she had desperately tried to convince him that subway tile was overdone and that he should choose something less trendy. Fleurs-de-lis were timeless. Unlike their marriage. "Oh," she managed to say. "Glad I could help."

He turned and shuffled for the door, casting one last glance over his shoulder. "You look really good, Eff."

Warm afternoon sunshine washed over her as the door opened and closed, leaving her in the rubble of his words.

CHAPTER 29
LOLA

July 30, 1962

Dear Patsy,

I think I'm beginning to understand why my mother was always in such a sour mood. Being an adult is far less exciting than I expected. I take two buses to get to work where I spend all day plugging little wires together until my fingers go numb. Then I come home plumb tired, only to be met by a sink full of dishes and a dinner waiting to be made. To say that things are far from glamorous is an understatement. Also, there's the matter of laundry. If it's not the washing, it's the hanging and the ironing. I'm convinced it's trying to kill me! You may think I'm fooling, but I am one thousand percent serious. Wallace will come home one day to find me smothered beneath a pile of his dirty long johns. The autopsy report will read "Cause of death: Laundry."

I suggested that perhaps he might help with the cleaning as he does most of the dirtying around here, but he only rolled his eyes as he flipped through a magazine with a picture of a man wrestling a dreadful creature of some sort or other. He said he was worn out from work. I can't help but notice that while I have about ten thousand jobs, Wallace only has one. Two if you count the lawn which I would prefer over laundry any day. I've told him this more than once, but he says it would be embarrassing to have his wife push the mower across the yard, like that would make some sort of statement to the neighbors about his own pushing abilities. I'd rather be just about anywhere than the kitchen. I should note, there was a minor incident last night with dinner. Did you know that garlic is flammable? I'm certain Mrs. Northrup never mentioned that! I would have remembered. I think Wallace is afraid to allow me near the stove again, so he took me out to dinner this evening under the guise of giving me a night off. I wore my orange knit blouse and tapered slacks. He prefers me in dresses, but I think he's beginning to realize that I'm different from other women. I like that I can bend over without having my dignity stolen by a gust of wind. In any case, he said he admires my spirit, even if my cooking leaves something to be desired. He said I'll make a wonderful mother someday, and from the way he was looking at me, I got the feeling he meant sooner rather than later. That scared me. It seems cruel to throw a baby into the mix now. At least until I figure out how to avoid explosions of all sorts. Besides, can you imagine the extra laundry?

I do love Wallace, and I don't mean to sound ungrateful as he is trying his best to adjust to married life, too. When he was promoted to foreman last week, he surprised me by bringing home a mahogany television set with a remote control. Modern advances never cease to amaze me. The picture is so clear and the sound so sharp, I feel as if I'm right there inside the screen! The best part is, we snuggle up on the sofa and watch the Grand Ole Opry; though I admit, I'd rather be making the music than watching it.

I did wonder why he didn't buy the Gibson. He knows how much I've been wanting it. But I suppose seeing you in my living room is the next best thing. I've saved thirty-one dollars, so that makes it a little easier to get through the day. Only forty-one dollars and fifty cents and it will finally be mine. Unless, of course, something else around here decides to go on strike. I've had to resort to whacking the air conditioner with a broomstick as it seems to have developed a mind of its own.

Sincerely,
Lola

CHAPTER 30
EFFIE / "TRY AGAIN"

"Be there in a minute!" Effie called. Cletus and Oscar were already worked into a fit of hysterics by the time the second knock thundered through the house. Jay was still at basketball practice, and Teagan was out with Harper. Brody was upstairs in his room, probably watching YouTube. Until Daniel left, she'd done a much better job of monitoring his screen time, but now she found herself rationalizing the hours she allowed him to zone out. For all she knew, maybe he was up there learning about the theory of relativity. It was a stretch, but it helped her sleep easier at night.

Blowing her hair out of her eyes, she did her best to open the door and hold the dogs back, but she lost her grip on Cletus, who promptly barreled into Daniel's waist. He was wearing a clean yellow polo and jeans; he must have gone home to freshen up after lunch.

"Whoa. Hey there, Cletus." Daniel stroked his black fur and patted his wiggly backside, then scrubbed a hand over Oscar's thick skull. "Hey, Eff." His gaze drifted over her until their eyes met, and he offered a tentative smile.

"Hey," she said, nearly out of breath. Pressed for time after Brody's appointment, she was still wearing her work slacks but had pulled on an oversize wool cardigan. Her hair was tied back in a messy bun with wisps flying freely around her face.

Letting himself inside, Daniel studied the living room as if he hadn't drawn up the plans himself and watched her agonize over seventeen shades of hardwood samples. After a few moments, his gaze returned to Effie, bearing a flicker of appreciation. She wrapped the sweater tighter around herself and rubbed her arms.

"No wonder you're freezing. It's an icebox in here."

Effie rolled her eyes. There were a few silver linings that came with her new single status, and having sole control of the thermostat was at the top of that short list.

With a familiar warmth about them, Daniel's eyes bored into hers, and her heartbeat quickened. She realized that the house was quiet. It had been almost ten months since she'd watched him clean out his dresser and empty his shoe closet. When she had begged him through tears not to go. And now they were alone in the home they'd built together.

"Thanks for seeing me," Daniel said, sticking his thumbs in the belt loops of his jeans. He rocked back on his heels, letting out a sound he only made when he didn't want to tell her something potentially explosive. "Listen, don't get upset"—he cleared his throat, letting his gaze drop to the floor—"but we have to ground Teagan."

Effie snapped her head up. "What for?"

He held up his hands. "Now, before I tell you, just know that I took care of it already. And I'm dealing with it." He attempted a soothing tone that did nothing to soothe her.

"You're starting to scare me, Daniel," she said, feeling more worried every moment he didn't respond. "Out with it already."

He released a long sigh. "Can we just . . . sit down first?" He gestured to the kitchen, and Effie nodded reluctantly. If Daniel was worried about Teagan, it must be bad. He had always been the calming voice in their relationship, the one who told her to stop micromanaging the kids' lives and let them make their own mistakes. He had been the one to teach Jay to drive because she hadn't been able to quell the visions of ambulances and crumpled metal and hospital beds.

As she lowered herself into a chair next to him, her mind raced with possible catastrophes. Unable to meet her eyes again, he laced his fingers together atop the table. "She's been cutting school. She and Harper have been going to these protests downtown—"

"What kinds of protests?" Effie heard herself ask, the alarm in her voice multiplying with each word. She was already imagining armed guards and looted stores and burning vehicles.

"I don't know . . . something to do with that damned museum. The girl's got her head in the clouds and the work ethic of a sloth."

Gripping the table with both hands, Effie began interrogating him the same way she might grill one of the kids when they were hiding something from her. "And how long has this been going on?"

"A while," he said, apparently not as bothered by this information as she was.

The apathy in his voice was beginning to irritate her. This was their daughter he was talking about, and anything might have happened to her while hanging out unsupervised with the likes of Lord only knows who in the middle of the day. "The school should have called one of us. Why did they let her get away with it for so long? I'm going to have a chat with the attendance secretary and give her a piece of my mind." She tugged her phone out of her pocket and pulled up her contacts. Perhaps she would get a head start and also send a strongly worded email for good measure.

Squirming in his seat, Daniel craned his neck to the side and winced. "They did call, Eff. Weeks ago. But when you didn't answer, they called my office line." He let out another long sigh. "Amber was the one who spoke to them."

Understanding slowly settled into Effie's vacant expression. Her throat grew thick with guilt. She'd been busy with work, distracted by emails and phone calls and dead people. Had she let her children slip through the cracks? Right into Amber's all-too-eager hands. She blinked a few times before she could formulate a coherent response. "Are you telling me that your girlfriend has been covering for our child to skip school?"

"I took care of it," he said, more firmly. "I can promise you it will never happen again."

It should have come as no surprise, but the idea of Amber plotting against her, telling Teagan how easily she could get away with fooling her poor simpleminded mother, set her heart on fire. Hadn't she done it once before? Stolen her husband and destroyed her marriage? Why wouldn't she try to take her children too? "How can you promise that? How do I know what she's teaching our kids? This is unacceptable, and quite frankly I don't feel comfortable with—"

"She won't be around anymore." His words came fast and sure, and the rest of Effie's sentence died in her throat. His eyes caught hers, desperate but firm. "Things between us lately have been . . . rocky," he went on. "The truth is . . . I left her weeks ago. That's why she never passed on the message about Teagan. I only just found out today when the school called again."

This information landed with the force of a freight train, and it took Effie a moment to recover her voice. "Am I to assume this means that you two are . . ."

"Not together?" He gave an ambiguous shrug. "Things would appear that way. Yeah," he said, seeming dejected.

Effie righted her shoulders and did her best to act as if this news weren't something to celebrate, but it was nearly impossible to keep the air of victory out of her tone. "Well, I'd like to say I'm sorry, but that would be a lie," she said. Her chest sank with the release of an exhausted breath. Closing her eyes, she melted against her seat. "And I am so tired of lies, Daniel."

"Me too, Eff." He swallowed hard, and his eyes darted. He was fidgety. Effie couldn't remember the last time she'd seen him this nervous. Maybe it was when her water had broken two weeks early with Brody and he'd raced home from work in a panic-filled sweat, scrambling to find her overnight bag. "I uh . . . I think I realize now that maybe Amber didn't really have the experience or the wisdom to be parenting our kids."

His admission took her by surprise, but she was still too angry to appreciate it. "You're just now realizing that? I am so glad you were able to learn this lesson at the expense of our family. What, do you want a gold star or something?" She eyed him, unimpressed. This was the part where she made him feel guilty, when he would finally understand just how much his choices had hurt them all.

He worked his hands together, not meeting her gaze. "You're right to be upset. I was . . . selfish."

"You forgot stupid and childish, but yes, selfish is a pretty good place to start." She cocked a saucy eyebrow, feeling vindicated but also irritated that it had taken him so long to come to this conclusion.

"I've been thinking lately . . . a lot actually." He touched a hand to her arm, and the shock of his warmth sent her mind swirling with questions she was too afraid to ask. "You remember those beach trips we used to take down to Galveston when the kids were small?"

Effie nodded, wondering what he was driving at.

"I took Jay out on the water in that paddleboat—"

"And that storm rolled in." She smiled weakly at the memory.

"He was so scared. Couldn't keep his eyes off the clouds. Was worried that a hurricane would blow us away. Then the wind turned, and we had to peddle against it so hard, I thought his little legs would give out. But we just kept at it until we saw you and Teagan and Brody on the shoreline waving us in. I never told you this, but I think I was just as scared as he was. Kept wondering what would happen if we couldn't make it back to the shore. Back to you."

His words clutched her heart, and she wondered if he was saying this for his benefit or for hers. "Yeah, well, that's parenthood in a nutshell, isn't it? Not knowing what the hell you're doing but pretending you do and praying the kids never find out you're just as clueless as they are." She had expected him to agree with her, but he only stared back, his brown eyes fixed on hers—steady and unrelenting. She couldn't remember the last time he had looked at her that way. It made her feel exposed, and she blushed.

Finally, he shook his head. "Effie, I don't think I ever told you how much I appreciated all you did for the kids. How much you did for me." His hand tightened around her forearm.

Her throat grew thick, but she let herself absorb the compliment—overdue but sweet. She hadn't realized how much she needed to hear him acknowledge the sacrifices she had made for their family.

"Do you think—" He sucked in his lips and made a face, like he wasn't sure how to say the next part. "I don't know . . . would you be willing to try again?"

The words hit her like a wall, splintering into a thousand jagged pieces. How could she want so many contradictory things to be true at the same time? As much as it angered her, part of her wanted everything to go back to normal, wanted the life they had before. But at the same time, she wanted him to suffer appropriately. Admittedly, she had no idea what the appropriate amount of turmoil was for a cheating husband, but she knew he hadn't paid his dues yet. Not like she had. Nevertheless, he was here now, saying all the right things, everything she'd wanted him to say months ago, before they'd enlisted lawyers to clean up his mess. But instead of relief, she only felt bile rising in her chest. When had she ever stopped trying? "You're the one who changed your mind, decided you were seventeen again." Her voice quavered. "I never left."

"I know. It's just that you were so wrapped up in the kids and—"

"*Our* kids," she clarified. "Don't blame me for your mistakes, Daniel." She pressed her hand to her chest to drive home the point. "I was wrapped up in our family."

"And I love that about you," he said more softly, reaching for her fingers. "The thing with Amber . . . it was never really about you. It was me. Somewhere along the way, things just . . . they got so predictable. I mean, didn't you ever feel like we were living on cruise control? Same thing every day. Work, home, kids. I'm almost forty-one, Eff, and I just kept thinking, is this all there is? Is this what I'll be doing when I'm sixty?"

"No," she said, blinking back tears. "Because the kids won't be around much longer. They'll be off living their own lives. And now, instead of giving them every precious second we can, we have to split our time with them. And it's slipping away from us, Daniel. All because you needed . . . something else." Her voice cracked, and she was unable to look at him.

She still couldn't wrap her brain around their situation because she had always thought their marriage was good—at least for her. Why had she stopped being enough for him? Through the ups and downs, the times when he'd put on a little weight or made a bad business decision, he had never not been enough for her. Even now, despite everything, she couldn't help studying his features when he wasn't looking—the slight dimple in his chin, the mole on his left cheek; it was the tiny imperfections that still sent her stomach fluttering. Why had he stopped looking at her that way?

"I'm sorry, Eff." Tears glistened in his eyes, making them look glassy and fragile, like the boy she fell in love with. "I wish I could do it over again. I'd do it differently."

"Me too," she said, wishing it were possible to turn back the years of the clock. But how many? Two? Ten? She didn't know where things had gone wrong, and even if she could have defied time, what would she have changed to make him stay? She wasn't even sure he knew the answer to that question.

"I know you don't have any reason to trust me, but I promise I'll make it up to you. Every day for the rest of our lives."

Words eluded her. She sniffed and tried to collect her thoughts. "I'll need some time. I'm flying out to see Lolly tomorrow morning, and I'll be gone the rest of the weekend." The timing couldn't be better. She needed space to cobble together what was left of her heart before she could decide if there was room there for him.

"Of course," he said, taking her hand and finding the place where her wedding ring had once been, the white flesh now the same sun-kissed shade as the rest of her finger. He rubbed it gently and smiled. "We were always good together, Eff." Holding her eyes, he leaned forward and rested his forehead against hers, the heat from his breath grazing her lips and making her shiver. He smelled the same as he always had—a musky cedar mixed with sweat and deodorant. A warmth spread through her, reminding her how safe she felt when they were breathing in the same air.

She nuzzled against him, letting him cradle her face and hold her the way he used to. Squeezing her eyes shut, she summoned a mental picture of Lolly and Pop, and her heart twisted into a confusing knot. Maybe Daniel could convince her that he loved her again. Maybe things could be different this time. Maybe they could even be better.

CHAPTER 31
LOLA

August 8, 1962

Dear Patsy,

I have wonderful and terrible news. Your new album came out, so today after work, I took the bus to Gus's and purchased *Sentimentally Yours*. But while I was there, I noticed that the Gibson was no longer in the window. In its place was one of those new electric guitars. I asked Gus where it went, and he said someone purchased it yesterday. As you can imagine, I was beside myself with anguish. Gus says he'll have another one in next week, and it won't be any problem to paint a pair of white fringe boots on the front. But I am skeptical they will look the same.

The saddest part of it all is that I was only five dollars away from earning my share of the money. I called Daddy to let him know, and he said he'll make sure the new one passes muster. But I'm in absolute mourning. If it weren't for that damn

Frigidaire, I'd have my guitar already. When I mentioned it to Wallace, he said I was being "unreasonable" and that any old guitar should do just fine. I told him that if it's all the same to him, it shouldn't matter if I made his sandwiches with peanut butter or Vegemite. I made it a point to slam the door loudly when I made his lunch this morning, but I have decided to be the bigger person and try to put it out of my mind.

I have also decided that cold milk is overrated.

Sentimentally Yours,

Lola

P.S. I have an update! It turns out that the man who purchased the Gibson was none other than Richard Montgomery, otherwise known as my father. He brought it over this evening, and I very nearly had a heart attack right there on my front porch. He said, "Scoop, I know you've been working hard for this, and I think it's been good for you to learn that you're capable of doing difficult things on your own." He said to consider it a belated wedding present.

The best part is, he told me to keep the money I'd already saved and that I don't need to tell Wallace about it. "Every girl should have a little insurance, and you never know when you'll need it," he said. I know I'm partial to him, but I do believe I have the best father in the whole world.

Right away, I started practicing my chords and picking around with a few different strumming patterns. It sounds even better than I'd imagined, and my fingers feel right at home on the strings. I'm going to Helen's this weekend so we can practice together. Louisa from work plays the fiddle, and she is going to come as well. We think we'll have a fine little band.

CHAPTER 32
Effie / "Leavin' on Your Mind"

As expected for a Saturday morning, the Dallas/Fort Worth airport was bustling—people in suits clutching their Starbucks, couples in loungewear, parents chasing after toddlers. It wasn't Effie's usual scene. She hated the whole business of flying—the confusing terminals, the stressful parking situation. Already, she'd gotten into the wrong line and ended up waiting twice as long to get through security. By the time she'd made it to her gate, there'd been nowhere to sit, and she'd ended up awkwardly hovering behind an elderly couple arguing about the size of the woman's carry-on bag. Effie resisted the urge to tell the woman that her husband was right and there was no way it was going to fit inside the overhead bin. She was done inserting herself in the affairs of others. From what she could gather, this couple appeared very much alive, but Effie wasn't going to take any chances after her experience in the grocery store. She would have preferred to drive to Kansas like she had when the kids were small, but now that she had a job that she needed to be at on Monday morning, flying was the only viable option. And surely dead people had no use for airplanes.

By the time she made it into the tight confines of the cabin, Effie's nerves were shot. It felt strange traveling without her family. She had strategically booked an aisle seat, terrified of having to crawl over strangers if her bladder couldn't withstand the hour-and-a-half flight. When she caught sight of her row, she saw there was already a thin wisp of a woman sitting in the window seat, who offered her a warm smile. A gray coiffed bun sat at the nape of her pearl-clad neck, and she wrapped a shawl around her slight shoulders and rubbed them. Effie returned her greeting with a polite nod that she hoped didn't appear too inviting. Exhausted from her late night with Daniel, she had planned to sleep, and the last thing she needed was to sit beside a talker. But from the way this woman was smiling at her, she presumed that luck was not on her side. Even before she'd begun attracting the attention of the dead, Effie had seemed to be a magnet for loners. At parties, she'd always been a sympathetic ear, unable to extricate herself from people who saw her as just the sort of person who would be most interested in hearing about a ruptured disc or a wayward child or a recurring migraine.

As soon as Effie had stowed away her bag and shoved her purse beneath the seat, the woman leaned over and said, "Beautiful day for a flight, isn't it? Are you traveling for business or pleasure?"

"Family," Effie replied, hoping to stave off any follow-up questions.

"A wonderful reason," the woman noted approvingly. "Me too. I'm visiting my son," she said, a frown taking shape on her face. "He's getting married, but I wasn't invited to the wedding. Can you believe that?"

"That's awful," Effie said, feeling herself being dragged into a problem she definitely should not care about. Even so, the woman was so congenial, it was hard to imagine how a family member—a son, no less—hadn't invited her to a milestone like that. *No*, she chastised herself. *Do not get involved. It's none of your business.*

The woman leaned over the middle seat, her eyes twinkling. "I'm Mona," she said. "And I must say you have the kindest eyes I think I've ever seen."

"Thank you." The compliment settled Effie's heart, and she could feel her pulse slowing as the captain's voice came over the loudspeaker. Even so, she did her best not to respond too cheerfully. "I'm Effie," she said through a halfhearted smile. "Lovely to meet you, Mona." Then she plugged in her earbuds and leaned her head against the seat rest, hoping to convey that she was a friendly person but also too tired to engage in small talk. She located a podcast and closed her eyes. When she opened them again, Cameron was occupying the middle seat, leaning over her, his thick eyebrows drawn together. If she hadn't known any better, she'd have thought he was inspecting her nose hairs.

A muffled scream escaped Effie's chest as she flailed into an upright position. Clumsily, she located the pause button on her podcast.

"So, where are we going?" he asked.

"*We* aren't going anywhere. *You* aren't supposed to follow me outside of work," she whispered. "Weekends are off limits!"

"That was never an official rule."

"It was implied."

Lifting an eyebrow, he appeared to give this idea some serious thought. "Well, I'm certain you said nothing about airplanes. Come on, Effie," he whined. "You can't leave me with that wet blanket brother of mine. I refuse to spend another Saturday night watching him gorge himself on my couch with basic takeout and *The Great British Baking Show*."

"Drew watches *The Great British Baking Show*?"

"It's so sad." He shook his head ruefully.

Effie didn't think it sad so much as endearing, but she kept this to herself. By now, she realized that Mona was probably wondering who she was speaking to. Not wanting to appear to be a lunatic, Effie gestured to her earbuds and dramatically mouthed the words, *Phone call.*

Then, keeping her gaze forward, she said, "This is the first trip I've taken alone in years, and you aren't going to ruin it for me."

"Who said anything about ruining it? I'm the perfect wingman on a solo trip because I can point out all the weirdos and axe murderers." She briefly wondered if Cameron was stalking Grace because it sounded exactly like something she would say.

"Absolutely not," she said, a little too loudly. "Besides, I have a lot on my mind." This weekend was supposed to be her opportunity to rethink her relationship with Daniel, and she didn't want distractions.

Cameron balked. "Oh, I'm sorry your life is so difficult, but are you invisible?"

"I mean it," she warned. "Besides, it won't be any fun for you. I'm visiting my grandmother."

Excitement flickered in his eyes. "I love grandmothers! And I have to say, they love me. I'm pretty sure it's the sideburns." He trailed a finger down his jawline and turned a cheek. "I think I remind them of Tom Selleck."

Her pulse quickened, coloring her cheeks. "I'm not going to say it again. Get out of here!" She said it loud enough that Mona shot her a look of concern. "So sorry. I wasn't talking to you." She gestured to her earbuds again, then caught sight of a flight attendant working her way down the aisle. Her face was all edges, but she was clearly trying hard to remain calm.

When she reached Effie's row, she crouched down and discreetly whispered, "Ma'am, we're about to take off, and some of the other passengers have expressed some . . . concern for your health. Is there anything I can do to make your flight more comfortable?" She smiled broadly, but Effie could sense the worry behind her eyes.

Embarrassment rippled through her. "Oh, I'm fine. Just a nervous flier," she reassured her, a little perplexed by the sudden attention. She hadn't been *that* loud. She smiled, then remembered Mona and gestured toward her new acquaintance. "But she might like something. Mona, would you like anything? Some headphones maybe, so you can watch a movie?" That would be just the thing to keep the woman from jabbering her ear off.

The flight attendant glanced at the window seat, her eyes widening as her smile glazed over. She turned again to Effie and opened her mouth as if to speak, but nothing came out. And that's when a fresh wave of goose bumps cropped up along Effie's arms.

Cameron pursed his lips and shrugged. "Probably should have mentioned that Mona here is dead too. We met at the gate, and she told me she had some unfinished business with her son. I thought you could help her out." Of course he did. A surge of heat swelled up from Effie's toes, threatening to erupt in a volcano of very bad words. *Fudgesicles.*

Mona gave a little wave, a guilty smile touching her lips.

Effie wanted to throttle Cameron, but it would probably result in her being escorted off the airplane. She would be one of those disruptive passengers that went viral for causing a scene, angering all the other travelers who had somewhere important to be. Effie did not want to be TikTok famous for choking invisible people, so she pasted on a smile and thanked the flight attendant for her thoughtfulness. "I apologize for my outburst," she said in the sweetest tone she could muster, hoping to convince the woman that she was entirely sane. Then, venturing to look up, she added, "A bag of pretzels would be lovely."

Surely by now, the warmth radiating from her face must be creating a furnace. Effie closed her eyes, then dropped her head against the seat rest.

It was going to be a long flight.

∼

It turned out that Mona wasn't invited to her son's wedding because the two of them had had a falling out. She'd quite publicly disavowed him last Christmas after he told her he was dropping out of divinity school and was an atheist to boot. It took the entire flight for Mona to finally understand that his choices were not a reflection of her parenting and that perhaps his soul was not destined for the fiery pits of hell. In their last few moments together, before Mona vanished into a beam of glittering dust motes, Effie felt the air lighten the same way it had when Iris had crossed over in the ambulance. Emotions carried a weight that was barely perceptible with the living, an intangible alchemy unbeknownst to most. But Effie was beginning to recognize the feeling that descended in the precise moment a person finally accepted the unacceptable, the way her skin tingled as if the tiny hairs of her arms were being lifted by a giant magnet. Effie suspected that the reason Mona had been eternally trapped on an airplane headed for a wedding she would never attend had nothing to do with her son and everything to do with her. It seemed what she'd needed most was to forgive herself.

Having made it through the flight, Effie retrieved her bag, then made her way to the loading zone, where a rideshare was waiting to take her to her parents' house twenty minutes outside the city. True to his nature, Cameron proved to be an obnoxious plus-one, taking every opportunity to comment on the pastoral scenery whizzing by. Apparently, rows of soybeans and corn were not the sort of milieu he had envisioned for a weekend getaway, and he kept asking if they would at least get to see a tornado. "I always wanted to go out with one of those storm chasers and take a photograph with a funnel cloud, you know? It was on my bucket list, but I never did it. Life is so short, Effie. You really shouldn't put off the things that matter most," he pointed out with an air of superiority that rubbed her the wrong way. He was the one who had cut his life short, after all. Besides, having cowered beneath a desk in her fair share of tornado drills, Effie bristled at the idea of someone paying a ridiculous sum of money to chase a deadly storm. It was only more evidence that Cameron was just the sort of person she would not have deemed worthy of her friendship if he were alive.

"Seriously, though." He looked at her, more discerning now. "What's something you always wanted to do but were too afraid to? Something everyone else would judge you for."

"I don't know." She mined her brain to humor him. "Eat chocolate Pop-Tarts, I guess," she said, remembering all those nights at Lolly's when she'd consumed them without a trace of guilt. What freedom, to be young. But after paying a medical professional to tighten everything that had gone loose over the years, it seemed irresponsible to eat junk food with abandon. If also joyless.

Cameron made a face. "I meant something *dangerous.*"

"Have you ever read the nutritional information on a box of chocolate Pop-Tarts?" she asked. "Dangerous is an understatement."

Every time she saw them in the breakfast aisle, she felt that familiar tug of desire as she passed by all the "pretend breakfast foods," reminding herself that good parents ate granola and egg whites and avocado toast.

Cameron gaped, his expression unreadable. "Your life is so sad."

CHAPTER 33
LOLA

September 5, 1962

Dear Patsy,

After much deliberation, our band has finally decided on a name. We plan to call ourselves the Pink Lassos which, I must admit, I didn't really like at first. Personally, I prefer yellow, but since Helen hosts our rehearsals, she tends to pull rank when group decisions are made. It's an unfair arrangement, but Wallace won't allow us to practice at our house. He says we would drown out his television shows, and we can't do it on the porch because the neighbors would "get ideas about his wife." I'm not sure what ideas he's referring to. From the way he talks about the Lassos, you'd think I'd up and joined the mafia or the communist party.

In any case, we've already bought matching pink cowgirl shirts and Louisa has expertly stitched our names onto the collars. So far, we've learned three songs including one on your new album that I think we pull off rather nicely. I sing the melody, and Helen and Louisa harmonize above me, though truthfully, Helen can be a bit of a diva sometimes and tends to overemphasize the importance of her part.

Now that we're beginning to look and sound halfway decent, I took the liberty of signing us up for an open mic night at a little honky tonk across the river. When I mentioned this to Helen, she gave me an earful and insisted we weren't ready for a public appearance, but I didn't back down. As I'm sure you understand, we need to perform in front of a live audience if we want to gain confidence and experience. I told them, "Hells bells, just look at Patsy! She wears pants up there on stage, stilettos, and bright red lipstick. If she can be brave like that, then we can, too."

Today, the three of us set to practicing a new song. It's an old Hank Williams tune, "I'm So Lonesome I Could Cry," which I'm sure you're familiar with. Maybe I chose it because the words feel very fitting for my life. I thought marriage was supposed to bring two people closer, but ever since we said those two little words, I feel more alone than ever. When Wallace comes home from work, he looks right past me, like he's looking for something better. It turns out it's the remote. And lately he finds any excuse to pester me about my guitar playing. While I was at Helen's, he phoned to say that it was too late for me to be out on my own and seemed to be in a tizzy over dinner which I hadn't yet made. I didn't mean to laugh, but it's a rather silly thing to say as we would both prefer a Salisbury steak TV dinner to my crispy tuna noodle casserole. If you ask me, the Gibson has truly proved a blessing for us all as my hands can now be put to much better use.

Even so, Wallace says ever since I got the Gibson, I don't pay him any mind which isn't true. He says I waste too much time at Helen's these days, and he doesn't appreciate coming home to an empty house after work. I beg to differ because it's not empty. There is a perfectly good television sitting right there in the living room.

  Sincerely frustrated,

  Lola

CHAPTER 34
Effie / "Then You'll Know"

When they arrived at Effie's childhood home—a two-story cream-colored farmhouse with a wraparound porch lined by boxwoods—Margie came barreling out. "How was your flight, hon?" She grabbed her by both shoulders and pulled her in for a kiss on the cheek, then checked behind her with a regretful frown. "I can't believe you didn't bring them."

"It's easier this way, Mama," Effie reassured her. "Besides, it was Daniel's weekend."

Margie tsked. "I'll never understand how that's easier, dividing up the days of the week like slices of pie. I still don't understand what went wrong between the two of you," she chided under her breath, as if Effie had been partly to blame. As if she had been the one to exchange naked pictures with a stranger and ruin nineteen years of a perfectly good marriage all because she was bored. Effie wondered what her mother would say if she told her that Daniel had fallen into her arms last night, practically begged her to take him back. She would probably pull out the red carpet for him, book the country club for a vow-renewal ceremony, and begin phoning all her friends. The thought induced a twinge of nausea. Under no circumstances was she going to tell her mother about last night, not until she was certain that her feelings were tidily squared away. Besides, she didn't want to give Margie the satisfaction. Then there was the matter of Cameron, whom she hadn't told about Daniel's change of heart. She had a feeling he wouldn't be too thrilled about a reunion with her ex. For now, she opted to keep this information locked in the safe confines of her mangled heart.

~

A pink-and-white balloon arch graced the gazebo of Margie's front yard, where tables rested beneath the shade. The afternoon light beat down upon their skin as Effie and her mother set out trays of meat and macaroni and cheese and potato salad. At Effie's suggestion, Cameron had decided to take a solo tour of her parents' farm, which wasn't so much a farm as a stable containing two geriatric horses, one cantankerous llama, and a dilapidated chicken coop. The animals were really just for show. Her parents grew sorghum, and this was the reason they lived on the outskirts of Kansas City, Kansas, a full fifteen minutes away from Lolly.

The lady of the evening had yet to make an appearance, but the other guests slowly began to trickle in. "When will Lolly be here?" Effie asked.

"Soon," Margie said, filling a mason jar with plastic forks. "Your father went to pick her up. She had a touch of a cold last week, but I think she's on the mend."

"How's she doing?" Effie asked.

Margie must have known exactly what Effie meant, because she drew in a deep breath, then let out a wistful sigh. "Oh, you know, same as always. Some days are better than others." She opened her mouth to speak, then closed it and started again. "We've been getting her house ready to put on the market."

Effie looked up from the tray of smoked pork she was slicing and gaped at her mother. "You're selling her house?" A sudden fear snaked around her heart. Lolly and Pop's little white clapboard was nearly as sentimental to Effie as her own parents' home. It was where Effie had spent so many long weekends, draped in one of Pop's giant T-shirts while Lolly serenaded them with ballads on her guitar. Pop hadn't been much of a singer, but he'd been just as enamored by Lolly as Effie was. Sometimes he would join in, off key and a beat behind, but the fact that he had tried always warmed Effie's heart. He loved the music because Lolly loved it, and it made Effie love her grandfather all the more.

Margie wrung her hands. "You know as well as I do that the bungalow is way too much house for one little old woman. Besides . . . I've been meaning to tell you . . ."

"Tell me what?"

Margie dragged out a sigh. "Honey, I've just had so much on my plate here." She hesitated before starting again. "Your grandmother isn't doing well, and I worry about her over there by herself. I leave a list of the important people for her next to her bed, but you know she's stubborn as a mule and won't read it. Then last week, Theresa came over and your grandmother locked all the doors and wouldn't let her inside. She had the stove on, for goodness' sake! We had to call the police, and the whole thing really upset her." Effie gasped, but Margie barreled ahead. "No need to panic. She's fine now, but she's losing her druthers faster than I can find them. I had to do something. She's liable to send the whole place up in flames."

"What do you mean?" Had she put Lolly in a home?

"Don't worry, Effie. I chose a good place," Margie said in the dismissive tone she used when she felt Effie was being dramatic. "She'll have people there to care for her around the clock. It's better for all of us this way. You'll see."

Effie suspected that what her mother really meant was it was better for Margie, easier than having to drive to Lolly's house every day and tend to her needs. But she couldn't fault her mother for making the call, even as her heart broke at the idea of her grandmother in a nursing home.

"That reminds me." Margie jerked her head toward the house, a tiny smile creeping in. "I have something for you."

~

In the kitchen, Margie opened a wide drawer beneath her china cabinet, pulled out a square wrapped in delicate tissue paper, and offered it to Effie. "We've been packing up her things, and I know how much you wanted it."

Effie's fingers recognized the bumpy ridges of the silver frame before her eyes confirmed what it was. Effie had liked to reach up on her tip-toes and run her fingers over its edges when Lolly wasn't looking. Patsy's letter. The one that had saved Lolly and Pop's marriage.

She gasped and pressed it to her chest, feeling grateful but unworthy. She hadn't expected to receive her grandmother's most treasured possession until after Lolly was gone. "I can't take this, Mama." Tears pricked her eyes.

"She wants you to have it. I've already cleared it with her. Besides, she won't be able to take many things with her."

Though she knew it was too much to hope for, selfishly, Effie still wanted to ask Lolly about the letter, about what had happened in her marriage to cause her to write to Patsy in the first place. Back then, she'd been too little to understand all the workings of a relationship and how much one person could hurt another. She had only witnessed the good moments between Lolly and Pop. But now she understood with painful clarity how much a person could lose when she gave her whole heart to someone else. Before Daniel's affair, Effie hadn't known all the ways her insides could ache. If something had happened between her grandparents, something big that tested the limits of their seemingly perfect marriage, she was desperate to know what it was.

"What happened between Lolly and Pop that upset her so much? Why did she write to Patsy in the first place?"

"Oh goodness, who knows," Margie said, irritation seeping into her tone. "Each time she told me the story, it seemed to grow bigger and better. You'd think the two of them were soul sisters, the way she went on and on about her."

"So, you don't know why she wrote to her?"

"Why is this suddenly so important?"

"It's not." Tucking a stray lock of hair behind her ear, she tried to sound casual. "I just always wondered."

Margie heaved a tired sigh. "All I know is that your grandmother was going through a difficult time. She said Patsy told her exactly what she needed in that moment. If it weren't for Patsy, she never would have been so happy in her marriage. So, I guess, in a way," Margie said, planting her hands on her hips, "Patsy saved us all."

Gingerly, Effie peeled back the tissue paper and lifted the frame closer to study it. Wedged between the glass was a wrinkled piece of cream-colored stationery embossed with gold roses around the edges. The message was written in blue pen with big curly capital letters and a slightly slanted cursive hand. Effie could picture Patsy Cline pressing the tip of her pen against the paper, stopping every so often to reflect and then adding another line as the words floated into her thoughts. She smiled knowing that someone so important, someone so successful and smart and talented, had taken the time to write these words to Lolly. Her Lolly.

> Dear Lola,
> Thank you so much for writing to me. I'm writing this letter while I'm out on tour, riding in the back of this old rickety Cadillac. I'm squished between the boys who keep picking out tunes on their guitars. Every time I try to close my eyes, we hit another pothole and I get a fret board in my

side. We've crisscrossed these southern states every which-a-way, and our next stop will be Toledo, Ohio. That's where I plan to mail this letter to you. If we ever get there.

I cried myself a river of tears when I read your letter because I know a thing or two about heartache. Lord knows, relationships are hard, and trying to understand the ways of men is like trying to understand why the earth goes round the sun. That dog just won't hunt. Some of them want to hold you down, and some of them want to give you wings. But only the really good ones understand that you were already born knowing how to fly all along, and all they got to do is get the hell out of the way.

Hoss, from everything you've told me, it sounds like you already know what to do. I wish I had more advice for you, but all I can tell you is that I've always followed my heart and it has never steered me wrong. Hang in there, little gal! It's never too late to set things right. Good luck.

With Love,
Patsy Cline

Goose bumps sprouted atop her arms. Carefully putting the letter down, Effie thought about how those simple words had led to decades of happiness and generations of children. Maybe Margie was right that Patsy had saved them all. In some sense, she had been Lolly's guardian angel. And if that were true, was it so crazy to think she could be Effie's too? *Time to set things right.* That had been Patsy's message for her, too, and the words echoed in her head, getting louder each time she rehearsed them. All this time, she'd lain awake at night and wrestled over the meaning of that phrase. But now it all made complete and total sense.

She couldn't give up on Daniel. She couldn't give up on their marriage and the legacy of family she owed to their children. Not yet. Not until she'd fought for the life all of them deserved—the life Daniel had forgotten and let slip away.

There was still time to make it right.

CHAPTER 35
LOLA

October 19, 1962

Dear Patsy,

I think you would have been proud of the Pink Lassos tonight. By all accounts, our debut performance was a raving success, even if Helen overshot the descant by about a mile. It took me a verse to overcome the jitters, but by the time the chorus rolled around, we were really on fire. The whole place was bouncing, and I got lost in the applause. At least until my eyes skimmed the back of the room. Wallace was leaning against the back wall with his arms crossed, watching me with a look I'd never seen before. His eyes were empty, like two black holes. He wasn't mad or upset. It was more like he was trying to work something out in his mind. I've never felt afraid to be around him before, but as soon as I saw him, I smudged away my lipstick and slipped off the stage. As we were leaving, he caught me in the parking lot and grabbed my arm. He said, "How do you think it makes me feel when you come to places like this looking like trash? It was real cute when you wanted to play superstar before we were married, but things have changed now."

Honestly, I couldn't disagree with him. Things have changed. I used to think I couldn't live without Wallace and my guitar. But now I realize, I could get along just fine without one of them.

Sincerely,

Lola

CHAPTER 36
EFFIE / "LOVESICK BLUES"

Guests began arriving in earnest, and the pasture behind the barn and silo was now converted into a parking lot. Vehicles were wedged into every available nook as families trailed onto her parents' ample front lawn—Helen's and Louisa's children and grandchildren, Margie's church friends, and some of Lolly and Pop's old neighbors. The smell of sweet hay and freshly cut grass hung thick in the air, transporting Effie to simpler times when she used to help her mother pull weeds in the garden out back or mow their three-acre lot on her father's John Deere. Purple milkweed dappled the perimeter of the lawn, and in a few months, the whole scene would be lit up by a halo of sunflowers billowing in the breeze.

At Margie's request, she'd busied herself tying pink and red bows along the stage, which wasn't so much a stage as it was a giant piece of plywood stapled atop a collection of old milk crates. It was just big enough to accommodate three octogenarians, a couple of foldout chairs, and a microphone. Effie's father had covered it in a white awning to provide some relief from the sun, which was out in full force. It wasn't a bar or a supper club like the ones Lolly and the Lassos had frequented over the years, but hopefully it would make her feel at home. Effie checked her watch, noting that her grandmother should be here by now.

As if on cue, she caught sight of her father ambling toward the stage.

Wearing a plaid button-up shirt and stiff jeans, he meandered through the tables, his brawny arms widening to take her in. "Hey there, darling." He planted a kiss on her cheek, the familiar scruff of his round face scratching her skin.

"Hey, Dad."

The shade of his Stetson hat shielded his eyes as he pulled back from her and looked at her over the crook of his sunburned nose. He'd always had the complexion of a man who worked the land and the calluses to prove it. "How's that sorry excuse of a husband of yours?" Effie's father had never quite forgiven Daniel for stealing her away. When the scrawny basketball player with seemingly no future in sight had asked for Effie's hand after graduation, Tim and Margie had thought they were being generous when they'd let the two of them live in the barn, then provided a loan so their only child wouldn't become the wife of a drifter. They'd expected Daniel to use the money to buy a home or invest in a farmstead, as they had. They had not expected him to abscond with their daughter and future grandchildren to a city eight hours away. While Margie could forgive Daniel for the greater good, Tim was not the forgiving type and had said on more than one occasion that *that boy* had gotten far too big for his britches. "I always knew he was all hat and no cattle." He frowned at her. "How's the divorce coming? He isn't trying to give you the slip, is he? Because he wouldn't have a job if it weren't for me."

"Everything's fine, Dad," she lied. The truth was, she had no idea what was going to happen anymore. But with Patsy's letter fresh on her mind, there was a good chance things with Daniel could work out after all, so she didn't want to encourage her father. She changed the subject. "Where's Lolly? Didn't you pick her up?"

"Inside, getting ready." He jerked his head toward the house. "You know your grandmother. She can't go on without her spangles and sparkles."

"Tim!" Margie shouted from the porch. "Stop lollygagging and bring out the rest of the canopies! That sun is vicious today. I told you we should have gotten more!"

"I'm working on it!" he shouted back, his jaw tightening.

Margie shot him a steely look. "If you were working on it, you'd be moving instead of standing there jawing as if there's no work to be done."

"Well, it would be easier to put up the canopies if *someone* had stored them away properly!" He turned to Effie for support. "She threw them in the barn without even bothering to take out the stakes."

Her parents could keep this going for ages. It was all just a part of the weird mating ritual they'd danced for forty years. She yelled. He cursed. Their relationship was complicated, but at the end of the day, Effie knew her parents loved each other. She could see it in the way her father carefully placed a glass of water at her mother's bedside each night as she read. She could see it in the way her mother would quietly sew a button onto a shirt or let out the seams of his pants when he'd put on a little weight. But was that enough? She'd always wanted something more, something easier. At one time, she'd believed she had it. But if her parents didn't exactly have a storybook marriage and she and Daniel had done it wrong, would she ever know how to get it right?

Margie glowered daggers. It was a look Effie knew all too well, and she sensed it was time to make her exit before an earthquake ensued. "Now, Tim!"

"Damn it, woman! I'll get to it when I get to it!" he thundered.

Effie shook her head. How had these people survived four decades of marriage when she and Daniel hadn't been able to manage two?

~

Effie found Lolly in the master bathroom applying a thick layer of black mascara. She leaned her head against the wall, considering her grandmother with affection. As expected, Lolly was wearing a pink cowgirl shirt adorned with white fringe and embroidered with matching stars on the collar. A red kerchief was tied snugly around her neck, and white rhinestone-studded boots adorned her feet. She was entirely in her element, but her cheeks were more concave than Effie remembered, her posture slightly bowed. That showstopping, larger-than-life version of Lolly that Effie held in her heart had been whittled down, weathered by the storms of life and the seasons of illness. Despite all that, she was still glamorous. Cornflower blue eye shadow stretched all the way up to her brow, and her lips were stained a cherry red.

A current of worry swirled in Effie's mind. She'd been hoping that today would be a good day, one of those rare windows when Lolly returned to herself and remembered more than just the music.

When Lolly caught sight of Effie in the mirror, her hands jolted, and the makeup applicator went flying to the floor. "Good Lord, Effie!" Lolly's shoulders collapsed, and she clutched a hand to her heart. "Don't you know not to sneak up on an old woman like that? I'm liable to stab myself in the eye with this thing."

"Sorry," Effie replied, unable to suppress a chuckle. Relief diffused her worry. Lolly had recognized her, had spoken her name unprompted. Hope swelled in her chest.

"Now get over here and give me a hug." Lolly smiled, calming Effie's heart, then wrapped her in a firm embrace. "I'm so glad you're here." Her blue eyes sparkled with excitement. "Where are Daniel and the kids?"

Guilt eclipsed her short relief. "Sorry, they couldn't get away," she said gently, unsure what year her grandmother was operating in today. Was she imagining Jay and Teagan and Brody as much smaller versions of themselves, frozen in the happiest parts of their lives? If that were the case, she almost envied her grandmother.

"You tell that husband of yours that I'm none too happy about him taking my granddaughter away from me," Lolly chided.

"I will," Effie promised.

"Speaking of Daniel, how is he?"

"Busy with work," she replied. It was the truth. Even so, a wave of guilt washed over her.

"Your grandfather is the same way, honey." Lolly turned to the mirror and picked up a blush brush, then shook her head. "Doesn't know what to do with himself unless he's piddling around with some project or other. One of these days, I'll convince him to retire, and he'll take me to California to see those redwoods." With trembling fingers, she applied a fresh coat of blush to her cheekbones.

Hope drained from Effie's chest, and she forced a sad smile. Her grandparents had already been to see the redwoods, the Rocky Mountains, the Statue of Liberty, and every national park within a thousand-mile radius of Kansas City, Kansas. Hearing Lolly speak of Pop in the present tense filled her with a bittersweet ache. But if it made Lolly happy, maybe it was better for her to live in the past. Just for a moment.

Studying Lolly's mood, Effie formed her next sentence carefully. "Mama said you wanted me to have Patsy's letter. But I don't want to take it. It doesn't feel right."

"Oh honey, it's just paper." She waved her away. "I've got her where it matters." She placed a hand to her bosom. "Right in here."

It was enough to convince Effie that perhaps she was telling the truth. "All right," she conceded. "But only if you're sure."

"I'm sure."

A warmth saturated her chest, but the question of the letter's meaning hung heavy in Effie's thoughts. With Lolly in good spirits today and Pop still alive in her mind, the moment seemed ripe for the asking. "Since we're on the subject," Effie said, working up her courage, "why *did* you write to her?"

An almost imperceptible frown crossed Lolly's face, but Effie was certain she had seen it. "Oh honey, I can hardly remember," her grandmother replied, brightening. "I'm sure it was some silly thing or other." But Effie suspected there was more behind the words. Maybe something she didn't want to remember.

"Yeah," Effie pressed, "but was there ever a time when Pop did something so awful, so terrible, that you thought the two of you couldn't come back from it?"

Putting a finger to her chin, she said, "Well, let's see. One time he mowed over my tulips, but that was an accident. At least I think it was. I had just donated a box of his Matchbox toy car collection, so I suppose we'll never know for sure." With a mischievous twinkle in her eye, she said, "Honey, every marriage has its problems."

"I know, it's just"—Effie dropped her gaze—"some problems are bigger than others."

Lolly released a deep sigh. "What I *can* tell you is that there isn't anything two people can't work through if both of them are committed." She put down the makeup brush and turned to face her granddaughter. "Is everything all right between the two of you?"

"Of course," Effie replied, hoping it sounded convincing. If she and Daniel reunited, it would do no good to confuse Lolly and tell her about their almost divorce. "You think we're good together. Right?" Lolly's opinion had always mattered more than anyone else's. If she believed in this marriage, then maybe Effie could too.

"Of course."

"I don't know." Effie shrugged. "I guess I just always wanted to have the kind of relationship you and Pop had, you know. I wanted us to complete each other the way you two always did."

Lolly flashed her a disapproving frown. "Oh honey, no one can complete you. That's much too big of a job to ask of anyone else. Besides, even if they could, would you really want them to? Your grandfather and I have always worked because he understood that I was already a whole person all on my own. Marriage is just . . . inviting somebody else along for the ride and seeing where life takes you together. And your Pop, well, I think he'd agree that we've had one hell of a ride." A tiny smile reached her eyes.

The words struck Effie's heart, and she was grateful for this sliver of time with the grandmother she remembered. "I miss you," she said, blinking back tears. "Sometimes I feel like I've gotten so far away from this place, from everything I used to be, like I can't see my way forward anymore." It had been easier before so many other people depended on her to make the right decisions.

"You'll find your way." Lolly leveled her gaze and flashed Effie a knowing look. "You know what I loved so much about Patsy?"

Effie knew what her grandmother was going to say before the words left her lips. She mouthed the phrase along with her.

"She sang the truth. The sweet, the sad, the bitter. The whole mess of it all tangled up together." Lolly's eyes sparkled with warmth. And though she couldn't be certain, Effie felt her grandmother was entirely lucid when she looked her square in the eyes, put a hand to her shoulder, and asked, "What's your truth, honey?"

Effie bit her lip, embarrassed to admit that she hadn't the slightest clue how to answer that question. Before she could come up with a response, Margie poked her head into the bathroom. "They're asking for the birthday girl."

Lolly smoothed down her shirt. "Well, that's my cue," she said, pulling back her shoulders. "My public is calling, and I can't disappoint them, now can I?" She squeezed Effie's shoulder one more time and flashed her a wink.

As Lolly glided away, Margie caught her by the arm. "Don't overdo it, Mama," she warned. "Everyone will understand if you need to take a break."

Lolly recoiled from Margie's grasp. "Don't you ever tell me what I can't do," she said firmly, a determined expression taking shape on her face. "Ever."

∼

If anyone had asked Effie to explain why a Pink Lassos performance was so magical, she would have said it was the way those three women carried themselves on a stage. Decked out in matching shirts and cowgirl hats, they always exuded an unbridled confidence that Effie envied.

And they loved the music. Helen was the engine of the whole thing. With her solid build and teased brown bob, she walked a steady bass line that never wavered. And tiny Louisa's nimble fingers could improvise a fiddle tune so lively even the most stubborn audience members couldn't help but tap a toe. Each of them knew how to work a room, but Lolly had always been the star, addicted to the spotlight. With her bedazzled boots and fringed leather earrings that nearly touched her shoulders, the woman was a born performer. Even when she was little, Effie had recognized that her grandmother's voice had the power to hypnotize. Lolly could shift effortlessly from a syncopated bluegrass melody to a soulful ballad with the ease of a master. At her fortieth wedding anniversary, she'd serenaded Pop with a moving rendition of "Blue Moon," and there hadn't been a dry eye in the house.

As Effie watched her grandmother strap on her beloved guitar and take her place on the makeshift stage between her two oldest friends, her throat constricted with emotion. She'd settled herself at an empty table at the back of the yard. Almost empty. Cameron had returned, and he began pestering her with questions about her rural childhood. "I just don't understand the point in owning a llama if you can't ride it," he said. "Did you raise them for their fur?"

"No," she whispered, annoyed. "He's more of a . . . pet."

Cameron threw up his hands. "Well color me confused, because I fail to see the point in owning a pet that you can't actually pet. He spat at me. Which reminds me: Is chewing gum made from sorghum?"

"Can you quiet down?" Effie whispered. "They're about to start." A few people turned around and flashed her a look she was becoming all too familiar with.

On the stage, Lolly clutched her guitar to her chest. She took a breath, closed her eyes for a beat, then threw a subtle nod to Helen and Louisa. As her fingers strummed a simple pattern, the first few chords of "Crazy" drifted over the lawn, subduing the audience. Effie smiled. Considering that she was conversing with an invisible man, she thought it a fitting choice.

"They're amazing," Cameron said after the first verse. He sounded truly impressed, and Effie knew he was a tough audience.

She couldn't disagree. "Lolly's the best singer I know in real life."

"Well, yeah, but that's not what I meant. It's the glamour of it all. Not many people can pull off fringe, but I've got to hand it to her." Cameron whistled. "She really sells it."

"You should have seen her when Pop was alive. She would have had him up there in a matching shirt."

"A regular Johnny and June, huh?"

"If June were the star of the show and Johnny were tone deaf." They exchanged a smile, and Effie's gaze drifted back to Lolly like a magnet.

"Who sings this song?" Cameron asked. "It's a real banger." She couldn't tell if he was being genuine or cracking a joke, but his head was swinging along in time to the beat.

"Are you seriously telling me you don't know?"

Cameron tilted his head as if in deep thought. "It sounds familiar."

"Familiar?" Offended on Patsy's behalf, Effie scoffed, the whites of her eyes on full display. "She was only the most amazing woman to grace the stage. Ever. You've never heard of Patsy Cline?"

Cameron shrugged. "I've heard of her. She was a singer."

Effie felt her heart rate tick up the way it always did when she was about to launch into a diatribe against one of the kids. "*Singer* isn't really the right word. Did you know she's the most played artist of all time on jukeboxes in this country?" she said with a bit of smugness. "God, she sang with so much feeling." Effie closed her eyes, letting the song trickle through her like medicine in her veins, then let out a wistful sigh. "They don't make them like Patsy anymore. She's . . . timeless."

By now, Cameron was staring at Effie as if she'd just had a nervous breakdown. "She sounds rad," he said, though his deadpan expression didn't really sell the word. "Country music was never my thing," he went on, crossing his arms. "Every song is so depressing. Take this song. The whole thing is about a woman pining over a guy who left her for someone else."

"Maybe because some of us can relate," Effie pointed out.

"Yeah, but . . . you don't want Daniel back." He raised an eyebrow. "Do you?"

It was the second time he'd asked the question, but now, the answer wasn't so clear. "I mean, it's not so much about wanting him back as it is about doing what's best for our family."

A shadow crossed Cameron's face. "How can you say that?" he asked with an edge to his voice. "He clearly didn't have your family in mind when he chose Amber."

Effie rolled her eyes. "You wouldn't understand."

"Try me." He leaned back in his seat as if he had all the time in the world. Which, she supposed, he did.

She considered the question thoughtfully. It was difficult to put her feelings for Daniel into words. How was she supposed to give up on two decades of her life? He had been the heartbeat of every precious memory—Daniel holding each of the babies in the hospital, so proud he'd sent out a company email with all their birth stats and a photo of their deliriously happy and exhausted new family. Daniel building her the house of her dreams with his own hands, installing that extra closet in the hallway because she'd said she was afraid to go in the attic. It was as if her thoughtful, attentive, and—most importantly—faithful husband had been taken over by body snatchers. Cameron would never appreciate her situation because he was young and gorgeous and single. At least, he had been. "You had the whole world at your fingertips." After a long pause, she looked up at him and sighed. "I married Daniel straight out of high school. My whole life is wrapped up in him."

Seeming unimpressed, Cameron shook his head. "Look, I've known you all of a month, but even I can tell that you're too good for him. He cheated! I've been slapped for less."

"It's not that simple. I've spent more of my life with him than without him. It's not like there's a switch I can just turn off and stop loving him. He's a part of me. And he always will be." A woman turned around again, flashing a concerned look that made Effie flush. Steeling herself, she fixed her eyes on the stage.

"Don't you see what's happening here?" Cameron pressed, more urgently now. "You've finally started to put your life back together and move on. And he's jealous. It kills him to see you doing OK without him."

"No, you're wrong. He messed up, but he realizes that now, and he wants another chance."

Cameron laughed. "He doesn't want another chance. He wants you to forget about all the shit he did so he can have his cake and eat it too."

"In all fairness, he did break up with her," she pointed out.

Cameron rolled his eyes. "Effie, I'm telling you, guys like Daniel are a dime a dozen. And if he did it once, he'll do it again. Which is why you have to cut him loose."

"You don't know what you're talking about."

Folding his arms, Cameron regarded her dubiously. "So, you're telling me if Daniel walked over here right now and wanted to get back together, you would say yes?"

Effie gave a noncommittal shrug. "Yeah. I think so." Of course she would. She would punish him appropriately, make him beg for her forgiveness, and then she would melt into his arms, enveloped in the scent of him. It was the scent of everything she loved about her old life. It was the scent of home.

She was about to tell Cameron that she had no use for his unsolicited advice, that he, of all people, couldn't possibly understand the importance of commitment and loyalty and devotion because they weren't glamorous and easy. But the music, or rather the lack of music, tugged her attention away. Lolly's voice had taken on a strange monotonous tone, her words slurring into a stream of unrecognizable syllables. Helen and Louisa stilled their playing, and Margie rushed onto the stage just as Lolly fell to the ground. She crouched at Lolly's side, checked her pulse with one hand as the other gently lifted her jaw, which had gone slack. "Call 911!"

Something sharp splintered inside Effie's chest. Her feet carried her toward the stage, but she knew even before she arrived at her grandmother's side that the world had just shifted beneath her feet.

CHAPTER 37

LOLA

December 15, 1962

Dear Patsy,

When I poured my heart out to you, I didn't expect you to answer. But you never cease to amaze me! I suppose that's just the sort of woman you are—a real class act. I read that you once visited a fan in the hospital when she was so sick, she couldn't make it to your show. If you ask me, that is the mark of a great woman—elegant enough to sing at Carnegie Hall but not too self-important to help out regular people like me.

In your letter, you told me to follow my heart which was wonderful advice. The only problem is, at the moment, my heart seems to be just as upside down as the rest of me. I can't seem to make heads or tails of my life or make any decisions at all for that matter. Yesterday, I stood in the cereal aisle straining my eyeballs between a box of Sugar Smacks and Bran Flakes until everything went blurry. I realize it was probably too much to ask of you, but I suppose I wanted you to tell me what to do. Any choice I make will only disappoint someone—my mother, Wallace, God the Father, the Son, and the Holy Ghost. Sometimes it feels like I'm being split in two, like I'm pretending to be one way on the outside but on the inside the real me is shaking my fists and screaming, trying to get out. I must not be doing a very good job of hiding it because at Thanksgiving my mother caught me in the kitchen, and she could see it in my eyes. She said, "You're thinking of leaving him, and you need to get your head on straight, young lady. You've made your bed, and you'll lie in it. Don't even think about coming back here." I can't expect her to understand a thing about love. Her and Daddy don't even sleep in the same bed. But I'm not made that way. I think a person needs to feel passionate about something in her life or she's liable to go mad.

Sometimes, I'm not sure where to put all these feelings, and I worry they'll consume me. Then I pull out the Gibson and close my eyes, and the notes flow from my fingers into the guitar and my voice carries them on a melody. For just a moment, the world stops spinning, and I catch a glimpse of the girl I used to be. And for just a verse or two, I can breathe again.

Sincerely,

Lola

CHAPTER 38
Effie / "I'm Blue Again"

What was supposed to have been a weekend trip had turned into a five-day affair. After administering a series of tests, Lolly's doctors confirmed that she had suffered a massive stroke, likely brought on by irregular stress. They told Margie they weren't sure if she would wake up, and if she did, she would likely require round-the-clock care in a rehabilitation facility. When it became clear that Lolly was as comfortable as possible, Effie kissed her parents goodbye and told them to call her immediately if there was any change.

It was all Effie could do to keep from falling apart in front of the kids. Daniel had kept them a few extra days, but now that they were back with her, there was still the matter of Teagan's crimes to address.

"Did you guys have a good week at Dad's?" she asked, testing the waters as the four of them shared a couple of pizzas.

"It was fine," Jay noted without meeting her eyes.

"Except Dad doesn't know how to make french toast," Brody pointed out with his mouth full. "Can you teach him how to do it?"

"Sure," she said, though she and Daniel had bigger things to discuss. They were supposed to have a serious conversation this weekend about whether this divorce was going to happen. Regardless, after Lolly's stroke, she was going to have to rely on him more than usual.

"I want to talk to you about Lolly." Effie struggled with how much to tell them about her grandmother's condition. She didn't want to worry them, but things looked bleak. "I'm going to be visiting her more than usual over the next few weeks, and I'll need you guys to help out more around the house."

"Sure, Mom," Jay said, his brow furrowed. "How's she doing?"

"Not great," Effie admitted. Then, turning to her daughter, she took a deep breath. "And I'll need you to start being honest with me, Teagan. No more secrets. Your dad and I have been discussing your punishment . . ."

Teagan stopped midchew, and her shoulders wilted. "Of course you have," she muttered under her breath.

"I want you to know that we are in lockstep on this. You're grounded at both houses. And I'll be calling the school every day to make sure you're there."

"So, you guys are only in agreement when you're torturing me?"

"We're in agreement when it comes to doing what's best for you," Effie said decidedly.

"If you knew what was best for me, you'd ask me why I skipped school in the first place. Me—a straight-A student taking AP classes, Mom. Do you think I'd be so callous about school if I didn't have a good reason? Admit it. You don't know anything about me."

Effie tried to keep her expression neutral, but the accusation scraped at her resolve. "This may come as a surprise to you, but I happen to know a lot more about you than you think."

"No, you don't. You don't care about saving the museum. And somehow, you manage to make everything about you."

Effie should have left it there, but with Lolly unwell, her cup was on the verge of overflowing. She couldn't handle one more drop of snark or sass. Heat burned in her chest, and before she could talk herself out of it, the words were in the air. "I make everything about *me*? Teagan, do you hear yourself? You cut school. You speak to me like I'm nothing. You are so . . ."

"I'm so what?" Her tone was accusatory, but she looked as if she were about to crumble.

"Spoiled!" Effie said, louder than she had intended.

Chewing slower now, the boys lowered their eyes. Teagan blinked as if she'd been slapped, then went silent for a few moments. "Well, maybe I don't want to live here anymore." Her lip quivered, but she didn't cry. In that moment, Effie briefly caught sight of the little girl who used to explode over the injustice of family game night, and she wanted to hug her. "I'm going to Dad's."

Effie softened her tone. She was beginning to regret her choice of words. "Fine. I'll drive you over later tonight."

"No, Mom." Her daughter's voice was more assured now. She sounded so grown up. "I mean I'm staying there. Indefinitely."

The words crashed into Effie with the force of a tidal wave. Teagan would prefer to live with Daniel. What kind of mother lived apart from her child? All those years she had spent holding on to everyone else's dreams, neglecting her own, only for Teagan to look at her with that stubborn tilt of her head and declare her independence. Had any of it mattered? For some reason, the only thing she could hold in her mind was Patsy's message. *Time to set things right.* But how would she ever begin to set things right if people kept abandoning her?

∿

Effie headed for her desk to settle in for the morning. On a whim, she'd picked up an extra cappuccino from Gordon's and dropped it off in Drew's office. It was the least she could do. He'd been so kind, allowing her to stay with Lolly for as long as she needed. Now that she was back, she hoped she would be able to make it through the day without crying. The thought of her grandmother attached to all those machines was almost unbearable. Every time her phone vibrated, she was filled with a fresh surge of dread. Then there was the matter of Teagan, who hadn't reached out since leaving last night. She'd texted Daniel to talk about her, and in his usual coolheaded way, he'd told her that Teagan would come around eventually. He'd also asked if Effie had made a decision about him, which she hadn't. She'd hardly had time to think about a reconciliation, with catastrophes following her like footprints. It felt as if everyone she loved had held a meeting and decided that this was the week to upend her life.

Approaching her desk, she discovered Cameron spinning around in her chair like a bored toddler. His usual winning smile was replaced with a pathetic sulk, his shoulders entirely limp.

"Where have you been?" she asked, setting her coffee down on the desk. "I thought maybe you didn't need me anymore." Since the flight home, he'd been MIA. And as much as she hated to admit it, Effie had been worried about him. After Lolly's party, he'd been almost pleasant. The following morning, she'd been surprised to find him standing guard at her grandmother's hospital bed. He'd been empathic and thoughtful, distracting her from her grief by divulging all the drama going on behind the scenes of the hospital: which doctors had slipped into the break room together, which PA had a crush on the cute tech that came to check Lolly's vitals. This wasn't the Cameron she knew. During those late nights at her grandmother's side, he'd proved to be so much more than the self-absorbed jerk she'd first taken him for. But today, he seemed all about himself again.

"I went to Cassidy's office," he said, his voice uncharacteristically lifeless. "She was showing off her ring to everyone like it was the Hope Diamond or something. And then I just . . . walked around town. Visited the crash site," he added with a tortured expression.

Effie studied him with pity. She knew from experience that watching the love of your life move on with someone else was soul crushing. The only thing worse would be death. And Cameron had been unlucky on both fronts. "I'm sorry. I know that must be hard."

Burying his face in his hands, he let out an anguished groan. "I've got to get out of here, Effie. I can't be here when she gets married. It's torture. You have to get Drew to accept my death so I can leave."

"I'm working on it," she said. Though in truth, since Daniel had shown up asking for a do-over and Lolly's stroke, Cameron's plight had been at the bottom of her priority list.

"Well, do something fast. I don't think I can take much more of this." He pulled himself up and began pacing the room.

"This may come as a shock to you, but I have a lot going on right now too. You're going to have to be patient."

"I've been patient! It's been almost a year," he said, his voice growing desperate. "Maybe this is just hell. If it is, it's a seriously messed-up version of it." Balling his hands into fists, he paced the lobby, stopping every so often to inspect the scenes hanging along the wall. He lingered in front of the biggest one—a rendering of a purple-hazed mountain range at sunset—and examined it thoughtfully. "What makes you able to see me when no one else can?"

"Believe me, I've been asking myself the same question for weeks. I died and came back to life during a . . ." She paused and debated how much to reveal before settling on "Routine operation. And ever since then, let's just say my life went from *Gilmore Girls* to *Ghost Whisperer* real fast."

Cameron seemed to be far away, and she wasn't certain he'd heard her. Finally, he looked at Effie, his eyes questioning. "What was it like for you? Dying, I mean."

The hairs on Effie's arms tingled. "You didn't see the light?" Ever since it had happened, her "death" was constantly at the forefront of her mind. And for some reason, it comforted her, like a well-worn blanket, wrapping her up in tranquility and love and home. It was a strange thing—thinking of her near-death was what now made her feel most alive.

Cameron nodded. "I did, but . . . I was too scared to go toward it. Wasn't ready, you know? I couldn't imagine leaving Drew after everything he'd been through. After the accident, I remember watching everything from above. It was so strange to see myself down there, trapped in that car, knowing there was nothing I could do about it.

I was so stupid." He shook his head. "When the light came, I guess I just . . . wasn't ready to give up yet. So . . . I ran."

Her chest dropped with a weighty sigh. She knew what it felt like to want to run away. "Well, to answer your question, it was kind of . . . beautiful." Though it wasn't just beautiful. It was a myriad of things all tangled up together she didn't have the vocabulary to describe. How could she explain color to a blind person? Or describe the sweetness and texture of an apple to someone who had never tasted before? "I mean, I'd always wondered, you know—what comes after. Is it just lights out? End of scene? I was raised a Christian woman, so I believed we live on, of course. I hoped, anyway." She gave a reluctant shrug. "But I was still afraid. I always imagined it like this huge mountain looming in the distance. I'd picture myself standing at the precipice, leaning over this giant cliff. And I knew at some point I would have to jump off. A part of me was convinced I'd land in a heap at the bottom, and the other half hoped that maybe I'd fly. But in the end, when I finally fell, it wasn't either of the two. It was like . . . catching the wind in my sails and just gliding down softly. I could have stayed there forever." Her heart fluttered at the memory, and she was grateful for the chance to finally talk about it. "I don't know if any of that makes sense," she said sheepishly.

"It does." Cameron swallowed, casting his eyes on the ground.

Sensing the emotion in his tone, Effie went on, hoping her experience would give the poor thing something to hold on to, even if it wasn't his own. "I wasn't alone. If that helps at all. There was someone else there in the light, guiding me." Patsy's rich alto voice floated into her thoughts, and she smiled. "Life's funny that way, I guess. We come into this world kicking and screaming, so afraid to blink our eyes open in the light, but someone is there to pull us into it. Death isn't much different." She thought of Jay and Teagan and Brody, the way their little bodies had stretched and wiggled into the world, how they had screamed like banshees, as if protesting their very existence, and her heart settled. "It makes me less worried now, for my family, knowing that we don't have to go through any of it alone."

Cameron nodded, though the movement appeared robotic. Closing the distance between them, she offered him a sad smile. "We're going to figure this out, Cameron. Because you aren't alone either," she said, though, not for the first time, she wondered if perhaps she was the right person for the job. After everything Cameron had been through, Effie couldn't bear to fail him. But for reasons unbeknownst to her, the universe had chosen her to be his guide. And just as she'd guided her children, she would do it, even if she had no idea how to drive this train. Already, a new thought had begun brewing in her mind, but it would be difficult to broach the subject with Cameron without upsetting him, so she chose her words carefully.

"Cameron, have you ever wondered if maybe Drew isn't the one who needs to accept your death?"

"What do you mean?" he asked, narrowing his eyes.

"I mean, maybe it's you," she explained, thinking of Mona, who had only needed to forgive herself to find peace. "You said you avoided the light, that you weren't ready to go. And I think that maybe . . . well, maybe now, if you're no longer afraid, you'll be able to make the transition."

Of course that was it. It made complete sense, a *Wizard of Oz* twist. Cameron had possessed the power within him all along. Proud of herself for puzzling this out, Effie flashed him a reassuring smile, but his face was twisted in a strange sort of grimace. It took her a few moments to register that he wasn't looking at her. He was looking at something or some*one* behind her. Slowly, she swiveled to face Drew, his mouth ajar in what she could only assume was horror. "Who are you talking to?"

Heat coursed through her veins, coloring her face a fiery red. "No one," she stammered, wondering how much her boss had heard. Hopefully not the dying part.

But his face had gone pale, his eyes hard like ice. "Why did you say my brother's name?"

"I didn't," she lied.

"You did." It surprised her a little to hear the edge in his voice. "Do you think you can . . . talk to him?"

Effie made a muffled sound—something between a groan and a polite cough. "Well, not in so many words."

"Do you think Cameron is here with us right now?" he asked, giving her the same baffled look Daniel had given her when she'd told him about her death. It made her jealous of Cameron. For the first time, she wished she were invisible too. She was pretty sure death was preferable to the disaster that was her life.

"Oh God, Drew. Stop being such a prick!" Cameron shouted to no avail. "You always were the boring one." Looking at Effie, he pointed to his brother and added, "You know, he's the one who ruined the tooth fairy for me. Santa Claus too. Said it was pointless to live in a world of illusions. Well, look who's living in a world of illusions now, buddy!"

"Not exactly," Effie started to say, but Cameron's outburst had unbalanced her. "If you'll just—"

"I told you about my brother because I trusted you, because I thought you cared. But you're just . . . crazy."

"That's exactly what I thought at first too. Look, I know this is totally weird, and I wouldn't blame you if—"

"Just stop," he said, backing away. He was nearly shouting now, and it frightened her. "I don't know what I was thinking not running a background check. I—I knew you were too nice not to have something wrong with you. And something is seriously wrong with you."

"Drew, I know it doesn't make any sense. It didn't to me, either, at first." Effie was speaking quickly now, the words pouring out as her heart hammered like a runaway metronome. But she could sense the conversation was already far off the rails. "If you'll just let me explain—"

"Cameron is dead," he muttered, his jaw tightening.

"I know it's scary," Effie tried in her sweet lilt, "confronting something you never thought could happen. Believe me, I know. But this is real. And it's really happening to Cameron. If you'd just let me spend some time with the two of you, I think I might be able to help him move on."

"The two of us?" He shook his head. "This is absurd." He chuckled at the ceiling, but there was no joy behind it. "You're actually serious, aren't you?" Then, leveling his gaze at her, he raised a trembling finger. "Effie, the only person you need to worry about helping is yourself. I don't know if you need medication or a psychologist . . . or . . . just leave."

CHAPTER 39
LOLA

March 1, 1963

Dear Patsy,

You're coming to Kansas City! After my shift today, I took the bus to Gus's to see about your latest record, and right there in the window was an advertisement for a benefit concert at the memorial building this Sunday night. I can hardly believe that after all this time, I'll finally be seeing you perform live! I mentioned it to Wallace, but he says he doesn't want to sit in some stuffy auditorium to watch a bunch of hillbilly pickers sing through their noses. I took offense to that as I consider myself an aspiring hillbilly picker of the finest caliber. It's for the best anyway. He would only ruin the experience. He wouldn't know a good song if it hit him right between the eyes. I showed the flyer to the girls at our rehearsal yesterday, and they were equally thrilled.

I've been thinking a lot about the letter you wrote me. I'm going to wait until after Wallace's birthday this month to make any decisions. I at least owe him that much.

Sincerely,

Lola

CHAPTER 40
EFFIE / "BACK IN BABY'S ARMS"

Perched in front of her vanity holding a tube of brick red lipstick, Effie cringed at the memory of that morning. Why hadn't she just denied the whole thing outright, said she was practicing a monologue or something, instead of insisting that Cameron had spoken to her? Of course she had sounded delusional, and she couldn't blame Drew for flying off the handle. Things at work had been going swimmingly, but now she was no longer certain if she even had a job anymore. She swept her hair into a low bun and studied her profile as her phone chimed on the counter. Her pulse quickened when she reached for it, and she wondered if it was Margie with bad news, or Drew texting to apologize, which was ridiculous since she was the one who owed him an explanation. Instead, Daniel's name flashed across the screen.

Can't stop thinking about you. On your way?

A nervous warmth saturated her chest as she lay the phone down. No need to respond right away. If Cameron were here, he would tell her to let Daniel sweat it out. Reaching for a tube of mascara, Effie composed herself as best she could and determined to put the whole Cameron-Drew debacle out of her mind. Perhaps she would call Drew later and apologize after the dust had settled, but for now she had more pressing things to do, like rebuild her marriage. There had been a spark there—more like a blazing fire—when Daniel had held her in the kitchen they once shared. When he'd called this morning to ask if they could talk, she'd said she would meet him at a park tonight. It was easier that way. Safer. Reuniting would be like navigating an emotional land mine where the kids were concerned. She wasn't sure what to expect from them, and it wasn't fair to get their hopes up if things didn't work out. She would not break their hearts twice.

She would never be able to shake the image of their faces in the days after he left, the way they'd tiptoed around her, careful not to send her to pieces all over again. And she had felt so guilty because she'd known it had been equally devastating for them, though Teagan had never cried in her room like Brody had or called her father a "self-absorbed prick" like Jay had. If she'd been upset about their new arrangement, Teagan had never shown it. As far as Effie could tell, the only thing that *had* changed was her daughter's newfound hatred toward Effie.

After carefully applying her mascara, she inspected herself in the mirror and smoothed her control-top underwear. She wondered if Daniel had noticed the changes in her body. If he even cared. He'd always said he loved her curves, but that was before he'd left her for a woman who had probably never even heard of shapewear. The differences would be invisible to anyone who'd never seen her naked, but Daniel had traversed every inch of her body, the stony ridges before the kids came and the soft plains after. Tonight, she'd gone for a classic look, in a sleeveless black dress and pearls. No point in trying to outdo Amber, since she would never win in a numbers game against her. Instead, Effie would lead with sophistication and grace, timeless traits earned through a lifetime of love and loyalty.

"Wow." Jay sailed past her before stopping to throw a nod of approval, soft curls loosely hanging about his face. "You look great, Mom. Where you going?"

"Just out with Grace," she lied, trying to sound casual. Though if she had told her best friend about this evening, Grace would have shown up armed with zip ties and held Effie captive as she recounted Daniel's betrayal in painful detail. Effie wasn't ready for Grace or anyone else to know about this. Not until she knew exactly what *this* was.

~

When she arrived at the park, Daniel hopped out of his truck in a blue polo and his signature ironed jeans. Sneaking around like this reminded her of all those times she'd broken out past curfew to "stargaze" with him. Back then, the only constellation she'd been interested in was the faint dusting of freckles on his nose. An approving smile played on his lips as he took her in, and she blushed.

"You look nice," she said, feeling reserved. She didn't want to appear too eager for a reconciliation, and he was going to have to put in a lot more effort than a pair of clean pants. Still, she couldn't deny how good he looked in a slim-fitted dress shirt, the way the stiffly pressed fabric hugged his slightly pudgy midsection so perfectly.

Clutching her black velvet handbag, she righted her shoulders. "So, where are you taking me?" He had been vague over the phone. Part of her was nervous to frequent any of their old stomping grounds, just in case they ran into any acquaintances. Not to mention dead people. They needed to have a real conversation, a painful one. And that would be difficult to do around prying eyes.

"Hold your horses, Mrs. Baker," he said with a secretive grin. "And turn around." He swirled a finger in the air. When she hesitated, he rolled his eyes. "Just trust me."

Reluctantly, she obeyed, though he could hardly blame her if she hadn't. A cloth mask fell over her eyes, and she could feel it tighten as he tugged the ends around the back of her head.

His lips grazed her ear. "Can you see anything?" he whispered.

The closeness of his breath sent a shiver through her limbs. "No. And I might add that it's a feeling I don't particularly enjoy."

"Give me your hand," he said, his voice low and assuring.

She took a shaky breath and reached out her fingers, uncertain as they lingered in the darkness. When his warm hand locked around hers, her entire body relaxed in his grasp. She had missed the way it felt to have him at her side, the two of them pushing through the unknown together—lovestruck teenagers who had no idea what health insurance or property taxes were. Gently, he led her along with tenderness toward what she thought was his truck. Steadying her with both hands, he tucked her into the passenger seat and reached across her chest to fasten her seat belt.

"You do realize I look like a hostage," she pointed out.

"Guess I hadn't thought of that," he said. "If we get stopped, we'll just tell the police that we're trying out some of that S and M stuff."

"I think you mean BDSM," she corrected.

"Well, look at you," he teased. "Only a few months apart and you're a woman of the world."

Effie laughed in spite of herself. She had always appreciated his quick wit, the way he could play off her quips and get her to loosen up. But tonight, she also found it irritating. She wanted to stay angry for as long as she could manage before letting him back into her good graces.

Keeping a firm hold on her hand, he wove the truck over bumps and around sharp turns until finally the ground stopped moving and the engine fell silent.

"Can I take it off now?" she asked, impatient to see where they had landed. Wherever they were, it was quiet. No other cars idled, and she couldn't detect any lights.

"You can take off whatever you like, darling. Except that bandanna." She could feel him smiling at her, and against her will, she smiled back.

"All right. I'm waiting. What's your next move, cowboy Casanova?"

A door opened and closed, and she was alone in the truck for a few moments before her door flew open and Daniel's familiar hands found hers again. Carefully, he guided her out, leading her along for a little while before he stopped.

"What's happening?" she asked, rooting around aimlessly.

Then his hands slid down the small of her back, tugged her closer until their bodies were flush. She could smell the mint on his breath as it grazed her neck. And though she couldn't see him, her body recognized the curve of his frame against hers, the way she had always fit so perfectly against the shape of him. His hands were firm and warm as they crept down her back and landed just below her waist. How was it possible that, after so many years, his body against hers could have the same effect? All her nerve endings were firing at full blast as a series of tiny earthquakes rippled through her. Instinctively, she tilted her head, parting her lips, waiting. All at once, it was as if she realized she'd been living without oxygen, and now that it was here within reach, the anticipation was enough to knock her over. When his lips met hers, an electric current pulsed through her body, filling her up with a familiar heat that made her skin tingle and her head go fuzzy.

But after the first few intoxicating moments, the dizziness gave way to something else. Something darker. Her stomach soured, and though she tried to will them from escaping, tears leaked out of her. Was this the way Amber kissed him? Was it better with her? Was she now only a three-star restaurant when her husband had become used to five?

Gently pulling away from her, he lifted the mask and trailed a finger down her wet cheek. "You're crying, Eff."

"I guess I am." She dabbed at the corners of her eyes, feeling silly that she'd allowed her emotions to get the better of her. She was supposed to be the one making *him* cry. Now that her eyes were open, she could see that they were in the parking lot of Marco's. Her heart clenched at the memory of the five of them huddled over a Sicilian pizza after Brody had accidentally scored a goal for the other team. He'd been so heartsick, and Daniel had agreed to let him choose whatever kind of pizza he wanted. They'd all laughed over a large pineapple with anchovies. "What is this, Daniel?" Still trying to wrap her head around the gesture, she waved a hand toward the restaurant, with its green, red, and white letters and the dark *A* that had given out years ago. "What are we doing here?"

"I remember how much you used to love this place when the kids were small."

Confusion and nostalgia had begun playing a tug-of-war in her mind, and she shook her head to clear it. "That's not what I'm talking about. I mean what are we doing *here*? What happened to us?"

His smile faded, and he grimaced, deepening the lines that had recently cropped up around his eyes. Suddenly, he seemed so much older. "I'm so sorry, Eff. I can't imagine what I put you through. I never wanted any of this." His words nearly bowled her over. Last summer, he'd made it perfectly clear what he wanted, and it had not been her.

"I never thought you would hurt me like that, and then . . ." She pressed her eyelids closed, trying to summon her voice, but the words clogged her throat. Somehow his betrayal felt fresher than ever. It was like a tragic movie she knew she shouldn't watch, but nevertheless she allowed herself to replay all the most awful parts.

"I screwed up. I know that now." Tucking a strand of hair behind her ear, he studied her, his face stricken.

She'd thought this was what she'd wanted to hear, had rehearsed the moment she would throw her hands around his neck. But now that he was standing nose to nose, it felt as if things were moving too fast. "I'm getting whiplash, Daniel. First, you tell me our life is boring, that you have to leave to find yourself. And now you tell me you have to come back because you didn't need to be found after all. What am I supposed to think?"

"I can't explain it, Eff. I wish I could." He fumbled through the words. "All I can say is that some lessons you have to learn the hard way. We got married so young. I think part of me resented the fact that I never really got to see what else was out there. But I know now that it wasn't worth losing you."

She had to admit that part of her had occasionally wondered what her life would have been like if she hadn't married so young, if she'd gone to college instead of helping Daniel grow the business and staying home with the kids. But she'd loved them all too much to break the promises she'd made. It sliced her to the center to know that Daniel had chosen differently.

The regret in his eyes gave way to a glint of hope. "I look at you now, and I think, How did I ever get so far from here? How could I forget my Effie?"

She examined him dubiously. "A pair of double Ds and a tiny waist have a funny way of making a man forget certain things."

"Forget all that, Eff." He waved his hand, seeming annoyed that she had brought up his indiscretions again. As if *she* had been the one to ruin things. "This is what I want to remember. You and me. Two kids in love and stupid as hell. Stupid enough to believe that love was all they needed to make it in the world."

She wanted to believe him, but the words felt foreign, like they were meant for someone else. "I don't know," she said, giving a tired shrug. "Maybe it was stupid."

"No, Eff. It's not." His jaw was set and determined now. It was the same game face he used to put on before basketball practices. "We were perfect for each other then. And we're perfect for each other now. I think God knew that I was too boneheaded to know what's good for me, and that's why he sent you to me when we were so young."

Effie was in no mood to theorize about God's timing. At the moment, the two of them were not on the best of terms. "Let's leave God out of it. I don't want you to feel like you're settling for me because of some predetermined plan." She didn't want to repeat the mistakes her parents had made, trapped in a predictable pattern that made both of them miserable—even if they did love each other in their own ways. For what? To satisfy a vow she'd made before she'd been legally old enough to drink? Lord knew they were both different people now. "All I've ever wanted is for us to be happy together. Grow old together. I thought that was what you wanted too. But if you're not happy . . . if you're not one thousand percent sure that this is where you want to be"—she bit back tears, hoping he would disagree—"I don't want you here."

Hanging his head, he dropped his hands from her waist. "Effie, I admit I was confused about some things for a while there. But I'm not confused anymore." He softened his gaze, reminding her of that skinny restless boy on her doorstep with the wide grin and endless heart. "This is where I want to be."

She wanted to believe him, but Cameron's nagging words drifted into her thoughts, and as much as it pained her to face the possibility, she wondered if maybe he'd been right after all. What if Amber had only been one of many indiscretions? Maybe she didn't know Daniel at all. The thought was even worse than the affair because it meant she had fundamentally misunderstood the first half of her life, when it had apparently been so obvious to a complete stranger. "And how do I know you won't go and change your mind again?" she pressed, her voice louder, more sure. "How do I know you're in this for the long haul?"

"Because now I know what life was like without you. And I don't ever want to live like that again."

"Even if I'm not twenty-seven with the skin of a goddess?" She arched an accusing eyebrow. "I mean, couldn't you have picked some-one a little less perfect? How am I supposed to compete with her?"

"You're doing better than you think." He grinned, his lips giving way to that contagious smirk that always melted her. "Have I told you how amazing you look lately?" He didn't come right out and say that the surgery had been good for her, but he might as well have. She hadn't imagined feeling so cheap and tawdry when he noticed the changes in her body.

Feeling braver, she heaved in a steadying breath. "This is who I am, Daniel. And it doesn't matter how many surgeries I get; it's only going to get worse from here. Are you prepared for that?"

"Only if you're prepared for liver spots and erectile dysfunction." He blew out his cheeks. "Time's a fair SOB, isn't it?"

Rolling her eyes, she started for the restaurant, but he blocked her with his chest. He laced his fingers through hers, then raised the top of her hand to meet his lips. "It's you or it's no one for me, Eff. I can't imagine being with anyone else."

Lucky him, because she *had* imagined him with someone else, and it had nearly killed her. Why had it taken him so long to realize this? Why did he have to break her to understand that she was already everything he needed? If he hadn't, maybe she wouldn't have gotten the surgery. Maybe she wouldn't have nearly died. It stood to reason that she wouldn't have transformed into an unwilling medium for lost souls when the only soul she'd ever really wanted to find was her own.

Pulling her hand away, she swallowed back tears. "I need some time to think." Things were different now. Muddier. *Time to set things right.* But how could she really be with him when all she could see were all the parts of herself that hadn't been enough for him the first time around? Other than Amber leaving, what had changed since then?

Inside her purse, her phone vibrated, and she fished it out. Margie's picture materialized on the screen, making her flinch. She had no intention of telling her mother about tonight, but she couldn't risk sending it to voicemail if there was news of Lolly. "What is it, Mama?" she answered, feigning normality.

"It's your grandmother." There was an air of defeat in her tone, so very unlike Margie.

Effie's heart dropped, and she braced herself for the worst.

"We were with her when she went. Till the very end." There were tears in her mother's voice, and it quivered. "Honey . . . she's with Pop now."

CHAPTER 41
LOLA

March 4, 1963

Dear Patsy,

I've never been much of a writer, and I don't really have the words to describe what happened last night as I watched you perform. You sang with so much feeling, so much anguish. I could feel it dripping from every word, and I realized that I didn't even know what that kind of heartache feels like. Because I'm not sure I've ever really been in love. Not in the way you sing about.

For the last song, you walked on stage in a white chiffon gown, and I swear you looked just like an angel, Patsy. I couldn't take my eyes off you. When you opened your mouth, the whole place vibrated with anticipation. It was like we all knew we were about to witness a miracle. Then as the song drifted over the audience, something inside of me slipped into place, something I didn't even know was missing. You sang "I'll Sail My Ship Alone," and I could picture myself on this great big ship of dreams venturing out into the ocean with nothing but my songs and guitar. And for the first time, I wasn't afraid.

Afterward I went home, and Wallace was drinking a beer and watching a western on TV. He didn't even ask me about my night, which didn't surprise me. I fell asleep dreaming about that ship, wondering if I'm brave enough to let it set sail.

Sincerely,

Lola

CHAPTER 42
Effie / "I Fall to Pieces"

A leaden sky hovered outside the sealed windows, the blinds and heavy curtains drawn so tight that not even the faintest ray of sunlight could seep in. The kids were at Daniel's. To his credit, he had held her last night as she fell apart and offered to keep them as long as she needed.

Her puffy eyes were rimmed in red circles, the product of a sleepless night crying in her bathrobe. Cocooned in her bed under a pile of thick quilts, Effie couldn't tell where the blankets ended and she began. She'd spent the better part of the morning with her box of tissues, watching reruns of *Mary Tyler Moore* and *The Golden Girls*. Lolly had always fancied herself a Blanche, while Effie envisioned herself more of a Rose.

She had hoped that a marathon of their favorite sitcoms could conjure her grandmother's spirit. It wasn't lost on her that she finally had an opportunity to use her troublesome new abilities to serve herself. But try as she might, she had been unable to will Lolly's presence into appearance. If Effie weren't so broken, she might have laughed at the irony of it all. Go figure. Able to see the dead, except for the one person she actually wanted to see. Did that mean Lolly had no regrets? Nothing that needed to be repaired? If Effie died today, she was pretty sure she'd have a litany of visits to make, starting with Teagan. Maybe she'd even have a few things to say to Margie about the way she'd tried to steer

Effie's life, always pestering, always pushing, always unsatisfied with Effie's choices. And she would definitely haunt Daniel for a few nights.

"How are you doing?" Grace asked when Effie finally answered the phone. She'd been pummeling her with texts all morning, but Effie hadn't had the energy to return any of them.

"OK," she sighed, because how else could she sum up the past year of her life?

"I'm coming over after work." This was not a request. "You shouldn't be alone right now."

Alone. It was an accurate assessment. She could envision herself in twenty years, sitting on this same couch beneath the same smelly blankets watching the same reruns with the same canned laughter. "I'm fine. Really, I promise."

"And how's Teagan? Have you talked to her since she left for Daniel's?"

"I called the kids last night to tell them about Lolly. She seemed . . . distant still. I have no idea how they're taking it." She'd been too wrapped up in her own grief to gauge theirs. Maybe they were OK, but that was only another reason to feel guilty. What if she hadn't done enough to keep her grandmother's presence in their lives, her familiar alto voice and the sweet country melodies she'd hummed as she held them? They were entitled to Lolly's legacy too. Effie dragged her palms down the sides of her face, rubbing at the bags beneath her eyes. "What if we totally screwed them up?"

Grace's response was swift and sure. "Oh, you definitely screwed them up. And I screwed up mine." Effie could feel the smile touching her lips. "But that's the universe's fault for sending kids to *us.* I mean whoever's in charge up there was either drunk or asleep at the wheel when they made me a mother with no instructions. Effie, we're all just making this stuff up as we go. Like our parents did, and their parents before them. No one has the answers."

"You're right," Effie conceded, her chest a little lighter. But surely *one* answer wasn't too much to ask, was it? Patsy's admonition rolled around inside her brain. If there was ever a time for the universe to explain itself, it was now.

Grace promised to check in again after lunch, ending the call with a command that Effie shower and put on clean underwear.

Alone with her thoughts, Effie picked up Lolly's letter and studied the curvy slant of the text again, her fingers lovingly brushing the glass as if it were a sacred relic. As her eyes trailed over the words, she wished she knew how to follow Patsy's advice, as her grandmother once had. *I've always followed my heart, and it has never steered me wrong.* She had no idea what her heart was saying because her head was throbbing with a confusing mix of jumbled memories—Daniel proposing to her beneath a sea of starlight in the bed of his truck, Daniel building this house for her with his hands, the same hands that had held her each time one of the kids had been born. The same hands that had once driven her to the hospital when she got food poisoning at that sketchy sushi place and cleaned her vomit off the floorboards while she'd slept it off in the guest room. But those same hands had held Amber too.

The thought burrowed into her, and she couldn't shake the image of the two of them together. Had Cameron been right? Had she wasted nineteen years loving a man, bearing his children, cooking his meals, only to be informed that they were suddenly and simply incompatible? A bad fit. A mistake. How silly she had been to have missed it.

～

A warbling voice startled her from a restless sleep. It was too deep to belong to Grace. From beneath her comforter, it sounded as if it were coming from deep inside a cave.

"Effie, are you in there?"

A muffled groan escaped her chest. Like a turtle emerging from its shell, she peeled back the blanket and, through one lazy eye, clocked Cameron at the edge of her bed. She studied him warily. A part of her had hoped he'd moved on after their conversation yesterday, but apparently she had failed at being a medium as well. No surprises there. "You broke our agreement," she mumbled. "You're not supposed to come to my house."

"I was crossing my fingers behind my back. Besides, you're forgetting the fine print."

"What fine print?"

"Every agreement has fine print. And in this case, it says that I can come to your house in the event that someone's life is in danger."

Rolling over, she heaved a sigh. "I hate to be the one to tell you this Cameron, but you're already dead."

"Not my life," he shot back, looking affronted. "Drew's."

Effie hadn't spoken to Drew since he'd caught her conversing with his dead brother and looked at her as if she'd grown a second head. Had she pushed him over the edge by dredging up a past he'd rather not remember?

"After you left yesterday, he went home and got totally pissed," he went on. There was a nervous urgency about Cameron's tone, so unlike him that it unsettled her. "I've never seen him like this before, Effie. I'm really worried he'll do something stupid. Then he left my place this morning and never came back. I have no idea where he is. I've searched everywhere."

A kernel of concern wedged its way into her gut. This was entirely her fault, but she had no idea how to fix things. After her cringeworthy performance yesterday, Drew would never trust her again. "Your brother made it pretty clear he thinks I'm insane."

"Look, I wouldn't be here if I wasn't desperate. You're the only person who can help me!" His gaze flickered between the empty take-out containers littering the end table and the pile of crumpled tissues at his feet. For a moment, he seemed to second-guess that statement.

Effie's shoulders shook with a bitter chuckle that made Cameron raise an eyebrow. "Why does everyone keep saying that? Look around." Propping herself against a stack of pillows, she waved a tissue toward the mountain of laundry that had accumulated at the foot of the bed.

"My life is a total mess right now. I can't help anyone else, much less Drew. He thinks I've totally lost it, and to be honest, I can't say I disagree with him."

"Look, I don't know what's going on with you, but it can't be nearly as bad as what I've been through," he pointed out. "You promised you would get me to the other side. News flash. I'm still here!"

Burrowing herself deeper into the mattress, Effie scoffed. "Which just proves my point that I'm entirely unqualified to help you! Let me spell things out for you. My daughter hates me. My grandmother died. I'm ninety-nine percent certain I'm now unemployed. And things with Daniel are . . ." Her voice wavered as Daniel's face drifted into her mind. She broke into a full sob, drawing a fist to her mouth, her shoulders shaking as she gasped for air.

"I'm sorry about your grandmother," he said, his voice uncharacteristically soft. "Lolly was a force, that's for sure. And I don't know what's going on with your kid, but she's a kid. She'll get over it." Lowering himself next to her on the bed, he let out a sigh. "But as for Daniel, you have to let him go, Effie. He doesn't deserve you."

"But he finally wants me," Effie protested, blowing into her tissue. "The other night, he looked at me the way he used to. And now I'm . . . confused."

"Welcome to the club," Cameron said, not looking especially sympathetic. "You aren't the only one in the midst of an identity crisis here."

She plucked another tissue from the box and dabbed her eyes. "It's my fault. I let things get boring. I got . . . complacent. People in my family don't get divorced," she pointed out. "My mother once threw a blender at my father, and they're still together. Chipped his front tooth." Her parents' marriage had always been a tornadic affair, full of screaming and threats, but once they'd expelled it all, the calm after the storm came, when they'd hold each other and whisper soft apologies. But Effie and Daniel had rarely fought. At least not audibly. When she was angry with him for getting home late or for forgetting to pick up one of the kids from school, she punished him with the silent treatment, which he returned in equal measure. It occurred to her now that maybe her parents hadn't been experts in conflict resolution, but at least they were passionate about each other. Somewhere along the way, the passion in her marriage had fizzled.

"You can't honestly think your parents are modeling relationship goals, Effie. There's no A at the end of the test for suffering through it till the bitter end."

"I know," she admitted. "I just always wanted to show the kids how amazing life can be when they find their person, you know? That love isn't just an idea in a song or a movie but a real, tangible thing."

A flicker of understanding crossed his face, and he nodded. "Look, I'm no therapist, but don't you think it's better for your kids to see the two of you happier apart than to see you miserable together?"

"But I wasn't miserable," Effie protested. At least she hadn't thought she'd been. But reflecting on it now, maybe a part of her had wished for more too. Maybe she missed the way Daniel had looked at her when everything was a new adventure. "I loved our life together, until he . . ." She held back tears as Margie's words pricked at her conscience. Did she bear just as much blame for everything that had gone wrong? "I think somewhere along the way . . . I settled. I let it slide when we stopped making time for dates. I put the kids first. I nagged at him for being late all the time and never helping around the house. I wouldn't even let him make love to me." Not in the easy, reckless way she had before she'd been concerned about stretch marks or her deflated chest or the soft folds of her stomach. Deep inside, she knew her body wasn't the source of her insecurities. But no amount of surgery would quiet the nagging sense of worthlessness that had crept in over the years. Maybe she hadn't cheated, but she'd pushed him away. She'd felt undeserving of his touch. And instead of talking to Daniel, she had ignored it, hoping it would go away, that life would go on as usual and she wouldn't have to change anything.

"So maybe you stopped paying him as much attention." He gave an apathetic shrug. "Big freaking deal. He's a grown-up. He didn't have to cheat."

"It doesn't excuse it," Effie said. "I guess I'm just saying I can maybe understand now why he left. He told me things got boring. That Amber was a symptom of the problem but not the reason he left. And he realizes that now." Effie braced for the hailstorm of criticism Cameron was sure to level against her. "The point is, I have half a life invested with him."

An incriminating silence hung between them until Cameron finally groaned.

"You can't look at it like that. So, you made a bad investment. It happens." He shrugged. "Take it from a guy who's had to cut his losses more than a few times. Before my restaurants went gangbusters, I had two others that failed horribly. The important thing is recognizing when it's time to move on."

But Effie didn't want to move on. There was so much good to salvage from their marriage, so much more that had gone right than wrong. Besides, it would be impossible to untangle herself from Daniel, impossible to decipher the exact space where he ended and she began. What's more, how would she ever be able to preserve the millions of memories he had been a part of without coloring them in regret? Pushing the thought away, she shook her head and wiped at the fresh tears that streaked her cheeks.

"Think of it this way." Cameron gesticulated the point with his perfectly manicured hands. "Let's say you buy a car and it doesn't work. You spend countless hours and thousands of dollars trying to fix it, but no matter what you do, it still won't run. At some point, you have to stop wasting your resources on fixing something that can never be fixed. It's a lemon. Effie, you've spent years with a man who didn't appreciate you. Giving him any more of your time would just be illogical. It's basic accounting."

In his usual arrogant way, Cameron was making a lot of sense, but she couldn't reduce two decades of history to a math problem. She pressed her eyelids closed, and a few more tears spilled out. "It's not that simple."

"It is. You're afraid to begin the next chapter of your life because you're terrified to do it without him. And I know you can. You are so much stronger than you give yourself credit for."

"I'm not. I'm afraid all the time." She blinked back tears. "I can't be alone. If I'm not Daniel's wife, then who am I?" With pleading eyes, she looked at him as if he might be able to tell her.

He pursed his lips and cut her a defeated look. "You're my friend. And right now, you're all I've got."

Her face softened as she absorbed the compliment. Against her will, Cameron had weaseled his way into her heart. Still, she couldn't discount everything that had happened over the last week. "But don't I owe it to him to give it another chance?"

"Effie, the only person you owe anything to is yourself." He looked at her in a way that made her heart squeeze, the way she wished her own mother had looked at her when she'd learned about Daniel's affair. "If anyone can start over again, it's you. Yolo!" He threw out his hands.

The reference was entirely lost on her, and she scrunched up her face.

"You only live once," he clarified. "Life is short. Way shorter than I could have predicted. Don't you get it?" A shadow fell over his face, as if he were just now realizing this depressing fact. He looked up at her and asked, "If you could do anything, what would it be? What's your chocolate Pop-Tart, Effie?"

Considering this, she drew a blank. Daniel had been the one to suggest the move from Kansas to Texas. Daniel had wanted to start the business. And when she'd considered going back to school for a degree in design, Daniel had been the one to point out how expensive day care would be and how he really needed someone to handle the paperwork for Baker's Builders. And how taking out a second loan would be a huge risk.

Cameron's shoulders sagged. "Look, if you really want to get back together with Daniel, fine. But do me a favor?" A few beats passed before Effie returned the question with a single nod. "Don't promise him anything until you decide who you are without him."

~

After she firmly explained to Cameron for the hundredth time that she was in no condition to look for Drew, he left in a mood, flickering the lights in her bedroom and setting off the alarm. She'd had to run downstairs in a panic to turn it off, cursing him the entire way there. Now, buried underneath her down comforter, Effie felt the heat of her breath. She could sense Cletus and Oscar waiting outside the door but muffled their whines with a pillow. She wasn't sure what made them hang around when she wasn't sure she wanted to be around herself. She had disappointed Drew, had failed at a marriage she wasn't even sure she wanted anymore, and had lost Teagan somewhere along the way too. It seemed that real living, breathing people wanted nothing to do with her.

Cletus let out a howl, and Effie responded by throwing a pillow at the door. In the process, her elbow grazed the glass of water resting beside Lolly's letter. It tumbled over, cracking the glass in the frame, and water trickled over the sides of the end table. Frantically, she lifted the edges of the frame and shook off the drops, but she could see that moisture had begun to seep through, reaching the border of the paper. Some of the ink began to smudge.

With shaky fingers, she pried open the tabs at the back of the frame, doing her best to free the letter before it was entirely ruined. In her panic, she imagined her inheritance gone, Patsy's precious words evaporating in a matter of seconds. As she lifted the cardboard backing, afraid to reveal the extent of the damage, her eyes caught sight of a familiar script on the back of the wrinkled paper. She recognized the shape of the letters instantly. They rolled into one another in a seamless, graceful pattern. When she had seen it printed in her childhood birthday cards, it had always made her feel so fancy, like a queen receiving royal correspondence. It wasn't Patsy's handwriting. It was Lolly's. Her heart quickened as she read, unable to absorb the words fast enough.

November 5, 1962

Dear Patsy,

I'm not sure how to begin this letter except to say that I am your number one fan and most devoted listener. I've followed you from the very beginning of your career before any of your songs hit the pop charts. These days, hearing your voice on the radio is one of the only things that keeps me going. With that rich, lonesome sound, I suspect you are a woman who knows a thing or two about heartache. But you're so brave, Patsy—baring your soul on that stage night after night in front of all those people. That's why I'm writing to you. I don't think I could write these words anywhere else, not even in my journal, so I'm entrusting them to you. I hope you won't mind.

Earlier this year, I got married. I was in a hurry, and I suppose I got swept away with the idea of finding a great love, the kind that makes every day feel like a new adventure. In the beginning, I thought I loved Wallace, but that was only because I was too naive to know what love was and because he was holding back the worst parts of himself—the parts that make me feel like I'm nothing. I thought that when you love a person, you're supposed to love all the things about them—their hopes and dreams. But Wallace doesn't seem to care about mine. In fact, I think he would prefer it if I didn't have dreams. It's easier that way for him. How is it possible to wake up next to a person every day and still feel as though he never truly sees me? Not the real me anyway.

Last night, I said my prayers and asked the Lord to forgive me for contemplating the worst, but if I stay with him, my soul will disappear little pieces at a time until I don't exist at all. I'll wither and die in this little house full of all the things I thought I wanted—everything except the one thing I can't live without—the freest version of myself, that stubborn wildness in my heart that just won't quiet no matter how deep I try to shove it down. If I follow it, I'll be left with nothing, and I won't have kept my promise to love Wallace forever. The sad truth of it is, I don't think I ever did. Not really. Not in the way you sing about in your songs.

Sometimes, I can't remember choosing any of this at all. In some ways, it feels like it was chosen for me, like I've just been waiting in the wings of my own life, hoping for something to change. Hoping for a miracle so I won't have to do the hard thing. But maybe it's worse to live the kind of life that makes you feel dead on the inside, like nothing you do is worth doing at all. Maybe it's worse to just go on living for someone else's dreams instead of living for your own. The truth is, I don't think I'll ever have that great kind of love you sing about until I make good on the promises I made to myself, the ones I made before the world got its hands on me.

I wish I had a big sister I could ask these kinds of things to, but these days I feel so alone, Patsy. I need someone to tell me what to do. Please help.

Your friend,

Lola

As she digested Lolly's message, one word stood out to her, the name so wrong it tasted sour on her lips. *Wallace.* No matter how many times she rearranged the letters, she couldn't make them make sense. Her grandfather's name was Henry. Tracing a finger over the date, Effie was struck by the image of Lolly and Pop in front of the Kansas City justice of the peace—Lolly wearing a simple sheath dress, a demure smile on her lips, while Pop held her waist from behind. The photo remained indelible in Effie's mind. *September 5th 1965.* Lolly had always said that Patsy was the reason for her idyllic marriage with Pop. But her letter was dated 1962, years before their wedding. Patsy's letter wasn't dated—a fact that had never seemed significant before. But looking back now, Effie realized she'd allowed herself to fill in the gaps, to tell the story as she saw it. How she wanted to see it. Maybe good marriages were in her blood, as Margie had said. But maybe bad marriages were too.

How was she supposed to move forward with Daniel now? Was this a sign from the universe that she was supposed to leave him? End a bad marriage and start over again on her own, as Lolly had done? The thought frightened her, but she couldn't shake the feeling that her grandmother was trying to tell her something.

CHAPTER 43
LOLA

March 6, 1963

Dear Patsy,

I went to bed last night still floating on a cloud, but when I woke up this morning, the whole earth had shifted beneath me. There was a heaviness in the air, and I could feel that something was different. It was Helen who rang first, before I'd even seen the papers. She was crying so hard, she could barely get out the words. She told me about the crash, how they'd sent out searchers to look for survivors. My fingers went lifeless and cold around the telephone, and everything went gray. With tears in my eyes, I looked over at Wallace, but he just shook his head and said, "Hell, Lola. You didn't even know the woman."

I can't expect him to understand what it feels like to lose a person you admire so much. But how am I supposed to imagine a world without your voice in it? How am I supposed to listen to your records without falling to pieces?

I just keep thinking that if one little thing had gone differently, you might still be here. If your manager had chosen to wait a day instead of flying through that storm, if you'd caught a ride back with someone else, maybe you wouldn't be gone. It's amazing how much one little choice can affect the rest of your life. But I suppose that's what life is—a million little choices that could send us in a million different directions, and we'll never know what could have been, so we have to choose carefully today. Because yesterday is gone, and tomorrow is never promised.

You had no way of knowing I was in the audience, but somehow it felt like that last performance was just for me. And now you're gone. It's unfair that while your life has ended, mine feels like it's finally beginning. And it's all because of you, Patsy. Because you showed me what it looks like to be brave. You showed me how to look the world in the eyes and dare to be yourself. You gave me the strength to step into my life, and that's something my own mother never did for me. So, from here on out, whatever choices I make will be the right ones, because they'll be mine, and I will hold you in my heart wherever they take me.

It won't be easy, but luckily, I still have my savings. Lord bless Daddy for having the foresight. I've already spoken to Louisa about staying with her a while until I work things out. It will crush Wallace, and my mother will probably never speak to me again. But I can't put it off any longer. I'd rather be disowned by her than disown my own soul. I think that would be the greatest tragedy of all.

Sincerely,

Lola

CHAPTER 44
Effie / "Today, Tomorrow and Forever"

The evening sun hung low in the sky as Effie made her way toward the swath of green earth ensconced by teetering pines. Gravestones jutted up around her like tiny forgotten temples. Sunlight filtered through the trees, setting their needles aflame in dazzling bursts of gold that shifted as the wind swept through their branches and rustled her hair. It hadn't taken long to deduce where Drew was. Today marked one year since Cameron's accident.

As she inched closer to the slab of gray granite bearing Cameron's name, Effie caught sight of Drew perched at the foot of the grave and tucked her arms around her chest. "Thought maybe I'd find you here," she said softly, planting her feet a safe distance from him.

"I'm assuming Cameron told you where I was," he replied, his blue eyes stubbornly fixed to the words on the stone. CAMERON BRYCE FIELDS. SON. BROTHER. FRIEND. The way he said this only confirmed her assumption. He still thought she was delusional.

He was wearing a ratty Stanford T-shirt and a pair of blue sweatpants, and he'd acquired a five o'clock shadow, a detail that worried her. "Or was that one of your other spirits?" He tossed back a swig from the bottle of whiskey in his hand, another concerning fact. Drew had never seemed like the sort of person to get drunk when the sun was still up.

"You could say that," she said, tossing a glance at Cameron, who flashed a grin. "Speaking of spirits," she said, "I think maybe you should lay off of them too." It felt wrong to reprimand her boss for day drinking. Then again, she still wasn't sure where they'd landed on the whole job front. Though he hadn't actually said the words *You're fired*, considering how he'd spoken to her yesterday, it seemed safe to assume as much.

"Well, I appreciate your concern, but all things considered, I think I kind of deserve this." He raised the bottle toward her in a mock toast. Then his shoulders deflated, and he drew his other hand to the back of his bristly neck. Without meeting her eyes, he asked, "Why are you here, Effie?" He sounded annoyed but firmly blinked as if he were trying to hold back tears. She wanted to hug him, then shake him to his senses.

Why did men always have to put up a concrete front? In nineteen years of marriage, the only time she'd seen Daniel cry was when the Warriors took the Mavericks in the 2007 playoffs. Maybe if they'd both been more honest about their feelings from the very beginning, things could have turned out differently. She knew that Drew would feel better if he just let out some of those pent-up emotions. "I just wanted to say that I'm sorry about your brother," she tried softly, padding closer, still uncertain how to go about consoling her boss. "Do you want to talk about him?"

Drew shook his head, his lips curled in a tight grimace. "I think you grossly misunderstood the job description when I hired you." There was a sharpness to his voice now, and it startled her. He'd been curt before but never cruel. "No offense, but I don't need you to delve into my personal life."

"I deserved that," she admitted, just as uncomfortable as he was that she had come here. Then, gathering her courage, she stole another glance at Cameron, who nodded for her to go on. "Can you just . . . do one thing for me? And then if you don't like what I have to say, I'll leave and you'll never hear from me again."

Drew studied her dubiously, then nodded, resigned.

She inhaled, deep and slow, hoping the words would take on a shape that made sense, and somehow everything came spilling out of her on a river of breath. "OK, this is going to sound ridiculous, but a while back, I nearly died—well, I suppose I did die. But then I came back to life. Maybe. I'm not really sure what happened, but ever since then, a lot of really strange things have been happening. Look, I know it sounds crazy, but Cameron came to me. He told me that you blame yourself for his death, that you feel responsible and that's why he can't move on. He believes that's what's keeping him here. But if you ask me"—she cut Cameron a nervous look—"I think he's just as scared to let you go. I think he wants to see you happy first."

Cameron dropped his gaze to his shoes. To his credit, Drew listened without interrupting or breaking into laughter. Finally, he took another drink and smacked his lips together. "And how do I know you didn't just read the news? How do I know you're not the kind of person who scours the obituary section every morning looking for gullible folks to scam by feeding them a bunch of crap about their dead family members?"

A tired smile graced her lips. "He said you would say that. He also said you took his keys away from him the night of the accident. Because you were a good brother," she said, more seriously now. "But he followed you inside the restaurant and dug them out of your coat pocket when you weren't looking."

Maybe the words had managed to pierce his foul mood, because he pulled his eyebrows together as if he were remembering. Then, lowering his drink, he hung his head. "Look, Effie, for what it's worth, I don't think you're crazy," he said, his voice a little kinder now. "Maybe you really do think you can see him. I believe that *you* believe you can. But it doesn't make it real."

Cameron swung his gaze from Effie to Drew, and a flicker of anguish crossed his face. "Tell him about the fishing trip," he urged.

Conjuring their conversation from a few weeks ago, Effie did her best to recount the story just as Cameron had told it. "He wants me to remind you about the fishing trip. You were in high school and had just gotten your license. Your dad asked you to run some errands, but you took Cameron out to the lake instead. And he got finned. You wrapped up his hand, told him it would be a secret between the two of you. And your parents never found out. You told them it was a dog bite, and they believed you."

By now, Drew was staring past her as if he'd just seen a ghost. Remembering Marty at the grocery store, Effie studied his chest for signs of a cardiac event, but he seemed to be breathing just fine. For a long while, he said nothing. Finally, his lips cracked into a broken smile. His eyes filmed over, and he sniffed hard, then smeared his hand quickly across his cheek.

Cameron's lips turned down at the corners. Seeing his brother in pain was clearly weighing on him, and now Effie was having trouble keeping her own emotions from spilling over. She forced a watery smile and zeroed in on Drew, wishing she could force the words to take root in his heart. "It's not your fault. He knows that you cared about him. He knows that you love him, and he wants you to be happy. But now it's time to let him go."

"I did let him go." Though his voice quivered, Drew's response came fast and hard. "But I can't forgive him. So don't ask me to." It wasn't a request.

Was that what this was about? Of course Drew would feel abandoned and angry at his baby brother for leaving him too soon. She should have intuited this. Effie inched closer to him, hoping to chisel away at some of his resentment. "If it changes anything, you should know that he feels awful about what happened. He made a terrible mistake, and it cost him his life. Isn't that punishment enough?"

"Is that what he told you?" Drew's blue eyes had turned to steel, his tone clipped. "Did he tell you he wasn't the only one whose life he could have ended? Did he tell you who else was in the car with him that night?"

Taken aback, Effie considered this new set of facts. True, Cameron was a bit aloof and self-absorbed, but had his recklessness put someone else's life at risk? One look at Cameron's face was all it took to confirm the worst.

"Samuel." Drew provided the answer before she could guess, so angry his voice trembled. "My son."

Suddenly, Effie understood exactly why Drew hadn't wanted to talk about his brother. Remembering the family photo in his office, she clutched a hand to her stomach. *Oh Cameron, you didn't.* If Cameron had harmed anyone else in the accident, especially Drew's son, she wasn't sure she could blame Drew for resenting him. If anyone hurt her children, even unintentionally, she would tear them apart.

"Our mother was getting remarried," Drew explained, seeming far away now. "Hank was a lot younger than her, and Cameron and I both knew he was only after her for the huge chunk of change our dad left her—the house in the Keys, the stocks and bonds. As the oldest, I was always the coolheaded one. I told Cameron Mom would come around eventually when she saw Hank for what he was. But Cameron always shot from the hip." Dropping his head, Drew let out something between a chuckle and a scoff. Then his eyes glassed over, and he set his jaw. "That night at the rehearsal dinner, he called the groom out in a drunken toast, pretty much threatened to kill him if he ever tried to take Mom's money. The whole time, Samuel was tugging on my sports coat, complaining about how much he wanted to go home, how he was tired of being around a bunch of adults. He was the only kid there, so I couldn't blame him for being bored. Somewhere around the death-threat part of Cam's speech, I gave him my keys and told him to go wait for me in the car and I'd be there just as soon as I said my goodbyes. I guess it was around then I caught Cameron on his way out, stumbling into the parking lot. I thought I was doing the best thing for him by taking his keys. Then I went back inside and hung my jacket on the back of my chair." Dropping his gaze to his feet, his face muscles contracted in a pained sort of grimace. "I lost track of time.

Stayed longer than I'd intended. That was my mistake. And I have to live with it every day."

As the missing pieces of the story filled in, Effie felt her heart clench. Remembering Cameron's need to outdo his brother with a twin BMW, Effie finished his sentence. "And instead of his own car, he got in yours by mistake," she said, casting a disappointed look back at Cameron. His normally electric eyes had gone lifeless.

"The car shouldn't have even started," Cameron protested helplessly. "But Samuel had the keys on him, and it's a remote start. You have to believe me when I say I didn't know he was in the car." His usual can-do attitude had vanished, his perfect face entirely broken. He was practically shouting at Drew, who couldn't hear any of the desperation in his voice. "Samuel was asleep, slumped over in the back seat. As soon as I saw him, I turned back for the restaurant, but I cut the corner too wide, and the tree seemed to come from nowhere," he explained, looking more pathetic than she'd ever seen him. She wanted to reach out and hug the both of them.

"What happened to Samuel?" Effie asked, not sure which brother she was addressing. Her breath hitched as she pictured Brody. What would she do if something like this had happened to him? She wasn't sure she would ever recover.

"He's OK," Drew answered. "Thankfully. Though not without a lot of physical therapy, not to mention counseling," he added. "He broke his clavicle and two ribs. It was six months before he could raise his arm above his shoulder. Missed an entire season of baseball. And all because my stupid brother couldn't see past his vices." For the first time today, Drew met her eyes and held them. They were full of pain. "Tell me how I'm supposed to forgive him, Effie?" he asked, almost pleading now. "How do you forgive a person you loved when they let you down in the worst way possible?"

Reflecting on the past year, Effie bit her lip. She didn't know the answer to that question. But since Cameron had come into her life, she'd learned a few things about herself—mostly that she was strong enough to do hard things. If that was true, just maybe she was strong enough to do the hardest thing of all. And if she could do it, maybe Drew could too. "It won't be easy," she finally said. "But the only way forward is to face the pain head on. You have to forgive him, Drew. And yourself. If Cameron were here right now, what would you tell him?" she asked, hoping she wasn't making things worse.

Drew cast his eyes around the graveyard as if searching for proof. "Can you, uh . . . can you see him now?" he asked. She still couldn't tell if he believed her or not.

Effie checked behind her once more to be sure, and as ridiculous as it felt to admit this preposterous fact, she nodded.

Drew pulled in a deep breath and released it slowly. "I'd tell him I was so tired of cleaning up his messes, of always having to be the adult in the room, of bailing him out of his failed business ventures because he was too impulsive to think past the woman he was currently sleeping with. I'd tell him he was stupid and irresponsible and way too self-absorbed. Most of all, I'd tell him . . ." His spine seemed to go slack. "I'd tell him that despite all those things, I miss him. And I wish more than anything that I could have been a better brother to him. Maybe if I had been, he'd still be here. I'd tell him I wish I could do some things over again. I'd do them differently."

As someone who understood that sentiment, Effie wanted to reach out and wrap her arms around his sinking shoulders.

"He *was* there for me," Cameron protested. "Just like he's there for his son. I see the way he is with Samuel, the way he looks at him like he's the only kid in the world. It's the same way he used to look at me." Cameron sniffled. "I'll never forget that." He looked to Effie, pleading. "Can you tell him that?"

Blinking back tears, Effie relayed the message, and Drew's eyes softened. There was a shift in the air between them, and though she wasn't certain if he believed her yet, he was looking at her in a way that made her think he just might respect her again.

~

Evening had descended in earnest now, and the shadows of the trees lengthened across the graves. Effie's skin prickled with goose bumps as a cool wind wafted over her. A few minutes passed in silence, and she was beginning to wonder if she should change the subject to something lighter, but she was at a loss for suitable topics. Finally, Drew moved toward the headstone, then raised the bottle and set it gingerly atop Cameron's name.

When he spoke again, it was more to himself than to her. "You know, after he died, everyone was so accommodating. People I'd never even met were bringing over casseroles and loaves of bread. For weeks. But when they looked at me, it was always with this pity in their eyes, like they felt sorry for me. And I knew it wasn't because my brother had died but because of the way he died. And then, after a while, the visits stopped altogether, and people didn't ask about him anymore. It made them uncomfortable. It was like it was . . . easier for them to just forget." He looked to Effie now, his red eyes searching hers. "You were the first person in months who asked me to talk about him. Besides my mother, who wants to talk about him all the time." Resting a hand on the stone, he looked back at her, his eyes softer now. "I don't know how you do it, but you're kind of good at that," he said.

"Good at what?"

"At getting people to open up to you. There's . . . an energy about you that's calming. That sounded weird," he said, dropping his head.

"No, it didn't," she protested. She was taken aback by the compliment but not willing to let it slip away.

"I guess what I'm trying to say is," Drew went on, seeming flustered, "I like having you around, Effie. I hope you'll still work for me even after . . . all of this. I'm sorry for blowing up at you earlier."

The admission caused a lump to form in the back of her throat, but she refused to let herself cry. After everything, she wasn't going to be fired from the first real job she'd had in nearly two decades, and the realization of this fact was enough to bowl her over. But maybe it didn't really matter. If she was being honest, she'd taken the job more for Daniel than herself. She'd wanted to prove to him that she was capable, that she didn't need him to make a life. But maybe somewhere along the way she'd been fooled into believing that the mark of a good life was something she had to prove at all. *See, I baked two hundred cupcakes for the auction, made a vegan pizza for my kid, and still had time to sew merit badges, all before Daniel came home from work. I'm worthy too.* She'd been so generous with her time and talents that she hadn't thought to save anything for herself. When she died, her legacy would be that she was a good mother, a decent daughter, and a loyal wife. But all those roles existed in relation to others. Who was *she*, really? Underneath the driving and the cooking and the scheduling and the worrying. She'd stayed so busy that she never had to ask herself the question: What do I need?

Filled with a new courage, she said, "No offense, Drew, but I have to quit." She wasn't normally the sort of person to add insult to injury, but in the spirit of truth-telling, she might as well begin with herself.

Drew seemed taken aback, then gave a subtle nod. "Well, I can't say I blame you," he said, raking a hand through his disheveled hair. "Although I am beginning to wonder what it says about me that I can't seem to keep an assistant any longer than a romantic relationship these days."

"It's not you," she said, and she meant it. She'd taken the job because she was desperate, not because she'd wanted it. "I can't be the notetaker in the room anymore, the person responsible for keeping up with everyone else's dreams. I have to follow my own. Or at least figure out what they are."

"I get that," he said, though he seemed surprised. Honestly, so was she. "You, uh . . . decide on what you're going to do yet?"

"Maybe," she said, casting a glance back at Cameron, an idea brewing at the edges of her mind. "I think I have an . . . unusual skill set that has the potential to help a lot of people." She didn't know what the rest of her life was going to look like, but if Cameron had taught her anything, it was that time was short. Cameron smiled and winked, sending a rush of confidence through her veins.

"Well, whatever it is, I think you'll be amazing," Drew said, meeting her eyes and holding them.

A wave of heat crept up the back of her neck, but she reminded herself that she was here for Cameron. "I know you miss him. You always will. But it's OK to be happy. It's what Cameron wants for you."

"And how do I do that?" he asked, looking at her as if he truly had no idea. "Just pretend like he never existed? Because it's too hard to think about him without falling apart."

"I get it. Believe me, I do," Effie said, feeling braver. "You think you can't hold on to the good times without getting lost in all the pain, but you can. Maybe not yet, but you will. Don't you see?" she said. "That's what life is. It's the happy moments mixed in with the sad. It's knowing that every second we have here is fleeting, but that's what makes it so precious. Your time with Cameron isn't wasted. It's not some bottled-up thing that you can never take out again because you're worried it will spoil. You'll have him in your life for as long as you make space for him." The words felt like they were coming from someone else. Someone wiser.

Daniel's face fluttered into her thoughts, but she blinked the image away, still unsure.

"So, what comes next for him?" Drew sniffed again, then bravely met her gaze. "What's after all of . . . this?" He waved a hand around in the space between them. The sun had already disappeared behind the trees, and from somewhere beyond the graveyard, a whip-poor-will trilled out its evening song.

"To be honest, I don't have a clue," she admitted. "But I'm not so sure it matters all that much. Maybe the point of all of this is to just . . . recognize heaven right now. Find the beauty in the people we care about, and tell them how much they mean to us while we still have the time." Maybe she needed to hear those words just as much as Drew did.

"You might be on to something," Drew admitted finally, dragging a hand down his cheekbone and tugging down the red sacks beneath his bloodshot eyes. He pursed his lips. "I guess this means I need to hire a new assistant. Again."

As she tried to formulate a witty response, a warm breeze wafted between them, sending a shiver through her limbs. And before she turned back, she knew what she would find. Even so, she waited a few seconds to confirm the truth, because she wasn't ready to let him go just yet either. A stillness settled over them, tranquil and full of unspoken love. She could feel it in the air all around her. She squeezed her eyes closed to hold in the tears, and when she finally dared to open them again, Cameron was gone.

CHAPTER 45

LOLA

July 6, 1963

Dear Patsy,

I suppose it's probably time I stop addressing these to you as you've been gone now for a while. But it's hard to let you go. I still listen to your records every day, though I admit I tear up every time I do. Three months ago, I packed my things and left Wallace a note telling him that I don't want anything from him anymore, just myself. All things considered, it seems more than fair. I knew I was doing the right thing because losing you hurt worse than leaving him, and I never even met you. What does that say about a marriage? For the time being, I've moved in with Louisa and her husband, just until I figure things out. But it's good because it means we can practice more.

As I suspected, my mother won't talk to me yet, but Daddy calls every now and then to see that I'm doing all right. Wallace keeps phoning and driving by Louisa's house. Sometimes he begs and cries for me to come back. Other times he calls me names and threat-ens to smash the Gibson. Looking back, it's easier to see that my life with him was just a record scratch, a mistake that taught me a few things about myself— mostly that I'm stronger than I ever thought I was. In fact, I think if this new version of myself had met the old me, she wouldn't even recognize her. It's hard, but I'm doing my best to put one foot in front of the other, even though I have no idea where I'm headed yet. I guess there's no easy way to start your life over. The only thing I know for sure is that I don't want to waste any more time on things that don't set my soul on fire. I'm tired of living small. I'm going places, Patsy. And if I can become half the woman you were, it will be enough for me. I hope I don't disappoint you. Thanks for everything, hoss.

Sincerely,

Lola

P.S. I almost forgot to mention that a few weeks ago, I ran into a fellow stocking cans at the grocery store. I asked him where they kept the deviled ham, and he said, "In the same place we keep all the satanic foods—near the angel food cake so it might be con-verted." I laughed, and when I did, I realized it had been so long since I'd done it that I almost forgot the sound of my own voice. I started timing my weekly grocery trip to when I knew he would be there. Even now, every time I see him, I get these little flutter bugs in my stomach, and I worry I'll forget to breathe. Henry is smart and kind and funny. He's the kind of man I wish I had married. Last week, we went on our first date, and he told me something that nearly bowled me over. He said, "Lola, the first time I saw you was at a dance two years ago, and you were wearing the most god-awful sleeves. You looked like you were going to fly away in those things." He told me he wanted to ask me to dance, but he could see I was with someone else, and he didn't have the guts to go up to me. Imagine that! I told him I was glad he finally worked up the courage as that was something I was working on myself. We're going out again next Friday.

CHAPTER 46
EFFIE / "YOUR CHEATIN' HEART"

Morning rays filtered through the kitchen windows, illuminating the slivers of blonde in Teagan's sandy hair. When she was little, it had always lightened a couple of shades over the summer, continuously bathed in sunlight from their outdoor adventures—afternoon swims and zoo trips and discovery hikes in the woods. But these days it was closer to Effie's toffee color. After Effie's talk with Drew yesterday, Teagan had called in tears, asking Effie to pick her up from Daniel's house. It was the cherry on top of an already emotionally exhausting day, but Effie had practically flown to get her, sailing through yellow lights as if her life depended on it. Though it pained her to admit it, a part of her felt vindicated. For the first time in months, Teagan had reached out, had begun to thaw the ice that separated them, and Effie hoped this was just the beginning.

Stooped over the table nursing a mug of coffee, she saw her daughter through a filter—that feisty little girl who'd once had dreams of becoming a part-time dog groomer / part-time news anchor / part-time waitress, because why shouldn't she be able to do exactly as her unfettered heart desired? In her young mind, there were no limits. Only possibilities. Effie had always done everything in her power to support her kids. It wasn't lost on her that she was a walking contradiction—demanding all the best things for her children, pushing for them to follow their dreams, when she'd let her own fall by the wayside. She missed those days when Teagan had talked her ear off about the magical future she envisioned, in part because she'd lost that ability to imagine the impossible for herself. But since Effie had picked her up from Daniel's last night, Teagan had hardly uttered a word.

"You sure you don't want to talk about it?" Effie asked again.

"I'm sure." Teagan sounded dejected, and it concerned Effie more than the lying or the talking back or the angry quips. She just nibbled her avocado toast, scrolling through her phone like a zombie.

"Is it Lolly?" she tried. "It's OK to be upset, honey."

"No, Mom, for the millionth time. I'm OK. Really."

Effie steeled herself for a backlash, but she couldn't let the moment pass without speaking her mind. "I know things have been . . . hard lately. But I want you to know I'm here for you if you need to talk. Did something happen at your dad's?" She studied Teagan's face for a clue, but all she got was an eye roll.

"No. Just . . . it's nothing," she muttered.

"Obviously it's something," Effie pushed gently. "I'm trying to understand you, Teagan, but you're making it really difficult." Mindful of her escalating tone, she gripped her mug a little tighter and pulled in a slow breath. "Whatever it is, you can talk to me."

"Not about this, Mom."

"Of course you can," Effie said. "There's nothing you could say that will shock me. I know it's hard to believe, but I was a teenager once too."

"It's not that." She pushed away her plate and chewed her bottom lip. Tears gathered in the corners of her eyes, and her voice trembled when she finally spoke, so softly that Effie wasn't sure she'd heard correctly. "I heard him last night."

"Heard who?"

"Dad," she said, her voice tinged with emotion. "He was upstairs talking on the phone with someone . . . a woman." She hunched forward and wrapped her arms around herself, making her look so much smaller. "And it wasn't Amber."

Something dark pierced the walls of Effie's heart. Her eyes danced around in search of an explanation, but in her bones, she knew there was only one. "Well . . . maybe it was . . . a client," she pointed out. "Or a potential investor. It could have been anyone, honey." Even now, after everything Daniel had put them through, she felt an inexplicable need to protect him, to keep their kids from seeing all the worst parts of their father. But she knew she wasn't being convincing.

"It wasn't, Mom."

Effie's heart dropped, taking her smile with it. "He was right," she said under her breath, shaking her head as Cameron's smile floated into her thoughts. If this was the second woman, Effie knew without a doubt there had been a third, maybe a fourth. Damn him. Was this what Daniel had meant when he asked her to try again? Of course. He'd meant that *she* should try again, that somehow she was the source of the problem, the thing that needed to change for him to want to stay.

Heat gathered in Effie's cheeks, her eyes burning from the effort of holding back tears. But she wouldn't let Teagan see her cry. Right now, she had to be the strong one. She had to show her that Daniel couldn't hurt this family any more than he already had. "I'm so sorry." Leaning in, she placed a hand gently on her back, hating that she couldn't absorb her daughter's pain.

Teagan's shoulders heaved through the sobs, and she struggled to catch her breath.

Seeing her daughter fall apart was worse than anything Daniel had done to Effie, and she silently cursed him for destroying their daughter's heroic image of him. "I'm sorry he disappointed you. I wish we could have made each other happy. I wish . . . things had happened differently. I wanted so badly to make it work for you kids."

"I'm glad you didn't."

A confusing mix of shock and relief tumbled around inside Effie's head. "You are?"

Tucking her bangs behind her ear, Teagan gave a single nod. "I always knew you deserved better. We all did. I mean, I love Dad, but he was never here like you were. When he's with us, I can tell he doesn't really want to be, that he's doing it because he has to. He isn't the one who spent all those hours with me at the museum just because I needed to see the giant turtle skeleton." She smeared the back of a hand across her cheek and sniffed.

"You said it was so big because it ate all the other turtles," Effie teased, drawing a guarded smile from her daughter. A realization entered her mind, so obvious that it nearly stopped her breath. How had she missed it? Saving the museum wasn't just about saving a piece of history. It was about saving a piece of her childhood. It had been Teagan's way of surviving the divorce.

"Honey, I'm sorry I didn't listen to you before. But from now on, whatever lights you up is what lights me up too. I wish I were more like Harper's mom, but I've never been very good at stepping outside myself to make a difference. Not like you do." She traced a finger across Teagan's cheek.

"Why do you always do that?"

"Do what?"

"Act like you aren't enough." Reluctantly, Teagan reached for her sketchbook, flipped it open, then slid it toward her. It was a penciled portrait of the two of them, drawn from a family photo of their time at the beach one summer, Effie wrapping her arms around a pudgy swimsuit-clad toddler, all soft edges and ruddy cheeks. Somehow, Teagan had managed to capture the devotion in her eyes, how her gaze was fixed squarely on her daughter's. It was obvious she was a woman in love with her child. A tear carved its way down her cheek as the image seared itself into her heart.

Teagan fixed her red-rimmed eyes on Effie's. "You're the one I look up to, Mom. The person I always wanted to be. But when Dad left, it was like you just . . . stopped living. I could tell you were waiting for him to come back. And then you went and got surgery for him."

Shame filtered through her. Teagan had picked up on so much. Somehow, she had missed the moment when her daughter had suddenly grown wiser than her.

"To see you just . . . give up on yourself," Teagan went on. "It hurt worse than Dad leaving."

A sharp twinge of regret swept through her. All that time she'd spent worrying that she wouldn't be enough for the kids, when all along she'd been everything to them. The heaviness of this realization was almost enough to undo her entirely, but she managed to keep her chin steady.

"I wish I could go back and do some things differently. But I promise"—locking in on her daughter's eyes, she drew in a long breath, feeling more determined than ever to do the hard things—"I will never give up on myself again. From now on, I'm going to be brave like you."

CHAPTER 47

EFFIE / "I'LL SAIL MY SHIP ALONE"

One Week Later

It was a strange thing to see a person hollowed out of all the things that made them distinctly them. By all accounts, it was Lolly resting inside the smooth mahogany box—her soft jawline petrified into stone, her gnarled knuckles interlocked peacefully atop her chest. Yet Effie knew with an unyielding certainty that Lolly was not here. Leaning in closer, she whispered, "Say hello to Patsy for me." Effie drew two shaky fingers to her lips and kissed the tips, then pressed them gently to Lolly's forehead. "And tell her I'm working on it." Picturing Patsy in her flowing dress with outstretched arms, Effie's mind drifted again to her words. *Not yet, hoss. You need more time to set things right.* She finally knew how to do that. Or at least how to start. It would be difficult and it was going to break her heart all over again, but it was the only path forward.

Brody wrapped his arms around her waist, catching her off guard. She buried her nose into his soft curls, and a wave of nostalgia threatened to set off her tears again. When had her babies grown up? When had they stopped reaching for her hand and following her around all day as if she were a celebrity, the center of their tiny worlds? Back then, she would have given anything for a break from her life. But now she wished she had frozen time.

Resting a hand on her shoulder, Jay gave her a pained smile. "Love you, Mom." He was wearing an old gray suit of Daniel's, one he wouldn't have filled out a year ago, and seemed more grown up than ever. She clasped a hand over his. "Love you, too, sweetie." On either side of her, Brody and Teagan laced their arms through hers, and together they walked solemnly from the chapel into a future Effie hadn't fully imagined yet. But it was there, waiting for all of them. And it was going to be scary and messy and amazing. But it would be worth it. Because this time, it was hers to choose.

~

The women of Lolly's church provided a feast of epic proportions. In the spacious fellowship hall, long white tables were generously filled with rotisserie chicken, green bean casseroles, fingerling potatoes, and scores of pies in every flavor imaginable. An army of volunteers wearing black aprons darted about the room, generously seeing to the needs of those in attendance. Settling herself at a round table across from the kids and next to Grace, Effie ironed out her napkin and looked up just in time to see Daniel slip inside the double doors. Drawing a hand to her updo, she pretended not to see him. But moments later, Margie hovered behind her, placing a stern hand atop her shoulder. "You must have done something right," she whispered, demurely shielding her words with the back of her hand. "Look who came."

Effie's mouth went dry, and she quickly chugged her glass of water. Her gaze flitted to Daniel again, who seemed to be scouring the room with no luck. "It's a funeral, Mama. This is not the time."

"Well, the man didn't come for Lolly. He came for you." Margie pressed her other hand into the small of Effie's back. "Go and talk to him!"

After her mother walked away, Grace elbowed Effie in the side. "Don't you dare," she whispered, her voice full of warning. Unsurprisingly, she had been a fierce advocate for the divorce when Effie had finally told her about their almost reconciliation and Daniel's new escapades. She'd even booked a ticket to Lolly's funeral before Effie had, worried that Margie would try to sway her. "He's lucky you're not suing him for emotional damages and taking him for everything he's worth."

From across the table, Teagan offered an encouraging nod, her lips tucked into a tepid smile. It was all Effie needed to steel herself for the next part. Placing her napkin down on the table, she pushed back her chair and headed in his direction.

"Effie." Daniel's stubbled face broke into a relieved smile when he saw her approaching. "How you holding up?" He moved to kiss her on the lips, but she tilted her head just out of reach, and he caught her cheek instead. This threw him off balance, but he covered with something that sounded like a cough.

"All right. The kids have been great," she admitted, wrapping her arms around herself. "Thanks for letting me have them this weekend."

"Of course. Lolly would have wanted them here." Sliding a hand through his hair, he cleared his throat. "Listen, Eff . . . I was hoping to catch you alone. I meant what I said the other night . . . about giving us another chance."

"Bullshit."

"What?"

"I'm calling you on your bullshit, Daniel," she said, more firmly this time. Grace was right. It felt good to curse when the situation called for it, like something wild in her had finally been set free. "You don't want to get back together any more than I do."

The cursing seemed to startle him, and confusion rippled across his face. "That's not true, Eff. I see how much you mean to me now. I'm sorry it took me so long to realize that. I don't know how I ever forgot. So, thank you . . . for not giving up on me. For making me realize what I was missing."

Heaving a sigh, she squeezed her eyelids shut. "The thing is, I shouldn't have to convince you. You should just . . . love me. For everything I am right now. Not for who I was or who you want me to be." She mined her memories, drifting back to happier times. "Daniel, do you remember when you took that photo of me on the beach in Galveston? The yellow bikini one?"

He nodded, though she wasn't sure if he had a clue what she was talking about.

"Every time I looked at that picture, I could see how in love with me you were. I know that sounds crazy, but I could. I've been thinking, when is the last time you took a picture of me? When's the last time you saw me that way, like I was worthy of remembering?" Her mind flickered to the photo Drew had taken of her, and something twisted inside her heart. "Sometimes I feel . . . like a ghost."

Daniel's gaze drifted behind her, his shoulders sagging. "I do love you, Eff."

"Daniel, stop gaslighting me," she snapped. "I can't do this. It's not like Amber just happened. It's not like she just *fell* into bed with you. You posted a profile on a singles site, for God's sake." Heart racing, she closed her eyes and steadied her breath, but her chest still trembled. "For nineteen years, I chose us. Every day. But the second things got boring for you, you just gave up. And I think I've finally realized that I deserve better. I deserve someone who's going to choose me every time. Even when it's hard. Even when things are boring." She closed her eyes for a beat. "I'm done trying to make this marriage work on my own."

This appeared to take him by surprise, because he stared back at her as if she'd just spoken in gibberish. And it was then that an infuriating realization itched at the back of her mind. Had he believed she would take him back? When things inevitably fell apart with Amber, had he just assumed he could come sauntering back into her life as if nothing had happened? Judging from his reaction, she realized that he had never expected her to reject him. But this little bit of power she now had was intoxicating, and she wielded it proudly.

"We're done," she said, her eyes penetrating. "I'll sign the papers after a few modifications have been made, of course. My lawyer will forward them over to yours."

"Effie, think about what you're saying," he pleaded.

"I know what I'm saying." A few months ago, she would have been as shocked as he was to hear herself. She'd been certain she would cease to exist without him, the boy in the lavender tie on her porch, with that contagious grin. But maybe that was only because she'd never allowed herself to imagine a life of her own, because she was afraid. Now that she'd glimpsed the other side, she realized she could still breathe, still move, still do hard things without Daniel propping her up.

Patsy's words bolstered her, and Effie imagined her—wherever she was—smiling and giving a nod of solidarity.

"I think . . . I think a part of me will always love us together. But that picture I keep trying to hold in my head is just a memory. You say you've changed, but I have too. And I can't go back to the way things were because I don't think I was happy either."

His face fell, his focus drifting to the floor as if searching for something to grasp on to. "Then let's start again." He looked up at her, desperate. "A clean slate. And I promise that things will be different this time."

"Oh Daniel. Honey, I hate to tell you this, but . . ." She struggled to pin down the correct thought until, all at once, it came to her perfectly formed. "You're a lemon."

Daniel looked pained, but Effie's voice didn't waver. "And I've got too much to do in my life to waste another minute trying to fix you. I can't make you happy. I tried. And now I owe it to myself to choose me." Cameron would be so proud.

Daniel's shoulders sagged under the weight of her words, until finally he gave a slow nod. "I uh . . . I understand." He cleared his throat. "I'll keep taking care of you all. I'll pay your fair share of the business." The fight in his voice had dissipated.

"I don't want you to buy me out anymore," Effie said, evenly. She'd prepared for this and took another beat to ensure she was not misunderstood. Filling her chest up, she straightened her shoulders. "I want a share in the company. My parents gave you the seed money for it, and I worked right alongside you all those years, helping you build it. It's just as much mine as it is yours."

"Now, hang on a second there, Eff. Let's be reasonable here—"

"I'll fight you on it, Daniel," she shot back. "And I'll win. So, I'm asking you to do what's right here. Half and half. I've got an eye for the remodeling side of things, and you know it. You always took my advice, and the customers loved you for it. All I'm asking is to do what I always did but actually get credit for it."

"How exactly is that fair? I put my blood, sweat, and tears into this business, worked right alongside the guys. I'm the one who brings in new clients."

Holding up a finger, she narrowed her eyes to slits. "Let me refresh your memory. Free childcare for seventeen years. Dinners. Transportation." She punctuated each service by counting it off with another finger. "I'm the one who pushed you to take a chance on Lakeside Landing. I've never had much of a head for numbers, but I'd estimate that I've saved you somewhere around a million dollars. Give or take. Would you like to pay that out in installments or just give me what I'm asking for?"

A telling silence hung between them, and she stared him down, satisfied. For the first time, she had delivered the words exactly as she'd practiced them in her mind—confident and unflinching.

Finally, he spoke. "All right," he grunted, his shoulders bristling.

"And I've got some ideas for how to bring in new business," she added, folding her arms across her chest, each word bolstered by the last. "I'm working on a few things of my own."

He cocked an eyebrow.

"I've been going over the numbers, and I don't think we're holding down our share of the market like we used to. We need to offer some holiday incentives to drum up interest. Get some fresh commercials out there, and new graphics. Don't worry," she said, sensing his concern. "I'll send over my notes."

"And how exactly do you know so much about business all of a sudden?"

"I know a lot more than you think, Daniel. You just never thought to ask," she said. "And I'm not stopping there. I've got a lot more plans."

"Which would be?" he asked dubiously.

Confidence pooled in her chest, giving way to a wistful smile. "I don't know yet. I still have time to figure it out."

EPILOGUE
Effie / "I'm Moving Along"

September 2024

The early morning darkness slowly drained away as the sun peeked out from behind the stretch of roofs and soft blue siding of Bright Horizons Construction and Renovation. The charming new office was nestled between a doughnut shop and a yoga studio. As she strode toward the entrance, Effie slowed her pace, plunging a hand into her slacks and jingling her keys. She loved this sliver of time between the night's shadows and the sun's first rays. Maybe it was the stillness of the street slowly being replaced by lulling engines and shuffling feet, the smell of coffee colliding with the heavenly scent of fresh scones from next door. More likely, it was because this was when it was easiest to imagine the living existing alongside the dead, past and present flowing together, both inescapable. Both equally exquisite.

Before that fateful day at Rosehaven, she had thought that her forties would just be the start of novel inconveniences—colonoscopies, weak knees, gray hairs, and mammograms. Starting her life over entirely and doing it alongside a cast of dead people had decidedly not been on that list.

As she opened the door and took stock of her corner desk, a shallow breath hitched in her chest. Lolly's face ebbed in her memory. Despite how often she'd wished for it, she'd never seen her grandmother's spirit, which she supposed was a good thing. It meant that Lolly had lived her life to the fullest, left nothing unwritten, no song unsung. And for Effie, at least, life after Lolly's death was filled with a greater sense of purpose, a stronger sense of urgency to do the things that made a difference instead of waiting for the next thing to happen to her. What's more, she was now confident that when it *was* finally her time to go, Lolly would be the one to sing her home.

Lolly was the reason Effie had been brave enough to suggest a new name and location for the office, someplace neutral where she and Daniel could grow the family business, which was just as much hers as it was his. Most days, her ex-husband oversaw a crew. The office was her domain, so she could focus on bringing in new clientele.

Clutching her tote bag, she shuffled to her desk, throwing a nod and a "Good morning" to Melissa, who smiled and handed her a piping hot cup of fresh coffee. Effie brightened at the sight of her assistant, with her stout stature, short brown hair, and eager eyes. Melissa was a member of Effie's book club and had gone through a divorce last year. Effie had agreed to let her work mornings so she could take classes before her kids got home from school. But Effie had gotten the better end of the deal. She would never regret hiring an assistant who firmly believed in carbs and strong mocha lattes.

Sipping her drink, Effie lit a jasmine-scented candle, then settled behind her desk, where pictures of the kids were sprinkled about—Jay in his maroon-and-white A&M jersey, posing with the new team; Brody in his soccer uniform; Teagan beaming in her feathered band hat, holding her trumpet, flanked by Effie and Daniel lacing their arms through her knobby elbows. Luckily, the woman Daniel had been dating at the time didn't make it into the picture. After Amber, he hadn't managed a relationship longer than the expiration date on a gallon of milk, but that was no longer Effie's concern. Daniel was a good father, and that was all she needed him to be.

"Any news on those tiles we ordered for the Rivas' kitchen remodel?" she asked Melissa. "We've got a crew scheduled to be there tomorrow. And if we don't start on time, we'll have to push the Khans' bathroom to October."

"On it," Melissa said, producing a notepad. "I've already contacted the supplier, and they're putting a rush on it. The tiles will be here in three days."

"Perfect." An inflated housing market and high interest rates meant more people were renovating in lieu of moving or building. At Effie's suggestion, the company had pivoted, and it was paying off. If business kept flowing at this rate, she might have to start turning down potential projects.

Melissa chimed in, "Oh, and you've got a consult for a remodel at four p.m. today." Pressing her palms atop Effie's desk, Melissa leaned over and waggled her eyebrows. "The guy specifically asked for you."

"Did you get a name?" Effie asked, her curiosity piqued.

"Just a minute. I wrote it down with the address." Melissa returned a moment later with a sticky pad, then ripped off a page and handed it to Effie. "But he would only give his first name, so hopefully it isn't a stalker situation or anything," she teased. "Want me to go with you for backup?"

"No, that's OK," Effie said, a hopeful warmth saturating her chest as she read the name. *Cameron.* She drew a hand to her lips as tears pricked her eyes. For the briefest moment, hope blossomed in her chest. She knew it was ridiculous to think he would come back one last time just to see her, but Lord knew stranger things had happened.

～

Effie rarely ventured uptown. This high-rise condominium boasted a massive infinity pool atop the roof, while the pretentious lobby had both a gourmet coffee shop and a bakery. When she'd visited the restroom, she'd seen a full-size velvet sofa in the sitting area and soft white towels in lieu of paper napkins. As she entered the glass elevator, clutching her purse, she had no trouble envisioning Cameron living here. Upon reaching the mahogany door of his unit, she took a deep breath and knocked, trying to manage her expectations. When Drew appeared wearing jeans, a Rangers T-shirt, and a baseball cap, Effie released a suspended breath, and her chest deflated.

Drew must have caught a hint of disappointment in her reaction because he flashed her an apologetic grimace. "Sorry to have gotten your hopes up. But I wasn't sure if you'd come if I left my name. Didn't know if you'd forgiven me yet for the whole firing-you thing."

"You didn't fire me. I quit. Remember?" she replied, trying to place this new version of her ex-boss. It was like seeing a zoo animal in the wild. But she couldn't deny that he looked good, happier than she remembered.

He pursed his lips as if he were holding something back, then dropped his head. "Effie, I mean this in the kindest way possible, but you really suck at formatting memos."

Drawing a hand to her chest, she mimed a heart attack. "Well, message received, Mr. I-Need-Three-Screens-to-Read-One-Email. Good luck finding anyone else who can decipher your handwriting. You aren't exactly perfect yourself."

"I didn't say you weren't perfect," he said, locking in on her, his face more serious now. Remembering the photograph he had taken at the fundraiser, Effie felt heat rush into her cheeks. She almost corrected him. In another life, she would have counted off the many flaws she'd incurred over the years until he realized his mistake. But she had a strange suspicion that it would take a lot more than that to change Drew's opinion. And she didn't want to. He cleared his throat, then held the door open with one hand while drawing the other to the back of his neck. "Well, in any case, thanks for coming." He gestured for her to come inside. "Figured it was time to sell his place, you know. No point in hanging on to it."

She made her way over the threshold and took stock of Cameron's things, noting a pool table in the far corner. The living room walls were painted an abysmal forest green and decorated with a few abstracts, a couple of tennis rackets, and a Warhol-inspired photograph of Marilyn Monroe. It all seemed about right. On the credenza behind the plush leather sofa were pictures of Cameron posing with friends and colleagues. She could easily imagine him reclining in the La-Z-Boy in front of the seventy-two-inch TV or pouring himself a shot of tequila from the wet bar dividing the living room and kitchen. A dry lump sprouted in her throat. He was gone, but so much of him was still here.

Trailing behind her, Drew brightened his tone. "I'm actually looking to buy a house near Samuel's school. It's got a pool and a nice backyard. If the sellers agree, I think he's gonna love it."

"I'm sure he will," she said, forming a mental picture of Drew playing catch with his son on a wide swath of green.

"So, what do you think? Can you help me transform this thing from a bachelor pad into something I can sell?"

In this area, Drew could sell this condo exactly as is and probably receive over asking price, but Effie didn't tell him that. It might be unethical, but the idea of having an excuse to see him intrigued her. Slowly, she ambled around the room, inspecting the place from bottom to top. "Let's see. The floors have a little wear, but they look like maple, so we could sand those down and refinish them. Light fixtures could use a facelift," she noted, throwing a glance over her shoulder. "A nice soft neutral in this room would make the whole place feel bigger. But yeah . . . I think I can turn this around in a couple of weeks."

"That's great news." He seemed relieved. "I was hoping you could work your magic."

The compliment made her flush, and a fresh wave of nerves coiled in her stomach when she turned around and saw him staring at her. "Not sure about that, but there's definitely enough here to transform this place into something beautiful," she said, sweeping her gaze across the ceiling. The longer she did this kind of work, the more Effie became convinced that renovating was the mission of her heart, uncovering the beauty in something that had been neglected and written off. Maybe sometimes the best-laid plans were meant to be upended because something better was waiting to take their place. Maybe a well-trodden course wasn't set in stone. Maybe choices weren't stagnant but fluid paths that would continually take her to new places, as long as she could find the courage to spread her map a little wider.

"So . . ." A mischievous grin tugged at the corners of Drew's lips as he rocked back on the heels of his tennis shoes. "Have you played any pickleball lately?"

Effie laughed. "Not since I almost died at the hands of Carl."

"That's a shame," he teased. "You had real potential." Plunging his hands in his pockets, he peered up at her. "I'd be happy to coach you, you know." She hadn't planned to set foot on a court anytime in the near future, but there was a softness in Drew's eyes that pulled at her resolve. "I mean . . . if you ever wanted to work on your game."

Effie shrugged, letting her mind wander back to that night when Drew had so carefully tended to her injury. "Maybe," she said.

He smiled at her in a way that made her heart lurch. In that moment, his blue eyes reminded her so much of Cameron's, it nearly stole her breath. She had to look away to keep from tearing up. After everything, she couldn't help but wonder if maybe Cameron had done just as much for her as he had for Drew.

As if reading her thoughts, Drew asked, "So . . . has he ever . . . come back to visit?" His face flushed, but if Drew was embarrassed to ask the question, Effie was mortified to answer it. After all, she was the one who had admitted in the clear light of day that she could talk to ghosts.

"No," she said. Since that day in the graveyard, she hadn't seen him again, though she often caught herself scanning crowds for that flawless face and smug grin.

Drew raised an eyebrow. "Any other spirits?"

She smiled. "Sometimes. But no one quite like him," she admitted. It was the truth. No matter how many other lost souls she helped, she'd never met anyone who'd burrowed their way into her heart as Cameron had. She would never forget him.

With a smirk, Drew peered around the room. "Are there any here now?"

"No," she said, checking just to be certain. "We're alone." A fact that made her skin prickle with a sudden heat. The way he was looking at her made her wonder if there was something more behind the question, but she was still too fragile to let herself believe it was anything more than an innocent exchange between friends. Were they friends? She wasn't certain what to call Drew anymore. All she knew was that she missed seeing his face in the mornings. And now that he was here, standing in front of her, she dreaded walking away from him again.

"Good." He nodded, slowly moving closer, his eyes skating across her lips. "That's good."

It was all she could do to nod her agreement. As he closed the distance between them, she felt her whole body lean in, pulled toward him like a magnet. Gently, he tilted her chin up to his, and before she could register the heat of his breath on her skin, his mouth brushed across hers. Softly at first, then more urgent with every movement, as if he couldn't quite get enough of her. She couldn't remember the last time Daniel had kissed her that way, taking his time to savor the feel of her lips. She'd thought the sweetest moments of her life were behind her, but that was before she'd felt Drew's warmth melding with hers. When he finally pulled away, an ember of desire remained in her belly, radiating out to her tips. Slowly, he threaded his fingers through her hair; then they landed on her cheekbone and lingered there until they trailed down her jaw. "Thank you, Effie," he whispered. "And I don't just mean for today."

Effie knew she would remember this kiss above all others, the one that brought her heart back from the dead. And while she wasn't impatient to dive headfirst into another relationship that could break her, Drew's lips were so warm and his hands so soft. She may just have to see where they led her. She hadn't planned to fall in love again. The wide ocean spread out before her, glittering and endless, and the rest of her course was uncharted. Now that she was firmly at the helm, she knew she could sail her ship alone. But she didn't want to. And just maybe, if the conditions were favorable, Drew's ship could drift in tandem alongside hers, pushed by a gentle wind that shifted them toward the same horizon.

ACKNOWLEDGMENTS

In many ways, publishing my sophomore novel has been more terrifying than my debut. That entire crazy experience felt like a dream from which I've not yet awakened. I was certain this time around I'd prove to everyone that it was just a fluke, that I'd somehow fooled them into believing I could make a career out of this thing I love to do. I'm so grateful to my amazing agent, Ann Leslie Tuttle, who believed in this manuscript long before I did. I'm so sorry you had to read those first disjointed drafts before this novel knew what it wanted to be.

Thanks to my fabulous editor, Alicia Clancy at Lake Union, for taking a chance on this unconventional "ghost story" and for pairing me up with Melissa Valentine and Laura Chasen. #TeamPatsy was truly a match made in heaven! Laura, your astute edits were spot on. You seemed to know exactly what I was trying to communicate on the page and helped me do it without all those extra gerunds I thought I needed. Karah Nichols, Jenna Justice, and Alicia Lea were instrumental in pushing this manuscript over the finish line and making it truly shine. A huge thank you to Eileen Carey for designing a cover that is so much better than anything I could have imagined.

Thanks to my sisters—Julie, Mandy, and Shelley—for reading this manuscript in its early stages and being way too complimentary. Now that I actually want you to say mean things to me, you're far too nice to be helpful! Thanks to my parents for teaching me that I can do hard things and for forcing my debut on everyone you knew and some people you didn't. To my writing group—Julia, Molly, Erin, and Kyla—you are the dream team, and I'm so lucky to have you all in my corner. Lucille Guarino and Nancy Fagan, your input has been golden! Chelsea Larson, you are a gem for reading an early draft of this, even if you were too kind to give critique. I'll be forever grateful to you for coining my favorite made-up curse word.

Thank you to my daughters, Annabeth, Camilla, and Scarlett, for keeping me motivated by continuing to ask provoking questions like "When are you going to finish your book, Mom?" You will be happy to know it's finally done! And to Brent, who, bless his heart, humors me every time I start a conversation with the words "Hey, what do you think about this?" You loved this idea because I did, and I love you so much for that.

They say life inspires art, and I would be remiss if I did not acknowledge the influence of my grandma Vera on this work. I've never met another person who owned more instruments than she did—and I was a music major! She nurtured my love of country music and the old hymns long before I'd ever heard of Mozart and Beethoven. She would have been tickled pink to know she had a hand in this book.

Last, but not least, I owe a huge debt of gratitude to the holy trinity of country music, Patsy, Loretta, and Dolly, who bucked against the establishment, paving the way for all the amazing women who came after them: Reba, Faith, Tanya, Martina, Trisha, Wynonna, Shania, and Emmylou. The list goes on and on. These are the women who provided the soundtrack to my childhood, the ones who unapologetically sang the songs my young, timid heart needed to hear. May we all find the courage to step out onto the stages of our lives and sing the songs we were meant to sing.

ABOUT THE AUTHOR

Laura Barrow is a former teacher and a lover of books. She received her bachelor's degree in music education from Centenary College in northwest Louisiana, where she grew up. She now resides in northeast Texas, just outside Dallas, with her husband, three daughters, and a houseful of pets.